# ENEMIES

is the story of John Flood, an award-winning newsman who wakes up in an alley one morning next to the body of a murdered young woman, who spends five days of bewilderment, terror, love, rage, guilt, and flight from enemies, known and unknown. John Flood has stumbled upon a secret so earth-shaking that he can tell only one man, the President—if he can get to him . . .

"A CORKING GOOD NOVEL—ONE GUARANTEED TO KEEP YOU ON THE EDGE OF YOUR CHAIR."
—*American Way Magazine*

"A WONDERFUL PAGE-TURNER . . . A MASTERLY SPY NOVEL."
—*Boston Globe*

"GRIPS LIKE A FIST FROM THE OPENING PAGES . . . AN INTELLIGENT, STUNNINGLY EFFECTIVE SHOCKER."
—*Cosmopolitan*

# ENEMIES

# ENEMIES

# ENEMIES

## RICHARD HARRIS

BALLANTINE BOOKS • NEW YORK

Library of Congress Catalog Card Number: 78-27831

ISBN 0-345-28435-6

This edition published by arrangement with
Richard Marek Publishers

Manufactured in the United States of America

First Ballantine Books Edition: August 1980

For Susan and Robert Lescher

If a man know not
who his friends be,
he should know at
least his enemies.
—Anon.

# Wednesday

# 1

Flood came awake slowly, in pain, then slid back into sleep again. A minute passed, and another minute. He moved his head. It throbbed and his neck ached and his mouth felt as dry as a rug. Again he began to emerge from sleep but fought to stay there, to preserve its narcotic against discomfort. Slowly nausea rose into his throat and prodded him awake. He had to get to the toilet. Coming awake suddenly, fully, his eyes open, he felt, then saw, that he wasn't in his bed or on his couch and that there was no bathroom. The nausea subsided.

He was lying face-down on concrete with his head sideways on the crook of his elbow. A few inches away from his head was a curb and Flood stared at it for a long time, puzzled. Two feet beyond the curb were some rows of gray-streaked asbestos shingles. He looked upward as far as he could without making the pain in his neck any worse and saw that the shingles were the siding of an unfamiliar house—rather dilapidated, three stories, pre-World War I. Pain shot down the back of his neck into his shoulder and he slowly lowered his head to his arm and closed his eyes.

As the pain diminished, Flood waited and when it was gone he raised his head once more, farther this time, to examine the curbing. It was attached to the cement foundation of the house—a three-sided box-like affair, about two feet by three feet in size. He tried to remember how he had got there. Nothing. Then he tried to remember where he had been that night and what he had done. Again, nothing.

Lifting himself up on one elbow, he peered down into the rectangle formed by the curbing and saw that it was about a foot and a half deep and formed the recess for a basement window. He stared dully into the recess, his mind glazed, until he saw that he wouldn't have to vomit.

Flood turned away from the ugly puddle and looked at the dusty black basement window and tried to remember. He waited but his mind was empty. Then he inadvertently glanced at the puddle and remembered that much—a furious surge of pain in his stomach and the torrent of its contents pouring out and convulsive retching until nothing was left and more dry empty retching.

Not in a long time, he thought, not since his college days in New Haven. For the past ten years there had always been too much to drink, except for two or three weeks now and then when he stopped entirely to pull himself back from that line he knew he would never be able to recross once he had gone beyond it. Nearly every night in the past few years he had felt at least a little drunk when he went to bed and nearly every morning he had a hangover. But not like this one. A historic hangover.

He had never passed out before. And he had never forgotten everything before. Flood groaned and rolled over very slowly onto his back, his raincoat rustling on the gritty concrete. The early autumn sky was a flat dead gray. It looked as if it might rain dust. He raised his left wrist to his face and stared at the Timex blearily: 5:22. His head throbbed again and he moved his hand up to press his temples. It didn't help. At last the throbbing stopped of itself and he moved his hand back and forth through his prematurely white hair until he touched a bump, almost a knob, on the back of his head. He winced. That's why it throbbed then. He must have fallen on the curb. Jesus, he thought, what a night. He moved his hand down over his scimitar nose and his long innocent face to his jaw. He moved his tongue back and forth to raise some saliva. It didn't work. A dark image—two men carrying something heavy—flickered into his mind and vanished. He tried to get it back but that didn't work either. What had they been carrying? His mouth moistened as he remembered a knee supporting his

4

back and a bruising hand gripping one of his arms as a door opened. They had been carrying him. Then he tasted something foul again—bitter, like tobacco in the back of his throat. He grimaced and realized that it didn't matter just now. He had to get out of there.

Raising himself to his elbows, Flood looked straight ahead and saw that he was in an alley between two houses. Parked twenty feet away was an old purplish-blue car, which blocked his view of the street beyond and—fortunately, he thought—blocked anyone's view of him from there. He gathered his strength to get up and felt something under one leg. Sitting up, he moved his leg and saw a woman's shoe—a black patent-leather pump. What the hell . . . ? he thought, and picked it up. Then he saw the foot and the leg and the body of a woman.

She was lying on her back, sprawled as if she had been flung there, a few feet away. The leg with the shoeless foot was bent awkwardly, so that the foot was under her other thigh. The skirt of her dark-gray suit was pulled up almost to her waist and Flood could see a dark triangle between her legs. He knew that she was dead. He got up and stumbled to her side and knelt down. Her eyes were open, her lips slightly parted. Her high cheekbones and straight narrow nose were waxy and when he touched her throat it was cold. There was no pulse in the carotid artery. He thought he was going to vomit and constricted his throat to stop himself. Then he saw the knife—or the small carved ivory handle of it—sticking out of her left side, next to the V of her jacket's lapels. Whoever stabbed her, he realized, must have pulled the jacket and the white silk blouse beneath to one side before plunging the knife into her, since they were stretched angularly around the base of the blade. Blood had run down the front of her clothes and dried.

Whoever stabbed her . . . "Jesus," Flood muttered.

He moved down toward her legs and saw that there was dried blood on her thighs and that her pubic hair was matted with it. He tried to pull the skirt down to conceal her nakedness but her bent leg stopped him. He paused, took it by the knee and shoved it out straight, then pulled the skirt down. What good will that do? he wondered. Getting up, he stared down at her face and her black hair fanned out on the concrete and shoved his hands into his raincoat pockets. He felt a wad of cloth in one and took it out: the panties. They were white cotton, bikini cut. He stared at them for a long time, then dropped them beside the corpse.

I couldn't have, Flood thought. I couldn't have. Rape? Murder? He had never hurt anyone—not intentionally at least. But why couldn't he remember? Could his mind have gone blank for the first time in his life without a drastic cause? He tried to think back to the last thing he could remember before he woke up. It was leaving the office. He had left around eight-thirty the night before—or he assumed it had been the night before.

Trying to remember, he looked down at the woman's face. But another memory—Ellen's dark hair and straight nose and high cheekbones—intruded. Flood tried to shake off that memory before it got to him again. But that didn't work either and he saw Ellen's face with its rictus smile of agony. Then, unexpectedly, the image faded and he saw the face below him in a dark corner somewhere, half-hidden by a floppy-brimmed hat.

Treats, he remembered suddenly. He had been at the bar. She had been sitting at a table in the corner at the far end of the narrow room. He frowned now, wondering again if he could have killed her. He recalled offering to buy her a drink. A note. There had been some kind of a note. From her? Now he remembered that, too. He had written a note on the back of a bar check asking if she would have a drink, perhaps dinner, with him. The waitress—it would have been Lily—had taken it to her. But the woman had refused, politely and firmly, by way of a note written below his. He remembered putting the slip of paper in his pocket and nodding toward her with a smile, as if to say it was all right, he understood. He searched his pockets. There was no note.

Flood's distracted glance was caught by something protruding from under the woman's shoulder. He bent down and pulled it out—a small brown-leather handbag not much larger than a man's billfold. He began to open it but realized that it was evidence and shouldn't be tampered with. He began putting it back, then stopped. Jesus, he thought, evidence against whom? He shoved the bag into his coat pocket, picked up the panties, and used them to wipe the handle of the knife clean of any prints. A steak, he thought, wondering at the foolish irrelevancy. But it wasn't. It was the knife. He'd had a steak at Treats. He'd had four or five whiskies, doubles, first and then a steak. Some wine. Then more whiskies. Alone? He couldn't remember.

Flood dropped the bikini panties beside the body, and stared at them for a few moments. Idiot! he said to himself and picked them up and shoved them into his other pocket.

Suddenly he was certain that he was being watched and took a step forward, ready to run. He caught himself and stopped, with a pretense of calm, as if he had just stumbled onto the last thing in the world he had expected to find. Glancing upward and scanning the windows on the second floor of the house across the alley, he saw a face in one of them not twenty feet away. He turned again and started off in a stiff walk, then looked back. The face was a white flowerpot.

A car horn honked in the distance. Flood glanced at his watch. It was only 5:30—eight minutes since he had last looked. He found it hard to believe. It was past dawn and the early-morning people—the maids and janitors, the firemen and coffee-shop workers, the policemen . . . Jesus, he had forgotten—would be moving soon. Quickly he looked steadily up and down the body to see if he had missed anything. Satisfied, he was about to leave when he noticed that one of the woman's hands was clenched. He knelt beside her and forced the hand open. It was amazingly difficult

7

and he held the fingers open, sure that they would spring back closed. Instead, they lay there, in one of his big hands, cold against it. Nothing. He bent closer and peered at the small palm. A few strands of white hair. Mine, he thought. He picked them out carefully, then moistened two fingers and a thumb and felt for any missed strands. Nothing. He searched around the body, his face close to the ground, but found nothing more that might incriminate him as far as he could tell.

Getting up, he turned and looked at the spot where he had wakened. There was a small bottle, about the size of a pill vial, lying on its side next to the recess curb. The bottle had grooves for a screw cap but no cap. He looked around the cracked concrete paving but saw nothing. Then he peered into the basement-window recess and saw the cap, or the shape of it, covered with vomit. Forcing himself, he picked the cap out of the vile stuff, wiped it off on his coat, and stuck the bottle and cap into a pocket.

Jesus, he thought, enough. He turned wearily to leave but stopped after a step and looked at the woman's shoe. Shrugging, he went over and picked it up and put it on the cold bare foot. It was difficult without the wriggling help of a live foot, and Flood wondered if undertakers put shoes on corpses before shoving them into their coffins.

It's like a goddamn flag, Flood said to himself, thinking of his white hair, and walked faster. The alley was on the west side of New Richmond, eighteen or twenty blocks from his apartment, and it took him just under fifteen minutes to get home. He passed the fake Gothic university buildings (donated half a century before by a railroad magnate who had helped build the city to its thriving peak of a quarter of a million people) but avoided the main business section. Flood no longer had any real friends, although he knew a lot of people —all too many, he thought, as he hurried through the gray streets. He had once calculated that he knew one percent of the city's inhabitants. The only favor those twenty-five hundred acquaintances had ever done him was not to run into him that morning. He saw no one at all, except a black man who drove past in a rattling old Ford pickup.

Flood let himself into the locked apartment building quietly and climbed the five flights to his apartment rather than take the elevator and possibly be seen. He thought he remembered something as he stopped halfway up to rest, his heart pounding, his head throbbing. But he couldn't think of anything except getting upstairs to safety, and resumed the climb. When he reached his door he was dizzy and trembling so that he could scarcely get his key into the lock. Once inside the apartment, he closed the door softly and leaned against it, letting his breath out and drawing in long gulps of air. It smelled of stale cigar smoke and old clothes and dust and sweat.

Flood switched on a small lamp on a table near the door and looked around the place with disgust. He had sold almost everything that he and Ellen had bought and was left with only the furniture he had taken from his parents' house. It was heavy cumbersome stuff—a large couch that he'd had upholstered in brown linen, his father's tall wing chair still in its threadbare dark-red velvet, a long marble-topped coffee table on thick legs, the oak dining table that he used as a desk, three glass-fronted bookcases in dark wood, a pair of wood-armed upholstered chairs, a faded floral carpet; all that was his were the books in the bookcase and the papers on the table.

Without taking off his coat, Flood went to the kitchen—a small room with a dining nook in which stood the enamel-topped table from his mother's kitchen and two of the cream-colored wood chairs he had sat on all his life—and took a large can of tomato juice out of a cupboard. He poured a tall glass half full, shook in several squirts of Worcestershire sauce, and unscrewed the cap of a pint bottle of vodka on the counter. The bottle was half full and he poured some of it into the glass, stirred the mixture with a forefinger, and lifted the glass with a trembling hand to his lips. Jesus, no ice. It was as warm as blood. Seeing the blood on the woman's breast and thighs, he dropped the glass into the sink and retched drily. He ran cold water until the red ran out of the broken glass, then gulped handfuls of water and splashed his face. Grabbing a dirty dish towel, he dried his face and hands. Then he lifted the bottle of vodka to his lips and drank half of it in two great swallows. Shuddering, he gagged at the end, put the bottle down on the counter, and leaned against it, his eyes closed, for a long time.

Flood stood in the beating hot water, as hot as he could stand it, for nearly half an hour and tried to remember. He could think of nothing but the woman's face and Ellen's face. Finally he gave up and got out of the shower and dried himself with a thick towel. The knob on the back of his head had stopped throbbing; now it was a steady ache. He put on a pair of pajamas and a robe and slippers in case anyone showed up. There were people who knew that he usually worked at home in the mornings and rarely dressed before noon. It wouldn't do to seem different today.

Now he had to have food. Always after drinking he was hungry but he was hungrier than usual this morning because he had left yesterday's meals behind. He made three scrambled eggs, with pieces of bread crust broken up in them the way his mother had done, four pieces of toast, and a pot of coffee. He sat down at the kitchen table and in ten minutes all that was left was one cup of coffee. He felt better. Still, he had to hold the saucer with both hands to keep from spilling the coffee as he walked into the living room. He put the saucer down carefully on the coffee table in front of the fireplace and went to the windows and pulled the curtains open. Ellen had made them and he had wished a hundred times that he had never put them up when he moved after the funeral. They were quilted brown-and-yellow-and-beige-and-black cotton. A stylized floral pattern. For some reason he was glad now that they were there and looked at them abstractedly.

Suddenly he remembered. "Dart missile," the woman had said. What the hell was that? When had she said it? Nothing more came. He would just have to wait. Sooner or later there would be more pieces.

He felt slightly encouraged by the scant recollection. At least it was something. But then he realized that if he could recall her words he must have been with her and if he had been with her he could have . . . His hopes faded.

Flood looked at his watch. It was a little past seven. He wondered if the dead woman had been found yet. He saw a swarm of policemen in the alley, the men from homicide. Lieutenant Flower would probably be there. Flood didn't like the idea of coming up against Flower. As a journalist, Flood had often dealt with the police in the past twenty years but now that he could write more or less what he wanted to write he kept away from them. Most of them, he discovered, were trying to punish the criminal in themselves. That was the worst kind of hatred—the relentless fear of oneself. It was the killer in every man's soul.

My own killer? he asked himself.

Flood turned away from the window and switched on three lamps. On his way to take a shower, he had flung his raincoat on the couch facing the fireplace. Now he went to it, took the handbag and the panties out of the pockets, put them on one end of the coffee table, and slumped down in the armchair facing it. The coffee was cold but he drank it anyway, slowly, and stared at the panties. At last he picked them up and examined them. There was no label. He put them down and picked up the wallet and opened it. There were a few bills—four tens, a five, and two ones—and some change. There were also two New York subway tokens. He looked at them, puzzled by something he couldn't put his finger on.

Flood ran a hand through his white hair and hit the bump. He winced at the sharp pain. Was that why he couldn't remember? That and all the drink? Then he remembered something more. She had said she had over a thousand dollars with her and she was going to New York. He waited. That was all. He sat, his eyes closed, and tried to recall more. Nothing came and he opened his eyes and began examining the rest of the contents: an imitation tortoise-shell comb, a thin compact, three black hairpins, a small gold metal pencil, a rubber band, one gold hoop earring, and a few pieces of paper. He took these out and put the wallet down on the table.

Why New York? he wondered. And where was the rest of the money, if there had been more? Once again, nothing. He looked at the papers: business cards from a moving company, a boutique, an employment agency, a beauty parlor, a gypsy palmist, a dentist, a gynecologist. All of them were from Philadelphia. There was no driver's license, no social security card. But then he came upon an identification card with a name and an address: Wendy Cameron, Hotel Winslow, Philadelphia. He stared at the card, knowing that something was wrong. Wendy Cameron? Impossible. Dart missile, he thought again. There seemed no connection. Wendy Cameron, Wendy Cameron, Wendy Cameron, he said to himself. It was impossible. She had a faint accent—Eastern European or Slavic, he'd thought as he listened to her soft rushing words. That was it, she had been in a terrible hurry about something. And very frightened.

Small wonder, Flood thought as he saw her sprawled body on the pavement again. Then he wondered if she had been frightened of him. It didn't seem right. Could he have done that to anyone? No, he said to himself, but he was no longer so certain.

The next card was a Greyhound Bus schedule between Philadelphia and New York. Behind that was a piece of folded paper, the last item in the wallet. Flood unfolded it. "TREATS" it said at the top, and just below that "Where Friends Meet." The back of the paper was taken up by the broad scrawl of his handwriting: "Just wondering if you'd be kind enough to have a friendly drink (and dinner?) with a friendly drinker." It was signed "John Flood."

Flood sat back in the big red chair. One thing he had

remembered—about the only thing he had remembered clearly so far—was getting that note back with her answer at the bottom. Something like, "Thank you very much but I must leave soon. Thank you." He looked closely at the paper on both sides. Nothing had been erased or crossed out. He held the paper up to the light and brought it close to his eyes. It had been torn off, probably folded and torn, just below his message.

He felt the most grateful sense of relief he could recall ever feeling. He *knew* the note had been in his pocket, the complete note. So someone—the men who had carried him?—had torn off the bottom part of the note and put the rest of it in her wallet and planted him, unconscious, beside her body in the alley with some strands of his hair clutched in her hand. He hadn't done it. Then who had and why? If somebody wanted her dead enough to murder her and try to frame him for it, then somebody was going to want him dead even more. Jesus, he thought, feeling sick again.

Flood put the note on the coffee table and got up and went to the kitchen to get a drink of water. Pieces of the glass he had broken were still pink from the tomato juice. He took a thick tumbler off the drying rack and filled it at the tap, poured its contents over the shards of glass, and refilled it. As he lifted the glass to his lips, he remembered the small bottle he had found beside the basement window. It must still be in his raincoat. He put the glass down without drinking from it and hurried back to the living room. The bottle was in the bottom of one pocket and the cap to it in the other pocket. He took them back to the kitchen and washed the last of the caked vomit off the cap and put it on the counter to dry. Then he looked closely at the bottle. It was just a bottle, perhaps two inches high and an inch in diameter. He lifted it to his nose and sniffed. Again he remembered the bitter pungent taste of tobacco. He coughed and turned away.

Wendy Cameron with a Slavic accent, he thought, dart missile, a thousand dollars, New York, "Thank you very much but I must leave soon. Thank you."

It wasn't much to go on—not nearly enough. Philadelphia, New York subway tokens, a small, empty bottle with a noxious smell, someone carrying him. He shook his head. He was going to need a lot more.

Flood put the bottle on the coffee table and went to the bedroom. The blind on the single window was closed and the room was comfortingly dim. He lay down on his back on the unmade bed and stared at the ceiling. Nothing more came to him and he was sure he was going to fail again. He was a man who saw himself through his failures. Groaning, he rolled over and buried his face in one of the two pillows, and smelled perfume. He sat up and turned on the table lamp beside the bed, as if that would help him smell better, and leaned over close to the pillow. It was unmistakably perfume. Then he saw a hair—a long black hair. He stared at it dumbly. Jesus, she'd been here. He certainly didn't remember *that*. He searched the bedclothes and found several more long black hairs. He got off the bed and looked carefully around the room; nothing seemed out of place.

Getting down on his hands and knees, Flood peered underneath the bed. He saw nothing unusual. But just as he began to raise his head his eye caught a glint of metal at the edge of the carpet below the head of the bed. He had to lie down to get his hand that far. It was a small enamel cylinder—a lipstick, he saw, as he slid the two halves apart. A very red lipstick. He saw her blood again and felt sick.

Flood put the lipstick on the coffee table next to the bottle and went into the bathroom. His clothes were in a heap on top of the wicker hamper, and he realized that he had to get rid of them at once. He paused, wondering if he was right, if the perfume and the hairs and the lipstick had been planted there. His blue shirt with the red-blue-and-white striped tie still in the buttoned-down collar was on top of the pile of clothes. Flood picked up the shirt and saw a dark reddish-brown stain on the right-hand cuff. There was another, just a tiny spot, on the collar but he couldn't be sure that it was the same color. Then he held up the shirt by its shoulders and saw a broad solid stain, the same color, on each of the tails in front. Dropping the garment to the floor, he grabbed his boxer shorts off the pile. The front of them, around the fly, was stained, too. His dark-gray trousers and the gray-and-black herringbone tweed jacket seemed all right. But he knew that he couldn't be sure.

Again, everything seemed beyond belief. He had slept with too few women to forget one, he thought as he stood in the middle of the bathroom, the trousers and jacket in his hands. He dropped them and pulled aside the shower curtains. There was no reddish stain on the bottom of the bathtub but he realized that the hot shower he had taken would have washed away all traces. He tried to remember washing his genitals. Surely there would have been blood on him if there had been blood on his shorts. Had he blanked that out, too? He stood staring at the bathtub. Had he done it?

Flood backed his car, a five-year-old gray Chevrolet, out of the wood garage behind his apartment building. He got out, closed the garage door quietly, and drove away. It was still too early for much traffic but he kept just under the speed limit.

It was clear that he had to prove his innocence to the world and it was even clearer that first he had to prove it to himself. He was certain that he had got back the note he had sent the woman with a message from her at the bottom and he was certain that he had shoved the piece of paper into his pocket. Unexpectedly he remembered the end of the scene at Treats and again felt his chagrin at the rebuff. Jerry, the bartender, had seen the transaction—Flood's giving the note to Lily, who took it to the woman sitting at the table in the corner. He couldn't remember if Jerry had seen Lily bring back the answer a few minutes later. Two witnesses to his approaching a woman who was murdered not long afterward. Maybe they hadn't seen her face clearly under the floppy-brimmed hat, he thought, and felt a bit of relief. How could they remember her—it would be from a photograph now, too, a photograph of the same dead face—especially with the concealing hat? Jesus, the hat. What had happened to it? He stopped at a traffic light on Genesee Avenue and clamped his eyes shut for a few minutes. Hopeless, he thought, it's hopeless.

Flood turned onto Genesee and headed out to the River Road, turned there, and drove north out of town. The narrow ill-kept highway wasn't used much now that the expressway, running parallel to it, had been built a couple of miles to the west. There were no other cars on the River Road and the few businesses that were still operating after motorists gave it up for the faster route—a couple of old gas stations with muddy yards littered with junked cars, a grim diner, an old-fashioned motel with separate cabins, an animal hospital—seemed deserted.

Flood slowed down, looking for the narrow side road, and saw it a few hundred yards ahead on the left. He turned there onto a rutted dirt path one car wide that ran in a long loop down near the river and then back up to rejoin the River Road a mile farther on. Glancing at the two brown paper bags on the floor beside him, he wondered if they contained not evidence of his guilt but proof of his innocence. The blood on his clothes might not have come from her vagina or even from her body.

Flood clenched his teeth and drove on slowly, praying that he wouldn't meet anyone. When he reached the great looming rock, he pulled up. He sat motionless for a minute, then leaned forward to turn off the engine, hesitated, and left it running in case he had to leave quickly. The rock was between the road and the river, a hundred yards beyond, so he was concealed on that side by the granite outcropping and on the other side by underbrush and a stand of birches interspersed with ancient apple trees.

Flood recalled the picnic he'd had there with a woman from the office the summer before last. She was in her mid-thirties, ten years younger than he, and had never married. She had long blond hair, bleached almost white, she wore large round horn-rimmed glasses, and she talked a lot. It was only nerv-ousness, he knew, for she was shy, frightened, as awk-ward with men as he was with women. After the picnic lunch and bottle of 'wine, he moved forward to kiss her—with a kind of lunge he hadn't intended—and she pushed him away wildly and wept.

The circle of small stones he had placed at the foot of the rock to contain the fire they built to cook hot dogs was still there. Someone had placed the lid of an old metal garbage can upside down on top of the stones and it was full of ashes. That would make things easier, Flood thought; he would empty the lid first and he could scatter the ashes he made afterward.

Looking down at the parcels on the floor beside him, he swore softly to himself. It was absurd. The smoke from such a fire would bring the fire department or the police before the first sheet was consumed. He shook his head wearily. He hadn't the cunning for it, he realized, and wished that he had called the police when he found the body. Gripping the top of the steering wheel with his hands close together, Flood rested his forehead on them and closed his eyes.

After soaking the panties with Charcoal-Lite, he lit them, they flamed high in the air and burned down to a white flaky ash in less than a minute. There was little smoke. The shirt was more difficult because of its size, so he tore it into four pieces and burned them one by one. The tie was next and it smoked more than he liked but it was consumed quickly enough so that he was able to fan the smoke into faint clouds that disappeared by the time they reached the top of the rock. Afterward Flood waited until the metal lid was cool enough to handle, then took it back through the bushes into the trees and scattered the ashes carefully, low to the ground, to keep them off leaves and branches. One decent rain would obliterate all traces.

He drove, more quickly now, around the second half of the loop, back to the River Road, and eased out onto it without stopping. There was not a car in sight until he got to the city limits, when three cars passed him going in the opposite direction. Crossing Genesee, he turned onto Washington Boulevard, past the university complex and on toward Miller Air Force Base, six miles out of town. When he had driven two miles, he decided that the place he was looking for must be in the other direction, made a sudden U-turn, and headed back toward the center of New Richmond. A few blocks past the intersection of the River Road he saw a Salvation Army storefront in a rundown two-story wood building. It was open already, its front door ajar. He saw the laundromat next door and nodded. An unexpected break.

Flood parked in front of the laundromat and got the two bags ready. One contained the towel, sheets, and pillow cases, the other the jacket and trousers. Shoving the can of Charcoal-Lite back under the seat, he got out carrying the bags. There were two women in the laundromat—one a fat woman with her hair in curlers and her stockings rolled to her ankles, who sat in a plastic chair staring fixedly at the whirling contents of a washing machine opposite her. Flood turned to the other woman—a slim black girl with a sullen look who seemed to be in charge.

"Do you sell soap?" he asked.

She handed him two small paper packets without looking up from the laundry she was sorting and said, "A quarter."

He took the packets and gave her a quarter. He dumped the sheets and pillow cases and towel into a machine, emptied the soap packets on top of them, shoved two quarters into a slot, and closed the lid. As the window in front began to fill with water and the suds rose, he felt relieved. He had done something. Even if it was all wrong, it was something.

Flood went back to the black woman. "I have to go off for a couple of hours," he said. "Could you take my load out and dry it and fold it?"

"One load?"

"Yes."

"A dollar."

He handed her a dollar and she tore off a pasteboard ticket and gave it to him. She still hadn't looked at his face.

Picking up the other paper bag from one of the plastic chairs, Flood left and turned toward the Salvation Army depot. He walked past slowly, peering through the front window. No one seemed to be in the room beyond, so he retraced his steps, slipped through the open door without touching it, and looked around. At one side was a large wood box, open at the top, with a rough sign on front saying *Contributions — Thank you*. Opening the bag as quietly as he could, he poured its contents into the box and hurried out. As far as he knew, no one had seen him. He wadded the bag into a ball and got into his car and drove slowly away. The light at the next corner was red and as he slowed down he saw a litter basket under it. He pulled up close, rolled down his window, and tossed the bag in. Then he tore the laundry check into tiny pieces and dropped them out the window, one at a time, as he drove on down Washington. The city was beginning to stir into readiness for the new day and now there were scores of cars on the streets he used. But he saw no one he knew.

# 2

The telephone began ringing as Flood closed the door of his apartment behind him. He hurried into the kitchen and put down the bag of groceries he had stopped and bought in case anyone questioned his going out that morning.

"Hello," he said, trying to sound natural.

"Your ineffable copy has to be in an hour earlier, Johnny—by three-thirty," a nasal voice said. It was Rogers, the city editor. Only Rogers called him Johnny and only because he was known to detest the name. Rogers had once been described by a *Herald* reporter as "A man who won't say anything about someone if he can't say something bad."

Flood grunted and Rogers went on, "One of the presses is out. So get your column in—early. If you can't do the thirtieth draft, your fans will never notice."

Flood didn't hear him. He had forgotten it was Wednesday. In twelve years of doing the column he had never been late; twice a week, forty-nine weeks a year, for twelve years, and he had never forgotten before. "Okay, three-thirty," Flood said. He hadn't an idea in his head for a column, he hadn't even thought about it on Tuesday as he usually did. Now he recalled that when he left the office the night before, dry in mind, he had meant to get up at five this morning to work. Everyone at the office knew about his slow tortured work and finicky insistence on having it right. He was aware that Rogers called him Cramp behind his back—writer's cramp.

"You there, Johnny, or off in your dream world?" Rogers snarled.

"I said, 'Okay,'" Flood mumbled. "I've been at it since five."

"How many drafts this time?"

"I didn't count."

Rogers cackled through his nose. "Don't feel bad about it, Johnny. Virgil wrote only four lines a day." The phone clicked.

Flood looked at his watch. It was 8:10.

He quickly unpacked the groceries to get at the can of Charcoal-Lite that he had put at the bottom of the bag. Opening the cupboard door under the sink, he knelt down on the floor to put the can back at the rear of the cabinet. He knocked over a bottle and swore. The place was jammed with cans and bottles. He put the Charcoal-Lite on the floor and picked up the bottle. What the hell . . . ? he thought, looking at it in the dim light. It was made of brown glass and had a cork in its neck. He had never seen it before. Holding it up to the light, he saw that it was almost full. Easing the cork out carefully, he brought the bottle closer to his nose and recoiled. It smelled like the small empty bottle, only far stronger. Now the odor was unmistakable: tobacco. Suddenly he remembered more: someone holding his head from the back, a terrific pain there, cold pressure of something on his lower lip, and the bitter stinging taste of sodden tobacco.

Flood sat down on the kitchen floor, his legs bent at the knee, the bottle between them on the linoleum. He had been forced to drink something out of the small bottle, his fingers had been placed around it to leave prints, and he had been left to die beside the dead woman. But he had vomited. They must have left very soon after giving him the drink—poison? he asked himself—and he must have vomited soon afterward. Otherwise . . . Thank God for booze, he thought. If he hadn't been sick drunk, he would probably be dead, too. No wonder he felt worse than usual after a binge. He got up and poured a large glassful of milk from the carton he had just bought and drank it without stopping.

He tasted something else now—the cloying sweetness of blood. It was only his imagination, he knew, the memory of long ago that was always with him. As a boy of ten, he had watched in helpless horror as a speeding car swerved off the narrow highway to deliberately strike his dog Ollie. The terrier was dead when young Flood reached it, blood trickling out of its mouth, and he felt the hatred and terror that was to pursue him forever afterward—hatred of human malevolence and terror of death. He looked down at the dog and at that moment he knew what dying was like, as if he were dying himself. There was a taste of blood at the back of his throat, a foul nausea, a swirling madness as final darkness overcame all. That memory returned at times—usually a dim awareness but piercingly clear when Ellen lay dead before him—and now it returned again. He fought it as it rose in him because he knew the fear it would bring, the desperation that could lead to panic. He was more afraid now than he had ever been in a life that was full of fear. He knew there would be no escape this time. It was not fate—nothing so dramatic, or romantic, as that. It was merely accident. He had tried to pick up a woman at Treats and because of that he was going to die.

Flood put the glass in the sink and looked around. When had they planted the poison in the cupboard? he asked himself, certain now that it was poison. The night before while he was with the woman, if he had been with her at all? Or early that morning while he was lying beside her corpse in the alley? Jesus, he thought, or just now while he was out getting rid of the evidence?

He picked the bottle up from the floor and went to the bathroom. Slowly, carefully, he poured the contents —yellowish-brown, noxious-smelling liquid—into the toilet and flushed it repeatedly to dilute the stuff and make sure no traces remained in the bowl. Returning to the kitchen, he cleaned the broken glass out of the sink and soaked the brown bottle in hot water and cleanser. He put on a kettleful of water to boil, let the soapy water out of the sink, rinsed the bottle, soaked it with cleanser and hot water again, drained the sink and when the kettle was boiling he poured the steaming water slowly over the bottle. After it cooled he put the rubber drain stopper in place and dropped the bottle from a height of two feet into the sink. It broke into several large and a scattering of small pieces; he picked them up carefully and put them in a stainless-steel mixing bowl, then pulverized them with the head of a ball peen hammer until they were the size of grains of sand. He dumped them into the coffee grounds in the paper filter of his Melitta coffeemaker, added three tablespoons of fresh coffee, and poured the remaining water from the kettle into the mixing bowl and dumped that into the filter. He peered at the result. Coffee grounds. Satisfied, he carefully placed the filter upright in the half-filled garbage can.

Flood slumped down in the red chair. Who wanted him dead? What had he done? If he needed any more proof of his innocence, the brown bottle provided it. The realization that he had just destroyed that proof struck him a moment before the realization that it was proof to him alone. It would have been evidence of his guilt to anyone else, he saw, because he could never prove that the bottle wasn't his, any more than he could prove now that the woman had answered his written invitation with a written refusal.

He stared into the empty fireplace. Had they merely wanted to get rid of the woman and he happened to be a handy passerby to blame it on? Only a small family of the mob was active in New Richmond and it confined itself mostly to loan-sharking and protection rackets, mainly of small bars and dubious businesses. But he'd been a newspaperman long enough to know that the mob didn't do things this way. They did it quickly, obviously, with a couple of bullets in the back of the head, not with ivory-handled knives and exotic poisons. Who else, though? he wondered. The attempt to frame him had been so clumsy. Who the hell would rape and stab a woman and then sit down beside the corpse in a public place and drink poison? For that matter, who would carry poison around like a bottle of aspirin? It was crazy.

Flood got up and took a long Dannemann cheroot out of a box on the mantel. He rarely smoked any-more, three or four cigars a week at most, but it tasted so good as he drew in the strong flavor that he absentmindedly took another one out of the box and slipped it into his shirt pocket. Perhaps it wasn't all so crazy, he thought a moment later. They must have been in a hurry and had used what they had handy. It would probably have worked if he hadn't vomited.

He paused, thinking of the furor that the case would stir up. He inhaled and coughed. After a few years on the force, most policemen believed everyone—except possibly other policemen—was a criminal. He tapped the ash off his cigar into the fireplace. There was his column, too. After what he had written about the mayor and the city council and the police commissioner, any evidence against him, no matter how bizarre, would be welcome.

Wearily Flood got up and went back to the kitchen. He tied the garbage bag closed with a twist-tie and left by the back door, quietly moving down the rear stairs two floors to the trash container for the apartments there, and buried the bag under several others. For the first time in his life he felt sorry for the person who lived by crime.

Flood sat down behind the old upright Remington at the long oak table, rolled a fresh piece of cheap office copy paper into the typewriter, and stared at it. His mind was as blank as the paper. Surely her body had been found by now. He glanced at his watch and saw that it was nearly nine o'clock. Then he realized that he had been waiting for a fist to pound on the door and a voice to shout "Police!" He looked back at the paper and softly muttered a string of dissonantly unconnected obscenities.

To his astonishment, by eleven o'clock he had finished the column. "While man rails at injustice, accident is life's true villain" it began and went on to describe an incident that he had been involved in when he spent six months, a couple of years earlier, in Moscow on assignment from the *Herald*. He had been walking along a narrow cobbled street one afternoon, going nowhere in particular, when a small boy clutching a tin of sardines ran out of a shop and bumped into him. A moment afterward the proprietor hurried out, waving his arms and shouting at the boy. Flood acted as if he didn't know what the man meant as he ran, screaming furiously, down the street after the boy. Flood walked away as though nothing had happened. The next day a policeman appeared at his hotel and insisted on his going to court to identify a thief. Flood was amused by that. Obviously he had been followed all along and obviously the followers had to choose between exposing their surveillance or letting a criminal go free. Bureaucracy had triumphed. The shopkeeper was there, flushed and still indignant, and the boy, thin and old-looking, waited in silent terror.

The encounter created for Flood one of those common dilemmas of life that sometimes determine one's own future more than someone else's. He had the choice of possibly destroying the boy's life for a dozen sardines to uphold a principle of law he happened to believe in himself, or of getting thrown out of Russia just at the time that he was doing his best work since Ellen's death. Flood told the magistrate that he hadn't seen the culprit's face at the time. Then he offered to reimburse the shopkeeper for his trouble and to pay any fine that might be levied against the child. The magistrate glared at him with furious contempt and Flood realized how foolishly wrong he had been. This foreigner—worse, an American and, still worse, a journalist—had presumed to instruct an official of the Soviet Union in how he should administer his nation's laws. The magistrate ordered Flood out of the room and he returned to his hotel, expecting to be thrown out of the country that day. Nothing more happened.

Now Flood reread the column, made a few changes, and sat back. A single draft in less than two hours. It had never happened before; in fact he had never before written a column in less than six hours.

He pushed back his chair and got up from the table. His head spun and he sat down quickly. Sleep, I've got to have some sleep, he thought. There were many things to do still but he didn't care, he was too tired to care. He got up slowly and stumbled into the bedroom and sat down on the side of the bed. He took off his shoes and fell back on the bare mattress and the bare pillow, asleep.

# 3

Ellen floated toward him laughing, her black hair streaming behind her in the pale blue sea. They embraced and parted and swam steadily side by side to a small cove. The beach at the foot of the towering craggy stone cliff was concealed from all but the seaward side and they took off their bathing suits and made love on the sand in the sun. Ellen's head was back and she stared past him into the infinite sky and screamed as he flowed into her. Then her eyes went sightless, the eyes of her dead in his arms on the mountain.

Flood woke up, his clothes soaked with sweat. How could a mind do that—the best and the worst moments of a life together at once? He turned over and buried his face in the pillow. Now he remembered. The hair in the sea, the hair on the concrete, the hair on his pillow. He had gone to bed with the woman— here. The sleep, or the dream within it, must have straightened out the kink that had blocked his mind, for now scattered fuzzy memories of the night before crowded into it. She was afraid and came here to hide. Her husband was going to kill her. Or had he tried to kill her? She was running away. To New York. She gave Flood a letter to deliver to her sister. He paused, wondering what had happened to it, and again remembered being carried. They must have taken it from him.

He rubbed his head and felt the lump. It was going down but it still hurt when he touched it. Was that why he had forgotten? he wondered, and realized that it didn't matter as long as he was beginning to remember.

She asked him to make love to her. There was a special reason but he couldn't remember that yet. He took her by the hand into his bedroom. He remembered that well enough—half-drunk and fumblingly awkward and too quick. Then she wept and fell asleep for a few minutes, lying beside him. "Dart missile," she said suddenly, very clearly, in her sleep and cried out, "Don't, don't!" When she woke up, with a start of fear, he asked her what the words meant. She was terrified but told him to forget it, it was only meaningless dream talk.

Shivering in his wet clothes, Flood sat up on the side of the bed and groggily rubbed his eyes. Had he done it again? he asked himself. Looking at his watch, he saw that it was nearly 12:30. He had slept too long. There were many things to do. He sat forward slightly. My semen is inside her, he thought, and wondered if semen was identifiable, like blood, by type. "Oh my God," he said softly, and rocked slowly back and forth.

It was a matter of life or death, she had said, "for many, many people." As he dug into his memory he saw her intense face and pleading eyes. He must make sure that her sister and no one else got the letter. He had promised her that but he wondered now if he had taken her seriously. She had pleaded with him so mysteriously. It was for his good more than her own, she had said. What could she have meant? Then he remembered more: she had written her sister's name and address on the envelope but he had scarcely glanced at it. There was a ballet school. The sister taught there Monday, Wednesday, and Friday from two to five. That was the only place that was safe to contact her. Under no circumstances was he to telephone or go to her home. He had put the letter on the coffee table, scarcely noticing his act, and then they had gone to bed.

Flood got up and went into the living room. He searched under the cushions of the couch and easy chair and on the carpet beneath them. As he had expected, it wasn't there. If the letter had been on him before he was carried into the alley, they would have been sure to take it, and if he had left it here, they would have been just as sure to take it when they came in to plant the poison.

Flood took off his clothes and got into a shower again. Something was stirring in his mind, darkly just below the surface, but each time he reached down to grasp it and bring it into the light it sank further. He must leave it alone, he thought, and it would rise on its own. What was it? A fact? An idea? A scrap of memory? He realized that he hadn't left it alone to emerge by itself, and to distract himself he stuck his head under the shower nozzle and let the hot water beat against his scalp and run down his face. Then part of the answer came to him in a question: Was he trying to bring back whatever it was that lurked hidden in his mind or was he trying to drive it further away? I must not know, he thought involuntarily. That realization created another: fear that he had caused the woman's death, as he had Ellen's. Flood stepped back a few inches and let the water comfort his shoulders and chest. Had he done it again? he asked himself once more, and this time he faced the question: Was his fear that he had murdered the woman a mask to conceal his fear that he had let her die by his negligence, by refusing to listen to her, as he had refused to listen to Ellen? Knowing now that finally there was a greater threat to him than the truth—his death—he saw that he could save himself only if he forced himself to remember what had happened. Exoneration was a luxury. There was only one necessity: survival.

Flood's recollections of what had happened came slowly, the facts scattered and out of order. But as he dug deep and probed still deeper—always aware now that he had to know—he remembered more and more and within half an hour or so he had largely reconstructed the events of that night.

The woman left Treats at around seven o'clock. Flood watched her go without looking at her directly. He didn't want to humiliate himself anymore by seeming to ask even for a smile, a nod. An hour later he left, too. He was a little drunk and decided to go home and watch television for a couple of hours to let the drink wear off, then go to bed so he could get up at five and write his column. As he came out of Treats, someone called his name. It was the woman. She was in a car, a dark-green car, parked in front of the restaurant.

Flood got into the car as she asked and she drove off slowly, not looking at him, her face still half-hidden by the wide brim of her hat.

"You are John Flood, aren't you?" she asked after they had ridden several blocks in silence.

"That's right."

"You write for the *Herald*?"

"Right again." He regretted his flippant tone as soon as he had spoken. Something was wrong. Her voice—soft and oddly accented—was urgent. He waited.

"Your articles from Russia—they were good," she said after another long silence.

"Thanks. I liked the Russians—a lot."

"And Russia?" She turned for a moment to look at him.

"Not much," he answered. "Not at all, in fact."

"At least you seemed sympathetic."

Flood wondered what it was all about. Why had she refused his invitation, then waited outside for him for a full hour?

He looked at her, hoping to see her face better, but it was too dark in the car and the light from the streetlamps they passed was too quick and distorting to help much. "I tried to be fair," he said at last. "I'm sick of the Cold War. And I'm even sicker of all those who make such a fat living out of it—all the politicians, the military-industrialists, and all too many of my colleagues in the press. It's the tired rotten old story—the bullies at the top on both sides getting the sheep ready, priming them, stirring them up so they'll go out and get themselves slaughtered without a bleat." He stopped abruptly. Only booze could make

30

him preach like that, he thought, embarrassed at himself.

There was another long silence as she drove on. Finally, she said, "Are you brave?"

Flood looked across at her surprise. "Not at all."

"I think perhaps you are."

"I'm a certified member, in good standing, of the American Cowards Association."

She gave him a tic of a smile. She looked pretty.

"Where are we going?" he asked.

"I don't know. It depends on you."

"I'm sorry to be so obtuse but I'm confused. You wouldn't have a drink with me but you waited outside more than an hour for me."

He saw her hat nod, and she said, "I didn't want to put you in any danger without your consent."

"Would you let me out at the next corner?"

She turned to him in alarm and he saw that she *was* pretty, perhaps more than pretty. Late thirties, he thought, maybe forty, dark and lonely and sad.

"You are too frightened to stay?" she asked. She half turned toward him as she spoke and the lights from an oncoming car swept her face, throwing its high cheekbones into prominent relief.

"A joke," he said flatly. He was beginning to feel drunk and rolled down his window a couple of inches. "That's so I can scream for help."

She laughed—an unexpectedly high nervous trill of a laugh.

They were silent again and he noticed that they were driving in the opposite direction on a street they had traversed only a few minutes before, through a large industrial section of the city.

"All right, what is this danger I may be in?" he asked at last, knowing that she wouldn't explain until he asked.

She didn't answer. Finally, after several more blocks of silence, she said, her voice taut now, "I didn't mean to ask anyone for help but I must. I was just going to run away, but I need help—a little help is all. It is dangerous for you but not too dangerous if you are careful. I turned to you because I remembered your writing when I saw the note. Not at first. Later. It was several minutes before I remembered who you were."

"I see," Flood said, not seeing at all. "And then?"

"I refused your invitation because it might have been dangerous for you if we had been seen together. It must never be known that we even spoke."

She pulled to a stop at a traffic light and turned to him. "Do you understand that? No one—absolutely no one—must ever know that you and I spoke together. It could be fatal."

"That's a pretty strong word."

"It is a very weak word," she said, pulling away from the intersection as the light changed. Then her voice went on in a rush, "I must escape. If I don't, I will be killed. I must warn someone else who is in danger and I need your help. I can't tell you what it's about but it may be the worst thing imaginable."

"For whom?" he asked, trying to sound casual but watching her intently.

"Everybody. Don't you see? No, of course you don't. I'm not sure but I think I'm right. Devastation." She was silent for a few moments, then said, "The worst cataclysm the world has ever seen."

Jesus, Flood thought, she's crazy.

At the next stoplight, she turned and faced him. "I have three hours before my plane leaves," she said. "I must get out of sight. I cannot go driving around like this. They will be out looking for me. They know the car."

"They?" Flood craned around to see if there was another car in sight. There wasn't—at least not as far as he could tell but the street was dark; they could be back there with their lights off. She didn't answer him and he asked, "Who are *they?*"

She shook her head impatiently. "Never mind," she said. "It's better for you if you don't know. They will kill me if they find me, and if you know who they are, or if they even suspect you know who they are, they will kill you, too. There's a plane at eleven-thirty for

New York. I must be on it. Until then I must hide. Will you help me?"

If he had waited for the light to change, he could have stalled her until he thought of some excuse. But she was staring at him beseechingly, her eyes luminous in the dark. Tears, Flood thought, why do they always use tears? Yet she was clearly scared, crazy or not. Now he was becoming afraid himself but he was also afraid of the look, the contempt, he would get if he refused. He nodded. "Okay."

The light changed and she drove on slowly. "Your place," she said. "Could we go there, just for two hours? They would never think of that."

"As you said, if they spotted your car——"

She shook her head. "I've been watching. No one has followed us." She paused and added, "At least I don't think so."

Now that he had agreed to help, he accepted her fear as more real and was anxious to get off the streets, too. "The first corner after the next light, turn right," he said.

"Do you have a family, a wife?"

Flood shook his head and it was a few seconds before he realized that she couldn't have seen the motion. "No," he said, "I live alone."

"Why did you hesitate?" She sounded frightened again.

"I was thinking. I had a wife."

"Divorced?"

"She died."

There was a silence. "I'm sorry."

"Yeah," Flood said, hardened against those two words. "Turn right the next corner."

She parked the car as he instructed, facing out at the far end of the line of wood garages behind his apartment house. The car couldn't be seen from the street, he told her as they got out and went toward the rear entrance of the building. He unlocked the door with the same key that fit the front door and they went into a small terrazzo-floored lobby. Flood pointed to the stairs and the woman nodded and took off her shoes. He did, too, and when he straightened up he saw that she was already at the top of the first flight. He hurried after her. She had narrow hips and slender ankles and her calves flexed slightly, enticingly, at each step. I'm too drunk for that, he thought, and wondered if that was what she wanted. He had once known a woman who had to concoct the most bizarre situations before she could go to bed with a man.

As they entered his apartment, he shut the door behind them, whispered "Wait," and went to close the curtains at the double window before turning on a light. She was standing slackly, her head down, by the door. Flood watched her as she pulled herself together, letting out her breath in a long murmuring sigh, then taking her hat off and shaking her hair loose. She raised her head wearily and looked at him. He went to her and took her by the arms—a gesture of comfort.

But she didn't want even that. She trembled and said softly, "Don't. Please."

Flood released her and stared at her face. He had been wrong, he saw. She was not pretty; her face was too hard, drawn, and she had on too much makeup. But he had been right in a way, too; there was a sad loneliness about her. He blocked the feeling. As he started to turn away, her eyes filled with tears again and her lips trembled.

"What is it?" he asked.

She shook her head. "Never mind."

"A drink?"

She shook her head again and he nodded and went to the kitchen to fix one for himself. At Treats he had been drinking Jack Daniel's but he didn't have anything that good at home, so he took out a bottle of cheap bourbon, filled a large old-fashioned glass with ice, and poured the whiskey up to the top. If it was sex she wanted, he thought, he should make coffee. Instead, he picked up the glass and swallowed a large gulp; then he filled it with bourbon again and went back to the living room.

The woman was sitting in the red chair, her head

back, her eyes closed. Her eyes were very large and
the lids were dark—whether from eye shadow or
fatigue, he couldn't tell. He sat down on the couch a
few feet away and at the sound her lids flew upward
like sprung roller shades.

"It's all right," Flood said. "You're safe now."

She nodded uncertainly. "Please don't ask me anything."

"Okay," he said and took a sip of his drink. They
were silent for several minutes and he wondered how
they would get through the time until her plane left.
Danger—if there was any danger—hung over them but
he couldn't talk about it and it was all he wanted to
talk about. "Do you want to watch television?" he
asked and felt absurd.

She looked at him sadly and shook her head.
"Please. You go ahead."

He shook his head, too, and took another drink.
They were silent again for several minutes. Finally
Flood tried another approach. "That accent of yours
—I don't recognize it. Is it Slavic?"

She seemed afraid again. Then she shrugged, as if to
herself, and said, "Partly."

"Now I know all about you," Flood said.

She sat forward abruptly. "You do?"

"Jesus, how am I supposed to help you if I don't
know what this is all about?"

"You don't have to know," she answered, sitting
back, relieved. "You don't *want* to know." She looked
at a small gold watch on her left wrist. "Two hours,
two and a half hours, that's all I need. That's the
help you can give me. Then I'll go and you need
never think about me again."

"Great," Flood said. "Cataclysm. Devastation. And
here I am, the uninquiring reporter."

She sat forward again, looking stunned. "You mean
you would write about this? In the newspapers? My
God!"

Flood shook his head. "One doesn't have to be
planning to write about a thing just because one won-
ders what it means," he said sharply, irritated by her

35

suspicion. "You can't fling those ominous words around like that without creating curiosity, you know."

He noticed for the first time that she was holding a small handbag, not much bigger than a man's wallet, on her lap. Now she opened it and took out a sheaf of bills.

"I have a thousand dollars—a little over a thousand dollars," she said. "If I give you half of it, will you help me—without any more questions?"

"Jesus," he said.

"How much do you want?" She held out the bills. "Here, you can have all of it."

Flood was suddenly very angry. "Why don't you get the hell out of here?"

She flushed deeply and put the bills back in the wallet. "I'm sorry."

"You're good at that anyway." He took a large drink of whiskey. The hell with delicacy, he thought, and moved in with the reporter's oldest tactic—asking a question when the subject is off-balance with embarrassment or shame: "Who's trying to kill you?"

It worked. "My husband. And Bell. His assistant. I don't think his real name is Bell. It couldn't be. Anyway he lives with us."

Jesus, Flood thought, nothing more than a marital squabble. And here he was, sitting with some crazy woman who had probably had her face slapped.

"You don't believe me of course."

"Of course."

She closed her eyes again and when she opened them she seemed resigned. "If I tell you—not all but some —will you help me?"

"What do you want me to do—kill him? Anything you ask." He knew he had gone too far. Whatever had happened, whoever she was, whether or not she was demented, she deserved better than this.

"Please," she said, "don't talk like that." She broke off and put a hand to her lips. "You don't understand," she said through her fingers and lowered her hand. Her lips were fuller now, as if she were aroused, and Flood felt a momentary flicker of desire. "It's serious, more serious than you can imagine," she went on. "I discovered something that he has to kill me to conceal. He *has* to. If you find out what it is, he will have to kill you, too. He has no choice, believe me. Please believe me."

She held out a hand in a small gesture of appeal. Flood looked at her without answering.

She lowered the hand to her lap and continued, "My sister—she lives with us, too—is away, somewhere in New York City. Thank God she wasn't here. If she had been here, he would be sure I had told her and he would kill her, too. But he knows I can't reach her. She didn't know where she was going to stay, so I have no idea where she is. She'll be back tomorrow. For her sake as well as mine I must get away from here tonight. If I wait and she comes back, he'll think she knows as well." She paused and opened her bag, then looked up at him. "Will you do one more thing for me?"

Flood noticed that she was wearing small gold hoop earrings. "Let's hear what it is first," he said.

She took an envelope out of the bag along with a slim gold pencil. She began to write on the blank front of the envelope but stopped and stared at Flood for a moment. "I hope I'm right," she said and resumed writing. She hesitated a few seconds and held the envelope out to him.

Flood put it face-down on the table without looking at it.

"It's for my sister," she said. "I put her name there and the address of her ballet school. She's there Monday, Wednesday, and Friday afternoons. Two to five. Will you see that she gets it? And tell her she must destroy it as soon as she's read it."

Flood didn't answer.

He turned off the shower and stood staring blankly at the wall and asking himself over and over, What happened to the letter? Often he hid things—money, a fine antique gold chain Ellen had always worn around her neck, her wedding ring—and sometimes he couldn't find them later. Once he had accidentally come upon two hundred dollars that he had stuck, God knows when, under the cover of the large unabridged Webster's, which was always open on its stand next to the table he used for a desk. He put on his robe and went to the stand and lifted both sides of the dictionary. There was no envelope.

Flood turned and stopped. Of course, he thought, of course. She had been wearing earrings when she sat in the red chair but there were no earrings on her in the alley and there was only one earring in the handbag. To make sure, he went to the bookcase and took the bag from behind the economics textbook, where he had hidden it before going to destroy the evidence. There was only one earring. He looked again at the papers in the wallet. Whoever she was, she wasn't Wendy Cameron, he thought, hearing her softly accented voice again. And she lived somewhere in New Richmond, not in Philadelphia.

Had they hidden the earring here? he asked himself. Had they planted the lipstick under the bed? Then he remembered the woman's watch. She had been wearing it the night before but there had been no watch on either wrist, he realized as he saw her body in the alley. And the hat. "I'll never make it," he muttered. He sighed and went to dress.

Flood found the second earring in the pocket of a freshly laundered shirt halfway down in a stack of shirts in his bedroom dresser. And he found the watch inside the hem of one of the living room curtains. But he didn't find the hat. For a few moments he was pleased with himself because he had outwitted them, but almost at once he realized that he had no idea of what else they might have hidden there. It could be something left out in the open that he wouldn't notice but that the police would recognize at once as evidence. Flood walked slowly around the living room, examining everything, and repeated the process in the other rooms. He found nothing out of the ordinary. That was just it, he thought, it wouldn't be out of the ordinary. He repeated the examination but again found nothing unexpected. All he could do was hope he hadn't missed anything.

Hope, he thought sourly. He went to the living room closet door, which had been locked ever since he put Ellen's things away. He turned the key and opened the door. Ellen's clothes—loosely wrapped in thin plastic sheets—filled most of the closet. On the floor were boxes of her other things and on the top shelf were more boxes. He couldn't remember what was in them. Shoes, he thought. The boxes on the floor contained shoes, slippers, handbags. In the boxes on top there were letters, papers, tax returns, a novel she had started when she quit her job as an editor. Wondering whether they had hidden something there, he knew he couldn't search that place; he would rather turn himself in to the police.

Her red suit, pinkish through the plastic, caught his eye and he saw her again as she had looked the only time she wore it—to the Pulitzer Prize award ceremony. She looked so beautiful in it, and he remembered her contradictory expression as he came down from the stage, his Pulitzer tucked under one arm—her eyes brimming with tears and her gentle smile.

His Pulitzer series won national attention almost at once, so Flood got the prize without the lobbying and infighting editors and publishers and writers usually have to engage in to win it. The political and financial corruption he uncovered throughout the state went back two generations and this time the villains weren't the ordinary political hacks and their appointees but members of the oldest and most prominent families in the Northeast. These estimable thieves, Flood demonstrated, had stolen scores of millions in public funds. To protect themselves, they further undermined society by rewriting parts of its laws and then hired a couple of noted, and deeply venal, historians to cover their tracks in public-school history texts. After the *Herald* ran the seven-part series, a grandson of a man who would have gone to prison if he had been alive attacked Flood on the street; he got thirty days in jail and served every day of it.

The night of the award ceremony, Ellen and Flood stayed at the Plaza, drinking Dom Perignon in their room and making love. The next morning they had brunch in the Palm Court—a caviar omelette for her and corned-beef hash for him and a bottle of icy Sancerre. Then they went for a walk in Central Park and did all the things that one does on a walk in Central Park: they watched the ducks in the lake across from the hotel; they visited the zoo and marveled at the slithering grace of the seals in the center pool; they watched delicate young men exercising their nervous Afghans and greyhounds; they watched youngsters and grownups sail their model boats in the oval pond; they ate hot dogs; they watched lovers spooning in the cold spring grass; and they rode on the carousel. Afterward they went back to their room and made love again, and he said to her, "It'll be even better in Stockholm with the Nobel," and they came into her laughter.

At the left side of the closet was a separate plastic bag and Flood took it out. It contained the jacket and trousers he'd worn on the trip west, their last days together before she died; he'd had them cleaned and put them away, out of sight. If he was right, he needed the jacket. He tore off the plastic and saw that he was right, or close enough for the difference not to matter. The herringbone pattern was perhaps a little larger than the one he had got rid of at the Salvation Army but no one would notice—not as likely as they would notice if the jacket he wore nearly every day suddenly disappeared.

Flood slipped on the coat. It was tight across the shoulders and it smelled slightly musty; otherwise it was all right. He shut the closet door—sad and relieved at once to close off the sight of her things. I should get rid of those, he thought, and knew that he wouldn't, not yet anyway.

Turning away, Flood saw his raincoat draped over the back of the couch. He stared at it in disbelief. Jesus, how could he have forgotten that? If he had been seen leaving the alley, he had been seen leaving it in a tan raincoat. If there was blood on his clothes, there would probably be blood on the coat. If he had lain on the concrete paving of the alley, there would be fragments of concrete in the weave of the material.

He grabbed the coat off the couch and took it into the kitchen, the brightest room in the apartment, and examined it carefully. There seemed to be no blood-stains but he couldn't be certain about a small dark spot behind the button at waist level. Feeling something he hadn't noticed earlier, a thick piece of paper in the inside breast pocket in the lining, he reached in and took it out. It was an envelope—a bill from his bookstore.

Flood stopped short and turned to stare through the doorway toward the bedroom. He remembered now. A few seconds later, he was standing beside the bed looking down at the night table next to it—a heavy old mahogany piece from his parents' house with feet the size and shape of half grapefruits turned upside down. He knelt on the dark-blue rug and studied the pile of it around the feet. It seemed all right. Drunk as he had been, he had made sure he put the table back precisely where it had been. Then he had taken her out to her car. Pausing now, he remembered how anxious he'd been for her to leave. He had opened the door to the driver's side for her. That was the last thing he remembered. They must have hit him then.

Getting up, Flood lifted the table by its top and set it down to one side. The marks left by the two feet on the end nearest the bed seemed undisturbed—deep smooth indentations, perfect circles with no overlaps. And the rug, extending nearly to the baseboard, lay flat. Reaching down, Flood gently lifted the rug a couple of inches and slipped his fingers underneath. He felt the paper.

The envelope was gritty with rug dust and he blew it clean, then sat down on the bed. The woman had printed, in shaky block letters on the front, *Marja's Ballet* and below that an address: *28 West Hannum.* He knew the street; it was at the end of Edwards, an area of old frame houses and rundown commercial buildings.

Flood held the envelope up to the light and saw a series of faint lines through the paper. He turned the envelope over. It was sealed. He took a pencil off the night table, carefully inserted its point under a gap at one end of the glued flap, and slowly slit open the envelope. Inside was a folded sheet of lined paper. He took it out and saw that it was covered on both sides with closely written Cyrillic script. It was Russian.

# 4

Before going to Moscow, Flood had studied Russian at the university for a year and after his year in Moscow he was fairly fluent in the language. He took the envelope and letter to his desk in the living room, got out his Russian dictionary and grammar, and went to work. In half an hour he had translated the letter:

My darling Marja:
  I can only pray that this reaches you and no one else. When you read these words, I will—I hope with all my soul—be far away and hidden forever from the fearful world we have lived in for so long together. I cannot tell you where I am going because it would be fatal to you if he found that you know, and it would be fatal to me if he learned my destination from this letter or forced the truth from you.

Flood reread the paragraph—pausing at the macabre irony of the words "hidden forever from the fearful world" and went on:

  I could not wait for you to return tomorrow. A few more hours, an hour even, in that house would have cost me my life. And if he had seen us talking—as we would have, of course, even though innocently—that would have cost you your life too.
  I beg you, my loving sister, do as I tell you. Only in that way can you possibly survive.
  Act as if you have not the slightest idea of why or when I fled or even that I fled. Act as if something must have happened to me, some accident. Insist on calling the police. If he suspects

that you know *anything* or wonder about *anything* you are in terrible danger. Pretend, my darling, pretend for all you are worth. Your life depends on it, I assure you.

Wait a few days or a week until he is confident that you know nothing and stops watching you. Then flee. Prepare the way carefully. Put money aside secretly. Plan. Then go and go quickly. To Europe, I think. There you can hide better among your own kind.

A year from today if I am still alive I will leave a message for you in the old place and in the old way.

I have discovered the answer to what we have asked ourselves so many times since we moved into that house. I have learned what is in the attic. The operation they call "Until the next time"—

Flood paused to look at the original. The Russian words for the parting salutation are *Do svidanya* but she had run them together as non-Russians often do. Operation *Dosvidanya,* Flood thought, puzzled by it. The sisters had been puzzled too, it seemed, as he read on:

They mean "until the next time" in the sense that it is often given, especially by Americans: "Goodbye."

He looked up her word—*proshchay*—in his dictionary and saw that he was right. It meant "good-bye." Then he looked up *Do svidanya* and saw that at the end of the definitions was one saying: "Sometimes, loosely, good-bye." He went back to the letter:

The operation means "Good-bye, America." I know why now. The coat hooks in Bell's room. I am sure I was seen. Bruce's love for me is very great, I know, but it can never overcome his loyalty, his belief, his duty. For Bruce to do that would be to deny his life. Now he must kill me if he can and I must escape if I can.

Flood stopped reading. It sounded crazy but the woman was dead, murdered as she had said she would be. Bell was the assistant who lived with them, apparently in the attic. But "coat hooks"? What did that mean? Was it a code?

He shook his head in bewilderment and finished the letter:

I will tell no one what I found, not even you. I am too frightened of what would happen to me and to you, the only person I have always truly loved with all my heart. It is in your hands now. If you want to know, you can find out as I found out. If you want to tell the Americans, that is up to you. I cannot. I am afraid of what they might do. And I am afraid of what will happen, must happen, if they are not told.

Beware, beware, my beloved.

Your adoring Natalie

She hadn't got very far in her flight, Flood thought, again seeing the sprawled figure in the alley. *"Dosvidanya,* Natalie," he whispered softly. He felt close to her, and he trembled slightly as he realized how close he was to her and to her fate.

Flood was quite certain he hadn't been followed, so they didn't know yet. He pulled into the garage entrance of the Hotel Bancroft, told the attendant he would be only a few minutes, and went into the hotel and through the main lobby to the Penguin Bar. He stopped at the door and looked at his watch: 1:43. He pushed the leather-padded door open and went in. Along the wall just inside the door was an oak half-beam with staggered rows of heavy brass coat hooks. The coat hooks in Bell's room, he thought, and wondered again what that meant. Taking off his raincoat, he hung it on top of one much the same as his. Two customers at the crowded bar who had their backs to each other let him get an arm in far enough to pick up the double Bloody Mary he ordered. Standing there uncomfortably, he drank quickly, holding the battered briefcase he had brought with him between his feet. He had another double, then paid.

Fifteen minutes after he had left his car Flood was back beside it carrying someone else's raincoat on his arm. He threw the briefcase onto the seat and slipped into the coat. Jesus, it fits, he said to himself. Taking it off, he looked at the label and smiled. It was from Van Bove's too. Its owner might never discover the switch.

Edwards Street bisected Hannum and when he got to the T-junction Flood swung right onto West Hannum. He looked at his watch again: 2:08. He would have to be quick about it if he was going to get to the bank in time. So there could be no persuasion, no argument. He wondered if he could manage it.

There were several parking places in front of No. 28 but Flood pulled around the corner and parked on the same side as the building and headed back toward downtown. He slipped the briefcase beneath his seat but it wouldn't go far enough in to be out of sight. Swearing, he pulled the briefcase out and reached under the seat to see what was blocking it. When he felt the obstruction he knew at once that it was the woman's hat. They had planted it there. Jesus, he thought, wondering what else they had planted and where. He couldn't do anything about it now, he realized, and shoved the briefcase under the seat beside him.

No. 28 was a five-story red-brick building with its entrance in the center. At the left of the entrance was an electronics shop with a windowful of television sets, stereos, and portable radios. At the right was a secondhand bookstore with a windowful of dusty books on art and music. Pausing there, Flood peered through the window into the interior and saw someone in the rear. He went inside and directly up to the figure, a frail man with pale thin hair and a pale thin face. He was leaning indolently against a bookcase examining his long yellowish fingernails and ignored Flood.

"Excuse me," Flood said.

The man glanced at him idly with a look saying that the last thing in the world he wanted to do was sell a book.

"I'm looking for something on the ballet," Flood went on, sure that his deceit was obvious. "For a girl. My daughter. She's twelve."

"Too old to start ballet," the man snapped. "Eight at the outside. And train. My God, how they train." His eyebrows slid upward half an inch. "Sometimes I think the ceiling's going to come down. Just listen to them."

He pointed to the ceiling and Flood cocked his head to one side. He heard a barely audible sound, like a muffled drum far away. He looked at the man inquiringly.

"Marja's Ballet," the man said, making a face. "All those sweaty little girls."

"Really—here?" Flood asked. "A ballet troupe?" He wished now that he had never come into the place.

"Not quite so grand. A ballet school. Marja's Ballet, I said." He made another face.

"Is it good? My daughter is wild about dancing."

"I told you, she's too old. Anyway, put her in a sack and drop her in the river first. It's a filthy business. Nasty, ruthless people."

"And Marja?"

"The pits. Oh, she's a good-looking bitch. But a bitch all the same. Used to be in some European troupe, they say. I wouldn't know. Yugoslavian, I think. She's gone, though."

Flood nearly gasped. "Gone?"

The man nodded. "Too old. Gone in the legs."

Flood paused. "Maybe I should go talk to her. Then come back and get some books, on her advice."

"Do that," the man said disinterestedly. "Don't slam

the door on your way out. Some idiot slammed it last week and cracked the glass." He began to examine his nails again.

Flood started away, then stopped and turned. "What does she look like, so I'll recognize her?"

"Who?" the man asked, not looking up.

"Marja."

He shrugged listlessly. "Oh, thirty-five or so. Tallish. Built like a dancer of course. Reddish-blond hair— strawberry blond, I believe it's called." He sneered.

At the top of the first flight of stairs was a frosted-glass door with the words *Marja's Ballet School. 2 to 5 Mon. Wed. Fri. Students Only.* There was a buzzer in the door jamb under a sign saying *Please Ring.* Flood tried the door and it opened. Beyond was a small foyer with a cracked brown-linoleum floor, on the left a counter with no one behind it, and directly ahead a door with a clear-glass top half. Flood went to it and looked through. It led to a short hallway ending in a doorway, past which swirled leaping, pirou-etting, running forms of youngsters, mostly girls, in black, white, pink, blue, green, yellow leotards. He stood for a minute, trying to catch a glimpse of any-one who fit the man's description of Marja. They were all far too young.

Flood opened the door and walked quickly down the hallway. At the end he stopped and scanned the large room. In the far corner a muscular girl was gesticulating at a tall woman with reddish-blond hair who was wearing black leotards. She was standing with her back toward Flood. He hesitated, looking around to make sure there was no one else who might be Marja, then strode the length of the long room to her side. She didn't notice him.

"If I don't feel like a flower how can I dance like a flower?" the girl was saying.

"Excuse me," Flood said, more loudly than he in-tended.

The girl turned first, one arm held up with the hand drooping languidly. "Yes?"

Flood ignored her. The woman turned to him. Her eyes were so green and so large that he scarcely saw her face. "Are you Marja?" he asked.

"Yes. Can I help you?" In tone and inflection, her voice was much like her sister's, although there was hardly any accent. Except for the same prominent cheekbones, she looked nothing like her sister. Her nose was a bit too broad, her great eyes set too far apart, and she had a slight gap in the middle of her upper teeth. But her hair was fine—curly and bushy and full of reddish-gold light—and her eyes made one forget any imperfections.

"I must speak to you," Flood said.

"Of course."

The girl stared insolently at him and waited. Flood waited too, and finally the woman turned and said, "All right, Alexa, why don't you practice being a toadstool for a while."

The girl glared at her balefully and stalked off.

Marja turned back to Flood. "As you see, I'm rather busy. So—"

One of the intimidators, Flood thought unhappily. He felt less sure of himself than ever.

"What can I do for you?" Marja asked, impatience in her voice now.

"Your sister—Natalie . . ." Flood began and broke off.

"Natalie? Is something wrong?"

She was staring hard at him and for a moment he thought he was going to blurt out the truth. Instead he said, "There's been an accident. I was sent to fetch you." He wondered why he had said "fetch." It was his grandmother's word. He couldn't remember ever having used it before.

"An accident? My God, what happened?"

"I think she's all right. I don't know for sure. I was in the bank. I work there. That's where she is. They said to bring you."

"What kind of accident? What bank?"

"First National," he said limply. He couldn't go

on with it much longer. He had to get her out of there. "They called you but there was no answer. I'll take you to her. We must hurry."

"Has her husband been called?"

"I don't know. I think so. Please hurry. They told me it was urgent. You must . . ." Flood's voice trailed off and he stared at her helplessly, as if pleading that she not make his unpleasant chore any more unpleasant.

Marja nodded. "I'll change."

He didn't want that. She might use a phone. "There's no time," he said, trying to make his voice imperative. "Just throw on a coat."

"I'll only be a minute. Maybe I should call her husband."

"There's no time, I tell you," he said frantically. "He's probably there already."

She nodded distractedly and he wondered if she had heard him. She turned and hurried away and Flood followed her, as closely as he dared, and she saw him as she looked over her shoulder to call to a woman and tell her to take over the class. At the door to another hallway off the far end of the room, she stopped long enough to say, "Wait here. I'll be only a minute." Then she left.

Flood stood by the doorway. What if she called the husband? he thought. He would be waiting for them at the bank. Or the police. "Jesus," he muttered, and felt panic rising in him. He wanted to bolt but he made himself wait by the door. He knew he couldn't leave now. She was the only person in the world who might be able to help him. Anyway, if he left she would remember him—at least his white hair. This goddamn hair, he thought, feeling more helpless than ever.

Marja came hurrying along the hallway toward him. She had put a wraparound dress on over her leotards and was tying the sash. She was wearing sandals and carrying a raincoat. As she reached his side, he turned and started toward the exit without speaking.

In the foyer she stopped. "Shouldn't I call Bruce?"

"Who?" His hand was on the knob of the outer door. He had to stop her from calling.

"Bruce. Natalie's husband. Bruce McCade."

"I told you, he's probably there already," Flood said. At least he knew the killer's name now.

"But you weren't sure they called." She hesitated, looking at him.

"It's very serious," Flood said. She seemed suspicious, so he looked back into the green eyes and said, "It may be too late."

Without another word, she followed him out of the studio and down the stairs. As they got into the car she said, "Hurry—please hurry."

Flood drove as fast as prudence permitted. Several times he checked the rearview mirror to see if anyone seemed to be following him. It was impossible to tell. There was too much traffic and a tail could be two or three cars behind him. He wondered if she had called when she went to dress. Of course McCade would have told her not to let Flood know she had called anyone. He felt her eyes on him and stared ahead, hoping she wouldn't speak.

"What's your name?" she asked.

"Flood," he said without thinking. "John Flood." He wondered if he should have told her but realized it was the only way. The lie he had used to get her out would have to be the only lie. He needed her trust above all else. "It happened in such a hurry I've forgotten your last name. I mean, I remembered only Marja's Ballet and the address."

She didn't answer but he knew that she was watching him. He wondered what he should do if there was no place to park in front of the bank. Obviously he couldn't expect her to wait for him to park while her sister was lying somewhere injured, perhaps dying. As he turned the corner and saw the bank and the full line of cars along the entire block, he shook his head. "I'm no good at this at all," he said.

"What?"

He realized that he had spoken out loud. He pulled up in front of the bank and double parked. Turning to her, he said, "Natalie is dead."

Marja looked at him uncomprehendingly. It was unimaginable to her, he knew; he hadn't been able to believe Ellen's death even when her body grew cold in his arms. "I'm sorry," he said and regretted the useless words.

Marja was beginning to grasp the horror of what he had told her. Her lips, parted slightly, trembled and her great eyes were dimmed with tears. But she didn't make a sound or a move. Flood reached over to touch her hand and she withdrew it. She took out some tissues, dried her eyes, and blew her nose once. She was composed again. He stared at her in astonishment.

"What happened?" she asked. "Where is Bruce?"

"Bruce killed her," Flood answered unhesitatingly. He wasn't sure but he was sure enough to say it. He had to stop her from calling McCade.

"That's crazy," she said angrily. "He loved her."

"I know. She left a letter for you. She knew he was going to kill her if he could."

Marja stared at him. "How do you know all this? Who are you?"

"She gave me the letter to give you. She was trying to escape."

"And you read it?"

Flood nodded. "I had to. You see, he tried to kill me, too. I had no idea why. I thought the letter might explain—"

"Did it?"

"Not really. Only you can do that."

"Who *are* you?" she repeated.

"I told you."

"Is that really your name?"

"It better be. It appears over my column in the *Herald* every Thursday and Monday."

Marja nodded. "I'm afraid I don't read the papers often."

"You don't miss much." He saw that she was uncertain now, not knowing what to believe. "Look," he said, leaning toward her, "it was an accident."

"Her death?" She looked immensely relieved.

"No, no, the letter—her giving it to me. We met by accident. She was very frightened. She had no one else to turn to. She asked me to hide her and then she gave me the letter and made me promise to get it to you."

Marja looked at him coldly. "Where is it?"

"In the bank—in my safety-deposit box." It was another lie but he had no choice now. Once there she would understand.

"Is this a trick?"

"Could you be safer than in a bank?"

She thought for a few moments, then said, "Park the car."

Marja looked at the briefcase suspiciously when he slid it out from under the seat. He was so grateful that he hadn't dislodged the hat and knocked it into view that he merely said, "Some stuff I want to put in the vault." That was true at least.

One of the two uniformed bank attendants in the vault gave Flood a slip of paper, he filled it out, and handed it back, together with the key to his box, and waited. A minute later Marja and he followed the attendant down a red-carpeted hallway to a small room with a table and two chairs facing each other across it. He put the metal box down and started out. "Just ring when you're ready," he said.

Flood placed the briefcase on top of the box and sat down. He nodded toward the other chair but Marja stood watching him uncertainly. She could leave now, he thought. She could turn and walk out and there would be nothing he could do.

She sat down and said, "Give me the letter."

"First I must tell you what happened."

"Everything?"

"Everything I can remember."

She waited and he began speaking, quickly, matter-of-factly, quietly, with more precision and brevity than he had hoped to muster. As he promised, he told her everything he knew and she listened intently, watching his face closely but betraying nothing on her own.

When he reached the point where Natalie asked him to make love to her, Marja interrupted. "Why did she do that?"

"I don't know. She didn't say. Maybe gratitude. Maybe she felt sorry for me. It wouldn't be the first time a woman took pity on me in that way." He stopped. If there was anything he had to avoid now it was self-pity.

"And you?" Marja asked. "How did you feel about it?"

Flood looked away for a moment, trying to remember. "I'm not sure," he said finally. "I was afraid to in a way. I'd had a lot to drink, as I told you. I wasn't sure I could."

"What difference would that have made?" she demanded. "She may have wanted only comfort. Or was your fear too strong for you to care about that?"

"I don't know." He felt his face redden. "It seemed important to her."

"You don't understand at all, do you?" Marja asked in a flat tired voice. She lowered her eyes to the briefcase.

"I guess not. Do you?"

She looked up at him and he saw that she was angry. She shrugged slightly, as if disinterested in the subject, and said quietly, "It was the only way she could leave him. She had never betrayed him in any way—never. Before she could leave she had to betray him."

Flood felt used, then foolish, for surely he had used the woman, too, even if reluctantly. He had wanted something—comfort, too, perhaps—he realized now as he remembered Natalie's gentle appeal to him across the dimly lit room. Her sadness and loneliness had been his.

"Go on," Marja ordered.

He finished the rest of his story quickly—pausing only when he saw her eyes mist over as he described what he had found upon waking up in the alley. He forced himself to tell her about the blood on the dead woman's thighs and at that Marja closed her eyes against the words. When he finished at last, he looked at her steadily, as if to implore her belief in him.

"You have left out nothing?" she asked.

"I don't think so. That's everything I remember. If I recall something I forgot, I'll tell you."

She nodded. "Give me the letter."

Flood opened the briefcase and took out the envelope. Marja glared at him. "You lied," she said.

"I had to get you here, out of sight. I couldn't think of any other way."

"All right." She reached for the envelope.

Flood pulled it back. "I'll read it to you. It's the only evidence I have of my innocence."

"And if I ring the bell and tell the guard to call the police?"

"You won't," Flood said, hoping he was right. He took out the folded notepaper, put the envelope on his lap out of her reach, and began reading in Russian.

Marja's eyes widened. "You know Russian?"

He lowered the letter. "I was assigned to Moscow a few years ago. Before I went there I studied the language." He went back to the letter but as he read it his sense of pronunciation faltered so often that she repeatedly asked him to read something over again.

Finally, as he was puzzling over a word, Marja snatched the letter out of his hand. "We don't have time," she said flatly. She leaned back so the piece of paper was out of his reach and slowly read the letter. Then she read it again and when she finished she handed it back to Flood. "I believe you now," she said. She lowered her hands to her lap and stared down at the table for a long time. At last she raised her head and looked at Flood. Her eyes had filled with tears again. "I knew it would happen—someday," she said. She was silent for a few moments, then added, "Now he must kill me, too."

"Not unless he knows you know," Flood said quickly. "Do you know what's in the attic? The coat hooks? Does that mean anything to you?"

She shook her head. "Nothing." She was quiet, then said, "I'm glad she didn't tell me. I don't want to know."

Flood was stunned. "But that's why he killed her."

His voice had risen to a half-shout and she silenced him with a gesture. "All I need to know is that, not the rest. It's too dangerous."

Baffled, Flood looked at her, waiting for her to go on, but she was silent again. "Who's McCade?" he asked finally.

Marja shook her head. "I can't tell you—not yet. Perhaps later. That's dangerous, too."

"Dangerous?" he shouted. "Jesus Christ, the man murdered your sister and tried to murder and frame me, and now you tell me he's dangerous?"

"Someone will hear you," she said calmly. "I told you—perhaps later. I need time to think."

"You've got to help me."

Marja looked at him coldly. "The way you helped Natalie?"

"At least I tried." The accusation sickened him. He looked away.

"By taking her to bed?"

Infuriated by the unfairness of the charge, he turned on her. "That's rotten."

Her expression didn't change. "Where is Natalie's handbag?"

Without a word he took the wallet-like bag out of his briefcase and handed it to her. She looked at it and nodded, as if to confirm that it was her sister's. She opened it and dumped the contents on the table. As she went through the papers, she looked increasingly puzzled, then held up the identification card. "Wendy Cameron?" she asked, staring at him, her green eyes eager now.

Flood realized that she was clutching at the last hope —that the dead woman was not her sister. "You've never seen those?"

"Natalie has never even been in Philadelphia."

"She didn't use the name Wendy Cameron?"

"No—never. Why should she?"

"Then he was trying to conceal her identity," Flood said. "Maybe so you wouldn't find out." Doubt clouded her eyes as he went on, "After all, there's the letter. Isn't it her handwriting?"

"Describe her," Marja said.

Hope gradually drained out of her face as Flood spoke. At the end she reached down and picked up the earrings. "I knew it was Natalie," she said softly. "These are her earrings. Bruce had them made for her out of two old wedding rings. You never find earrings this heavy." She nodded to herself and then, at last, she wept.

It was raining when Flood came out of the bank— thin, wind-blown, slashing rain—and pedestrians were hurrying, their heads down, faces tense. He passed a small haberdashery and stopped, then turned in. A few minutes later he emerged wearing a brown slouch hat with the brim turned down all around. It looked rather foolish, he had thought as he bought it, but it might help. He patted his breast pocket to make sure he had the envelope with the thousand dollars he withdrew after Marja left and hurried on, bent against the wind and rain like everyone else.

She had tried to conceal her striking hair, too, he saw as he slid into the car beside her. She was wearing a black knitted cap and looked quite different—older, rather drawn. She gave his hat a nod of approval and said, "Better."

"So's the rain. No one can see into the car now."

"They won't have to—not if they know the car."

Anger toward her arrogance rose in him but he tried to ignore it as he pulled out and drove through the shining streets, checking the rearview mirror constantly. "I'm sure they haven't followed us," he said as they got near Hannum. "There were several clear blocks behind us most of the way."

"They are very clever."

Flood pulled into a small parking lot behind the building where the ballet school was located and turned off the engine. The thin rain beat at the car and a mist of steam rose from the hood. They were silent. Finally, he turned to her. "You still haven't told me the rest of your name."

She didn't look at him. "Is that so important?"

A sense of futility overcame him. "Are you going to walk away, just like that?" he asked, careful to keep the anger out of his voice.

Now she looked at him but said nothing.

"Are you?"

"I haven't decided."

"But McCade—"

"I shouldn't have told you his name."

"You did though. Now I can find him."

She smiled faintly. "I think you'll wish you hadn't."

They were both silent again and Flood tried to think of something to say, anything to keep her from leaving. "I thought we could help each other," he said at last. It sounded like a plea.

"I don't need help," Marja said.

"I certainly do," he burst out.

She nodded.

"You may, too," he added lamely.

She turned. "From you?"

The insult was like a slap. "Why not?" he asked, his voice defensive. "How was I to know? It sounded, it seemed . . . so crazy."

Marja shrugged, disinterested again.

Inflamed by her composure, he said, "You may want a man at your side."

"A man at my side!" she cried, her eyes blazing with contempt. "What man has ever been anything but trouble? What can you do that won't make things worse? You and your childish machismo! You disgust me."

Flood pulled back in his seat. It was as if all the pent-up anger of womanhood had burst upon him. "I need you," he said. He had meant the words to be plain, straightforward, but they sounded plaintive. He was disgusted with himself.

"What good can I do you?" she demanded. "If he sees you with me, he'll kill you."

"He'll kill me anyway."

"That's true."

"And you."

"Not if I have nothing to do with you. That's probably my only chance."

Flood hadn't thought of that. It was true. He was horrified at himself but he said it anyway: "He killed your sister. I tried to help her and now he wants to kill me. Doesn't that matter to you?"

She didn't speak for a long time but stared off past him at the rain, her eyes blank. Like Natalie's, Flood thought and shuddered involuntarily. At the movement she turned to look at him. "You're frightened," she said.

"Very."

"Good."

"And you?"

"Yes. But not so frightened I can't act. And you?"

"I think I can."

*"Think?"* She looked at him contemptuously. "Is this the male assistance you offered me?"

Tough, Flood thought. Jesus, she's tough. He stared into the green eyes until he lost himself and said calmly, "Nothing like this—nothing—has ever happened to me before. I woke up beside a dead woman this morning at half past five—" He paused to look at his watch: 3:14. His column was due at the office in fifteen minutes. He was amazed at the thought—to be distracted by something so ordinary now. "A lot has happened," he went on. "I think I've done pretty well. Maybe this sort of thing is in your line. I don't know. But it's not in mine. I'm exhausted. I'm bewildered. And I'm very, very scared." He stopped.

"All right," she said. "As long as you see that much about yourself. Anyway, I suppose I have no choice."

At first Flood thought she meant that she owed him

this because of what he had tried to do for her sister but then he realized that she knew McCade couldn't let her live now. She needed help, too, and there was no one else. At least they were equals in that way.

"My name is Voll," she said. "Marja Voll. You could have found that out for yourself easily enough."

# 5

"Eight minutes late," Rogers said, looking at the digital clock on his desk. Among the shifting, mounting, disappearing mounds of papers on its cluttered surface only the clock was always visible. Time was Rogers' god.

"I was waiting for you in the space ship," Flood said. Over the years he had found that banter was the safest way to deal with Rogers; it was either that or the garrote.

Rogers picked up the copy for Flood's column and began reading. He read at a phenomenal speed and looked over everything that went into the paper before it went in. Flood hated the business of waiting, standing beside the desk like a schoolboy while his copy was read, but it was a rule. He glanced at Rogers from time to time with distaste. The editor was a tall pot-bellied man with a shiny bald head, a pug nose, and loose lips that looked like pieces of raw liver; they wore a permanent sneer. "E. M. Rogers" said a plaque on the outer side of his desk. No one knew what the initials stood for but there had been many guesses, ranging from "Ego Maniac" to "Enemy of Mankind."

"Not bad, not bad at all," Rogers said, tossing the copy into his out-basket. "For hand-me-down Emerson, that is."

"You're sweet," Flood said. It was hard, at best, to keep up his end with Rogers and under the circumstances it was nearly impossible. If I could only get some sleep, Flood thought.

"Copy!" Rogers suddenly roared. A boy ran up and stopped. He looked terrified and picked the copy out of the basket gingerly, as if hoping that he could get away without having to speak to Rogers. "Get Ormond over here," Rogers snapped at him. Then he grinned at Flood. "Something more I can do for you?" he asked with a moist floppy grin. "A fifty per cent raise? A three-month vacation with pay?"

"I'd settle for a little milk—"

Rogers screwed up his face quizzically.

"—of human kindness."

"Clean out of the stuff," Rogers snarled and turned away.

Just as Flood started off, Ormond—a young reporter who hadn't yet learned to conceal his curious innocence with even a pretense of cynicism—hurried up to the desk. "You wanted me?"

"That is not quite the word I would use," Rogers said nasally. "More like 'called' or 'summoned.' Peremptorily of course. And due only to a pressing need and the absence at this late hour of anyone with a modicum of experience, judgment, and the ability to write a simple declarative sentence."

Ormond looked perplexed, then smiled nervously. "Sure," he said.

"Sure what?" Rogers demanded indignantly.

The Torquemada of journalism, Flood thought and went to a nearby drinking fountain. He drew a paper cupful of cold water, drank it, and drew another.

"Murphy just called from headquarters," Rogers went on. "He's on the case of that woman they found in an alley off Stark Street. He can't leave. He wants someone to go over to the alley—it's between Williams and Scott. Get a description—what it looks like, who lives nearby. Talk to the neighbors to see if anyone noticed anything. The cops, too, if any are still around. The usual. Phone it in. You've got forty minutes. Hop!"

"Right, Chief," Ormond said and started off.

Rogers screamed, "Don't call me 'Chief'! Never call me 'Chief'! Nor 'Bwana' either! Once more and you're fired! Understand?"

Stricken, Ormond nodded and fled. Flood stood at the drinking fountain. It was real then, he thought. Rogers' words were like the death certificate that had been missing. Flood strolled over to the editor's desk.

"What's this about a murder?" he asked, trying to sound casual.

"Who said anything about murder?" Rogers retorted, not looking up from his work. "I said a woman's body was found in an alley. Even in these vile days death occasionally occurs naturally."

Flood turned away quickly and went to his desk at the far corner of the city room. Because he had a column he also had a six-foot-high partition around three sides of the space allotted to his desk and he sat down, grateful for the relative privacy. He realized he was trembling and wished again that he could get some sleep. Nothing else would help. The story would be in tomorrow morning's paper. If they didn't know he had escaped, they would know tomorrow. He looked at the large clock across the room: 3:48. It was not quite half a day since he awakened beside the corpse. It seemed impossible that so much could have happened in half a day. Now he had another half a day, maybe a little more, before they got up and saw the paper. Maybe fifteen hours.

Flood sat forward abruptly. Jesus, television. Or radio. He rarely watched television and never listened to the radio, so he had forgotten. The news of the murder must have been broadcast by now. The sense of futility overcame him again and he sat, his elbows on the desk, his face in his hands, for a long time.

"Waiting for your muse to speak?"

Flood looked up. Rogers was standing there, grinning nastily.

"Here's her inspiration: 'i before e except after c.' "

"You've got a million of them, haven't you?" Flood said. "And every one at least fifty years old." Maybe he had gone too far this time, he thought, seeing Rogers' face go dark. The line was an exceedingly uncertain one and to cross it meant real trouble.

Rogers' lips moved wordlessly, as if he were chewing his frustration. Then he said, "I know reality isn't your beat, Johnny. Heaven forbid that facts should ever clutter your aerie. I also know you don't like being told what to write about, so far be it from me—a poor demented old editor—to tell the house Emerson where his thoughts should flow. But the publisher might be pleased if you actually wrote something our readers could understand."

Flood stared at him without speaking for a minute. "What sort of thing?"

Rogers shrugged. "Anything that might sell a few newspapers."

Flood nodded. "I'll think about it," he said. He hesitated, then asked, "The police have any leads on that woman's death?"

"If they do, they're keeping quiet."

"Who's running it?"

"Flower."

Flood repressed a shudder. "He's pretty good."

"Surely you're not thinking of writing about crime?" Rogers asked, grinning. "Not with your delicate sensibilities. What would Ralph Waldo say?"

" 'Commit a crime and the earth is made of glass,' " Flood said.

"Cute. Who said it?"

"Emerson." That made Flood feel better, especially when he looked at Rogers and saw how much worse he felt.

Flood's telephone rang and he picked it up automatically. Then it occurred to him that it could be McCade trying to find out if he was there. Flood clamped a hand over the receiver and looked inquiringly at Rogers, who gave him another nasty grin and left. Flood stared at the receiver, tempted to put it back on its cradle and leave. Instead he put the instrument to his ear and waited.

"Hello? Hello?" a woman's voice said. "Is that you? Mr. Flood?"

It was Marja. The fear drained out of him and he said, "Yes."

"Is something wrong?"

The absurdity of the question made him want to laugh. "No," he said. "Nothing more so far."

"Can you meet me at five?"

Then she was going to help. "Where?"

"A bar. Behind my school. Called Tony's."

"Right." He hung up before she changed her mind.

Flood leaned back in the old wood swivel chair and looked at his shoes. Beyond them, at the back of the knee space under the desk, he saw his travel bag. He hadn't been out of town in a long time and wondered if he had remembered after the last trip to replace the dirty clothes with clean ones. Bending forward, he pulled the bag out. It was a scuffed tan-canvas-and-brown-leather carryall—big enough to hold a few shirts, some socks and underclothes, a toilet kit, and odds and ends, and small enough to fit under an airplane seat. Flood unzipped the bag and saw that the clothes were clean. He noticed the neck of a bottle and pulled it out. Jack Daniel's and nearly full. He couldn't remember when he'd bought it; probably sometime on the road when he'd felt flush. Anyway it would mean one less stop. He zipped the bag closed and looked into one of the outer pockets. His Sony tape recorder. He had forgotten it was there; it was a good one—two hundred dollars with an office discount—and too valuable to leave lying around like that, he thought. In another pocket were some tape cassettes and extra batteries and in still another were three small notebooks and two fillers for his ballpoint pen. Fully equipped, he thought. Now if he only knew where to go.

Flood rose and picked up the bag and started out. Pausing at Rogers' desk, he said, "I'll be away for a couple of days."

Rogers looked at the bag. "No typewriter? A lovers' holiday?"

Again Flood felt stupid. It would be a small misstep like that, he was sure, that would send him sprawling. "I left it home," he lied. "No, maybe not." Nervously he turned and went back to his desk and unlocked the double-sized bottom drawer. The Olivetti was there, as he knew. He took it out, unzipped the cover part way, and slid in a half-inch-thick sheaf of copy paper. Rogers didn't look up as he left.

Flood took the same route out of town that he had used earlier and followed the River Road past the city limits until he came to a weather-beaten sign saying Guardian Motel and turned in. At the side of the small yellow house was a door with a sign above it: *Office*. He stopped and went inside. The office was a small room divided in half by a Formica-topped counter. Behind it was a row of filing cabinets and above those were three dime-store pictures of wild geese flying in Vs. He didn't remember the place at all.

An emaciated man in his sixties with dyed-black hair and watery eyes came in through a door behind the counter. He had a toothpick in his mouth and was chewing something. "Afternoon," he said.

Flood didn't remember the man either. "Any vacancies?" he asked.

"We got nothing but vacancies, mister. Place is empty as my wife's head." He smiled, revealing a set of inhumanly regular false teeth. "Take your pick. Eighteen dollars a night. You alone?"

Flood nodded.

"So far, huh?" He started to laugh but apparently thought better of it. "Don't matter actually. One person or six, it's all the same—eighteen dollars."

Flood took out his wallet. "I'll pay for two nights," he said.

The man wrote out a receipt. "Thirty-eight sixteen with tax."

Flood gave him two twenties and asked, "The cabin at the far end of the rear row facing the river—is that free?" Was he trying to get closer to Ellen? he wondered. For years he hadn't been able even to look at the place when he drove by.

"Said they're all free," the man replied. He took a plastic disc with a large key attached from a board on the wall and handed it to Flood. "Fifteen," he said, and shoved the register forward.

Flood signed it W. Cameron, Philadelphia.

He drove slowly along the driveway between the two rows of cabins. They were identical—yellow clapboard with steeply pitched roofs, each about twelve by fifteen feet. The row on his right faced the main road and contained eight cabins, spaced just far enough apart to park cars in between them. The row on his left faced the other way, toward the river, and contained seven cabins; these were staggered so that they were opposite the parking spaces of the cabins across the driveway. Pulling into the space before the last cabin on the left, Flood turned out his lights and looked back through the car's rear window. The cabin opposite blocked the road beyond. Each cabin had a single window underneath the roof of a small porch in front. The car was hidden from the River Road and no light from his cabin could be seen there.

He put the carryall and typewriter on the aqua chenille bedspread and looked around. The bed had an old white-iron tubular frame of the kind that was once common in hospitals. Next to it was a blond-wood nightstand, its top marked by innumerable cigarette burns; on it was a small lamp with a wood base and a paper shade with deer running around it. In one corner was a white wicker armchair with a thin cushion on the seat, under the window was a small table painted white, and on the floor was a dark-blue cotton rug the size of a bathmat. The bathroom was small, with a miniature wash basin and a narrow shower whose yellow paint was peeling. Flood shook his head. He might never have been in the place before.

It had been a long time since the last drink, he thought, and opened the carryall. Then he remembered that it had also been a long time since he'd had any food. He couldn't take the chance. He glanced at his watch and saw that he was due at Tony's in less than half an hour; it was a fifteen-minute drive. He looked out the window toward the river. It was getting dark and the water, visible for brief stretches through the trees along its bank, was turning black. He longed to sit on the porch and drink whiskey and think.

The hell with it, he thought, I need one. He went to the bag, took out the bottle, got a plastic glass from the bathroom and poured it halfway full. Putting the bottle away, he ran cold water in the basin and filled the glass the rest of the way. He went onto the porch and sat down on the edge, his feet on the second step, and stared out at the river.

A poem he had written years ago when he was in college ran through his mind. It was entitled "Doom" and it went:

> Inside these city walls
> Along cigar and cabbage halls,
> Softly, a foot falls.

Flood smiled in self-depreciation as he recalled those days. He had been a solitary boy, defiant, touchy. The other young men at Yale were too anxious to belong to pay attention to someone who didn't know how and they left him alone. Except for Phil Briggs, his roommate for two years, and they had fallen out at last. It had been a lonely time but Flood hadn't even known it—or that he had been lonely for most of his life—until his senior year when Briggs introduced him to Ellen. Flood had always been awkward with girls, too, but from the start she let him be himself—made him be himself actually, by gently turning aside his posturing and his defensive sarcasm. After a month he knew that he had to marry her but it was she who asked him.

His father tried to talk him out of it. She wasn't Catholic, he said, even though he hadn't been near a church for as long as Flood could remember. It wasn't that, he realized later; it was that she was too strong for his father to control and he refused to be around anyone he couldn't control. He warned his son against her, then behaved with cold propriety toward them after their marriage, unbending, stern, always judging. His judgment, as usual, had been wrong, for Ellen was the best thing that had ever happened to Flood.

Only six years of her, he thought, turning to look back at the cabin behind him. Again he couldn't remember ever having been there.

Tony's was bright and noisily cheerful. Most of the customers were laborers—loud men in rough clothes

—along with a few office workers, mostly young men and younger women each sitting in separate groups. A row of booths ran along the wall parallel to the bar on the opposite side of the room and Flood saw that the rear booth was empty. As he walked toward it, two men facing him in a booth stared at him. Not good, he thought. It was a neighborhood bar where most people knew each other at least by sight; strangers weren't really welcome in such places. He would be remembered. He left his coat and hat on and slid into the seat facing the door. It was just past five.

When Marja came in a few minutes later he had finished half of a double bourbon. The men who had watched him watched her, too, and one of them made a small whistling sound as she passed their booth. Three men at the bar swiveled around on their stools to stare at her. It wasn't that she looked so wonderful, Flood thought, because she didn't. She had the cap on and looked older than when he had left her. But that didn't matter to the men, he knew; they spent half their time at work—up on construction jobs, peering out of manholes, leaning out of truck cabs—whistling and shouting at women, all kinds of women. It was merely a male game, he thought, and remembered Marja's scorn.

"Who is Bruce McCade?" he asked as she sat down across from him.

"Natalie's husband." Her voice was flat, as if it held back some internal pressure she was afraid to release.

"Why tell me the only thing about him I already know?"

Just then the waitress brought the hamburger and French fries that Flood had ordered. "I haven't eaten since early morning," he said in apology. "You want some food?"

Marja glanced at the plate in front of him with distaste. "A ginger ale," she told the waitress.

"McCade," Flood said. He took a large bite of hamburger and grimaced. "Dog meat," he said. "Not for dogs but from dogs." He took the top of the roll off and poured a thick layer of ketchup over the meat.

"I have never understood how Americans survive teenage," she said.

"By remaining teenagers." He chewed quickly to get the noxious stuff down. "What do they eat in Yugoslavia?"

She was more surprised than he expected—and more nervous. "How did you know? Natalie?" She rested her hands, which had long untapered fingers and short nails like a man's, on the table before her. Her right thumb stroked the side of her forefinger for a moment until she saw him watching it and stopped.

"The man in the bookstore below your school," Flood said. "I stopped in there before I went to see you and asked a couple of questions."

"What else did you learn?"

"He doesn't care for sweaty little girls in leotards." Marja nodded.

Flood put down the hamburger. "Okay, how about McCade?"

"Yes, I'm Yugoslavian," she said, putting off the moment again. *Donau Schwaben.*"

"What?"

"For centuries fairly large numbers of people living along the Danube on its passage through Yugoslavia have called themselves *Donau Schwaben*—Danube Swabians. They are Germans who migrated down there long ago from Swabia, in Prussia. They retained their old ways and few of them married outside the community. My father was one of the exceptions."

"Herr Voll?" Flood asked through a mouthful of potatoes.

Marja nodded. The waitress brought her ginger ale and left.

"Your mother was Yugoslav?"

"No, Russian. My father was a schoolmaster— near Belgrade. He spent a summer holiday before the war in Leningrad. She lived there. They met." She shrugged.

That explained her looks and the odd accent. "Mc-Cade?" he asked once more and pushed the plate of half-eaten food away from him.

"He killed Natalie, didn't he?" she asked unexpectedly. She took a sip of ginger ale and looked at him over the top of the glass. Her manner was quite different from her manner of an hour or two ago. She was less confident, edgier, and he wondered if it was the shock of what he had told her. He waited and finally she went on, "Since you told me, I've done nothing but try to prove to myself that he wouldn't have . . . couldn't have . . . done that. But her letter disproves me."

"What could she have seen?" Flood asked in a low voice, hoping to lead her back to McCade. "What could be in the attic?"

"I told you I don't know. We were ordered to keep away. Bell lives there. If you met Bell, you would want to keep away."

"But Natalie didn't keep away, it seems." Her eyes clouded and he realized that he had taken the wrong tack. "Tell me about Bell," he urged.

"A man of squares and rectangles," she said shortly. "An absolutely square body and a smaller square head. Two rectangles for the arms, two rectangles for the legs. About fifty. Close-cropped gray hair, gray eyes. Very strong. And very, very silent."

She wasn't going to help, Flood thought. He waited a moment, then asked, "What does McCade do?"

Marja was silent for a long time, staring down into her glass. When she looked back at him, she shook her head slowly, not so much in refusal as in bewilderment.

"How can I help if I don't know anything?" he asked. He realized that he was pleading again and stopped. Sooner or later she would tell him.

"His name is not McCade," she said softly a moment later. "It is von Hoffen—Emil von Hoffen." She stopped.

"*Donau Schwaben?*"

"No. He's from Silesia."

"Prussian?"

"Originally," she answered. "He's perfectly English,

though. Oxford educated, a faultless British accent, all the typical mannerisms of the proper Englishman."

Her voice faltered and she stopped again. Then, recovering, she leaned forward, looking into his face, and spoke softly and rapidly. "During the war he was a captain in a Panzer division. It was stationed in Yugoslavia, trying to put down Tito's partisans. His father was a senior general—one of the old Junkers—in command of an army at Stalingrad. When the Russians turned on the Germans there and pushed them back, his father was forced to retreat or see his army annihilated. He retreated and Hitler ordered him executed. The SS would not even allow him the usual grace of suicide. He was strangled with a wire and his body flung into the pit of an outhouse. His wife died of grief a month later and when Bruce—or Emil—learned of their deaths he nearly went mad. He defected to Tito with eight of his men and three tanks. I'm told Bruce was a decent man then. He was a great friend of our father's. When the Germans found out about his defection they killed my father and two other *Donau Schwaben* in retaliation. So Emil came back in the dead of night and took Natalie and me off into the mountains. He left us with an old woman who had lost two of her sons in the war. We didn't see him for several years and then one day in nineteen fifty he turned up. He had come to take us away with him to England. By then Natalie was sixteen and I was nine. He told us he had lied before about his name to protect himself in case he was captured by the Germans and he was really Bruce McCade. He said he had been on secret detachment from the British Army but we must never breathe a word of it. We went to live in London. I suppose Natalie had been in love with him all along. He was nearly fifteen years older but it didn't matter. When she turned twenty-one they were married. The wedding was in a garden at Oxford."

Flood listened to her with mounting disbelief and then, hoping to throw her off guard, he asked, "Why were you away last night? Where were you?"

Marja looked slightly surprised, nothing more. "I

went to New York to see about renting some costumes," she explained. "The school's having a recital next month. I took the train down on Monday and came back today at one o'clock. I haven't even been home."

They were silent, looking away at the men at the bar, then back at each other.

"What if I go home and find Natalie there, perfectly all right?" she asked.

"What if you go home and find that she's missing?" From Marja's expression he knew that was what she expected to find. "What will you do?"

"Act as I would have acted if I had never spoken to you."

"That will be hard."

She nodded.

"If he suspects?"

"Why should he?"

They were back to McCade and Flood took the opening to ask, "What does he do—for a living, I mean?"

"He's a businessman. He owns United Flags. You may have seen the factory. It's out on Lincoln Avenue, this side of the airport."

Flood had passed the place dozens of times—a one-story cinderblock building painted white with a large sign on top in red, white, and blue. "They make flags or just sell them?"

"Both," Marja answered. "All sorts of flags—club flags, business flags, fraternal flags, military flags, flags for local, city, state, and federal public buildings. You have no idea how many people want flags. Then there are the flagpoles. Some are made to order and equipped with electronic devices that raise and lower the flags at pre-set hours. Those are usually for installation on tops of buildings that are difficult to get to."

"An active business?"

"Very."

"And profitable?"

"That's the strange part," Marja said. "It's lost money every year—some years quite a bit of money."

She paused, then added, "I know something about keeping the books but not the overall picture."

He was surprised. "You work there?"

"Mornings," Marja said. "As bookkeeper. And I do some things Bruce won't entrust to anyone else."

Flood was interested for the first time since she began talking about the flag factory. "What sort of things?"

"Making sure that certain orders are expedited."

He felt suddenly nervous about the time that was passing. "What kind of orders?" he asked impatiently.

"The most important ones—from the government mainly, for public buildings, military bases, places like that. Bruce says those orders create other orders. He says our product is the best on the market but he must sell low to build up a clientele. So the prime customers—that's what he calls them—get equipment for less than cost. That's where the losses are. He says we'll make up for it later. It's taken nearly ten years to build up the business, and now he has lots of contacts—government purchasing officers mostly." She broke off and looked at him curiously. "It's a dull business really," she said after a moment. "Why all the questions?"

"I don't know," Flood answered, quite truthfully.

The waitress came to clear off the table and Flood ordered another drink, hoping she wouldn't ask him if he wanted this one double, too. She didn't but when she returned with the drink Marja looked at it, and then at Flood, with disapproval.

"Is that how you're going to help?" she asked.

"I'm glad to see you are your old self again," he said, taking a swallow.

"It would be a mistake to make me angry."

Her voice was cold and he looked at the green eyes and saw that they were, too. "This name change of his—Emil von Hoffen to Bruce McCade," Flood went on quickly, "Did you believe his story?"

"I suppose so. I was only a child."

"And later?"

"No."

"But you pretended to?"

"Yes."

"And Natalie?"

"Yes."

"Didn't you have a theory?"

"We wondered."

"Is this how *you're* going to help?" he asked. She didn't answer, so he went on, "The attic. Natalie wrote you she had found the answer to what you had both wondered about for so long. If neither of you believed his real name was McCade, why did you think he changed it and concocted that story for you? What did the two of you think—what do *you* think—is in that attic? What did he kill his wife to conceal?"

Marja hesitated. Her tough assurance was gone, her face slack. But as she looked at him her defiance returned. "A transmitter," she said matter-of-factly.

The same thought had occurred to Flood an instant before but he decided to dismiss it for now to see if he could taunt her into a further admission. It was all going far too slowly. "So Bruce is a CB freak," he said, sitting back.

Marja's face went hard with contempt. "A long-range transmitter," she said. "Long enough to reach a spy satellite."

"One of ours?"

"Yours is not mine," she said flatly.

"Russian?"

She nodded.

"KGB?"

She nodded again. "I think so."

Flood slumped back in the booth and rubbed a hand across his mouth. "Jesus," he muttered. If it were only the Mafia, he thought.

Marja watched him closely, as if trying to decide whether he was worth bothering with any longer. He sat up and took another swallow of his drink. Marja looked at him with contempt.

"I don't know," he said at last. "I just don't know."

"You look it."

"I don't think I like you at all," he said suddenly.

"The man in the bookstore was right—a nasty bitch."

She smiled thinly, revealing the slight gap in her teeth. "Do you actually think I care what that fool says? Or you?" She started to get up.

Flood reached for her. Whatever happened, he couldn't let her go. "When you said our satellite isn't yours did you mean—?"

"That I'm one of them—McCade and Bell?" she finished for him.

He nodded.

Marja sat back, still tense, and looked at him levelly. "No. I'm not one of them. But I'm not one of you either. If it came down to a choice—" She hesitated. "I don't know." She looked at him again in the same appraising manner, and said, "When I told you about Bruce—or Emil—taking Natalie and me to hide in the mountains you never asked about our mother."

Flood thought back and nodded. "I didn't think—"

"You had better start thinking," she said sharply and went on matter-of-factly once more, "One night nearly a year before my father was killed by the Germans you Americans came over our village near Belgrade to bomb von Hoffen's Panzers out in the woods five miles distant. When the first wave of bombers came over, my mother was at her sister's across the village and she ran home to be with us, because she knew we would be frightened. One of your planes dumped its bombs short and they landed on the village square and on our church. All that was found of her was one hand. She was identified by her wedding ring."

No wonder she was bitter, he thought, and looked at her more kindly, even admiringly. "An accident," he said lamely.

"I prefer the viciousness of Germans or the brutality of Russians to the stupidity of Americans. Negligence is unforgivable."

Flood thought of Ellen. Was he never to be forgiven?

"Are you an agent, too?" Marja asked, staring at him. "CIA? FBI?"

He was astonished, then amused. "I'm not *that* incompetent," he said.

She smiled. "Couldn't you go to them?" she asked. "Explain what happened and get their help?" She reached out as if to touch him but withdrew her hand.

Flood wished she hadn't stopped. He asked, "Explain what? That I didn't kill Natalie? That there's a nest of spies who did, that they make American flags as a cover, and that they can be rounded up tonight, all unsuspecting, with complete plans for taking over the YMCA?" Suddenly he realized that he hadn't got the address or description of the house from her. He felt sleepy. The drinks had picked him up for a time but now they were letting him down. He ordered black coffee and asked Marja to tell him about the house.

"It's at the corner of Barnard and Trevelyan—Two twenty-four Barnard. A large old Victorian place, the largest house in the neighborhood. Do you know the area?" Flood nodded and she continued, "It's painted gray. You can't miss it. There's a large garage back in the rear and more land around the place, nearly an acre, than any of the other houses in the neighborhood. That's why Bruce bought it, I think. It's private but not isolated enough to stand out."

"A fence?"

Marja shook her head. "There's no need for a fence, not with Damon around." He was about to ask who was Damon when she went on, "Damon is a dog—a very large, very unpleasant dog. A Doberman."

"Of course," Flood said wearily. "There would have to be a Doberman." Maybe he should call the Bureau, he thought. But then he thought of Keller, the agent in charge, a big bluff man with the kind of arrogant assurance that masked his utter incompetence. Lieutenant Flower had once said of Keller that he couldn't find his own footprints in the snow. There was Busby at the Agency in Virginia, but Flood realized that he wouldn't allow himself to believe the story, not with the corpse of a woman included. Why should he? Flood wasn't sure he believed it himself.

"When we moved into the house, it was equipped with all sorts of alarms," she said. "Burglar alarms on all the doors leading outside and all the ground-floor windows. And several fire alarms. Bruce is terrified of fire. I asked him about his fear once—otherwise he seems fearless—and he muttered something about getting trapped in a burning tank during the war. There's also an alarm on the door to Bell's room at the top of the attic stairs."

"I thought you were forbidden to go up there."

"One day Natalie couldn't bear their secrecy any longer. Bruce and Bell were out in the garage trying to fix the car. It's the only time I can remember at least one of them not being in the house. Natalie crept upstairs and opened the attic door. An alarm went off and she shut the door and it stopped. She ran back downstairs and sat at the tea table with me in the small parlor. When Bruce and Bell came racing in we were calmly drinking tea. Bruce asked if we had heard an alarm and Natalie said, cool as could be, that there was a ringing sound but it stopped, then sipped her tea and took a biscuit. He sat down to have a cup with us, even though he detests tea. I suppose he wanted to see if it was hot. It was. I had made sure of that. Bell was nervous. He clenches his hands into fists when he's nervous. I thought he might never get them unclenched. Bruce said something to him—about an electrical short, I think. That was all. He watched us for a few days but he never said anything."

"How about the factory?" Flood asked.

"There's no dog, no guard or watchman," she answered. "There are only two alarms—very simple ones. The first is attached to the main outside door and works by a key next to it. The second is the same kind but inside, attached to the door to the safety room. That's where the safe is with all the records and some special equipment for the more expensive installations." She reached into her bag—a large canvas satchel—and took out two keys on a ring, one large and round, the other small and square. "The big one is for the outside door, the small one fits both alarms. Do you want them?"

All he wanted was sleep. He took the keys tentatively and asked, "Do you think I'd find anything helpful there?"

"I don't know." She looked at him squarely. "I've never tried. When you're walking along a precipice you don't look down."

He nodded. She had suspected for a long time that something was going on then. He was silent, thinking. "And the operation called *Dosvidanya*?" he asked.

"That's all I know," Marja answered. "Bruce goes away occasionally—on business trips, he says, to get new orders. But I don't know—"

"What?"

"As far as I can tell from the correspondence no orders have resulted from the trips. Once when he left he said to Bell, 'Operation *Dosvidanya* is yours.' He didn't know I was nearby. Luckily neither did Bell. And Natalie heard him use the same phrase over the telephone twice. She also heard Bell address him as 'Colonel.'"

"A KGB colonel. He must be in command of the operation." He paused, then asked, "If it's a transmitter, what are they transmitting? I thought they sent information they collect by way of diplomatic pouches. The air waves must be monitored by the feds."

"It could be in code." She looked at her watch. "I must go. Bruce will wonder." She started to get up.

Flood put a hand out to stop her. She sat back, waiting for him to explain. He wondered if he should tell her about the motel cabin. "Stop and get something on the way home," he said. "Food or wine or something, to account for the delay."

Marja nodded.

He didn't want her to go. Taking the key to the cabin out of his pocket, he showed it to her and explained the layout of the motel. As he talked he watched her eyes closely for a glint of triumph but she seemed scarcely interested. Clearly she wanted to leave. "There's no phone in the room," he went on. "If you have to get hold of me—urgently, I mean—I've registered as W. Cameron."

She looked at him suspiciously. "Why that?"

"It was the first name that came to mind. Is there any way I can call you?"

"No, no, you mustn't," she said. "Bruce has a private line in his room. The other line is open. It's too risky." She paused, thinking, then said, "You could call me—if it's a real emergency—at the plant. But you must be careful. Don't say anything openly. Talk about flags." She paused again. "If things are all right ask about green colors we have. If things are uncertain and you want me to be careful ask about yellows. If things are bad, dangerous, ask about reds."

Flood stared at her admiringly. "You're pretty good," he said. "It's Miss Voll?"

She nodded. "You're calling from Herbert Reiner's office in Chicago. He's the purchasing agent for Cook County. We're negotiating with him for a large order. You want to know about the delivery date. That's my bailiwick. Remember the colors." She started to get up once more.

"Jesus," Flood said and slumped back.

She stopped. "What is it?" She turned and looked behind her in alarm.

"How do I get the keys back to you?" he asked.

"We're not good at this at all, are we?" she said, her voice flat with dismay. She thought for a moment, then nodded to herself and said, "There are three trees —maples—halfway down the block from the house, on the same side. Between the sidewalk and the street. The center one—in the crotch of the first branch. It's above eye level but not too high. Leave them there. I walk Damon early in the morning, usually around six-thirty to seven. Make sure the keys are there by then."

She paused and grabbed the keys from him. "My God," she muttered. "I forgot. Sometimes—rarely—Bruce sends me to the plant at night to pick up something he's forgotten."

"Can't you leave them in the tree tonight, after it's too late for him to ask you to go out?"

Marja nodded uncertainly, looking into his eyes. She was afraid, he saw, maybe as afraid as he was. To involve her in at least the prospect of action, the only relief for fear, he said, "The layout of the plant. I can't go in blind."

Quickly she described the floor plan and how the keys worked. "Do you have any idea what you're looking for?"

Flood shook his head. "None."

She got up and hesitated at the side of the table. "Be careful," she said.

He looked at her. "You, too. Good luck." Jesus, the banalities of life, he thought. There were no words for fear like this.

Marja tried to smile at him but it came out tremulously awkward and she turned away. He felt her shock and pain and loss then, and remembered hearing a story about a woman having a nightmare in which her murdered sister appeared moaning, over and over, "There is nothing worse than being murdered." Flood watched Marja walk quickly down the length of the room and out the door. He wished they could get into his car and drive off into the night and emerge in the sunlight somewhere far away. We'll never make it, he thought. A moment later, though, he realized that at least now he wasn't alone.

# Thursday

# 1

The keys were wrapped in a small square of brown paper twisted at the ends. Flood assumed the paper was meant to keep the keys from glinting in the light but when he was safely back in his car and heading toward Lincoln Avenue it occurred to him that Marja might have enclosed a message. He pulled over to the curb behind a row of parked cars and turned off the lights. Taking the keys out of the wrapper, he smoothed it out on his knee and flicked on the small flashlight he had bought after leaving Tony's. "B says N was tired, wanted to get away. He sent her to an inn up-state. We are to drive up there for the weekend. Friday night. Hurry."

Even after several hours' sleep, Flood felt sick with exhaustion. His sleep had been restless, fitful, as he lay, sweating heavily again, on the creaky iron bed, waiting for the door to open. Finally he had fallen asleep, his eyes fixed on the door, his shoulders hunched with tension.

He read the note again and tore it into tiny pieces. As he drove off, he dropped the pieces, one by one, out the window. Marja must know that she couldn't go off with McCade. He could only mean to kill her, too, once they were far enough away.

United Flags was in an area of small factories, gas stations, retail outlets for cheap carpets and cheap furniture, auto-repair shops, used-car lots, and a couple of dingy roadhouses—stretched out in drab spacious-ness along the highway to the airport. Slowing down as he got closer to the plant, Flood saw that the sign on a roadhouse next door was still on. *Patsy's—Wine & Dine* it said in flickering red neon; the windows were dimly illuminated and in each was a lighted Schlitz sign.

He turned in sharply and backed between two cars

in a row closest to the plant. He looked through the rear window of his car; the factory was no more than a hundred feet away—thirty running paces, he calculated—across open ground. The ground was macadam, a parking lot for the plant, with nothing to hide behind.

He ordered a glass of beer. When the bartender brought it, Flood asked, "How far's the airport?"

"Mile and a tenth," the bartender answered, gesturing in the direction Flood had been driving. The man looked at the clock above the bar: 1:40. "Nothing going out or coming in this hour of night," he said.

"I know," Flood said, though it hadn't occurred to him. "I've got to drop off a package for someone."

Flood finished the beer and ordered another. He was just delaying, he knew, and when he finished the second beer he put a quarter tip on the bar—enough not to anger the man, he hoped, but not enough to make him remember the customer—waved, and left.

Three minutes later Flood was inside the plant. He shone the light around and swore at its diminutive beam. He was in a hallway, about six feet wide and a little longer, with double swinging doors at the end. He moved forward and pushed them aside slowly to avoid any sudden noise. Certain that someone was inside, he flicked off the light and waited, sweating again, his shirt clinging to his back and under his arms. After what seemed like ten minutes—but was probably no more than half a minute, he realized—Flood flicked on the flash again and quickly stabbed its beam here and there around the room. No one. He lowered the light to keep it away from the windows and made his way slowly around the room. There were three modern desks made of Formica, two with typewriters on built-in extensions. Nothing, he thought. For the secretaries. Whatever he wanted wouldn't be there.

Moving on carefully toward a door that said *Bruce McCade—President,* Flood opened it slowly, the flash off, and sidled through. Again he waited in the dark, trembling. He turned the flash back on. Again no one was there. Heavy curtains covered one wall and Flood

86

crossed the room to them, turned off the flash, and felt through the fabric every foot or so. Windows the entire length of the wall. He shone the flash on the lower part of the curtains, below the window ledge, and examined their thickness. He couldn't be sure they would keep even the weak beam of the flashlight from being visible outside, so he didn't turn on the room lights as he had hoped to.

A red-leather couch was along one wall; next to it was a small table with a lamp on it; and next to that, against the adjoining wall, was a red-leather chair. In the far corner were two filing cabinets. A pair of wood armchairs with seats and backs upholstered in black leather faced the front of McCade's desk—a long French provincial table set out from the wall and facing the door. Behind the table was a high-backed swivel armchair in black leather. Walking around the table, Flood sat down in the swivel chair and flashed the light along the side just below the table top. There was no drawer.

He swept the light along the surface of the table; apart from the usual desk artifacts all that was on it was a stack of papers. He looked at the top one: a letter from the fire chief in Grand Rapids asking about the delivery date for his 16J-3 Modified Special Flagpole and Medium S-1 Flag. Flood riffled through the rest of the papers and found that they were mostly letters of inquiry, asking for information on the costs of various designs; the rest were orders. These came mainly from the Northeast, with a few from places elsewhere in the country. He took out one from the Quantico Marine Corps Development & Education Command, at Quantico, Virginia. It was for an A-1 Special Electra Flagpole and a Medium S-1 Flag. Stapled to the order was a three-page government form headed "Order for Supplies or Services." Typed in below were the words: "Blanket Purchase Agreement." At the bottom of the first page, under the printed words "Contracting/Ordering Officer" was a scrawled signature and, typed beside it, "Captain, U.S.M.C."

As Flood was about to put the order back in its place

in the stack, he noticed a penciled note in the upper left-hand corner: "M: Special Handling."

Marja? he wondered. He put the papers back as he had found them and went to the filing cabinets. They were locked.

Flood left the office, passing through the secretaries' outer office and making his way down a long narrow corridor. Halfway along it he came to the wide doorways on either side that Marja had described. She had told him that these rooms had no windows, so when he went into the one on the left he shone the flash on the wall beside the door, found the switch on the opposite side, and turned on the lights.

The bands of fluorescent bulbs built into the ceiling went on in twos and threes, flickered out, then back on. Flood stood uncertainly, startled by the brilliant light. The room was perhaps twenty-five feet wide and twice as long. The wall opposite him—the long side of the room—was covered from floor to ceiling with metal risers containing bolt upon bolt of fabric in every color. Running along the length of the room were two long tables. The one on the far side was about six feet wide and forty feet long; on either side of it were rows of sewing machines. At one end of the room was a black-steel grommet machine.

The nearer table, eight feet or so from where Flood was standing, was also about six feet wide and forty feet long. Its top was brown linoleum with a steel rim along the edge and here and there were bolts of material, metal T-squares, long wood rulers, large seamstresses' scissors, and a few partly made flags or banners. Flood went over and picked up a white silk embroidered banner with two black prancing horses facing each other under a gold eagle; below was the inscription *Virtue, Liberty, and Independence* and above was *The Governor—Commonwealth of Pennsylvania*. Next to the banner was a three-by-five-foot felt square with a Knights of Columbus shield on top and, below it, in black appliquéd letters: *Father McGivney —Council No. 6548*.

Here and there between the tables were large cardboard boxes heaped with partly finished American flags. At the end of one table were wood spools of different-colored silk thread. Lying beside them was a silk square with a rich embroidered design—two green-red-brown-and-black parrots facing a shield under a grinning gold lion. At the bottom was the inscription: *Après Bondie c'est la Ter.*

The room across the hallway was the same size as the other. But here was only one table, running nearly the length of the room along its center. Here, too, the far wall was covered with risers filled with bolts of silk, cotton bunting, satin, felt, nylon. Half the table was given over to folded banners and flags, apparently ready to be boxed and shipped, for the center of the table was stacked high with flat red boxes in different sizes. Piled along the underside of the table and filling the space there entirely were hundreds of rolls of paper; he pulled one out and saw that it was a pattern for an Elks banner.

Along the wall at one end of the room were shelves stacked with spools of rope and string; halyards, he decided. And there were scores of boxes of thread in various colors. The other walls were lined with narrow metal shelves filled with flat boxes like those on the table. Flood went over to examine them and ran down the labels: Afghanistan, Albania, Algeria, Argentina, Australia, Austria, Bahamas, Bahrain, Barbados, Belgium, Bhutan, Bolivia, Botswana, Brazil. He moved over to another row: Costa Rica, Cuba, Cyprus, Czechoslovakia, Dahomey, Denmark, Dominican Republic. Then another: Ivory Coast, Jamaica, Japan, Jordan, Kenya, Kuwait. Jesus, he thought, the whole world's here.

On another wall were green, white, blue, purple boxes containing flags and banners of states and cities. And on still another were more for clubs, businesses, airlines, hotels, banks, ships and yachts, and fraternal organizations.

Flood turned out the light and headed down the hallway to that part of the plant where Marja had said the flagpoles were assembled.

There were windows in this room, she had said, on the south side facing Lincoln Avenue. The street was a good hundred and fifty feet away but the absence of traffic at this hour and the lack of flashing car lights meant that any light here would be more likely to be seen by a passing patrol car. Flood kept the flashlight beam, as small as it was, down toward the floor as he traversed the room to get a sense of its layout. It seemed to be about thirty by forty feet in size. The first thing he saw were two tables, each ten feet long and placed end to end with a five-foot gap between them, along the center of the room. Lying across the tables and reaching nearly to the outer end of each was a long slender tapered white cylinder. It was a flagpole, or most of a flagpole; the base and top were missing, Flood saw as he examined it. It seemed to be made of aluminum, with a white baked-enamel finish.

He walked along the tables until he got to the narrow end of the pole. Cupping his hands around the light, he aimed it at the tip; it was threaded on the outside. The light suddenly glinted and flashed off something and Flood turned it off. He felt around the table until he found the object—a large, cold, metal ball. He picked it up; it was heavy. He turned his back to the windows at the far end of the room to conceal any light and turned on the flash. The object was a brass ball, about eight inches in diameter. He turned it around and saw a hole, roughly three inches across. He put a finger inside. It was hollow but the shell was much thicker than he expected, perhaps three-eighths of an inch, and the hole was threaded, too. Flood peered into the hole and saw that the thick shell was solid brass.

He fitted the hole over the end of the pole and turned it carefully; the threads caught. As the ball revolved, he saw a smaller hole about three inches down from the top. It was an inch and a half or so across and when he slipped a finger inside he found that its circumference was threaded, too. He unscrewed the ball and put it back on the table. Flashing the light over the end of the table, he looked for something that might fit into the smaller hole but found nothing.

A memory flickered through Flood's mind—a fallen flagpole, an American flag lying on dusty pavement at Miller Field. Two or three years ago he and Colonel Garrison had been coming out of headquarters there when the flagpole above the main entrance fell, narrowly missing them. A civilian work crew—several on the roof of the building with tackle and several on the ground below—had just finished mounting a new flagpole on the building's brick facade. They'd had it secured, they thought, and ran up the flag just as a sharp gust of wind caught it and pulled the mounting out of the wall. Garrison seemed unperturbed by his narrow escape. "The flag!" he shouted. "Get it off the ground!"

Now Flood realized what had triggered the memory. The brass ball atop the fallen flagpole had been crushed like a Ping-Pong ball. He felt the heavy ball on the table and recalled what Marja had said about the superior quality of United Flags' products. If the brass ball was an example, they were superior indeed —probably made to order under rigorous specifications. But why? he wondered. The question, even though unanswered, made him feel better. Maybe the risk he was taking would be worth it.

Flood examined the rest of the room. On the wall behind him were steel shelves stacked with small boxes of screws, nuts, stainless-steel eyelets, brass eyelets, and various fittings. Next to these were long boxes containing "Parade Poles," "Presentation Poles," and "Wood Poles, Plain;" beside them were boxes of gold and chrome tips for the poles, including "Round Spear," "Zionist Emblem," and "Church Cross." Stacked on the floor under the bottom shelf were boxes labeled "Gold Eagles." They came in three sizes—5 inches high, 7 inches high, and 11 inches high. He opened one of the largest boxes and took out the eagle. Kneeling down, he shone the light on it and saw that it was a stylized caricature of a bird, its head flat to one side, its wings open stiffly. It was extremely light-

weight and when he examined the label on the box
he saw the words: "Aluminum—Gold Finished."

At the end of the assembly room opposite the windows were three doors—one to the women's lavatory,
one to the men's, and one unmarked. Flood shone the
flashlight beam down at the lower right-hand side of
the third door and saw the small box Marja had
described: the alarm. He hesitated, staring at the box,
and felt for the keys in his pocket. Nodding as he
found the square-headed key, he knelt down on the
concrete floor and slipped the key into its place. He
paused, uncertain, his hand trembling.

Marja had said the room beyond had no window, so
he decided to prepare for an escape from the building
first. He got up and walked down the long end wall,
past a double steel door with a two-by-four plank
slotted into a pair of steel brackets at the center so
that it couldn't be opened from the outside, past racks
where various-sized flagpoles wrapped in heavy brown
paper, including several poles like the one on the
tables, were stored, to the windows at the far end of
the room. They were steel casement windows and
came down nearly to a workbench against the wall.
Flood got on top of the bench on his knees and
unlocked the closest window, so he could get out fast
if he had to.

He was halfway back along the room when he heard
a door slam and then another. He ran back to the
window. Sixty or seventy feet away, parked in front
of the main door to the plant, was a police car. An
officer walked from the near side of the car toward
the plant, and his partner came around through the
headlights to join him. Flood clambered onto the
workbench and slowly pulled the window closed, then
more slowly lowered the handle to lock it. He slid off
the bench and onto the floor and stared, half-crouching,
back into the darkness, wondering where to hide. He
heard footsteps coming closer. He fell to the floor and
rolled under the bench.

A moment later they were at the window. Flood,
lying with his back to the cinderblock wall, his head

on a piece of piping, his hands clasped at his chest, began murmuring a Hail Mary under his breath. He was unaware of what he was doing until he came, for the sixth time, to the words "pray for us sinners . . . at the hour of our death." He stopped. It had been twenty-five years since he had spoken those words.

There was a thump on one of the windows and a voice said, "Okay here."

"Check 'em all," another voice ordered. "You know what happened last time."

There were several more thumps, then the second voice said, "The light, too."

Suddenly a beam from a powerful flashlight swept through the window and around the assembly room. The keys, Flood thought, Jesus the keys. He had left them hanging in the alarm slot. The light swept across the room in the opposite direction, then hit each of the far corners twice. Flood thought he could see the keys. His stomach knotted.

The light went out and he heard footsteps receding. They must be going around the end of the building to make a complete circuit, he thought. A few moments later one of them thumped on the steel doors and Flood could dimly hear a voice but not the words. After that there was a silence. Just a routine check, he thought, and released his breath. A few minutes later he heard two doors slam again, an engine start up and die out into the night sounds.

Flood crawled out of his hiding place and crossed the room. He knelt by the alarm box, turned on the flash, and took hold of the key. He stopped, wondering if he had already turned it, and tried to recall which way she had told him. To the right, he thought, but he wasn't sure. If he had switched the alarm off and now turnd it back on and opened the door . . . Clockwise? he wondered. Counterclockwise? He sat back on his haunches, staring at the box. The charges that could be leveled against him were mounting, he thought irrelevantly: rape, murder, tampering with evidence, leaving the scene of a crime, flight to avoid prosecution, breaking and entering, and gross incompetence. He turned the key to the right.

Standing up, Flood reached for the doorknob, then paused. He went to the nearby double steel door with its simpler lock—the two-by-four plank—and waited. If they came he might escape that way. It shouldn't take them more than a few minutes after the alarm went off; he checked his watch: 2:04. He stood waiting for what seemed an interminable time and looked at his watch again: 2:06. His mouth tasted stalely of beer and he wanted a drink badly. He wondered if Marja had told him the truth, all she knew, and was sure that she hadn't. His head turned sharply toward the locked room. McCade could be in there waiting for him. Or Bell. It was a perfect place—a sudden soundless end. He stared at the door in the dim light coming from the windows at the opposite end of the room.

No, he thought, if they had been waiting they would have been in McCade's office, not here. They would assume that he might lose his nerve long before he got this far and flee. He shone the light on his Timex: 2:09. Seven minutes. He gave them three more.

No one was waiting in the safety room. Flood closed the door behind him and shone the light around. As Marja had said, there were no windows, so he switched on the overhead light. The safe—about six feet wide and six feet high and built into the far wall—had double doors. On one wall were two metal cabinets. He tried their handles—locked. Across the room was a long table with a single sheet of paper on top.

It was another government order form headed "Order for Supplies or Services," and again it was for an A-1 Special Electra Flagpole and a Medium S-1 Flag. It was signed, under the designation "Contracting/Ordering Officer," William MacKenzie, Captain, Lowry Air Force Base, Denver, Colorado. On the upper left-hand corner was written in pencil, "M: Special Handling." He put the paper down; it must be for the pole being assembled in the room outside.

On the wall above the table was a large fiberboard map of the United States with dozens of red-head pins stuck on it. He found Denver. There was no pin. He looked at New Richmond. There was a pin.

The safe opened at the first try. In the center section were six drawers in two rows of three, each with a keyhole. They were locked. The rest of the safe's innards was divided into various-sized compartments. In one at the left was a stack of ledgers. Beside them were some manila folders. Down at the bottom of the safe were thirty or so small cardboard cartons. Flood decided to start with the ledgers.

He took the top one to the table and sat down on a straightbacked chair at one end. A red-edged label glued to the cover of the ledger said "Private." When Flood opened the book he saw that the word meant not "personal" but rather "private orders"—for flags, banners, bunting, yacht burgees, flagpoles, carrying harnesses, mounts. Leafing through the pages, he found several hundred names of individuals, most of them from the state.

The label on the next ledger said "State, City & Town Govts." The entries here were for orders from a wide variety of government offices throughout the Northeast, with several dozen others from across the country; most of them were for American flags, some were for state flags, some were for governors' flags, some were for city and town flags, and the rest were for ceremonial bunting and banners.

The third ledger was labeled "Organizations" and contained lists of outfits in New Richmond, around the state, and again to a lesser degree scattered throughout the Northeast. He flipped through the pages and saw records of orders from high school and college clubs, teams, and bands; stores and hotels; and hundreds of others from various fraternal, religious, and social organizations.

The last ledger in the r' was entitled "U.S. Govt." Flood went through its pages more carefully. They contained over a hundred entries and some of them, perhaps half, were again for the A-1 Electra Specials.

Purchasers in Washington included the Treasury Department, the two Senate Office Buildings, the Labor Department, the Department of Health, Education and Welfare, the Supreme Court, the Capitol, the three House Office Buildings, the Department of Defense, the Central Intelligence Agency, and the White House.

Then McCade had penetrated every significant building in the capital, Flood thought. But why? What could he do with a bunch of flags and flagpoles?

After flipping through dozens of blank pages, he was about to close the ledger when he came to more entries. "Military" said a heading on a separate page. Following it were several pages of recorded orders from military installations. He read through them with mounting alarm: Maxwell Air Force Base, Montgomery, Alabama; Chanute Air Force Base, Rantoul, Illinois; Williams Air Force Base, Chandler, Arizona; Lackland Air Force Base, San Antonio, Texas; Columbus Air Force Base, Columbus, Mississippi; Marine Corps Air Station, Cherry Point, North Carolina; Fairchild Air Force Base, Spokane, Washington; Marine Corps Air Station, Santa Ana, California; Marine Corps Air Station, Beaufort, South Carolina; Mather Air Force Base, Sacramento, California; Nellis Air Force Base, Las Vegas, Nevada; Sheppard Air Force Base, Wichita Falls, Texas; Webb Air Force Base, Big Spring, Texas; Marine Air Corps Station, El Torro, California; Craig Air Force Base, Selma, Alabama; Laughlin Air Force Base, Del Rio, Texas; Marine Corps Air Station, New River, North Carolina; Randolph Air Force Base, San Antonio, Texas; Moody Air Force Base, Valdosta, Georgia; Reese Air Force Base, Lubbock, Texas; Vance Air Force Base, Enid, Oklahoma; Marine Corps Air Station, Yuma, Arizona; Keesler Air Force Base, Biloxi, Mississippi; Naval Submarine Base, New London, Connecticut; Andrews Air Force Base, Virginia. The final entry was Lowry Air Force Base, Denver, Colorado, dated the week before. Each of the orders included at least one Special Electra.

Flood sat back and rubbed his eyes. Why did it have to be him?

Since he had almost missed this batch of entries, he flipped on through the remaining pages of the ledger. Near the back he came to a long list of numbers that began:

| 34 20 04 | 75 28 06 |
|----------|----------|
| 45 48 00 | 108 20 12 |
| 24 54 18 | 96 33 58 |

Flood stared at the figures uncomprehendingly for a long time. Finally he took out a small notebook and a pen and carefully copied the entries. He was about to put the ledger back in the safe when he remembered there was a red pin at New Richmond on the wall map but he had seen no entry for that base. Leafing back to the military installations, he went through them again and found it, dated March 24th of the previous year: two poles, including one Special Electra, and eight flags of various sizes.

Flood returned the ledger to the safe and took out the manila folders. Most contained originals of the orders in the ledger. But two folders seemed to contain simply private addresses around the country. All were in small towns, mainly in sparsely populated states, or on various local roads nearby—Route 1, Highway 69, and so on. The contents of the final folder were the most puzzling of all: a batch of clippings from the New York *Times* between November 10th and November 16th, 1965. All of the clippings were about the Great Blackout that fall throughout the northeastern United States and part of Canada. Puzzled, Flood examined them and finally put the folders back in the safe.

He knelt down to look at the cartons stacked at the bottom of it. Each was stamped in purple ink "Dartmoor Electronics—Transistor Play Kits—The Kids Delight." The boxes were sealed with tape and after brief hesitation Flood took out his pen and ran its point down the concealed edges of the two flaps under the tape. He took the box to the table, sat down, and opened it. Inside was a brown plastic cylinder about the size of a container of frozen fruit juice. At one end were six vent-like apertures and at the other end was a hole from which two rubber-coated wires emerged, ending in tight coils of eight or ten loops each.

Flood sat back again, the cylinder held in both hands, and studied it. It meant nothing to him. Finally he saw, in tiny raised letters on either side near a seam that ran the length of the object, the word "Press." He pressed. Nothing happened. He turned the cylinder around and pressed again. Still nothing. Then he pressed the two sides of one half and pulled the other half out. The device came apart an inch and stopped. Flood held it up to the light and peered inside. Several wires crossing between the two halves prevented him from separating them completely. Inside each half was a maze of tiny cylinders, glass bubbles, and silver lines. A transistor, he thought unsurely. He put the cylinder back together and was about to replace it in its box when he noticed more tiny raised letters. He raised the cylinder close to his eyes and read "Transmitter Type 154J–0."

Was the device designed for a child's walkie-talkie? he wondered. It seemed unlikely. Why lock a child's toy in a safe place in a locked room in a locked building?

Swearing under his breath, Flood put the cylinder back into its box and the box back into the safe at the bottom of the rear stack. It might be months, even years, before McCade found it and saw that it had been opened. Or it might be hours.

As Flood, still in a crouch, turned away from the safe, he saw that the table concealed several sizable wood boxes tucked underneath its far corner. He scrambled over to the table and pulled one of them out into the light. A label on top said "Firmo Brass Works" with an address in New York. The box was nailed shut. He shoved it back under the table and pulled out one at the end of the pile. Its lid was open, set loosely on top, and when he lifted it off he saw nothing but wood shavings and at one end a foot-deep crevice where something had once been. Reaching down into the shavings in the middle of the box, he felt an object. Carefully brushing the shavings aside, he uncovered the gold wing of a bird. He lifted it slowly, brushing the shavings off it into the box, and pulled out an eagle.

He held it up to the light. It was a stunning piece of work, even without being compared to the flimsy gilt-coated aluminum birds he had found in the other room. This one was heavy, clearly made of solid brass. The bird was in flight, its wings two-thirds spread to a width of a foot, its head poised as if it was about to dive onto its prey, its eyes protruding, its beak open. It was a fine piece of sculpture, incomparably superior to others of its kind he had seen.

The eagle's legs were tucked under its body to simulate a bird in flight. Between them and extending downward at a slight angle was a post, half an inch thick, which ended in a round base. Flood sat on the chair and turned the eagle over to examine the bottom of the base. It was about an inch and a half across and threaded around its outer circumference. He thought of the brass ball and the hole that size and realized the eagle was to be mounted on it. It seemed strange, though, that McCade didn't mind leaving the ball in full view of his staff but kept the eagle concealed here. Flood examined it closely and finally saw a faint line, no larger than a thin scratch, around the body of the bird just in front of the shaft coming out of its belly. Holding the bird with one hand at the rear and the other hand at the front, he twisted them in opposite directions. Nothing happened. He reversed the twist and the bird came apart, slowly unscrewing at the line.

Flood put the head and wings of the bird on the table and examined the rear half. As he had figured, the metal was thick, perhaps a quarter of an inch, and also solid brass. It was a precision job, for the threading had to be exact if the two halves were to fit as they did. The indentation was a perfect cylinder. Just behind the threaded opening was a small hole, about an eighth of an inch in diameter. He held the bird to the light and peered up through the bottom of the shaft and saw light. He picked up the front and looked inside; there was another hollow cylinder. He held the thing up and saw light, apparently entering from the bird's beak.

Getting up quickly, Flood went back to the safe and took out the small carton he had opened. He removed the plastic cylinder and returned to the table. The device fit exactly into the hollow in the front of the bird. He slipped the rear half of the bird over the rest of the cylinder. It stopped before he could screw the halves together. The coil of wires was in the way. He had put the cylinder in wrongside to, he saw. He reversed it, uncoiled the wires, slid the ends of them into the small hole inside the rear of the bird, then slipped the cylinder into the back half first and enclosed it with the front half. The wires emerged from the base and the bird screwed together easily.

Once again Flood held the bird up and gazed at it admiringly. A moment later he saw something he hadn't noticed before—a calendar hanging on the wall at the far end of the table. It had a color picture, a photograph, of the White House. On top of the building was a flagpole with a flag fluttering in the breeze. Above that was *UNITED FLAGS—ONLY THE BEST FOR THE BEST*. Off at one side of the photograph was a circular insert showing a blown-up portion of the picture. In it was the end of a flagpole and an attached fluttering flag. On the end of the pole was a gold ball and perched atop it was an American eagle, its wings spread, its beak open.

Flood stared at the eagle in his hands. Marja had been wrong. It wasn't a transmitter in the attic, it was a receiver. Miller Field! "Jesus," he said softly, looking back at the calendar. Somewhere near the White House was an attic with another receiver. He thought of all the entries in the ledgers and slowly lowered the eagle. They were listening in on everything being said in every military and government office of any importance across the entire country. Flood felt chilled and shuddered. No wonder they had to kill him.

# 2

The travel-clock alarm rang cheerily. Flood tried to incorporate the sound into a dream he was having by making it a bumblebee in a clump of field daisies. The bee rose, turned gradually into an airplane, coming directly at him, its roaring motor anything but cheery. He sat up abruptly and turned off the alarm and sank back onto the pillow. Light filtered grayly through the curtains. He looked at the luminous dial of the clock and saw that it was almost seven. Yawning, he groaned and reached out to switch on the lamp.

The running deer on its shade snapped his memory open and he saw Ellen's lips open to his, her slender body tautly graceful beneath him, her breasts naked in his hands.

Flood lay back, his eyes closed, and forced himself to remember. It was their fifth anniversary and they drove north to a small restaurant beside the river. The place was too quiet, though, and so were they. For the past few weeks something had been wrong between them—neither knew what it was—and they had hoped the celebration would provide a festive trigger to release the tension and bring them together. But it hadn't happened. Flood felt himself going tight in the jaw, as he did when anger and helplessness overtook him at once. He looked at Ellen and she looked back and recited:

> How barely they do feel pleasure
> Where love lies past all true measure.

Driving along the River Road on their way home, Ellen suddenly sat forward and said, "We *must* check in at that old motel just ahead." A woman of about fifty was on duty in the office and she looked with sour suspicion at them and especially at Ellen's thin gold wedding band. Flood knew she was sure that they weren't married or, if they were, that they weren't married to each other. Ellen loved that part most—"to be so explicitly illicitly licit," she said as they came into the cabin and laughed and flung themselves onto the bed.

Now he sat up and swung his blue-veined bare legs off the bed and planted his white feet on the cold floor. Was the motel owner that woman's husband? Flood tried to think of the old man's youthful joy. It was impossible to imagine.

Flood remembered the brass eagle with the wires hanging out of the base and wondered again if he was right. The brass ball would hold the batteries or maybe they were in the upper end of the flagpole . . . hundreds of eagles around the country . . . every word, every secret transmitted to the Russians.

A pounding on the door brought Flood to his feet, panicked. The police! Then a man's voice called, "Mr. Cameron, you in there?" and he realized that it was the motel owner.

"What is it?" He grabbed his pants off the wicker chair, slipped into them, and picked up his shirt.

"Phone call," the man shouted. "A woman. Says it's urgent."

Buttoning his shirt, Flood opened the door. The man had a raincoat on over his pajamas. He looked aggrieved. "Pretty early for phone calls," he said.

"What time is it?" Flood asked, as if he, too, had been asleep.

"Seven. She says it's urgent. She waiting on the other end." He motioned back toward the office, as if that were the other end. "She said you'd pay me for my trouble. It's trouble all right, this hour." He turned away.

"I'll be right with you." Flood slipped into his shoes, without socks, and took his jacket and left the cabin. The man was already walking away and Flood hurried to catch up with him. Then he wished he hadn't. What was he to say? They walked in silence through the cold morning air and when they got to the office the man walked in without holding the door. He jerked his head toward the receiver lying off its cradle on top of the counter.

Flood paused. "Here," he said, taking out his wallet and handing him a five-dollar bill. The man brightened and nodded his thanks. "D'you mind my taking the call in private?" Flood asked. The man nodded again and left through the door into the house. Flood picked up the receiver. He waited a few moments nervously. "Hello," he said at last.

"The keys—they're not in the tree," Marja cried. "What happened? Where are they? Did Bruce—Oh my God!"

Flood's mouth fell open and he put a hand to his eyes. He had forgotten. He had been so relieved to get out of the plant, so exhausted, so eager to get back to the safety of the cabin. . . . He had never felt like such a fool. . . .

"Jesus," he said into the phone.

"What?"

He hesitated. "I forgot."

There was a gasp in his ear. *"What?"*

"Where are you?"

"I don't believe it—I just don't believe it," Marja said in a low ugly voice. "Are you insane? Putting me in a spot like this! Are you trying to get me killed? My God!"

Flood couldn't take much more. "Do you want me to leave them someplace or not?" His voice was tense, on the edge of becoming ugly, too. "We don't have time to quarrel."

Marja's filthy epithet stunned him. But he forgot it as she ordered him to drive immediately to a gas station at the corner of Trevelyan and Elm, where she was in a telephone booth just off the sidewalk, and to throw the keys toward the booth without stopping. "Now!" she shouted. "After that, stay away from me!"

Flood ran out of the office and down to his car. Marja was standing by the phone booth, her face white with fury. She had a huge Doberman with her, holding it with both hands on a choke chain. Flood had forgotten the dog, too. He would have to start thinking or it would be all over. He had already rolled down the window and now slowed the car, coming almost to a stop as he flung the keys toward her, praying they didn't fall through a sewer grating. As the keys hit, Damon plunged forward, snarling, his teeth bared, and Marja jerked him back furiously. Flood heard her curse him again and as he drove on he looked back. She was picking up the keys from the sidewalk and Damon was licking her cheek.

It was hopeless, Flood thought for the hundredth time. He had better go to the police. But then he remembered the night before and got angry at Marja. He had learned more about what went on at United Flags in an hour than she had in several years. His resentment deepened as he recalled her curse. What had she ever done except avoid looking down from the precipice? He would tell her that.

Flood skirted the downtown section and stopped near the abandoned railroad station, where there was still a newsstand, and bought a *Herald*. He folded it so he couldn't see the top of the front page and drove a few blocks farther on to the bus station and a diner stuck in the middle of a large parking lot behind it. Again he resisted the temptation to read the story and went inside.

He took a booth at the far end of the narrow room, facing forward so that he could see anyone coming in, and shifted his feet away from the aisle to conceal his bare ankles. When the waitress—a thin woman with a lifetime of frustration in her clamped lips—came to his booth, Flood ordered a large glass of grapefruit juice, fried eggs, bacon, potatoes, whole wheat toast, and coffee. As she left, without a word, he felt his unshaven jaw and only then realized that he hadn't even had time to comb his hair. He smoothed it down as best he could and waited.

The paper was folded on the seat beside him and it was all that he could do not to open it. The waitress came back and slapped a glass of juice in front of him, slopping it onto the table, and left. Flood mopped up the liquid with a paper napkin. Then he picked up the *Herald* and unfolded it. The main headline, as usual these days, was about the Mideast. A third of the way down the front page, on the left, was the story. A three-column, two-deck head ran: "Mystery Beauty Assaulted, Slain Here. Police Baffled." The article was dated the previous day and read:

The body of a beautiful brunette was discovered early this morning in an alley in the 1800 block of Stark St. by a resident, Anthony Polizzio, as he was leaving for work shortly after 7:30 A.M.

According to the police, the woman, age about 40, was apparently sexually assaulted before being stabbed to death by an unknown assailant sometime late Tuesday night or early Wednesday morning.

Lt. Bertram Flower, head of the New Richmond Police Department's homicide unit, stated that robbery could have been the killer's motive. The Department had no comment at this stage on the apparent sexual assault. The Department spokesman stated that the identity of the victim was unknown.

The dead woman was between 40 and 44 years of age, according to the Department crime laboratory. She was 5'8" tall and weighed 122 pounds.

The police are waiting for the body to be identified.

Flood wished he had finished his breakfast before reading the article. He saw Natalie's body again, the ivory handle of the knife in her breast, the blood caked on her thighs. The waitress shoved a platter of food in front of him. He looked at it with revulsion. She slapped a cup and saucer down in front of the plate and the coffee slopped out and filled the saucer. Not looking up, he blotted it with a folded napkin and casually opened the paper to the editorial page.

"That all?" she demanded, a pencil in one hand poised over an order pad in the other.

"Put down another coffee," Flood said, still not looking at her.

She added up his check, put it on the table, and left. He wondered if she had seen his picture at the bottom of the editorial page beside his column's head: "Today and Tomorrow." It didn't matter, though; the photograph was ten years old.

Flood ate as he read his column and wished that he had done neither. The food slid greasily down his throat and the words swam before his eyes. He was embarrassed as always—not by the column's quality but by his inability to resist reading it. Nearly twelve hundred of them had been printed by now and he had read every one—sometimes two or three times—after they were published. Now and then, when he had been particularly pleased with one, he had even read it aloud to Ellen. He winced at the recollection and put the paper down.

"Hey there, John."

Startled, Flood saw a policeman sit down on a counter stool a few feet away. It was Sergeant McLaughlin, from the traffic division. He had been promoted to sergeant partly because of a column Flood had written about him as an expert of the logistical modern world who got people to their jobs and back to their homes again day in and day out.

"Hello, Pete," Flood answered, trying to sound natural.

"I see you'll eat anywhere," the sergeant said.

Flood smiled. "And you?" He took out some change and put down a tip, larger than he would have left if McLaughlin weren't there.

"Coffee's all. Got to stay awake during the rush. I got a recurring nightmare—a twelve-car crash at the corner of Washington and Genesee and me there sound asleep."

Flood slid out of the booth and only then remembered his bare ankles. But McLaughlin didn't seem to notice. He glanced at the paper, folded open with the column showing. Jesus, Flood thought, he knows I was reading it.

"How's business?" the sergeant asked, smiling.

"If you read me once in a while, you wouldn't have to ask."

"C'mon. You know cops can't read."

Flood didn't mind the taunt; McLaughlin was his only friend on the force. He touched the officer lightly on the shoulder and said, "See you."

As he was paying his check, the waitress came up. "You said another coffee," she told him accusingly.

"I'll take it with me."

"Take-out's a nickel more." She looked as if she were marking him down on her death list and waited impatiently until he gave her the nickel before she filled a paper container with burned coffee.

Flood parked beside the cabin and got out. As far as he could tell, no one he knew except McLaughlin had seen him in town and the River Road had been clear all the way back. He looked at his watch: 8:10. He went inside. The coffee was cold but he drank it anyway, sitting in the wicker chair and wishing there was something he could do. He couldn't call Marja before nine. He sipped the coffee and wondered if she had meant that curse. He couldn't blame her if she had, anymore than he could blame her for her rage toward men; after all, he thought, men had brought nothing but ruin to her life. There was more to her than that, he was certain, and wondered why she had stopped herself from touching his hand the day before at Tony's. He had needed that kind of contact with her, he realized, and was surprised by the awareness that he missed her.

Mr. Reinhart from Chicago, Flood thought, and tried to remember the first name. It had vanished. So had the message he had devised. Green, yellow, red. Certainly it wasn't green; he didn't know enough yet and when he did the signal would probably be red. Yellow, he decided—a brilliant cautious yellow. He wished he had a gun and wondered what he'd do if he did.

He looked at his watch and swore. Not quite a minute had passed. Then he realized that it was an hour earlier in Chicago, so he would have to wait until ten before calling. He swore again. Two hours. He had to talk to someone before then. Colonel Garrison out at Miller? he wondered. Surely he could be trusted with a national-security case like this. Flood would persuade him to have the eagle over headquarters removed and dismantled. . . . He shook his head wearily. That would mean telling him about the break-in at United Flags and that would mean telling him about Natalie. Garrison was too much the simple soldier; he would never grasp the implications of what might be in that attic. It would be the same with anyone from the FBI or CIA. All they would be able to grasp would be one fact: murder.

Exhausted, Flood got up and poured the coffee down the basin. He lay on the bed and in a few minutes he was asleep. If he dreamed this time, he was unaware of it and when the knock came at the door he was instantly awake, again certain that it was the police. He got up slowly, trying not to make any noise, but the bed creaked and he cursed it under his breath.

It was only the maid, a plump cheerful young woman who wanted to talk. Flood put her off and went into the bathroom to brush his teeth and shave. When he came out she had finished the other room and was waiting patiently.

"You in town on business?" she asked, smiling pleasantly.

Flood nodded and tried not to look at her breasts. She was wearing a shapeless dress and a heavy cardigan but even so her breasts thrust out prominently. Ripe, he thought, and for a moment he wanted them so much that he was amazed at himself. He looked away, realizing now that his desire was not for sex but for comfort. He wanted to lie with his face buried in them. He looked at her face again.

She glanced at the bed and back at him, catching

his eyes on her chest once more. "It's all right," she said.

Flood wondered if she was the owner's daughter. Was this the way she lived, waiting for an occasional guest, a traveling salesman? Did she lie in her bed waiting, longing for someone like Flood?

"I'm late," he said, taking the raincoat off a hook on the wall at the end of the bed. "I've got an appointment in town."

She smiled at his nervousness. "All right," she said. "I'll just finish up in the other room."

As she passed him Flood could smell her—a smell of soap and disinfectant—and saw the tantalizing softness of her throat leading down to her breasts.

# 3

Flood turned left on the river road and headed toward Bay City, thirty miles north. He drove steadily at forty-five, keeping an eye on the rearview mirror. Now and again a car came up fast behind him and each time he waited, gripping the wheel and staring ahead down the black strip that ran alongside the river to Bay City. One by one the cars sped past and finally he relaxed, sure that he hadn't been followed.

Bay City, about half the size of New Richmond, had a Holiday Inn downtown and Flood drove to its garage to leave the car. While waiting for the attendant to check him in, he slipped Natalie's hat out from under the seat, rolled it up, and put it in his raincoat pocket. He told the attendant that he would be leaving the car for three or four days, though he might want to use it occasionally, then went into the main lobby to a telephone booth. Flood called the inn and watched a desk clerk across the room take the call, reserved a room under the name T. Barnard for Friday and Saturday nights, and said that he would probably arrive sometime the following morning. Then he called the local Avis office and ordered a medium-sized Chevrolet, to be picked up within an hour.

He dialed 0 and waited a long time until the operator came on. "Is it a toll call to New Richmond?" he asked.

After a slight pause the operator said, "I'm sorry, sir, but that's a toll call."

Grimacing at the receiver, he hung up, went to the cashier for change, and returned to the phone.

Ormond wasn't at the office but he reached him at home. Ormond answered just before the last two coins clicked through the phone box. Good, Flood thought, he won't know how long the distance is. "It's John Flood. I'm out of town. I wanted to ask you a favor. I've been thinking of doing something on that murder—the woman in the alley—for my next column. I heard Rogers talking to you about it yesterday. I may want to keep in touch with you in the next couple of days to get any facts I might need."

"Why sure, Mr. Flood," Ormond said eagerly. "Anything you want."

"Any more developments?" Flood asked.

"She died of a stab wound in the heart. She may have been raped but they can't be sure. She had intercourse sometime not long before her death. They have the semen type. They aren't sure it was a forcible sexual assault. Her vagina was torn slightly but the coroner thinks that was done after her death with a blunt instrument of some kind."

Flood felt sick. How could McCade do that to his own wife? Probably Bell. Even so . . .

"The funny thing is there was vomit at the scene of the crime," Ormond went on. "But it wasn't hers. Her stomach was full."

Flood saw the vile puddle again.

Ormond said, "Whoever vomited had been poisoned. Nicotine poisoning. It's pretty clear Lieutenant Flower doesn't know what to make of it. The police seem to think the poisoned vomit is connected to the case but they don't know how—not the last I heard anyway."

So that was it, Flood thought, tasting the bitter taste of tobacco again. "What are the properties of nicotine poison?" he asked. "How does it work?"

"The medical examiner says it's very simple to make. Just take a pound of tobacco and boil it in water for a while. Boil it down and strain it through a paper filter and that's it. Simple. But the problem is no one in their right mind would drink the stuff— not unless they wanted to commit suicide in a real nasty way. It's foul-tasting and it hurts like hell. Kills you in a few hours, depending on the dose of course."

"Any suspects?" Flood asked, his voice uneven.

"Flower is acting very mysterious," Ormond answered. "You know how he is. I think he doesn't have a clue. They're pretty sure that whoever it was carried the woman there after she was dead."

"Why?"

"The concrete in that alley seems to be an old kind that isn't used anymore. There were no traces of it on the bottoms of her shoes."

Again Flood saw the black pump as it had been lying when he came to in the alley. He looked down at his shoes. He would have to get rid of them. His apartment and the rugs must have picked up some of the concrete dust. But he remembered his long walk across town to his place; whatever traces of the alley concrete had been on his shoes may have been obliterated, covered over, mixed up by that walk's accumulation of other concrete dust.

"You there, Mr. Flood?"

"Yeah, I was just thinking." *Commit a crime and the earth is glass,* he thought.

The telephone clicked and a woman's voice said, "Your three minutes are up. Signal when through, please." It sounded like the same operator.

When the line cleared Flood said, "I'm on my way to the Cape for a couple of days. You mind if I call you again on this?"

"Sure, sure, Mr. Flood," Ormond said again, with increased eagerness. "Oh, I almost forgot. The police think they know the woman's identity."

Flood's hand tensed on the receiver. He had forgotten even to ask that.

"A man called in from Philadelphia late yesterday afternoon," Ormond explained. "Said his wife had come to New Richmond three days before and was supposed to be back the day before yesterday. He was worried. She wasn't staying at the hotel she said she'd be at. She drank sometimes, he said. The sergeant on duty asked him to describe her. He did and the description fit the dead woman exactly. Absolutely, in fact. It turns out she had an odd birthmark on one buttock—almost a perfect *fleur-de-lis.*"

Ormond pronounced the last word "liss" and at first

Flood didn't know what he meant. When he understood he asked, "The man knew about that?"

"Right. He was supposed to fly in last night. Flower told Murphy the guy—Cameron's his name—could probably take the body back with him today. The autopsy's being done. They've got all the vital organs."

"Did you say Cameron?"

"Uh-huh. It seems her name was Wendy Cameron."

After Flood hung up, he stood in the booth, dazed by the news. Was it all a mistake? Was Natalia McCade actually at an inn upstate? It was impossible. Then he realized that McCade must have arranged this with a confederate. Undoubtedly he had dozens of them, Flood thought, recalling the records in the flag plant. If there were receivers hidden near government and military installations around the country, there would have to be a lot of people manning them.

The phone rang. He picked up the receiver and the operator said, "Sixty-five cents more for overtime, please." Flood counted out the change and slipped the coins into the proper slots. When he finished the voice said, "Thank you." He hung up and a moment later he heard a clinking of coins falling inside the box. Without thinking, he put a finger in the coin-return slot. It was full. He took out the coins and just then the phone rang again. When he answered the same voice asked, "Sir, did a dollar and fifteen cents just fall into the coin-return?"

Flood counted the coins in his hand. "Yes," he said.

"There's been a mistake, sir. Would you kindly redeposit them?"

He looked at the money and said, "If you give me your name and address, I'll mail them to you."

It was a quarter to ten when Flood parked the rented car—a tan Chevrolet not too different in appearance from his, he hoped, though he could scarcely tell one car from another—in the space next to his cabin. He took his tape recorder out of the carryall, fitted in a fresh cassette, good for forty-five minutes per side, and inserted the plug in a wall socket. Sitting down on the wicker chair, Flood put his head back, thought for a few minutes with his eyes closed, and at last sat forward. He clicked on the recorder and began dictating into it quietly, the microphone mesh close to his mouth. It took nearly an hour to tell everything he could remember of the events following his encounter with Natalie at Treats. It was dangerous, he knew— especially to Marja if the tape fell into McCade's hands. But it had to be done. If anything happened to him, there would be at least this record. Someone in authority would find it; it would be checked.

Twenty minutes after he finished, he was in the vault at the First National again. This time he asked the attendant merely to put his safety-deposit box on a table in the vault room and slipped the cassette inside, on top of the letter from Natalie to Marja.

The Bancroft was half a block from the bank and Flood went there to make his call to Marja. A woman answered and he said, "Miss Voll, please, this is Mr. Reinhart calling from Chicago."

"Oh, yes, Mr. *Reiner*. What can I do for you?" It was Marja.

Flood cursed himself for getting the name wrong. She would hold that against him, too.

"We'd like an extra banner," he said.

"What kind of banner?"

"One changing from yellow to red."

"I see. How soon?"

"As soon as possible. Lunch time. One o'clock."

"That may be difficult, Mr. Reiner. But I'll try. What kind of material?"

Flood thought of the bolts of cloth on the risers at the plant. "Felt, I think," he answered, wondering where she was sitting. "At Tony's?"

"Bemberg silk might do better," she said. "The colors would blend more suitably."

"Not Tony's?"

"I don't think that can be done—at least not that quickly. Perhaps later."

"The cabin then? At one?"

114

"That might be possible. If not, then the later date could be met."

"If not the cabin at one, then Tony's at five?"

"Yes, I would think so. All right, Mr. Reiner. I'll let you know by letter. Thank you so much for calling." She hung up.

By the time Flood drove up the driveway to the motel it was nearly eleven-thirty. As the car came abreast of the office, the door opened and the owner came out. Flood swore and stopped. He had known this would happen sooner or later. He rolled down the window.

"Got a new car, I see," the man said accusingly.

"Mine broke down," Flood said. "The garage lent me this until mine's fixed." He cursed himself again. The license probably had a code letter identifying it as a rental car. A lie like that, even a small lie, could create suspicion.

The man nodded. "Goddamn cars they make nowadays, you're lucky they don't break down on the way home from the showroom."

He looked at Flood sagely and waited for a reply. Flood waited, too, without speaking. Finally he tried out a smile but it didn't work. "Well, got to go," he said. "Work to do."

"What's your line?" the man asked, moving a step closer.

"Line?" Flood asked, nervously watching him.

"Business, I mean. Line of work."

"That's why I'm here—looking for work."

"Oh." He looked more disdainful than suspicious now. "What kind?"

"Selling," Flood answered. "Just about any kind of selling."

The man nodded, disinterested. "Yeah," he said. "If you can sell, you don't need no trade." His eyes gleamed at the insult.

Flood gave him a curt wave and drove off. In the mirror he could see him looking at the back of the car, probably realizing it was rented.

Still wearing his hat and coat, he sat in the wicker chair for ten minutes. Then he got up and eased out of the front door and, keeping close to the front wall of the cabin, jumped off the end of the small porch. Fifty or so feet from the far side of the cabin was a row of scraggly bushes that apparently marked the boundary line of the property. The bushes, with here and there a gap, ran in a straight line down a gradual slope to the river. Walking rapidly, Flood went through the nearest gap and hurried toward the river, moving in a slight stoop to keep his head below the bushes. A copse of beeches ran along the river, back in the direction of the motel's opposite boundary, some five hundred feet away, where there was an identical row of bushes running back up the slope beyond the owner's house.

Beyond the trees and the river were some large rocks and Flood sat down on one and took Natalie's hat out of his coat pocket. It was dark gray with a thin black grosgrain band. He turned it over. Inside was a broader grosgrain band in pale gray with a label sewn to it: "Printemps. Paris."

Something caught his eye and he looked up, across the river. It was about two hundred feet wide at that point and on the far side was a fringe of rushes; beyond was flat farmland strewn with dead cornstalks. Far off was what he had seen—a truck speeding along a dirt road, leaving behind a trail of dust.

He turned back to the hat. Tearing off the outside band, he put it beside him on the rock and then ripped out the inside band, too. He tried to break the thinner ribbon but couldn't and finally put a loop of it under his heel and jerked the other end until it parted. Then he did the same with the wider band. After that he picked up a round stone, about six inches in diameter, and put it into the crown of the hat, folded the brim over and tucked it around the stone, and tied the bundle together with the two bands. Satisfied, he stood up, looked back to make sure he couldn't be seen, and flung the weighted hat, in an underhand softball pitch, as far as he could. It went perhaps thirty feet, skidded on the surface of the water, and sank.

Flood looked back toward the motel. He found that if he moved two feet to the left he could see his cabin, the car, and a dozen feet on the other side of the cabin but couldn't see the owner's house. He looked at his watch: 12:40. He would wait here, to make sure Marja was alone. A few minutes later he heard a sound. He ducked behind a tree and looked around it, back the way he had come. A figure—a boy with a turtleneck sweater and black hair—was coming toward him along the riverbank. He was carrying something; it looked like a shopping bag. Then Flood saw that it wasn't a boy. It was Marja. She was wearing blue jeans and a dark sweater; the black hair was her knitted cap and the shopping bag was her canvas satchel-handbag. She walked with her head down, carefully picking her way among the rocks, and he watched as she reached the line of bushes, peered through them toward the motel, then made her way up the outer side. She was alone.

When she reached the cabin, he ran to the bushes and followed her path. As he got to the end of the row, opposite the cabin, she was coming out the door and saw him. He ran to the porch and pushed open the door. Without a word she went in and he followed her.

"You were down there watching me?" she asked.

Flood nodded. "I didn't expect you to arrive that way," he said. "When I saw you I didn't know who it was. Then I recognized you when you got to the porch."

Marja looked at him speculatively. "What were you doing down there?"

"Thinking," he said. Thank God he had got rid of the hat before she turned up. "Where's your car?" He realized that he didn't even know if she had a car.

"By that diner up the road a little way," she said.

"Smart. I never thought of that." He should have, he realized. Of course he should have thought of a lot of things.

Marja opened her satchel. "I brought some food." She took out two brown paper sacks and handed him one. "Your favorite."

He opened the bag and took out something wrapped in white paper. It was a hamburger—a thin gray piece of meat in a small sodden roll. There was also a container of milk and two containers of coffee. The coffee was black. He looked at her, wondering if she thought he'd been drinking again, but she was busily unpacking her own lunch—a grilled-cheese sandwich, which looked uncommonly tempting to him, milk, and tea. He sat on the side of the bed next to the night table and she sat facing him in the wicker chair. They ate quickly, without speaking, and when they finished she filled her paper bag with the sandwich wrappings and paper containers and dropped it into the tin wastebasket.

"Well?" she said, turning to him.

Flood got rid of his debris, too, sat back, and in a slow voice told her everything that had happened—what he had found at the flag plant, his conclusions about its meaning, the conversation with Ormond, and what that meant, too.

"But why?" she asked at the end. "Why does Bruce want to conceal Natalie's identity?"

"If the murderer—supposedly me—had been found with the body, McCade couldn't have let it be known who she was, because the police might have insisted on searching his house. And once the supposed murderer got away it was even more important to conceal her identity."

Marja thought for a few moments and nodded.

"I'm still puzzled, though," Flood went on. "Surely Natalie must have been known around town."

Marja shook her head.

"Not at *all?*"

"Bruce hardly ever let her go out—and never alone. I think he didn't trust her. She had changed in the last couple of years."

"Since you moved into that house?"

She looked at him in surprise. "She was afraid—

more and more afraid. I would find her weeping. And sometimes she had hysterics and locked herself in her room. Bruce finally had Bell remove the lock. And she had begun drinking, too. I don't know if he was aware of that."

"He must have been at night—when they went to bed."

"They had separate bedrooms. They had begun to drift apart. It was hard for her. And then she became afraid." Marja paused. "It was the attic, I think."

"I must get in there," Flood said, surprised at the words, even though he had known that he must.

She ignored him. "I think she was losing her mind."

"All the more reason for him to kill her."

Her eyes glittered with anger for an instant, as if it was insensitive of him to speak reasonably about such a matter.

There was a knock at the door. Both of them froze, staring at one another in alarm. Finally Marja nodded at the door, and whispered, "You'd better find out."

Flood went to open it. He paused, his hand on the tin knob, and asked, "Who is it?"

"The maid, sir."

He opened the door and saw her, standing close, a towel held in front of her breasts. "I thought you might like a decent towel," she said, with a shy smile. "The others are so skimpy." Then she saw Marja and flushed. She looked at Flood as if to say "So that's why" and handed him the towel. She turned away.

Embarrassed at her look, Flood called, "Thanks," but she didn't acknowledge it. He closed the door and went back to sit on the side of the bed facing Marja. She had her hand in her satchel and when he was seated she took out a small automatic and pointed it at his chest.

"Did you kill Natalie?" Her eyes looked crazed. "If you did, I'll kill you."

"I told you—" he began and stopped. She was crazy and she was going to kill him.

Marja stared at him in silence for a long time, the

119

gun aimed unmovingly at his chest. "I'll kill them both," she said at last, her voice flat.

Flood was afraid to move. She meant to pay someone for her sister's death and he knew that it could be him if he frightened her. Slowly he put his hand out, palm up. "Give me the gun," he said.

Marja looked at him listlessly and put the gun back in her satchel. "It's only twenty-two caliber—a Beretta," she said. "Not much use unless you're close. As close as we are."

"I must get into your house tonight," he said. "Can you think of a way?" It seemed best to ignore her outburst.

"There is no way," she answered. "An alarm system. Damon. Two men, one of them always armed."

"Bell?"

She nodded and repeated, "There is no way. I must kill them. That's the only way."

Flood was touched by sorrow—she had lost so much —and by pity. He knew he must never let her know how he felt. She would despise him for that and he realized again with surprise that he wanted her to like him.

Her voice was still flat, coldly unemotional, and yet she seemed out of control, that implacable composure gone. He had to help her restore it if there was to be any hope at all. "All right," he said briskly, "we have to silence the alarms and take care of Damon. First, the alarm system. How does it work?"

She looked at him disinterestedly but after a moment's hesitation she described it: all the ground-floor windows and four windows and a door on a second-floor porch off McCade's suite of rooms were wired on the same system, which was controlled from a wall panel in his study. He had three rooms—a bedroom, a bath, and a study. The main outside doors— one at the front, one at the back, and one at the bottom of a flight of outside stairs leading to the basement—were on a separate system. Unlike the system at the flag plant, this one had no outside key to turn it on and off. Instead, when the system was on, the doors could be opened without any alarm being triggered at once; but if a switch concealed behind curtains inside each of the three doorways was not turned within thirty seconds, the alarm would go off.

"It's a high piercing scream," Marja said. "Nearly unendurable to the human ear. I came in the back door with an armful of groceries one day and forgot to turn the key. The alarm went off. Within seconds Bell was there in the hall to the kitchen, crouched down, both hands aiming a long pistol at me."

"And Damon?"

"Beside Bell, ready to strike." She put a hand to her throat.

"An attack dog?"

She nodded.

"He would attack even you?"

"He's Bell's dog."

"What's the attack order?"

She looked at him and quivered slightly. "Kill."

Flood let his breath out in a long sigh. He had got her back into the realm of possibility at least but it wasn't doing much good. "The alarm on Bell's door?" he asked.

"All I know is what I told you about the time Natalie tried to go up there. Obviously it has an alarm, too. How it works I have no idea."

"The garage?"

"There's no alarm there. It's a fairly good-sized building, about a hundred feet from the house. You know, back when it was a stable they didn't want the smell of horses so close."

"Describe it."

"It has room for three cars. The old stable doors have been replaced with overhead sliding doors made of some light metal—aluminium, I think." She used the English pronunciation. "There's a window on each side and two windows in the back. There's a loft running out halfway from the rear of the building." She paused to think for a moment. "That's about it."

"Anything in the loft?"

"Some boxes, I think. Some old furniture. I'm not sure. I've never been up there."

"How do you get up?"

"A ladder nailed to the wall at one side."

"The place is kept locked?"

She nodded.

"Are the windows barred?"

"No. Just plain windows—the kind that slide up and down."

"Sash windows."

She shrugged. "Whatever they're called."

"The cars?"

"Mine—a green two-door Ford. Bruce's—a dark-brown Mercedes six nine."

Flood whistled softly. "And Bell?"

"A gray panel truck. I don't know what kind. It's always kept locked. There's an antenna on top, so it must have a radio telephone."

"That's all?"

She nodded.

Again he wondered if she had told him everything. "I've got to get into that attic," he repeated. "There has to be a way."

After a pause, Marja asked, "Do you have any paper—big enough to make drawings?"

Flood gave her a sheaf of copy paper he had taken from his office and she took a pencil from her bag and sat at the little table facing the window. She began sketching swiftly and a few minutes later she cocked her head to examine what she had done, then handed him the drawing. It was a remarkably well done plan of the ground floor of the house.

He looked at her in surprise. "This is really expert."

"I got tired of ballet while we were in London and studied art for a couple of years," Marja explained. "I turned out to be a wretched artist but a skilled draftsman. Mechanical drawing, they called the course. I seem to be extremely mechanical."

The floor plan was detailed and so clear that Flood found what he wanted immediately: the basement entrance. An outside flight of steps led to it from a landing on the right side of the house, beside the driveway. "I'll need a plan of the basement and then the second floor," he said and returned to the drawing as she resumed sketching.

Flood studied the drawing carefully for several minutes. There were four fireplaces on the ground floor, he noticed, and imagined the Victorian grace of the house—heavy oak doors and paneling, high ceilings, tall windows, polished floors, spaciousness. Most of all he was interested in the stairways—a broad one in the central hall near the front and a narrow one back by the kitchen.

"Does the rear stairway go all the way from the basement to the attic?" he asked.

"Only to the second floor." She handed him a plan of that floor and pointed to the stairs up to the attic, above the broad main staircase.

Flood looked at the sketch. It was perhaps ten feet along a narrow corridor leading from the top of the rear stairs to the second floor, then another thirty feet or so along the main hallway to the attic stairs. At their top . . . He shook his head wearily. The chance was so small.

Marja finished her drawing of the basement and handed it to him. All he was interested in down there was the passage from the outside door to the rear stairs. It was direct—a narrow corridor across the width of the basement, bisected by the main corridor running from front to back—and led straight to the stairs. It should take only a couple of minutes from the basement entrance to the top of the attic stairs, he thought—if he wasn't stopped.

He glanced up and saw that Marja was watching him. "What is it?" he asked.

She hesitated, then smiled a little. "I was just thinking. Your hair."

"I know." He put a hand to the thick white thatch and now he said the words aloud: "It's like a goddamn flag."

"You could dye it." She paused. "It would be a shame, though. I rather like it."

He was surprised by the personal remark and felt his face flush. "I'm not supposed to have anything to hide, remember?"

"Even from Bruce?"

"If I could hide it only from him and wash it out when I got back to the office—" He broke off, wondering if he would ever go back to the office.

Flood turned to the plans, saying, "You don't know what the attic is like of course."

"Only where the stairs to it are." Again she pointed to the staircase. Her forefinger was unusually long and the close-clipped nail was also long, making the finger seem almost unreal. Flood placed the tip of his right forefinger beside hers and as she drew her hand away he traced the row of steps to the top. "Comes out in the middle of the attic?" he asked.

"Roughly. If my calculations are right."

"Is there a door at the bottom?"

"No, just at the top. That's where the alarm must be."

Flood looked up at her. "Do you hear footsteps above your room?"

"That part of the house is only two and a half stories. I think it's just empty air space above my room."

"Bell's room and whatever Natalie saw up there are above McCade's suite?"

"I told you, I don't know anything about the attic," she said edgily.

Flood sat back. He hadn't an idea in his head about how he might get into the house—or if he got in, how he might get out again. "It will take some thinking," he mumbled.

"It will take more than thinking," Marja said matter-of-factly. She glanced at her watch and jumped up. "I'm late."

Flood remembered the warning about McCade in Natalie's letter. "Has he been watching you?" he asked.

"You don't know when Bruce is watching you." She picked up her bag, then paused, looking down at him. "When?"

"Tonight," he said. "It has to be. He's looking for me. There's no more time. I'll figure out something. Can you be at Tony's again—at five?"

"What if he sees us together?"

"I'm sorry," Flood said, hating his futility. He waited, feeling weak again. Their talk, the intent scrutiny of the floor plans, her presence had dispelled his fear, but it was gathering again. "Tony's?" he asked.

"No!"

Slowly Flood got up and faced her without speaking. He knew that he could do nothing without her help. And he knew that he probably could do nothing with her help. It was time now to leave her alone if that was what she wanted. He stood slackly, waiting.

"Not Tony's," she said. "We can't be seen there again."

Relieved of both guilt and the prospect of going on alone, Flood looked into her green eyes and hoped she understood his gratitude. Again he wanted to touch her but refrained. "There's an old red-brick church—St. Bartholomew's—near the railroad station. Do you know it?" he asked.

"Yes."

"Make it the third pew from the rear on the left if no one's there. As soon as you can after five."

Marja looked at him in surprise. "Are you Catholic?"

"I once was—long ago."

"All right," she said, and was gone.

# 4

Flood made a drink and sat on the wicker chair. He studied the three floor plans and sipped the whiskey and got nowhere. Finally, after half an hour, he put the drawings down. He finished the drink and made another. It was two-thirty. Only two and a half hours before he was to meet her, with a plan ready. He took the glass and left the cabin, returning to the river edge by the same route. He sat on the low rock and stared at the dark water and across at the farmland beyond.

The house seemed impregnable. The alarm system and the dog and the two men. Flood sat, waiting for a light to go on in his darkened mind—the flashing idea that would point the way. Nothing came to him. The lights are out, he thought. He sat forward. That was it. He stared at the whiskey without seeing it and drank some without tasting it. Nodding to himself finally, he got up and hurried back to the cabin to get his coat and hat.

A little before three-thirty Flood reached Bay City and parked in front of Morley Brothers Sporting Goods. In a short time he had bought a dozen boxes of paraffin cakes, of the kind used to start wood fires; two five-gallon plastic jugs with handles and screw caps; a pair of black cotton pants; a navy wool turtleneck; a navy windbreaker; a black ski mask; a flashlight with a heavy black steel casing and batteries; a Shur-Fire propane cigarette lighter; and a slender pocketknife.

While the clerk was wrapping his purchases, Flood gazed into a locked showcase full of handguns. Guns like these had always seemed to him the most menacing objects, size for size, in the world and he had repeatedly written columns pleading for a national law banning them altogether. But now he stared at the assortment with fascinated longing and remembered the large pearl-handled revolver that his father had kept hidden in a shoe box in his closet. As a boy Flood had found the gun one day and occasionally he furtively took it out of the box and pointed it at himself in the long mirror inside the closet door. He could almost feel it in his hand now—the amazing sense of power and terror it gave him. He had to have a gun, some kind of gun.

At the corner next door to Morley's was an old-fashioned pharmacy and inside were two old-fashioned wood telephone booths. Marie, the head switchboard operator at the *Herald,* answered and Flood disguised his voice as he asked for Ormond.

"Mr. Flood?" Ormond asked in surprise when he came on.

Jesus, Flood thought, Marie had recognized him anyway. "Just checking in," he said. "Anything new?"

There was a silence on the other end, then Ormond said, "I don't know what to say, Mr. Flood. Something's wrong."

"That fellow—what's his name, Cameron?—she wasn't his wife?" Flood asked.

"No, that isn't it. She was his wife all right. The police have released her body. He's taking it back to Philadelphia in the morning."

"Does he know anything? I mean, about what might have happened?"

"Nothing. But, Mr. Flood—"

"Have you talked to him?"

"Yes. He's clean. Works nights and was at his job when she was killed. Flower checked of course."

"Any suspects?"

"Just a minute. Someone—"

Suddenly another voice came over the phone. It was Rogers. "*Mr.* Flood?" he said in a half shout. "What the hell is going on? Where are you?"

Taken aback, Flood quickly said, "The Cape—on the Cape."

"Now goddamnit, I want to know where you are—

exactly where you are—the phone number, address, everything."

Flood wasn't Johnny now, he realized, and missed the comfort of Rogers' familiar contempt. Controlling himself, he said evenly, "Who the hell do you think you are? Where I am, what I'm doing is my business." He was surprised by the cool anger in his voice.

"Oh yeah?" Rogers snarled. "Lieutenant Flower was here not an hour ago. He wants to talk to you. I don't know why but he was very insistent. *Very*. Something to do with that woman's murder. He mentioned a warrant. Now, what the hell is going on? Are you interfering in a police case? If I find out . . . Your job is at stake, Flood. The publisher won't back you this time."

If it were only his job, Flood thought, and began to feel the sense of hopelessness again. They must have tipped off the police. An anonymous call. More evidence planted in his apartment.

"Where are you?" Rogers demanded. "Get back here, wherever you are. Flower said one of his men saw you this morning here in town. Now, I want to know—"

The telephone receiver was like a gun at Flood's head and he removed it, staring distractedly at it and hearing Rogers' nasal, intent voice recede. Slowly, deliberately, Flood placed the phone on its cradle.

He bought a pair of gold-rimmed faintly tinted sunglasses and a bottle of brown hair coloring and left the store. On the south side of town he stopped at a small gas station and had the plastic jugs filled with high octane. When he drove off, heading back toward New Richmond, it was not quite four o'clock. "Time," he said aloud. If he could get through the night and find the answer, he might . . . But he knew that his time had run out. He could feel despair rising, not like before when fear had been compounded and confused by desperation and bewilderment and fatigue. Now it was simply despair, the flat certainty of reality.

Flood swung left, to the expressway, and headed south again, driving fast. He had plenty of time before meeting Marja, if Flower didn't get him first, but he wanted to wait somewhere in the vicinity of St. Bartholomew's. If he was late, she might get frightened and leave. He took the broad loop around New Richmond and left the expressway just south of the city onto a bridge across the Richmond River. At the far end he took the first turnoff, onto a narrow back road that ran parallel to the river, and headed north toward town. Now he was only ten minutes or so from the church.

He had never approached the cemetery from this direction before, and when he saw the broad gate ahead, with the ornate wrought-iron sign above—THE GROVE—he turned in. It had been a long time since he'd been there, at least a year, and again the lost warm longing hurt amalgam of feelings overtook him. He drove very slowly up the crunching gravel drive, past large marble and granite crypts, past tall monuments with angels or crosses or plinths on top. As the road wound up the knoll, he wondered if he should stop or go on. He parked and got out. Looking around, he could see no one; it was too late for funerals, and mourners didn't visit eternal resting places during rush hour. He looked up the knoll at the tombs there— older, smaller, slanted, weathered, for this was the original part of the cemetery—and hesitated. There might not be time. But his need to go on pressed at him and he wondered if this was where he had been headed all afternoon without knowing it.

Flood stopped by Ellen's grave. The headstone— polished gray granite and sunk even with the surface of the earth—was out of keeping with the gravestones around it, most of them from the eighteenth and nineteenth centuries—pale cream, white, dark brown, corroded, the inscriptions eaten away by time. Ellen had been fond of this spot. The faded symbols of mortality made death seem a comfort, not a terror. They had come here occasionally to sit and talk about the lives of those beneath the stones or to gaze in silence at the river and the farmland beyond receding distantly into the dark hills.

This part of the cemetery—like most of the state and the colony before it—had belonged to the Babcocks. William III had given Captain John Babcock, one of his faithful soldiers, tens of thousands of acres in the colony in 1692 and he and the Babcocks following him had prospered mightily. The revenues from the landholdings were immense and were made immeasurably more immense by the industrial development that transformed the region throughout the latter half of the nineteenth century. Flood had chronicled it all in his Pulitzer series, especially the Babcocks' plunder of the public during the family's final spree in Wall Street finance.

The Babcocks lying beneath his feet were all that remained. Flood glanced at old Tyler Babcock's tomb —a three-foot-square, white-marble block—and re-read the incredible epitaph: "In Death Even a King Is But a Man. Here Lies a Man." The conceit that death did not reduce all to humble equality but might raise one to the grandeur of kings amazed him anew, as it did each time he read it.

Susannah Babcock, Tyler's widow, had outlived him by twenty years but she wasn't here. She had other ideas, she'd told Flood when he went to see her just before Ellen's funeral and begged a bit of earth to put her away in. Ashes scattered from a great liner at sea as the sun set, Mrs. Babcock said. And afterward champagne for everyone as long as they could stand up. She had been twenty-nine—an upstart showgirl, not fit for the Babcocks—when Tyler, then in his early sixties, married her just after the First World War. He was the last of the Babcock line and he claimed she was meant solely for an heir but everyone had known there would be none, not after his two previous wives proved barren.

"I once thought of giving him a son by adultery," Mrs. Babcock told Flood without a flicker of compunction. "But I hated him too much to give him the satisfaction of even a bastard." Her black eyes glittered and she asked, "You say you're a journalist, Mr. Flood?"

He nodded, hoping she had forgotten the Pulitzer series.

But then she said, "You wrote those pieces that won that prize."

He nodded again and gave up.

"I loved it," she said flatly. "Wiped out the Babcocks. Oh, their fury, their impotence. I wish you'd come to me. I'd have given you enough to roast them all." She paused to slip a cigarette into an ebony holder, light up, and take several long drags. "Are you Irish, Mr. Flood?"

"Half," he answered. "The other half Scotch."

"Half will do," she said cryptically and went off into a tremulous little dry cough. "Tyler hated the Irish even more than he hated reporters. I don't suppose you're Catholic, too."

"I once was."

"In that racket once is always. Tyler hated them, too. Called them mackerel-snappers."

Flood held his tongue. Only the very old, who had nothing more to lose, were capable of such malice. "Is that all?" he asked and got up.

"Not quite," she said, glaring at his impertinence. "You shall have a plot in the Grove, Mr. Flood, this very day. Two of them, side by side. For a dollar. I'll ring up my lawyers at once." Then she burst out into a cracked peal of laughter. "Oh, to see his ghost!" she cried delightedly. "To spend all of eternity beside an Irish Catholic journalist." She choked over her laughter and waved him out.

Flood hadn't minded the vicious insult. He cared about nothing now except to make up to Ellen, even in this small way that was so late, by putting her away decently at least, someplace she had loved, where he could visit her in peace. Nor would the presence of the Babcocks have bothered her. She felt no animus toward anyone. "There is no such thing as evil free in the world," she had once said to him. "There is only good and bad mixed up in people, only their confusion and ignorance." It was a most un-Catholic idea for him, almost incomprehensible, but he accepted it from her.

Now he looked at her grave and once more off toward the river. At last he realized why he had chosen the great rock upstream to get rid of his clothes, why he had taken the cabin by the river, why he had drowned the hat there, why he had gone to sit on the rock and drink whiskey and think there, why he had come here. His life was ebbing away. All that was left for him was the dark water running into the oblivion of the sea, this place, that earth, the thought of her.

Flood knelt before the grave, tears coming at last, and he wept in silence, his shoulders heaving slightly, and tried to pray. He had forgotten how, it had been so long, and now, as he had done the night before, he repeated the Hail Mary over and over, mindlessly. It didn't matter. One needn't think, he told himself. It was the words, the talisman that unlocked the corrupted soul to save it from condemnation forever. A minute later he rose unsteadily and walked back to the car.

At the door of St. Bartholomew's, Flood glanced back to see if anyone was following him. An old man was picking through a wastebin at the corner. A woman with a child was crossing the street. A telephone company repair truck went by. He entered the church, into the dim solemnity, past the font, and saw lit candles at the altar far away and the bent backs and bowed heads of worshipers here and there. No one was at the rear. Flood moved down the length of the third pew on the left and sat at the far end.

A dark form stopped next to him and for a moment he felt panic clawing at him. It was Marja. She slid onto the seat and hunched over to whisper in his ear.

"Bruce called me at school. Natalie's gone, he said, missing from the inn. He left to drive up there."

Flood accepted the news complacently. "Of course," he said.

"Shhhh!"

He had spoken out loud. Turning to her, he whispered, "So she disappeared up there, not here. Very smart. He's here, looking for me."

Marja turned sharply to stare into the darkness behind them. Flood put a hand on hers to calm her. She stiffened at the touch and he took his hand away.

"Not *here*—in town," he went on. "He tipped off the police. Trying to frame me about Natalie again. They're looking for me."

She said something he couldn't make out. He looked at her inquiringly.

"Do you have it?" she asked.

He'd forgotten something else. "What?" he asked weakly.

"A plan!" she hissed.

Flood put his head closer to hers, close enough to smell her unperfumed skin and her hair. Very quickly he told her that she must take the dog out for its walk at exactly eleven-thirty that night and must stay out for at least half an hour. Before leaving, she must turn off the alarm on the basement entrance and leave the door there wedged slightly ajar.

Marja pulled her head back and stared at him. "Bell will kill you."

Flood ignored her. With McCade out of the house, he had a chance. "Where's the fuse box with the main power switch?" he asked.

"In the basement. On the wall in the main hall. Around the corner—to the right—when you come in from the outside door." She stopped and looked at him in surprise. "Of course! The electricity." A moment later she looked perturbed again. "But he'll know. The lights—when they go out."

"He won't be there." Flood hoped that he was right.

"But—"

Flood raised his hand to silence her and hastily explained about the gasoline and the paraffin blocks and asked where her car was. It was still behind the school; she had walked. "Does McCade suspect you?"

"No," she said certainly but added, less certainly,

"I don't think so. He's irritable, withdrawn. He scarcely notices me."

"We'll have to risk it." He went on to describe the rest of his plan—to put the flammable materials in the trunk of her car after they left the church separately, for her to leave the key to the trunk on the narrow ledge of the car between its rear bumper and the trunk, just below the lock, and then to unfasten the window in the back of the garage, the one farthest from Trevelyan. "Is there any cover behind the garage—bushes, trees, long grass?" he asked.

"A hedge—taller than a man and clipped square. Along the back of our yard. About thirty feet behind the garage."

"The other side of it?"

"The Binghams' yard."

"Any dog?"

"No." She faced him fully and he could see her eyes, dark green in the dimness. "You're going to burn our garage to draw Bell out."

Flood nodded without speaking.

"My car, too?"

He nodded again. It was only a car but he felt sorry for her. It was all she had now. It was her escape. He had been repressing the thought but now he faced it: if he got away and Marja didn't because of his negligence . . . it would be over for him.

Again she had said something that he hadn't heard. "Afterward?" she repeated.

"The cabin maybe. I'm not sure."

"And me?"

Flood had been expecting the question. The danger he'd been in and the danger he now faced had seemed reason enough to put her second but he knew he couldn't do that any longer. He sat back, thinking. She leaned next to him, waiting stiffly.

"Is it time?" he asked at last. "To get out?"

She was silent for a minute, then said, "It's time."

Flood told her about the room at the Holiday Inn. "T, for Trevelyan, Barnard," he said. "The streets at your corner. Say you're Mrs. Barnard."

"Too close. Bruce—" The words hissed sibilantly into silence.

"Don't go tonight," he said. "Too suspicious. Bell won't try anything without McCade. Act as if it was just a fire. Go to work as usual. At lunch—go!"

"By taxi?"

Flood looked at her to see if she was mocking him. He couldn't tell. She reached into her bag and a moment later slipped the small automatic into his hand. For its size it was very heavy—and very comforting. He put it into his raincoat pocket and nodded at her in thanks. He had forgotten to ask her for it but he knew why. Now she was truly alone. Or was she? Flood looked at her again, wondering if she had given him the gun so that he would have some small chance, at least, to alleviate her guilt.

# 5

With dark-brown hair, Flood looked astonishingly different. The task of dyeing it—twice to make it darker—was infinitely more difficult than the advertisements claimed. It had taken him more than three hours but as he stood in front of the mirror in the bathroom of the cabin he was more pleased with himself than he had been since he figured out how the transmitter worked from the brass eagle. Turning to the side and contemplating himself from one eye, he thought, Jesus, I look pretty good.

Whether he looked good or not—with the sharply curved nose and the long face—was open to question. But that he had been transformed was not. He seemed ten years younger, almost boyish, for his face was still unwrinkled except for the beginnings of fine webs below his eyes. He slipped on the tinted glasses. "Okay," he said aloud.

When he saw that it was ten to eleven he felt anything but okay. He checked the safety catch on the Beretta and put it in the right-hand pocket of the windbreaker. The flashlight went into the other pocket, the knife in the right pocket of the black pants, and the propane lighter in the left. He picked up the ski mask and tucked it in the windbreaker pocket around the gun.

The motel office and the house behind it were dark and Flood, using only his parking lights, let the car coast past the place and down the drive. At the exit, he switched on the low beams and turned onto the River Road toward New Richmond. Traffic was light on the way into town and not much heavier as he made his way around the main section and headed toward Barnard Street. He hit only two stoplights but at the second a police car pulled up beside him. Flood stiffened slightly, forcing himself to act naturally—or unnaturally natural as most people act, even when innocent, in the presence of the police.

He glanced toward the window two feet from his and met the eyes of a policeman with a bushy mustache and a cigarette dangling from thick lips. It was Tony Vito. Flood faced ahead and waited. Vito had been broken from sergeant for beating a suspect and fracturing his arm. He was as tough as only men with all the physical and legal advantages can be. Flood had written about the case and now he remembered the look of hatred Vito had given him as they sat in the public hearing room.

The light changed and he waited for a second or two for the other car to move. It didn't. He started up and drove steadily at thirty, keeping an eye on the rearview mirror. The police car was behind him, a hundred feet away, and keeping the same speed. Suddenly, several blocks farther on, its roof lights flashed on. Flood hunched forward ready to go, one hand on the headlight switch. The police car made a rocking U-turn at the next intersection and roared off, its siren screaming, in the opposite direction.

Flood's hopes rose a bit. Maybe McCade wouldn't recognize him either. Or Bell. He swore under his breath. He had forgotten to ask Marja to describe the two men. His disguise wouldn't deceive them if they found him someplace where they expected to find him.

Marja's description of the house had been like a photograph. As Flood drove along Barnard to the corner of Trevelyan he saw the place looming up grayly in the night. Several windows on the ground floor were lit up, he saw, but the second floor was dark and so was the attic. Heavy curtains or inside shutters, he thought as he looked up at the black rectangles under the roof line. He slowed down as much as he dared and drove past the front of the house. If she had made any mistake it was in the size of the plot of land, which seemed to him closer to two acres than one. The house was set nearly in the center, with a long straight driveway passing from Barnard down the right side of the house to the stable-garage, which he could see dimly at the rear. There were spacious lawns dotted with large trees; on the right side of the property was a long squarely trimmed hedge that ran straight back to the rear of the plot; there it joined another hedge running along the rear to Trevelyan.

Flood drove around the block and came up toward the house from the back, on Trevelyan. The garage was perhaps seventy feet in from the street, a story-and-a-half building with a steeply peaked roof. As he drove past the house itself he saw the back porch, then the semicircular side porch off the dining room, and, above that, McCade's rooms—all as clearly described in Marja's drawings. A hundred feet farther on, at his right across Trevelyan, was the only fire hydrant he had seen. It was at least two hundred feet from the garage. That would slow them down.

At the corner of Barnard he drove straight on rather than risk suspicion by passing the house in front again. The street was deserted except for a few parked cars. He turned left at the next corner, then left again, and parked between two cars, leaving a good ten feet in front of him. He was on Barnard, two blocks from the house.

At twenty minutes past eleven, Flood—now wearing the ski mask—slowly eased up the window at the far side of the back of the garage and climbed inside. He closed the window. Flicking on the flash just long enough to get his bearings, he saw the gray van at the far side and the green Ford immediately in front of him, both backed into the garage. Between them was a space for the Mercedes. Where was McCade? Waiting in the house? Marja had been holding something back, he was sure. But the key to the car trunk was exactly where he had told her to leave it. He opened the trunk, cursed as a light went on automatically inside, and quickly closed it again. The second time he grabbed the two jugs of gasoline and dropped them on the floor, then took the boxes of paraffin and closed the trunk. He took out the keys and put them in the ignition and went back to the rear of the garage.

Flood crouched behind the car for a minute, waiting to see if anyone had been roused by the noise. When nothing happened he got up and went around the car to the wall ladder. It took two trips to get the jugs to the loft. He splashed the gasoline from one of them over the boxes there and the other's contents along the base of the wood wall. Climbing quickly back down the ladder, he broke open and crumbled the paraffin blocks along the base of the wall by the ladder, then along the opposite wall by the van. He flicked on the propane lighter and looked at his watch. It was 11:32. He hurried to the wall by the van and lit the far end of the strewn chunks and crumbs of waxy paraffin. They puffed into a foot-high flame and he ran across the garage and lit the paraffin strewn along the opposite wall.

Seconds later Flood patted the trunk of Marja's car, murmured "Sorry," and clambered out the window. He closed it and peered in. Flames leapt up the side walls. If they didn't ignite the gasoline in the loft, he would have to go back in and do it himself. But the fumes from the gas would be collecting and a spark might touch off an explosion. Crouching below the window, Flood looked behind him at the tall dark hedge along the rear of the property.

There was a muffled whooshing roar, the window above him rattled in its frame, and he felt the side of the building tremble against his shoulder. The loft had caught. He ran to the end of the garage and peered around. There was no sign of anybody, no shouting, no alarm. Turning, he ran back to the rear hedge, fell to his hands and knees, and crawled to the corner and the long hedge that ran, parallel to the driveway, up to Barnard. Pausing a moment to collect himself, he stood up, then moved slowly forward along the hedge, watching the back porch and waiting.

When Flood reached a point opposite a tree beside the driveway and across from the spot where he figured the basement steps must be, he stopped and looked back at the garage. The side window was brilliant orange, the light from the flames spilling out to form a bright trapezoid on the side lawn. Soon, he thought, very soon. Then he heard a siren in the distance but couldn't make out whether it was growing louder. He waited.

A moment later the back-porch light went on. The door was flung open and a figure hurtled out, took a few running steps, and stopped. It was a man made of squares. Bell, Flood thought, watching him. His square head thrust forward, the man peered toward the garage, and ran to the door on the side where the van was. He bent down and grabbed the handle, stiffened, and groaned. He had gripped it too firmly to let go at once and when he did he shouted an incomprehensible word that sounded like a curse and put his hand to his mouth. Flood grinned—his gun hand. The metal door must be nearly red hot. Bell gripped his right hand with his left and ran around the far side of the garage. Abruptly he stopped, still within view. Flood realized that he was looking at the window there and the flames inside.

Flood had been watching so intently that he had lost track of the siren but now he saw the red and white flashing lights as a fire engine roared around the back corner onto Trevelyan and slowed down. Bell ran toward it, waving his arms, his broad square back toward Flood.

"Now!" Flood ordered himself and dashed across the lawn to the tree. He stopped there for a moment, peered around the trunk to see that the way was clear, and ran across the driveway to a spot just forward of the porch and out of the light spreading from above its steps. He flung himself against the gray clapboards and turned toward the front of the house. There were the basement steps a few feet away. He ran to them and slowed as he descended them. The door at the bottom was open an inch, a small stick holding it ajar at the bottom. Flood opened it all the way, kicked the stick out, entered, and closed the door behind him.

Panting, he leaned back against a wall in the darkness. A few moments later he flicked on the flashlight. The walls of the narrow hall were smooth brick, painted yellow, and the floor was concrete. A dozen feet away, at the end of the hall, was the broad main corridor. Flood moved forward into it. He shone the light on the wall to his right, just around the corner as she had instructed him, and saw the fuse box. Stepping up to it, he took the handle on its square door and pulled sharply. It didn't move. Locked. Cursing, he pulled again. Nothing. He turned the small handle and the door swung to. There were twenty or so fuses inside; none of the labels under them was marked "Alarm." Of course, he thought. It would be disguised under some ordinary heading. He looked at the main power lever for a few seconds uncertainly.

Turning away, Flood went back to the outside basement door, opened it slowly a few inches, and peered up. Just then the rear end of a great red fire engine passed on the driveway toward the garage, its lights flashing, its bell clanging. The bell stopped suddenly and he could hear another siren, perhaps two sirens, approaching. There were shouts and the sounds of running feet. It had to be time, he thought. The flashing lights, the fire, the confusion, the trucks between the garage and the house. He ran back to the fuse box and pulled the main switch to "OFF."

Pausing, he shone the light at the stairs across the broad control hallway and leaned back against the wall to calm himself. God knows what those steps lead to, he thought, drawing in a deep breath and letting it out slowly. It was a moment before he felt the pulsing throb of the wall against his back, then heard a low humming sound. He stiffened. With the electricity off, there should be nothing running in the house.

Flood aimed the beam of the flashlight down the main hallway, past the fuse box, and saw a door. He hurried to it and tried the knob. It turned and he shoved the door open and went inside. Near the other side of the wall he had been leaning against was a large bright-red machine. He ran the light across the side of it and saw that it was a generator. Of course.

They couldn't risk having the electricity go out in a storm. Whatever was installed upstairs must need a continuous electric supply. Suddenly it occurred to him that the alarm system was probably hooked into the private energy system—at least on a fall-back basis in case the main electricity line went off.

What else hadn't he thought of? he wondered and again he wanted to flee. A moment later he pulled himself together and turned the light back on the generator. Beyond it a long black tank about six feet high extended along the wall adjoining the one he was standing near. Fuel, he thought. He went to the control panel above and behind the generator and pushed the main switch to "OFF." Within seconds the motor stopped.

At the top of the inside stairway, Flood turned out the flashlight and slowly opened the door. It was dark. Visualizing Marja's drawing, he knew this was the cloakroom; at the other end was a short hallway between the kitchen and the dining room. About four steps out to the hall, a step to the right, and he would be at the foot of the stairs to the second floor.

He could hear sounds from outside and see flickering light coming through the rear windows of the house, across the kitchen, and along the hall. Flood took a long step forward just as he heard the door open. Footsteps came toward him. He flung himself into a row of coats hanging at his side, stumbling over some boots at the bottom.

There was a shout, a man's harsh voice: "Hey, you!"

The steps paused. "Yess?" another voice said.

"Are there cars in the garage?"

"Yess. *Zwei*—two."

"The keys to the doors! Where the Christ are they? We gotta get those cars out before they blow."

"The van, the van," the second voice said anxiously. "The keys, yess. But the lights. Why did the lights go out?"

"The fire must've cut the main line. The *keys,* man!"

The footsteps receded rapidly and a door slammed. Flood emerged cautiously from the coats, paused to peer around the doorway into the narrow hall, and saw that the brilliant light was coming through the thin curtain over the window of the kitchen door. He turned and ran up the stairs to the second floor. He left the flashlight off until he got to the top, then flicked it on. The door was open. Leaving it that way, Flood moved quickly out into the central hall and ran down it to the main staircase.

Flashing the beam up it, Flood saw that the door at the top was closed. He ran up the steps two at a time and took the doorknob. It gave way, swinging inward slowly, and he could feel its weight. He tapped a knuckle against its side: steel.

Flood closed the heavy door behind him and locked it. He turned and shone the light around the room he was in, keeping it low to the floor until he saw the condition of any windows that might be there. A recessed dormer at the far left was the only one. It was covered with a heavy brown curtain and when he checked behind it he saw that he had been right: inside shutters. Lifting the beam and sweeping the room—about twenty by fifteen feet and paneled with natural pine boards set vertically—he concluded that Bell must have been a soldier. A narrow bed covered with a taut khaki-colored wool blanket stuck out from one wall. Beside it was a night table with a brown-shaded lamp. Next to it, against the brickwork of a chimney, was an electric heater and next to that was a long wood table painted white, with a small white wood chair facing it. Centered on the top of the table were a blank legal pad and three sharpened pencils. Across from the table, beside the window, was a stiff-looking armchair covered with the same material that had been used to make the curtains. Nearby was a chest of drawers, also painted white. Most of the wood floor —it was a new floor, he saw, was covered by a rectangular gray rug. On the wall across from the chimney were three doors, the far one near the easy chair open. Flood shone the light in and saw a bathroom. The next door opened into a small tidy kitchen. The third was to a long closet.

Flood looked around the room again, puzzled. In a house this size the attic should be very large. Then he saw the coat hooks and remembered Natalie's words in the letter: "The coat hooks in Bell's room." They were on the wall at the right of the stairway door, five of them, made of heavy brass and attached to a board about four feet long and six inches high; it, too, was painted white. "The coat hooks in Bell's room," he repeated to himself. What the hell had she meant?

Striding over to the hooks, he examined them. The two next to the one in the center had clothes hanging on them—a long black-leather coat with one end of its leather belt dangling nearly to the floor and a maroon wool bathrobe. Flood took hold of the two end hooks and pulled them. Nothing. He pushed them. Nothing. He tried to turn them in either direction. Nothing. He had the same results with the hook in the center. But when he gripped the other two he felt something give under the clothes. He moved the coat and robe to the end hooks. Then he took the newly empty hooks and turned them, the left one counter-clockwise and the right one clockwise. They moved smoothly, without resistance, and behind them a section of the vertically paneled wall swung inward. He shone the light through the opening. A few feet away was a blank wall.

Flood entered the long hall. Pausing, he turned back to the door and saw a handle on its inside surface. He reached for it but decided not to pull it shut; it might lock him in. As he started down the hall he noticed that the floor was concrete, not wood. They must have put steel crossbeams under it and steel uprights all the way to the basement, he thought. Moving quickly, he came to what seemed to be the end of the hall, some twenty-five feet farther on. The wall on the right continued on as far as the light shone, but on his left was a massive concrete wall, six feet high and a foot and a half thick. He turned the light on the narrow side facing him and saw small dark circles embedded in the cement: steel reinforcing rods. He flashed the light down the length of the cement flank; it extended perhaps ten feet and beyond its far end was a space between it and another wood wall. The outer wall of the house, he thought. Two feet from the cement wall and running parallel to it was a gray steel panel about the same height. He walked around the panel and turned the light to his left.

He was in a control room of some sort. Puzzled, Flood moved forward, playing the light from one side to the other. The steel wall was the back of a large machine covered with dials, gauges, switches, buttons, lights, and two television screens: a computer. Turning behind him, he found a U-shaped counter a few feet away and went to it. A control panel, with more dials and switches. Moving down to one leg of the U, he saw that it contained a high-frequency radio. With all this equipment, no wonder they needed a generator.

Jesus, Flood thought, this was it. He bent down to examine the radio and saw that it was a receiver. There would be a recording device somewhere inside. The apparatus was divided into two sections. One was clearly a receiver and the other a transmitter. That was odd, he thought, and straightened up. What did they need a transmitter for? A moment later he realized it didn't matter. He had found what he was looking for. It was time to get out.

Looking around, he realized something was wrong: this room was too small as well. There must be more to the attic. He shone the light at the end of the computer and the thick cement wall behind it at the end opposite to the one he had entered by. There was a passageway about three feet wide, ending at a door at the back of the concrete wall. He went to it and put his hand on the knob. Time was closing in. He had to be quick. He pushed the door open and flashed the beam down the length of a room along its outer wall. Twenty-five or so feet away, on the floor in the corner, was a small motor of some kind. A storeroom, he decided, and started to close the door.

A glint of something caught his eye and he took a step forward through the doorway and shone the light into the center of the room.

"Jesus Christ!" he gasped.

Poised there on a steel cradle and aimed toward the slanted roof at an angle of about thirty degrees to the floor was a great gleaming silver cylinder with a pointed black nose ending in a long needle. A missile.

Flood stumbled and fell to his knees. "Holy Mother of God," he muttered and bent his head to get the flow of blood back to his brain. The dart missile . . . a nuclear warhead . . . Hail Mary, full of grace . . . Miller Field. Quantico, Lowry. The Pentagon . . . Jesus, the White House. Everywhere. The whole country.

"Oh my God," he mumbled, his head sinking lower. At last he forced himself to look up and to shine the light at the great evil thing. It was at least twelve feet long. There were four small fins just behind the nose and four longer ones near the tail, which was about a foot in diameter and hollow. Jet exhaust, he thought. The concrete wall behind it was a heat shield. But what would heat matter then?

Flood got slowly to his feet, swaying unsteadily, and made his way forward to the nose of the missile. Shining the light at the long black needle, he realized that it was an antenna. The only information transmitted by the brass eagle at Miller Field then was a radio beam to guide the missile to its target. The missile had to be armed with a nuclear warhead. He thought of all the brass eagles around the country. A war would be over in two minutes.

He had to get out. The only warning system left was John Flood. But he forced himself to shine the light on the motor he had seen from the doorway. Connected to it was a long telescopic rod extending upward and fastened at the roof on the near side of a narrow aluminum strip descending to the floor. At the right of the roof, directly above the motor, was a series of hinges. Shining the light across the end of the room, he saw an identical arrangement in the far corner. The roof opened up of course. The two parts of it, separated by the opening beneath the seam, swung outward or inward. Which way? he wondered pointlessly.

The beam of light caught a glint of metal on the far wall and Flood stepped forward until he was directly beneath the nose of the missile and shone the light across the room. On the wall was a large fiberboard map of the United States, like the one at the flag factory. Stuck into it here and there were small darts painted silver. A dart game—McCade's deadly sense of humor.

Flood turned a step and shone the light on the black needle above his head and down along the sharklike body of the nuclear missile. America was gone. *"Dosvidanya,* America," he whispered groggily. *"Dosvidanya."*

Flood closed the concealed door behind him and flashed the light around Bell's room, then turned it off. He would have to make his way out in the dark. Bell might be back in the house by now, even on his way upstairs. Slipping the flashlight into his pocket, Flood took out the automatic and slid the safety catch off. He unlocked the door to the stairway and slowly opened it. There was no sign of anyone, only silent darkness. With his free hand on the wall at the left, he crept down the stairs. At the landing he paused and tightened his grip on the gun. A corner to be turned—a danger spot. He thought he heard a soft footfall on the carpeted hall and bent forward, the gun thrust out at the darkness as if that were the enemy. It wasn't, he realized. It was the best friend he had. Moving out stealthily from the wall, he made a wide half-circle around the corner; if anyone was here he would be waiting close to the wall for protection and concealment.

Behind Flood, at the end of the hall, was a large bay window facing Barnard Street. It was covered with a heavy curtain and as he had come downstairs it had seemed as black as the rest of the hallway. Now, though, his eyes were becoming accustomed to the dark and he saw that light from the street outside filtered through the curtains. He was silhouetted against it, he realized, and quickly moved forward toward the rear of the house and the back stairs. He was safe for the moment at least, he thought; his silhouette must have presented a perfect target and yet no one had struck.

At the doors to McCade's and Natalie's rooms, Flood paused, his mind returning to the floor plan; the main stairway down to the first floor was there, two steps way, beside Natalie's door. If Bell came upstairs, he would probably come by the back stairs—the shortest way—as Flood had on his way up. It might be better then to go downstairs to the first floor by the main stairway. He hesitated, realizing that would mean having to find his way along the front hall, through the dining room, past the swinging door to the narrow rear hall and the stairs there. Too much chance of a misstep—stumbling into a table in the dark, a lamp or a vase crashing to the floor. He would have to take the chance and go the way he had come.

The spot on the back of the head where they had hit him began to throb again. He paused. There was no sound, only the dark, and once more he moved forward, this time keeping close to the wall on the right, his left hand out in front, his fingers spread like antennae to probe the darkness.

His fingertips touched something and he crouched down, ready to fire. Nothing happened. He reached forward slowly. It was the wood frame of the doorway. He felt to the right. The door was open. Had he left it that way? He began to straighten up but thought he heard a sound and crouched again, waiting. Feeling the panic begin to rise, he quickly moved forward, unconsciously sensing that the only way to subdue fear was through action. He felt the door jamb on his left and realized he was standing squarely in the doorway. One more step and he might have fallen down the stairs.

Jesus, Flood thought, careful, careful. He felt for the top step with a toe, found it, and started down. A few seconds later he was at the bottom and a moment after that he was back in the cloakroom.

He waited, listening. There were shouts outside still and he could see the flickering lights along the hallway wall outside the cloakroom at the far end. But it was quieter than before—no longer the frantic tumult. They must be getting the fire under control. He had very little time.

Beneath the noises from outside, he suddenly heard a footstep somewhere fairly close. Quickly he slid in between two long coats. Pressing himself back against the corner of the walls, he listened intently. Silence. He parted the coats and leaned forward.

The steps resumed. They came toward him and he pressed back against the corner, letting the coats fall into place. Overcome by fear, he could hardly breathe. He raised the gun to his chest. If Bell poked the coats . . . if he had a flashlight and shone it that way . . . he would have to fire blindly at that instant. They would hear the shot outside. He would have to move fast. He drew in a long breath and held it.

A light flickered over the ceiling and a voice muttered a string of guttural syllables that sounded like a curse. German. Flood tried not to pull the trigger too soon. The light moved off the ceiling and he heard rapid footsteps going up the stairs over his head. Bell was headed for the attic. Flood couldn't remember if he had left everything as he had found it. It was too late now to worry about that.

He flung himself out of the coats and ran into the hallway and down the stairs to the basement. Noise was unimportant now. He stopped at the outside basement door, trying to calm himself. He was too close now, almost there, to make a mistake. Hesitating for a moment, he slowly opened the outside door and looked upward into the stairwell. Nothing except dark sky, the branches of a tree, the muffled sounds of firemen calling to each other. Tearing off the ski mask, Flood walked slowly up the steps, pausing as his eyes came above ground level. To the rear of the house stood the huge back end of a fire engine parked at an angle. Above it were great puffing black clouds of smoke. He felt his eyes burning and wiped them with his sleeve and turned to look the other way, toward Barnard. There were three people, their backs to him, walking away. Curious neighbors probably. If they were leaving, the show must be nearly over. There was no more time.

Flood hurried back down the steps and into the basement. He put the gun in his pocket and stuffed the ski mask over it. Taking out the flashlight again, he flicked it on and went to the fuse box, pushed the main switch up to "on," hoped the firemen would have a handy means of explaining to Bell why the lights had gone back on of their own accord, hurried into the room with the generator and turned it on, then ran back to the outside door. He found the key to the alarm on the left side of the door jamb, turned it, went outside, and pulled the door closed behind him.

He fell back against the door, terrified that he had set off the burglar alarm. Realizing that it was lunacy to wait, he ran up the steps. Four firemen were carrying a hose from the back of the driveway toward the engine. Flood turned and walked quickly, but not too quickly, away from them up the driveway toward the street, waiting for someone to call him, waiting for a blow on the back of his head.

He was thirty feet from the street when a car came along Barnard, slowed, and stopped directly in front of the driveway. McCade, Flood thought. But it wasn't a Mercedes and certainly not a Mercedes 6.9. McCade must have more than one car, though, or the use of others. Flood walked on, feeling his legs pump stiffly. He tried to appear natural. His hair . . . the different clothes . . . he would have a few seconds at least. He put his hands in his windbreaker pockets and took hold of the gun. Had he put the safety catch back on? he wondered. Jesus, he thought, he'd never . . .

The window on the driver's side rolled down and a man's head emerged. Flood was near the sidewalk now and as he reached it he turned to the left, toward his car.

"I say, excuse me," the man said.

Flood stopped. Was it a British accent? He turned, gripping the gun in his pocket.

"A fire?"

Flood couldn't be sure. It was an accent of some kind. He nodded and said, "The garage." His voice was clotted; he hadn't spoken for hours, except to mutter to himself. He cleared his throat. "It's nearly over. Destroyed the garage."

"Not the Mercedes!" the man cried. "Oh, poor McCade!"

"They got the cars out," Flood said. He waved abruptly and quickened his step.

A pair of headlights swung around a corner two blocks up Barnard and headed toward him. There was no place to hide, he saw. His fear of what was coming, his terror of what he had seen in the attic were driving him to a crescendo of panic. He stopped suddenly. Then he grinned. Of course. He even had the costume for it. Quickly he crossed the grass strip between the sidewalk and the street and began jogging toward the oncoming car. The perfect disguise for an escaping marauder, he thought, raising his knees higher into a bounding stride as the car approached. Like any dedicated jogger, Flood kept his eyes straight ahead as the car sped past. A few steps farther on, he swung his head around and looked back. The car had stopped by McCade's driveway. It wasn't him, Flood decided; he would have pulled into the drive.

Flood slumped down into the seat of his rented car, then pulled himself together and started the engine. Hearing a sound, he froze, his pulse thundering in his temples, his throat constricted. He eased the gun out and slid the safety catch off. Swinging around suddenly, he swept the gun back and forth across the rear seat. No one. Jesus, he thought unbelievingly, he had made it.

He slowly drove the length of the block, away from the house, before switching on the headlights. A couple of blocks farther on, he put his wrist under the dashboard. It was one minute before midnight.

# Friday

# 1

Once on the river road, Flood headed for Bay City and the Holiday Inn. But as he passed the grounds of his motel he realized that he couldn't go on; the release of the tension he had been under made his fatigue irresistible. He knew he wouldn't be able to sleep, not with what he had seen, but he had to stop. His nerves were gone. Abruptly he swung into a darkened gas station next to the diner where Marja had got their lunch the day before. He pulled in beside two cars parked in the yard, got out, and locked the doors. He opened the trunk to get his bag but decided to leave it and reached down inside to get his razor. His fingers touched something cold, unfamiliar. Then he remembered: it was the pewter flask Ellen had given him one birthday; it was full.

Something drove him on past his cabin and down along the row of bushes to the river and the flat rock. Wearily he sat down and opened the flask and took a long drink. It was comfort, reward, reassurance, relaxant all at once. But it was a stimulant, too, and he felt acutely awake again. That would pass soon, he knew, and he would get drowsy as the depressant effect took over. He gazed at the black water, gurgling softly in the night silence as the weak current drove it slowly on. Downriver a few miles was the Grove. He wondered if her tombstone gleamed in the dark.

"Jesus," he muttered, seeing the great gleaming missile again. The enormity of its meaning was beyond comprehension. Yet he believed it as he believed that his own death would come.

Gloomily Flood took another drink and in a minute felt better. He had done well, he told himself, amazingly well, given the odds. He nodded, as if to acknowledge his accomplishment, and stared out at the dark water and the darker shoreline across the river. His satisfaction vanished as he realized that now McCade had only one chance: to find Flood and kill him before he got to anyone with his story.

Flood longed for a cigar and to assuage the craving he took another long swallow of whiskey. The firemen would suspect arson of course, he thought; they might even be able to prove it . . . traces of the plastic jugs, scraps of the paraffin boxes, the unlocked window that had been locked before, the quickness of the fire. Maybe not, though. The fire could have destroyed the evidence. McCade might not suspect him at all.

Flood shrugged. Speculation was pointless. He sat, hunched against the cold, then smiled suddenly at another thought: Here he was, a reporter with the biggest story in the history of the United States and he couldn't write a word of it, not a hint. Some of his colleagues in the press wouldn't hesitate to tell it, he knew. They would be driven by the magnitude of the story to disclose everything, without a thought about the consequences. That there would soon be no country to laud them wouldn't cross their minds.

He saw the maps again—the one at the flag factory with its red pins marking the missiles' targets, the one in the attic with the silver darts. Flood shivered. Scores, perhaps hundreds, of enemy missiles hidden in attics and barns and factories across the country. He felt as if he knew the day and hour and minute the world was to end. If the story got out, society might collapse. Panic. People fleeing cities in terror, soldiers abandoning military bases, Washington deserted, public lawlessness of a kind the nation had never known. Worse than war, he thought, because there would be nothing to rally the people to. He paused. Was it all a fear of phantoms? he asked himself. Again he saw the great sinister missile and felt the same stricken fear that had driven him to his knees then. No, it was all too real.

At last Flood faced what he had been trying to avoid since he left the house. He had to get to the President. He shook his head. The idea was absurd. He would never get inside the White House grounds, let alone into the presence of Gilfedders. The security people would check him out with the New Richmond police and that would be the end. He would be held and turned over to Lieutenant Flower.

Anyway, Gilfedders . . . Again Flood shook his head at the absurdity of the notion. It was hopeless.

Everyone had said that no man with a name like Gilfedders could become President of the United States. But Gordon Gilfedders had bludgeoned the American people into accepting that—and a lot more. Even his alien accent. Although he had been born in the United States, his parents had taken him back to Glasgow when he was two years old and he had remained there, on the waterfront of one of the toughest cities in the world, until he was twenty, when he returned to America. By the time he was twenty-six he was a city councilman in New York, a congressman at thirty, a senator at forty, and then President four years later. The small piercing blue eyes in the square pugnacious Scottish face mesmerized the public. There hadn't been a politician with that overpowering force of personality since Napoleon.

What could he give as his reason for seeing the President? Flood asked himself. The Russians have won? A plot to destroy the United States? A two-minute nuclear war that was about to start? It was ludicrous. Another crank. One of thousands who turn up at the gates of the White House with mad tales of conspiracies, plots, doomsday.

He took out the flask, unscrewed the top, and sipped at the whiskey. If he had done what he had done so far, surely he could find a way to get to Gilfedders, he thought. But maybe that wasn't necessary after all. Someone lower down, someone in the FBI or the CIA. He shook his head. It was too risky. Then everyone would know and it would get out to the public. He thought of Phil Briggs, his college roommate and once his friend. He was Senator Briggs now and a person of considerable influence in Washington. But Flood knew it wouldn't work, not after what happened. Katie Briggs had been Ellen's best friend and after her death there was no friendship with either of the Briggses. Only silent recriminations. The Senator would never believe him even if he listened. And, besides that, Flood wasn't sure he could be trusted. And if he could be, there was still Gilfedders to deal with. He had become more and more reclusive, suspicious, convinced that everyone was against him. Of course all Presidents got paranoid sooner or later, he thought. It seemed to come with the job.

The sedation of the alcohol had begun to work on Flood. He had to sleep or at least try. But he couldn't move, not just yet. He needed an idea, a notion of what he should do, ready in his mind so it could simmer there while he slept. This was the big one to sleep on. His mind kept probing what he had found, then reeled away from it each time and went off into one irrelevancy or another—the brilliance of the flag factory as a cover, Ellen's grave, whether Marja had told him everything, Rogers' nasal snarl, the great green eyes, McCade's next move. Flood finished the contents of the flask. His head ached and the spot at the back where he had been hit began to throb again. He sat moodily staring at the water without seeing it and realized that he was drunk now—not much but enough to put his mind and body off balance.

The Timex stood at 2:42 when he fell onto the bed, fully clothed except for the windbreaker and his shoes, and fell instantly asleep.

# 2

Flood came sharply awake at five-thirty, moments before the first light of dawn. He got up and went to the bathroom and turned on the cold water. Letting it run until it was icy, he splashed his face and the back of his neck repeatedly. The gas station might open early, he thought as he dried his head. He should leave now. He looked at himself in the mirror; he couldn't check in at the Holiday Inn looking like that. Making a thin lather of hot water and a small cake of hand soap, Flood shaved quickly—too quickly for his still bristly whiskers. He cut himself on the jaw and swore. He soaked the corner of a towel and held it to the cut for a minute. Then he tore off a piece of toilet paper, folded it into a tiny square, and stuck it to the thin red gash. If he got out of this, he thought, looking at himself again, maybe he'd leave the hair brown. He put on the tinted glasses.

Slipping on the windbreaker, Flood sat down on the side of the bed to put on his shoes. Then he searched the room, behind the wicker chair, under the bed, and in the bathroom to make sure he hadn't left anything behind. He was at the front door when he cursed himself and went to the bed. The gun was under the pillow. He put it in his pocket and stepped out onto the porch.

He saw the figure sitting in the green metal chair before he heard the voice.

"Good morning, Mr. Flood. You're an early riser these days." It was Lieutenant Bertram Flower. A big man with thick black hair and thick black eyebrows, he was sitting calmly, his brown hat on his lap, and smiling at Flood. "Titch, titch," he added in a parody of the sound, "you've cut yourself."

It was over, Flood thought, surprised at how empty he felt. And he had done so well—almost all the way. He put his hands in his windbreaker pockets without thinking and felt the gun. He knew he couldn't do it.

"I wouldn't if I was you, Mr. Flood," Flower said. The hat tipped and fell off his lap and he pointed a snub-nosed revolver at Flood's chest. "I like your hair-do, by the way. Very becoming." He got up, looking even bigger than he was in the brown suit that was a size too large. He moved toward Flood, still pointing the revolver at his chest. "Take the hands out—empty."

Flood obeyed. Flower came closer and removed the flashlight and then the gun. "My, my," he said holding it up. "A wop pea shooter. Lucky you didn't try it out. Or did you?" He put the gun to his nose and sniffed it. "Not recently anyway. I figured you might have one. So I waited. No sense breaking a door down and getting one in the gut when all you got to do is wait. Get inside."

He was the meanest cop Flood had ever known. It was because of his name when he was young, they said. The other kids had called him "Wall" and "Pansy."

Flood turned and reached for the doorknob. He heard a slight grunt and a swishing sound and flinched, waiting for the blow. Nothing happened. As he opened the door he turned halfway back and saw that Flower had merely stooped to pick up his hat. It was on his head now and made him look even more menacing.

"Inside, I said!"

Flood turned and suddenly the palm of Flower's hand on the middle of his back sent him sprawling across the room and onto the bed. He rolled over and looked at Flower in terror.

"Sit up and listen," Flower said and crossed the room to the bed.

Flood sat up, the man looming over him, and waited. He had done so well, too, he thought again, self-pity welling up in him. If only he had gone to the Holiday Inn last night . . . "How did you find me?" he asked, and wondered why. His voice sounded odd to him—flat and yet pleading. As if there were any chance now.

Flower grinned. "Simple. You assign two desk cops to call every hotel and rooming house and motel in the area: name and description. The name didn't work of course but the description did. You're a fool, Flood. All you newsboys are. There won't be a next time but if there was, you should pick a big place, the bigger the better." He leaned forward, gloating. "You think you could get lost in a rinkydink place like this?"

"What do you want?" Flood wondered if Flower was alone. Cops came in pairs but maybe because of the hour . . .

Flower put the small automatic in his pocket and his revolver inside his coat. "I remember that column you wrote defending that stinking Miranda warning. You like it so much I'm going to read it to you." He took a card out of his breast pocket.

"You're arresting me?"

"You guessed it."

"What for?"

"For impersonating a brown-haired man." Flower was enjoying himself immensely. He held up the card and read with the stilted delivery of a near-illiterate, "I advise you that you have the right to remain silent. Before being questioned you have the right to a lawyer. If you can't afford a lawyer, one will be provided to you free of charge." He paused and grinned at Flood. "If at any time during questioning you wish to assert any of these rights you are entitled to do so." He put the card away. "The charge is murder. Then there's rape—after the act." He grimaced and went on, "Destroying evidence, leaving the scene of a crime, flight to avoid prosecution. Anything else I've forgotten?"

Flood saw the woman's body again, then saw himself in court. He had to talk to someone. A top-notch lawyer, he thought. But who would believe him? And the time—there wasn't any more time. "You've got it all wrong, Flower. And when the truth comes out, it'll be your badge. More."

Flower's grin widened. "I'd like a hundred bucks for every time that's been said to me. We got it all, Flood. No reason not to tell you. Nothing I like better than smashing a guy's hopes, a guy like you anyways. Yesterday afternoon Judge Warner signed a search warrant for your apartment. We found the stuff. How could you have been such a goddamn idiot?"

McCade had been back, then, or Flood had missed something in his haste. He waited.

"First, the ivory-handled knife that matches the murder weapon. They were a set. A dealer we showed them to said they're very rare—'exotic' was his word. He'd never seen anything like them before. Hiding it behind your books! Christ, a goddamn child would be smarter."

"I don't know what you're talking about," Flood said. "What knife? Who—" He stopped hopelessly. No lawyer could help now.

Flower waved a hand to dismiss the question. "Second, her panty hose under your mattress. I suppose you never saw them either. The pubic hairs match."

Flood saw the body again and remembered the bare legs and the bare foot with the pump lying nearby. But she'd had on stockings when she sat across from him at his apartment. He couldn't recall whether he had seen her put them on after they went to bed. It didn't matter, not anymore. He thought of Marja and wondered what she would do. The Holiday Inn. He hoped she had the sense to flee.

"You weren't satisfied, were you?" Flower said, glowering at him in a sudden rage. "It wasn't enough the first time."

Flood stared at the face above him and the anger contorting its features. The words made no sense.

"Not enough just killing a woman through negligence," Flower said. "This time you had to do it yourself, straight out. You been waiting to do it ever since she died."

Flood leaped up but Flower stuck an open hand on his face and shoved him back onto the bed.

There was a popping sound and Flower looked immeasurably surprised. His eyes protruded and his mouth opened as if he were about to speak. But he said nothing. Instead, he fell forward, on top of Flood.

Flood tried to push him away but couldn't get his arms free. "Okay, Flower," he groaned. The detective's hat had fallen onto the bed and his face was turned away. Finally Flood got a hand and a forearm out and shoved him off. Flower rolled onto the end of the bed, then toppled to the floor, face-down. A small dark spot between the shoulders of the brown suit spread out wetly.

Flood sat up and leaned forward. A man was standing in the doorway.

"Mr. Flood," he said. That was all.

The light of the dawn sky behind him obscured his features until he moved into the room and closed the door. Slender, carrying himself like a soldier, bald, in his mid-fifties, and smiling, he was holding a pistol with a silencer. The popping sound, Flood thought. Bruce McCade. Or Emil von Hoffen. The Junker captain turned KGB colonel. He had followed Flower then, hoping he would lead him to Flood. Now it was clear why they had planted the knife and the panty hose. McCade had used the whole New Richmond police force to do his work for him.

Flood knew he had been given false hope to make these final moments worse and again he felt his life ebbing away. The river flowing to the sea. Exhaustion overcame him; he wanted it over with. Natalie and now Flower. Both deaths were his fault. All he could do now was protect Marja. He must not implicate her. But as soon as he had made that promise to himself he knew that it was foolish. He wouldn't be able to stand up to this man.

Flood sensed McCade's hesitation, even uncertainty, as he stood, unmoving, silent, just inside the door. The smile was fixed on his lips as if forgotten. Flood tried to speak but couldn't. He knew he shouldn't try. A wrong word and Marja . . . He waited. It was too late now, even for fear.

McCade quickly stepped forward and pressed the cold muzzle against the middle of Flood's forehead. "Oh my God, I am heartily sorry for having offended Thee," Flood intoned to himself, his eyes closed. "I detest all my sins . . ." Again he tasted blood and felt nausea rising. Then the muzzle was withdrawn. He waited, his eyes still closed tightly, his lips moving slightly as he prayed the ancient prayer. When twenty seconds passed and nothing happened he opened his eyes. McCade had stepped back. He gestured toward Flower's feet.

Flood stared at him in bewilderment. He had been ready to die but once more the terror, the unreadiness, seeped back into him. He had no idea what McCade wanted. Why didn't he speak?

McCade motioned to him to get up. Slowly Flood rose and McCade gestured again toward the black shoes on the body beside the end of the bed and pointed to a spot just inside the door. Flood looked at him. Did he want the body moved? Suddenly McCade stepped forward and put the gun back against Flood's forehead and shoved it until he sat down. "I firmly resolve to confess my sins, do penance . . ."

Again the gun was removed and when Flood opened his eyes he saw McCade bent over the body, his free hand grasping the back of Flower's suit at the collar. With the gun held on Flood, McCade quickly pulled the body around in a half circle, so that the head was toward the door, then dragged the body to the spot he had pointed at. Bending down, he turned over the dead man, crouched beside the corpse, keeping the gun and his eyes on Flood, and searched its clothing. He found the Beretta and looked at it for a moment, puzzled.

Flood wanted to say something, anything to distract him. Did he know that Marja had such a gun? "You'll never get away with this," Flood said, knowing the words were melodramatic and absurd.

McCade ignored him. He put the automatic in his pocket and removed Flower's revolver from its shoulder holster. Looking at it, too, he stuck his own gun inside his jacket and transferred the revolver to his right hand. Aiming it at Flood, McCade slid his left arm under Flower's body and, grunting softly, lifted the dead man until he was nearly standing up, facing Flood. McCade raised the snub-nosed revolver and aimed it at Flood's head. Flood realized now what McCade had been arranging: the proper angle for the trajectory of a bullet from Flower's gun, so that he could leave his own gun with the silencer in Flood's hand or beside his body. A gun fight . . . two dead men . . . Flood a cop killer now, too . . . He lowered his head until his chin was nearly on his chest. In the dim light he stared blankly at the small white scars on his hand where Ellen had bitten him at the end. He began again: "Oh my God, I am heartily sorry . . ."

There was a soft knock at the door and as Flood's head came up sharply the door opened. It was a woman. The maid. Jesus! Moving without thinking, Flood clasped his hands tightly and swung them back over his right shoulder just as McCade whirled around toward the door. Flood leaped in an arc across the room and as he landed he brought his doubled fist down with all the power he had onto the back of McCade's neck. He grunted and fell, unconscious, across Flower's chest as the body slumped back to the floor. Flood grabbed the revolver off the floor where it had fallen, then he retrieved the gun with the silencer and the automatic.

The maid turned and started to run but he caught her before she got to the edge of the porch and dragged her back into the cabin. She stared at him in terror, her eyes pleading, and he realized that she didn't recognize him with his dyed hair. He shoved her onto the bed and ordered, "Be quiet and don't move!" She cowered there, her face in her hands, and began to sob.

McCade groaned and turned over onto his back. Flood hurried to his side and as his eyes flickered open

Flood hit him on the temple with the butt of the silencer gun—a short, sharp blow. McCade gave a little moan and his body went slack. Flood held the gun with the muzzle at McCade's ear. He had to do it, he told himself. But he couldn't. He knew he couldn't. If the man had been coming at him, armed, ready to kill, he could have done it but not like this. He straightened up, staring down at McCade. If he killed him, that would make it worse; they would blame both deaths on him, not just Flower's. Besides, there were people who would want to question McCade.

Flood turned to the woman. She was staring at him and hiccoughed as she saw his face. "It's you," she whispered.

Flood hurried to the bed and grabbed her arm. "Come on," he muttered, taking her arm.

She drew back, still staring into his face. "But—"

"I'll explain later. We've got to get out of here." If Flower had a partner waiting, he thought, or if McCade had brought Bell along . . . Jesus, there was no end to it.

Remembering the guns, he released the woman and went back to the sprawled bodies. He took out the police revolver, wiped his prints off with his handkerchief, pressed the dead man's flaccid fingers around the butt, and put it back in Flower's shoulder holster. McCade wouldn't think of that, he hoped. Getting to his feet, Flood slipped the gun with the silencer down through his belt, at one side so that it wouldn't impede his movements, and pulled the windbreaker over its handle.

He stopped. Jesus, he thought angrily, that's wonderful. It was the gun that had killed Flower. If he was caught with it . . . Taking out the gun, he wiped off the prints, then knelt beside McCade and put his hand around the butt to leave his prints there. He slid the gun under the bed.

Flood got up and took the woman's arm again. She looked at him listlessly and he saw that she was in shock. He pulled her to her feet and with the other hand drew the bedspread down over the side to block

McCade's view of the gun under the bed. Turning, he half-dragged the woman past the two figures on the floor and out onto the porch. She tried to pull away and he gripped her wrist tightly as he looked back down the row of cabins. No one was in sight. They had probably both been alone. There wasn't time to worry about that now. Turning, Flood pulled her after him and jumped off the far end of the porch. She fell and just then he heard a snarling growl and saw the Doberman, crouched beside the cabin wall. The dog sprang at him and Flood fell to the ground. The dog flew through the air, its jaws gaping, then whirled around as the chain fastening him to a faucet pipe at the side of the cabin went taut. Damon fell, rolled over, and leaped to his feet. His teeth were glistening as he shuddered with leashed fury, the hair on the back of his neck standing up in a ruff, an almost purring growl rippling his throat.

Flood crawled away and got up. He pulled the maid to her feet and ran, dragging her behind him, to the row of bushes at the edge of the motel property. Damon started to bark and Flood flung himself through a gap in the bushes and fell to the ground again at one side. The woman rolled past him, her eyes bulging, her mouth open as if she was going to scream. He clapped his hand over it and crouched above her.

"I'm your friend," he gasped. "Understand?"

She stared at him in terror. He tried to smile at her reassuringly.

"Your friend," he repeated. "Do you remember me?"

Her eyes relaxed a little and she tried to nod, under his hand.

"That man I hit killed the other man—a policeman," Flood said, his voice suddenly harsh. He tried to soften it as he saw the fear come back into her eyes. He took his hand away. "It's all right," he said and remembered when she had said that to him as she looked at the bed. The words meant nothing to her, he could see by her face. Her mouth was open and she gasped for breath. "It's all right," he repeated.

Unexpectedly she nodded, too. "I know," she

whispered. "It's you." She stared up at him, waiting for something—a blow, a kiss, death. He could see the bewilderment flashing through her slow eyes, terror making them quick.

"I'm a federal agent," he whispered. "The man I hit—he will kill you if you don't get away. Murder . . . treason . . . away . . ." Flood's voice fell off into silence as he looked at her, waiting for a sign that she believed him. This is madness, he thought. He had to get away but he couldn't leave her here to die for him. He got to his feet and dragged her to her knees. "Get up!"

She rose unsteadily and clung to him, her face buried in his shoulder. "What?" she asked. "Who?" Her voice sounded numb, as if she were drugged.

Flood pushed her away and held her by her arms, feeling their plump softness. "Is the owner your father?"

She stared at him uncomprehendingly.

"The motel owner!"

Then she understood and shook her head.

"Where do you come from? Around here?"

Again she shook her head.

"Far away?"

She nodded. "Far enough," she said, the words hardly audible.

"Does the owner know that? Know where you're from?"

"No." She looked suddenly sad, distraught. "I lied. I got in trouble there."

"Good." She looked at him, dazed, and her eyes filled with tears, as if he had rudely enjoyed her infamy. Flood looked back over the hedge toward the cabins. Damon was straining toward them. Flood turned to her and said, "Do you know that rock, down there by the river?" He swept a hand upriver.

She nodded and shivered.

Her eyes were still glazed and he wondered if she had heard him. "It's life or death," he said, trying to sound harsh enough to convince her. "Mine and yours. Do you understand?"

She nodded again but he was unsure if she understood.

Gripping her arms more tightly, he said, "Go there. Right now. I've got a car. Hide behind the rock on the side by the river and wait for me. I'll pick you up. In two minutes. Hurry!"

She looked at him dumbly, beseechingly.

Flood struck her in the face with the back of his hand and she stumbled backward, her cheek reddened from the blow, her eyes brimming with tears and hurt. "Trust me!" he muttered. "You must trust me. Or we both die!" He took her arms again and turned her toward the river. "Down there!"

She hesitated and he gave her a push. She ran awkwardly down the slope through the ankle-length grass. He watched her for a moment, then turned and ran in the opposite direction, down the other slope toward the River Road.

As he got near the highway he slowed to a walk. He mustn't be seen running. There were no cars in sight. He walked quickly across the road and turned to the left toward the diner and the gas station next to it, a hundred yards away. Moving off the road onto the shoulder, he looked for a cover in case he heard a car. Hurrying on, he glanced back across his shoulder to the top of the slope, where he had left the maid.

The figure of a man was there. He waved his arms, then stumbled and fell face downward. McCade. He had passed out. Concussion, Flood thought. And then he saw the dog. It was racing diagonally down the slope, directly toward him. Flood turned and ran toward the gas station and his car. It was locked, he remembered, and swore loudly. He was fifty feet away from it when he looked back and saw the Doberman crossing the road the same distance behind him. Its mouth was open and he could see the white teeth and the pink tongue. It had been given the order to kill, he knew, and flung himself forward. He wouldn't make it. Too far. Too slow.

Flood could hear the dog's feet slapping softly as it came nearer. The car was only a few feet away now but there wouldn't be time to get the door open. Lying on the pavement just ahead was a piece of wood—a two-by-four about six feet long with one jagged end as if it had been broken off a larger piece. Flood ran for it and picked it up and turned just as the dog leaped for him. The jagged wood caught it on the chest and Damon shrieked in pain and fell to the pavement. Flood backed toward the car and a moment later the dog was on its feet, blood dripping from its chest. It crouched and crept forward, ready to spring again. Holding the plank under his left armpit and thrusting it back and forth toward the animal with his left hand, Flood felt for the keys in his right pants pocket. Jesus, they were actually there. The dog snarled, its teeth glistening with saliva.

The key turned in the door and Flood pressed the button to open it just as Damon attacked again. Swinging the plank sharply, Flood caught the dog alongside the head and it crashed into the rear fender and fell onto its back. Flood dropped the plank and flung himself into the car. He felt the dog's teeth graze his ankle and slammed the door against its head. Damon fell again and Flood pulled the door closed. Cursing his trembling hands, he finally inserted the key in the ignition and started the engine.

Suddenly the dog leaped onto the hood and moved forward, barking and snapping at the windshield directly in front of him, its toenails clattering on the metal of the hood.

Flood slammed the gear into reverse and backed up. Damon slid backward onto his haunches, righted himself, and came forward again, snapping at the glass in front of Flood's face. The animal couldn't get at him now, he knew, but the presence of the beast so close—its great snapping jaws, its fury, its mad desire to kill him at any cost to itself—was still terrifying. Flood swung the car to the left, the dog crouched swaying in front of him, and sped toward the road. When he had gone fifty feet, he slammed on the brakes and Damon shot forward off the hood, legs flailing in the air, and hit the far side of the road and rolled over and over into a shallow ditch beyond. Flood drove away and looked out the window toward the top of the slope. He thought he saw a dark form huddled on the ground but wasn't sure.

Perhaps it had been a mistake to meet her at the rock, Flood thought as he swung onto the narrow dirt road. If a car was there, he would be blocked; if anyone was following and had seen him turn in, they would be waiting for him at the exit. He swore but drove on. He couldn't leave her behind. Flood remembered the motel owner staring at his license plate and swore again. Once Flower's body was found the car would be traced. Then he realized that as soon as Flower was found roadblocks would be thrown up. A cop killer. Local police, state police, the FBI—the entire network would be put on alert. He had to get rid of the car. The police wouldn't know about his disguise . . . unless McCade told them . . . but if he was still unconscious they might find him up there . . . or dead, the sudden exertion too soon after the blow to his temple . . . They would find the gun that he had killed Flower with . . . his fingerprints on it . . . the maid, why had she come to the cabin so early? . . . Marja.

Jesus, he thought, he had forgotten. If McCade suspected her, Bell would have gone to work on her. Flood felt a surge of guilt. There was no way to get in touch with her now, not until she went to work— if she went to work. He jerked his left hand forward to reveal his watch. It couldn't be, he thought, seeing that it said 6:06. A little more than half an hour since he wakened? But the second hand was moving, and he realized that what had happened had happened very quickly.

He saw no one at the rock when he pulled up. Rolling down the window, he stuck his head out and called, "It's me. Hurry!"

The woman peeked around the far end of the rock and scurried out, her head down as if she were under fire, and ran around the car. Flood unlocked and opened the door on the passenger side and she clambered in. Her long hair had half-fallen out of its bun and hung in disarray around one shoulder. There were pieces of grass in it and he saw more grass and burrs on her clothes. She must have fallen. He wanted to ask her why she had come to the cabin so early but instead he merely looked at her—the same loose, lumpy beige cardigan, a brown wool skirt, a white shirt like a man's, stockings, flat brown shoes. She looked terrified still and he smiled in reassurance.

"You were so long," she murmured. "I thought you weren't coming." He realized that whatever her fear or suspicion of him she was now wholly dependent on him, too.

"He let the dog loose," Flood said as he drove off.

"That dog? My God! Did you kill him?"

"I don't know. But he nearly killed me."

She stared at him in wonder, her brown eyes wide, as if to say that she had chosen the right man.

It wouldn't hurt to let her think she had made a choice, Flood decided, and asked, "What's your name —just your first name, the one you use here?" He paused at the exit to the River Road and headed north.

"Sally. That's the name I use. It's my real name. I changed only my last name. It's—"

"Don't tell me," Flood said sharply. He glanced at her and saw she was hurt, as if he had rejected a gift. "If I'm caught they may force me to tell them," he explained.

"Oh."

He glanced at her again and saw that she was smiling slightly. He was taking care of her. It was all right then. Flood was heartened by her simplicity; at least he wouldn't have to explain, justify everything. She wasn't going to be like Marja. Absently he stuck a hand in his windbreaker pocket and felt the gun. Jesus, he'd forgotten that, too—even when Damon was coming for him. But then he was glad that he'd forgotten it; a shot, several shots, would have alerted someone. Anyway he knew he would have missed.

"Since you're a federal agent—" Sally began and stopped.

Even in her terror she had remembered. Flood nodded and waited.

"Well, you don't have to run away, do you? I mean, can't you call someone? Get help? You said I had to go. I mean . . ." Again she stopped.

"No one must know what happened," he said sternly, without looking at her. "I'm on an undercover assignment. It's vital. National security." He had never expected to find himself using that excuse—the patriotic refuge of half the scoundrels in Washington.

"Oh," she said again. "Okay, then where are we going?"

Flood looked at her in amazement. From her tone they might have been setting off on an excursion. Ignoring her, he asked, "Did you leave anything important at the motel—any identification, letters, things they could trace you by?"

Sally thought for a minute and shook her head. "I don't get any letters. Nobody knows I'm here." She was quiet again, then went on, "My clothes is all. They don't matter. I didn't have many anyway."

"Money?"

She reached into a pocket of the bulky sweater and took out a worn change purse. "It's all here. I carry it with me. Mr. Moriarty—he's the owner—he snoops. He won't leave me alone."

Flood glanced at her and saw that she had flushed. He imagined the old man with the dyed hair and the pusillanimous eyes. So he had wanted the comfort of those breasts, too. Flood glanced toward them, then quickly back to the road. "How much money?" His voice was curt with embarrassment.

She showed no surprise but snapped open the purse and took out some bills. She counted them laboriously. "Sixty-eight dollars," she said at last. "And, let's see, nineteen—no, twenty-one cents."

Flood was appalled by her prospects: sixty-eight dollars and twenty-one cents and the clothes she was wearing. And a companion wanted for two murders. He knew that he had to help her. But he knew even better that the best way to help her was by keeping away from her. He would be safer with her, though, he realized; they would be looking for a man alone. He put the thought aside. She had already saved his life once.

"What were you doing there—at my cabin—so early?" he asked.

"What?" She looked at him, then averted her eyes and said, "It turned colder during the night. I thought you might want another blanket."

Sure that she was blushing, Flood didn't look at her. He hadn't noticed the blanket but given the circumstances of her arrival at the cabin that was small wonder; she must have dropped it when she tried to run away. "You're okay, Sally," he said finally to comfort her and looked into the rearview mirror for a police car.

She put a hand to the back of her head and tucked the loose hair into place. Now he turned to her and she smiled shyly at him. Once more Flood was amazed by her—this time by how quickly her terror had turned into calm. She was a creature of the moment, he realized.

"Bay City," he said abruptly and felt her questioning eyes on him. He remembered Flower's advice about staying away from rinkydink places at such times. "We're taking a bus to New York."

As he turned he saw that Sally was staring at him with a look of gratitude. It was so intense he was embarrassed but a moment later he felt grateful, too.

He took a small bridge across the river, then picked up an access road to the expressway and headed north. The highway was clearly deserted and he drove on, taking the loop halfway around Bay City and turning off at the last exit so that they came into town from the northwest. The bus station was only a few blocks from the Holiday Inn and when they got there he parked at the far end of the lot, away from the terminal, and got out. "Wait here," he said and went to the trunk of the car. A couple of minutes later he reappeared wearing his tweed jacket, the stolen raincoat, and the brown slouch hat and carrying his bag and typewriter.

Sally looked at him in surprise. "You look nice," she said.

He nodded to her to get out and they walked to the terminal. Just inside the entrance was a bank of wall lockers. Flood found an empty one and shoved the luggage into it and locked it. "I've got to get rid of the car," he said. "You wait inside. Get a schedule and wait. I'll be right back."

He turned and walked quickly back to the car and drove out of the lot. As he pulled past the entrance he saw that she was standing where he had left her, peering through the glass door at him. He cursed. She was going to be a liability. He shook his head and glared at her and she turned away, abashed, to go inside.

Flood parked ten blocks away, on a downtown side street where there were no meters. He left the car unlocked and put the keys in the glove compartment. If someone stole it, so much the better. A few minutes later he was back at the terminal. It was nearly seven o'clock, he saw from a clock inside. Half a dozen people were there—a ticket clerk behind a counter and a handyman lazily sweeping up, and in the small waiting room were an old man who needed a shave, a leather-jacketed boy of about sixteen who kept tapping the pointed toe of one high-heeled boot and humming, and a worn-out-looking young woman with a fat baby asleep in her arms. Sally wasn't there.

Stifling the rising panic, Flood stood waiting. She was probably in the ladies' room, he thought, and realized again how tired he was. When it was over he would sleep for three days. He sat down, away from the others, in a blue-moulded-plastic chair and a minute later Sally came out of the ladies' room, paused to look around, saw him, smiled broadly, and came to sit beside him. She rested a hand softly on his arm and he looked at her face. Her eyes were lustrous—gentle animal eyes full of simple trust and simple needs. Flood looked away, off at the clock. It was seven.

"The schedule?" he asked. His tone was too curt, he realized, and smiled at her to make up for it.

She looked abashed again. "I'll get one."

As she started to get up, Flood put a hand on her arm and leaned close to her. "A policeman just came in. Don't move. Act natural. Probably just part of his beat."

Her eyes were full of simple fear now. Flood put an arm around the back of her chair and leaned back, yawning widely. He glanced at the policeman, who stopped, looked around the room, and went to the ticket clerk at the small counter. They spoke together for a minute, then the clerk laughed loudly, and the policeman gave him a wave and left.

Flood got up and went to a rack across the room where the schedules were kept. He took one and returned to his chair. A boy came into the terminal carrying two bales of newspapers and tossed them in front of a locked grate across the window of a small gift shop. The *Herald,* Flood thought, and the Bay City *News Chronicle.* He wanted the *Herald* badly but knew that it would probably be an hour before the shop opened. Then he realized that he didn't want a paper after all. If Sally saw it . . . There might be a picture of him by now, a description. If she believed he had killed Natalie . . .

He opened the schedule. Just then a voice announced over a loudspeaker, "Greyhound bus number one-sixteen arriving from Hartford at Gate Two. Passengers for Albany please wait at Gate Three for departure at seven-fifteen."

Flood found the Bay City-to-Albany section of the schedule and ran a finger across the page under the seven-fifteen departure. The bus arrived in Albany at eight-forty. He closed the schedule and said, "Go buy two one-way tickets to Albany. I've got to make a phone call." He gave her a twenty-dollar bill and as she headed toward the ticket counter he turned and went to a bank of telephones on the far wall.

Mrs. Barnard hadn't arrived yet, the desk clerk at the Holiday Inn told him. Wondering if Marja would ever arrive, Flood asked him to take a message for her and make sure that she got it as soon as she checked in—that her husband would call her there at nine o'clock.

Flood got his bag and typewriter out of the locker and rejoined Sally, who was standing in the middle of the waiting room looking lost.

"Oh!" she gasped when he touched her arm, then smiled as she saw who it was. "I thought we were going to New York City."

"We are," he said, "the long way."

He steered her toward Gate 3 and stopped behind the old man and the young woman with the baby. The boy in the leather jacket was still sitting lost in dreams of Nashville, tapping a foot and strumming his thigh like a guitar. Strobe lights, screaming fans, Flood thought, a gold record. He gave Sally the typewriter to carry, saying, "You look naked without a handbag." She flushed at the word and again he imagined her full soft breasts pillowing his face. It was possible now, he realized; they were together, going off like furtive lovers. But as he looked at the nape of her neck with its golden down and the side of her soft throat as she half-turned to make sure he was still there, he knew that it wouldn't happen. She was too vulnerable, too ready to accept any hand that seemed strong. He wasn't going to hurt anyone else.

There were only eight other passengers on the bus: the three people waiting in line and those already aboard —an elderly couple, two middle-aged workingmen, and a gaunt-faced young woman with a scarf over her rollered hair. She was chewing gum violently and gave Flood a look of general contempt as he passed. He pointed to a seat two rows from the back and Sally slid in next to the window. Flood put the carry-all and typewriter on the rack overhead and sat down next to her.

"Jesus," he said.

She looked at him anxiously.

"Nothing—just these tiny seats. Worse than an airplane. Do you remember when buses had those big comfortable seats?"

"Uh-huh," Sally said uncertainly.

She was too young to remember, Flood thought, glancing at her. Thirty, thirty-two at the most. Scattered over the floor across the aisle were cigarette butts, a candy wrapper, an empty Coca-Cola can, some tissues. Leave the litter to us, he thought, and leaned back.

Flood could see the gentle rise and fall of her breasts and closed his eyes. He wanted to sleep but he knew he couldn't have that either. He had to think. And he had to talk to distract her. There wouldn't be a lot of thoughts going through Sally's head, he was sure, but there might be one or two fairly simple questions: Where are you taking me after New York? What will I do when you leave? He didn't want to have to answer those. Or, worse: Do you have to leave me?

Standing at the front of the bus and facing the rear, the driver counted the passengers and was about to close the door when a man in a well-cut three-piece dark suit who was carrying a navy-blue raincoat hurried toward the bus waving a ticket. He was about forty, with dark hair, gold-rimmed glasses, and a thin, rather handsome face. Something was wrong, Flood thought and sat forward, wondering what it was. Then he realized that one doesn't often see such people on buses except in resort areas or at airline terminals; the man was too prosperous, too self-assured to use buses: the transport of the dispossessed. It was all wrong.

The man boarded and made his way toward the rear of the bus. Flood sank back in the thin stiff seat, hoping he didn't sit near them. The man glanced at him and sat two rows ahead across the aisle. His look had been noncommittal, the usual glance passersby give someone in their line of vision, nothing more. But of course that would be exactly the way he would look if he were following them, Flood knew. He tried to relax, telling himself that anyone who had been following wouldn't have waited that long before getting on the bus. Anyway he certainly wasn't a cop, not with those clothes and that face. Federal maybe, he could be that. The idea unsettled Flood until he realized that he would at least be safe in the hands of federal agents, even if they didn't believe him and refused to let him speak to anyone in authority. Safe for a time. But they would probably turn him over to the New Richmond police, too, and he would be anything but safe.

"Are you all right?" Sally asked in a whisper, her breath soft on his cheek.

Flood nodded; her concern was a burden now. The man opened a newspaper and folded it. It was the *Herald*. Flood wanted a drink, then sat forward a couple of inches. Jesus, the flask. He had left it on the table in the cabin. His initials were on it. Ellen had said it was for an emergency when she gave it to him; in those days he rarely drank anything stronger than wine, and not much of that, and the flask had seemed a modest luxury. The emergency had come, though, and Flood had gulped down the whiskey while the doctor and the state trooper watched him with disgust as he fell weeping beside her body. The flask would have his fingerprints on it, too, he thought, then realized that it scarcely mattered; his prints must be all over the room.

Suddenly he saw the silver darts on the map in the attic and turned to look out the window for distraction. The bus was on the outskirts of town and he studied the small houses intently to avoid Sally's look. It would do no good to dwell on the missiles; that was up to others. All he could do, and he was sure it would take all of his mind and energy to do it, was get the information to someone who counted. The rest—what McCade might do if he believed, or knew, that Flood had seen the missile, whether they were in place throughout the country, what the likelihood of an imminent attack might be—none of that was his concern. He hadn't the information, much less the power, to do anything about it and he was instinctively aware that the time he spent thinking about such matters would be subtracted from the time he had to fulfill his sole task: getting to President Gilfedders.

Sally was looking out the window, too, and as Flood glanced at her he saw that she was being good, trying to please him. Her hands, small for her size and slender, lay clasped loosely in her lap. What in the name of God was he to do with her? he wondered. He couldn't take her with him but he couldn't leave her alone to fend for herself.

"Why did you leave home?" he asked quietly, so the man ahead wouldn't hear.

She looked down at her hands and said, "My father threw me out."

Flood saw the standard cartoon scene: the front porch of a house on a snowy night, a woman with an infant in her arms, a stern old man pointing to the street. "Was it serious?"

She nodded. Then she turned to him with a look that begged him not to ask more about it and he knew that she would tell him if he did. Flood wanted to drop the subject but he couldn't. If the trouble she'd been in was serious, she might be a fugitive, too. The irony of being captured incidentally because he was in her company was too absurd. "Was it a crime?" he asked.

Her face fell; he had let her down. "The worst kind," she answered. "That's what he kept telling me."

"Who?"

"My father."

Flood nearly smiled. If that was all, he could drop it.

But now she couldn't. "He said that it was the filthiest crime a person could commit. He said that I was condemned forever."

"You got pregnant?"

Again she looked surprised. "How did you know?"

"And you weren't married?"

The surprise turned to consternation. "We couldn't," she said, her voice suddenly dull.

"There's nothing so terrible about that," Flood said

and took her hand. He felt drawn to her. She seemed decent and kind.

Sally looked at him gratefully again. "You don't know."

"Did you have the child?"

She took her hand away slowly. "Yes. It was dead."

Jesus, Flood thought, she *was* wanted. She'd had the baby and killed it. "It was stillborn?"

"No. It died two days later. It was a monster."

"Holy Mother of God," he muttered, wishing he hadn't begun the conversation. "I'm very sorry. But it couldn't have been your fault."

"Its father was my uncle, my father's brother."

Flood felt sick. The love of a good man, normal children, a decent life might diminish her horror but it would never leave her entirely. He took her hand again and held it.

The bus swung onto an access road and then onto the expressway and headed northwest. Flood glanced across the aisle and saw that the man had finished his newspaper or at least had put it down.

"My father killed him," Sally said suddenly.

At first Flood thought she meant the baby but realized it was the uncle, his brother, whom he had killed. Flood didn't want to know any more but he was sure she couldn't stop now. It had been inside her too long. "How did he find out?" he asked, trying to sound gentle.

"I told him. He beat me half to death and I told him."

"What happened to him?"

"He went to prison. For fifty years." Tears began running, then pouring, down her cheeks and dripped onto her sweater.

There was no comfort for this, he knew. He felt an insane impulse to slip his hand inside her shirt and hold her breast, as if that might help, and as insane as the idea was he knew that it might accomplish what nothing else could. But she would misunderstand. Instead he took out a handkerchief, turned her face gently toward him, and wiped away her tears. Obeying another impulse, he leaned forward and put his lips softly against hers. Sally placed a hand on his shoulder, then buried her face against his chest and sobbed quietly. A minute later she collected herself and sat back. She wiped away her tears and smiled tremulously at him and turned away to the window.

Flood saw how she had been able to accept the corpse in his cabin, the threat of more murder: nothing would be as horrifying as what she had been through. He was touched by her suffering and realized that in the past two days he had come to know two women who had lost far more than he had without hoarding their grief, without self-pity. Once more he felt drawn to Sally and a desire to give and take all that he could as generously as he could overtook him.

Again he saw the gleaming missile pointed in the attic and again he put the memory out of his mind.

"My father couldn't stand the disgrace," Sally went on. "He told the police he caught his brother stealing money and they had a fight and he went crazy—you know. Billy, my uncle, didn't put up a fight at all. He just stood there and let himself be killed. I think he wanted to die—the shame, I mean. I know I did."

"You saw it happen?"

Sally nodded slowly and he knew that she was seeing the murder as he had seen the missile a minute before —still disbelievingly. He asked, "How long had it been going on between you."

She looked away and was silent. "Since I was fourteen," she said at last. Turning back, she stared at him squarely. "We couldn't help it."

Flood saw now why she had come to his cabin: an older man . . . perhaps some resemblance . . . a few minutes of passionate memories.

"So no one back home knew the true story?" he asked.

She nodded.

"Then you could go back there."

"I won't. Not ever."

"I know it'll be hard but it's the best solution," he said gently. "Your memories must have passed—or weakened anyway." He felt his hypocrisy and hastily added, "You know people there, they can help you start over. Where did you live before you came to the motel? How long were you there?"

His assurances and questions didn't distract her as he had hoped. "I have nightmares about it all the time," she said. She was quiet for a few moments and went on, "I worked here and there. I was a maid in a couple of hotels and a waitress."

How would she live until she got a job? he wondered. She had less than seventy dollars. That would last a few days. She needed clothes, rent money, food money. He took out his wallet, slipped two fifty-dollar bills from it, folded them, and inserted them in her loosely clasped hands.

Sally opened the bills and stared at them. Two deep lines rose above the bridge of her nose and she shook her head. "I can't." She looked at him, smiling apologetically.

The money was too little, Flood realized and gave her two more fifties. "You saved my life, remember?" he said, trying to sound matter of fact. "You don't owe me those. It's I who owe you." He stopped, feeling too awkward to go on.

"You're a nice man," she said and kissed his cheek. The man across the aisle glanced back at them.

As the bus crossed the Hudson over the Dunn Memorial Bridge into Albany, Sally asked, "What time's the bus to New York?"

Although Flood knew the answer, he delayed by taking out the schedule, unfolding it, and slowly studying the long rows of arrival and departure times. "Nine o'clock," he said at last. It was true in a way.

Sally snuggled down in the thin seat and smiled in anticipation.

The bus terminal was in a desolate slum beneath one of those elevated highway systems that allow Americans to get in and out of their cities without having to look at them. The bus pulled into the yard of the terminal, a one-story cinderblock structure with a flat overhanging roof that was supposed to make it look modern, and stopped at Gate 13.

As the passengers in front began moving forward, the man got up and again glanced at Sally and Flood. That was natural, Flood thought; he might only be making sure he didn't bump into someone. He left the bus without looking back again and then Flood got up and took the typewriter and carryall off the overhead rack. Silently he handed the typewriter to Sally and waited for her to precede him. She wasn't used to that and looked at him questioningly until he jerked his head to signal her to go.

Inside the terminal Flood paused, watching the man cross the waiting room to a bank of telephones at one side. That was natural, too, Flood thought; he had arrived at his destination and was calling someone he had an appointment with. But Flood knew it was foolish to assume anything. He should leave at once, while the man's back was turned, quickly walk out one of the rear gates and get away. But he couldn't leave Sally, at least not until he had explained. It was true, he thought: most people would risk death rather than do something odd. The man turned from the telephone and his eyes met Flood's.

Flood looked at the terminal clock: 8:36. He looked at the row of gates along the rear wall—with signs to Poughkeepsie, Binghamton, New York City, Buffalo & West, Montreal, Burlington, Boston, Hartford-New Haven, Springfield-Providence—and casually asked Sally, "If you were going home, which gate would you use?"

She stared at him suspiciously for a moment and when he smiled reassuringly she scanned the line of gates and said, "That one," pointing to Gate 8, Buffalo & West.

Flood nodded. "Let's get some breakfast."

Ignoring the man at the phone, he took Sally's arm and they walked across the waiting room to the cafeteria. He ordered tomato juice and scrambled eggs for both of them and filled two cups with coffee while they waited for their food.

"You okay, Sally?"

She nodded, grateful again, and smiled.

Flood took out the schedule and found the entry: 9:05 departure for Buffalo.

When their breakfast came, he led the way to a corner table. They ate in silence, with Sally watching him covertly. He finished his food quickly and looked at her across the table.

She smiled again. "I like your hair that way."

Jesus, was that what she had been thinking about all this time? "I thought you'd never mention it," he said with a simper.

She laughed.

My God, he thought, she's actually having a good time. He knew he couldn't put it off any longer. "Sally, I want you to go and get a ticket home," he said, his voice almost angry. "No, get a ticket two stops beyond the one you want to get out at. Don't tell me where you're going."

He could see by her face that this was what she had been expecting, dreading. Her remark about his hair, her laughter had been attempts to forestall it. She had known all along. "Why?" she asked softly. "You said—"

Flood raised a hand to silence her. "I think someone's following us."

Sally looked startled. She hadn't noticed the man then. Now she looked around the room quickly; no one else was there except a woman behind the food counter.

"He was on the bus with us," Flood explained. "He's out in the waiting room. If he's following anybody, it's me. We have to split up. I'll lead him off and get rid of him."

"Then we can meet later?"

Flood nodded, hating himself for the lie. "I'm going out to one of the telephones and make a call. I'll take down the number of the phone and a week from now at exactly noon I'll be at that phone if everything's all right. You call me there. Understand?"

She nodded. "Okay," she said listlessly, as if she knew that it was pointless to resist.

"Your bus leaves at five past nine—in fifteen minutes. Remember, get a ticket to the second stop *past* your destination. Keep your eyes open on the bus. If you're sure no one's following you, get out at your real stop. If he checks with the ticket clerk and finds out where you bought a ticket to, you won't be on the bus when it arrives there. Just in case he has someone waiting."

He paused and stared at her. She was frightened again.

"Do as I say. They will kill you without a thought. Believe me. *After* they've tortured you to find out what you know."

"But I don't know anything!" Hope filtered back into her eyes.

"They won't believe that until they've finished with you. The less you have to say the more they'll hurt you until they're satisfied you don't know anything. But you do know something. You saw that man in the cabin— the one with the gun. He will do anything to shut you up."

At that she nodded, finally convinced.

"Go on," Flood said gently. "It's all right. Just do as I say."

Sally nodded again and got up and started away.

"Take the typewriter," he told her. "Keep it with you. It looks like a bag of some sort at least."

Without a word she took the typewriter and left. A moment later Flood did, too, and went to a bank of phones across the waiting room from the one the man had used. He was nowhere in sight. Flood called information and got the number of the Amtrak station at Rensselaer, back across the Hudson from Albany. He dialed, asked when the next train to New York City was, and was told that it left at 9:30. There would be time, he thought. It wasn't quite five to nine. He dialed the Holiday Inn and asked for the desk. A man answered and Flood said, "Has Mrs. Barnard checked in yet?"

"Just a minute, please."

Flood saw Sally at the ticket counter. There was still no sight of the man.

"Yes, she checked in a half an hour ago but said she wasn't to be disturbed."

"This is Mr. Barnard," Flood said. "She's waiting for my call."

"Oh, yes, Mr. Barnard. Just a moment, I'll connect you."

Flood saw Sally walking slowly, dejectedly across the room toward Gate 8 without looking in his direction.

"Hello? Is that you?"

Flood smiled. He hadn't realized how anxious he'd been about Marja. "Yes. Are you all right? Did they suspect anything?"

"I don't know. It was terrible when I got back last night—all the firemen, the garage almost gone. Bell was suspicious, I think. But he said nothing. Bruce wasn't there of course. They got my car out. It's scorched a little on one side, but otherwise—"

He hadn't even hoped for that break. "Listen, I don't have much time," he said.

"Where are you?"

Suddenly he had the feeling that she wasn't alone. Someone was there. He could see McCade with a gun at her temple.

Quickly Flood said, "Never mind that. The less you know the better for both of us. It's nine now. Get out of there as soon as you can. Drive west a few miles to any back road heading south where you won't be expected. Go to New York. I'll meet you—" He paused and cursed himself for not being ready. Then he said the first thing that came into his mind. "The seal pond at the zoo in Central Park."

"I've been there but I don't remember where it is."

"On Fifth Avenue in the sixties. Ask someone. At two o'clock. That will give you plenty of time." It would give him enough time, too, to make sure she was alone.

"Two o'clock at the seal pond. And from there?" she asked.

"I don't know," he said flatly. That was one thing he couldn't tell her—not until he was sure she was alone. He needed her still, both to get him to Washington by car and to be available as a witness in case Gilfedders doubted his story. "Make sure you're there." He hung up before she could ask anything else. Then he wrote down the number of the phone.

Flood went out the main door to a line of three taxicabs. He took a ten-dollar bill out and handed it through the window of the first cab. "I'll be five minutes," he said. "You want to wait?"

"Sure."

Flood put his carryall in the back. "No other passengers," he said and headed back toward the waiting room.

Sally was waiting at Gate 8. The man in the raincoat had gone. Encouraged, Flood started toward Sally and tried to ignore the way she looked: drooping shoulders, bowed head, slackly hanging arms. He went up and kissed her cheek. She turned to him expectantly. Hating himself more than ever, he handed her the slip of paper he had written the number of the pay phone on. She shoved it into her sweater pocket. He was sure that she knew he wouldn't answer if she called.

The terminal clock said 9:02.

A minute later the driver climbed down from the bus, opened the gate, and the loudspeaker announced the departure for Buffalo and points west. Sally turned to Flood and began to speak but stopped as he shook his head. "I know," he said. He leaned forward and kissed her lips gently and she clung to him. "I know," he repeated. "Me, too." He pushed her away slowly and looked into her eyes. They were full of tears.

"Okay, folks, okay, time to board," the driver said.

Flood gave Sally another light push and without speaking she turned and left. As she reached the top of the bus steps, she looked back. Her lips were trembling and tears were running down her face.

# 3

Trains were still the only civilized form of transportation man had devised, Flood thought as he saw the gleaming white Turboliner with red and blue stripes down its length. Undoubtedly that was why Americans had practically stopped using them. He reached for his notebook to jot down the idea for his column, then stopped himself as he realized that there wouldn't be a column—not for now anyway.

He swore softly. He had forgotten to buy the *Herald* at the bus terminal. Glancing at his watch, he saw that the train was due to leave in eight minutes and went back into the small station to see if there was a newspaper stand. There was but it carried only the Albany *Knickerbocker News* and the *Times-Union* and the New York *Times* and *News*. He bought all four.

Wondering about the man in the dark raincoat, Flood boarded the train and went to the forward section of the smoking car, past a mid-car snack bar tended by a black barmaid; there were only two people, both men and sitting apart, in that section. He put the carryall on the rack and his coat and hat on the aisle seat, then slid into the seat next to the window facing the river.

The car was clean and comfortable and seemed almost new. It was done in reds and browns and deep purple and had capacious seats with high winged headrests. Slowly the train pulled out of the station and picked up speed and soon it was moving fast and smoothly. Flood eased the seat back and closed his eyes. He needed sleep badly but couldn't risk it, he knew, and let the seat come back forward. His body would have to hold out until he was safe—perhaps tonight. Somewhere by the sea, he thought longingly.

Flood picked up the *Times* and went through it carefully; there was nothing about him or the murder of

Wendy Cameron. There was nothing in the *News* or the Albany papers either. He put them down and leaned back and closed his eyes. If only he could get to Phil Briggs before the story broke, he thought. Once it was out, Briggs wouldn't help. Whatever the obligations of past friendship, Briggs was still a politician and Flood knew that the true politician has no friends. A woman raped and stabbed to death, a policeman murdered. There would be no help from anyone.

Flood saw Ellen's face, then Marja's, then Sally's. He was nothing but trouble for everyone. He sighed softly and leaned back and in an instant he was asleep. He slept heavily, dreamlessly, and awoke with a start of alarm, seeing the silver missile poised in the attic and the doors in the roof swinging open.

The train was coming into a station; Poughkeepsie, he saw on a platform sign. He had slept nearly an hour. Looking around, he found that one of the passengers had left the car but nothing else seemed changed. As the train stopped he saw a long old-fashioned gray-brick building beside the railroad yard. One end was taller and painted a bright yellow; on it, in large letters, was: *J.D. Johnson Co. Plumbing—Heating. Buy Where the Professionals Buy.* That was the trouble, he thought: he was an amateur.

Flood slipped out of his seat and went to the bar. The black woman smiled at him. "Good morning, love. What'll it be?"

Flood smiled back admiringly. She was stout and handsome and good-natured, with beautiful teeth, and was wearing eight or ten gold bracelets on one arm. He looked at the shelves behind her and saw miniature bottles of liquor. "Bourbon and water, please," he said. "Make it a double."

She filled a plastic glass half full of ice and water and handed it to him with two bottles of Old Grandad. He handed her a ten-dollar bill, and their fingers touched for an instant. She smiled and gave him his change and their hands met again. "Thanks, love," she said.

Feeling better than he had since he woke up in the

cabin that morning, Flood lowered the small table from the back of the seat in front of him, put down the glass and bottles, and took the tin of Dannemann's out of his carryall. He lit a cigar and sat back comfortably and emptied one of the bottles into the glass. He took a long drink, then puffed on the cigar for a few moments, then took a longer drink.

Suddenly a freight train roared past, two feet away, headed north and as it vanished, leaving relative quiet behind, Flood saw a man standing with his back to the tracks by the riverbank a dozen feet away. He was wearing suntans and a blue windbreaker and a baseball cap, and he was utterly motionless, so lost in contemplation of something—maybe only the river itself—that he could ignore the rattling screaming roar of two trains passing him a few feet away. As he disappeared from sight, Flood had the feeling that it had been he himself standing there. He shook his head and took another drink and puffed on the slim cigar. A few minutes later the train swept past a ruined castle-like structure on an island a couple of hundred yards offshore. The hills across the river were higher now, more rugged and deeply wooded. Cut out of them at the less steep points was an occasional meadow running down to the water's edge. Then the river widened abruptly, its far bank nearly lost in mist. Just as abruptly it narrowed and a great treeless granite bulb of a hill loomed up, steamy clouds dripping tendrils down its crown. The land fell again to a series of more jaggedly irregular hills and the riverbank became a sheer stone cliff. God, the earth is beautiful, Flood thought, longing for a place on it to hide.

A little later the train slowed and entered a rail yard with dozens of tracks widening out the space between him and the river. Then the train slid into the Croton-Harmon station.

Suddenly Flood felt someone watching him. He looked down the aisle, directly into the eyes of the man in the dark raincoat who had been on the bus. He was standing at the end of the car a dozen feet away.

He stared at Flood for a moment then opened the door and left the car.

Stunned, Flood sat without moving. Was it the same man? he asked himself. Was it only a coincidence? Fear rose in him again and he tried to stifle it before it turned into panic. The man could be merely an innocent traveler who had paused, wondering where he had seen Flood before.

Realizing it was no time for such questions, Flood jumped up, took his coat and hat, hesitated, dropped them on his seat to make it appear he hadn't left, grabbed his carryall, and ran back along the aisle toward the door at the opposite end of the car.

"Bye, love," the barmaid said.

Flood nodded and hurried on, hoping the rear door was an exit. It wasn't. He ran through the next car and got to its vestibule just as the conductor was about to close the outer door. Flood got off the train and a moment later it pulled out. No one resembling the man in the dark raincoat was on the platform. Another train was standing beside the far platform and he ran up a flight of concrete steps to a passageway over the tracks and down another flight to the far side. Two conductors were standing fifty feet away beside an open door to the train. Flood waved and one of them motioned him to hurry. "Local to New York?" he gasped as he ran up to them.

One of the conductors nodded and said, "Nearly missed it this time."

Flood made his way down the car to the middle, past half a dozen other passengers, and sat down by the river side again. He would have to get off the train before it reached Grand Central, he realized. They would be waiting there. At all the train, bus, and air terminals. Flood paid the conductor and wondered if he should ask where he could get off and catch a city bus or subway. But if the man in the raincoat had somehow got on the train or asked the conductor . . .

A minute later they stopped at Ossining. He remembered that Sing Sing was nearby. Jesus, the trip was full of fun. He closed his eyes and leaned back, trying to calm himself. He had come this far . . . Soon he would be lost among the millions . . . if he could get there. He remembered Flower's sarcastic advice and the look on his face as he fell dead on top of him.

Flood went back to a man who was sitting alone and leaned over so he could be heard above the clatter of the train. "Is there a stop before Grand Central where I can get a subway train?" he asked.

The man, dressed in rough working clothes, nodded. "Where to?"

"Columbia University," Flood said. That sounded right. At least it was on the West Side, near the river.

"Marble Hill," the man said. "Couple of stops before the end. The Seventh Avenue subway's right there. Can't miss it."

Flood thanked him and went back to his seat. That would take him to Times Square, he thought. He saw Flower again. There was nothing rinkydink about Times Square.

After a stop at Spuyten Duyvil, the train swung away from the Hudson to follow the Harlem River. Flood glanced back, looking for the man in the dark raincoat; there was no sign of him.

"Next stop," the workman shouted and waved.

Flood nodded quickly to silence him. Now everyone would be aware of his departure. He swore softly and walked to the exit. As the train stopped, he stepped off and quickly walked behind a small waiting room with clear plastic walls that were opaque with scratches and dirt, crouched down, and pretended to tie his shoe. The train pulled out and he stood up and ran to a long flight of stairs to an overpass leading to the street far above.

At the top—Marble Hill Avenue and 225th Street —was the subway station, a small green building perched above the street a short block away. A train covered with graffiti trundled off over the elevated tracks toward a bridge across the Harlem River and, on the other side, Manhattan. He hurried along the street, ran up the steps to the station, bought four tokens, and pushed through a turnstile and went out onto the platform. A dozen people were waiting. He walked to the far end and looked back. No sign of the man in the raincoat.

There was a ten-minute wait for the next train. Flood began pacing and stopped himself. Too goddamn long, he thought. If the man on the train found him gone . . . a walkie-talkie signal to someone . . . Would a radio like that work on a train? Flood wondered. He didn't know. Christ, there was so much he didn't know.

At last the train rattled in and Flood boarded it and sat next to a door. He smelled the sweet pungent odor of marijuana and saw two black men at the rear end of the car passing a joint back and forth. Someone at the other end was playing Spanish rock on a radio. A walkie-talkie would work then, he thought uneasily. The train hurtled on and at 125th Street the passenger with the radio got off. A tall black man with a goatee wearing a long white gown and white pants and a white turban got on and when the train started up again he stood in the middle of the car, just in front of Flood, and announced that he represented an organization that looked after homeless children. He made a long, stilted speech in a singsong voice and ended with a shout: "You who believe be helpers of Allah!" Then he thrust a plastic cup in Flood's face.

Flood looked up at him impassively. After the KGB, this was a piece of cake, he thought. He shook his head slightly and the man glared at him for a few moments, then sneered and shoved the cup at a woman sitting nearby. She put some coins in it and he moved off.

A clock on the subway platform at Times Square said 1:01. Flood walked quickly to the rear of the platform, up the stairs, and toward a row of wall lockers. He locked the carryall in one and headed up another flight of stairs into Times Square.

He looked around at the garish mélange of depravity.

The asshole of America, he thought. Here the nation deposited its excrement. He wondered if a dart missile was aimed at the city. Probably not. It was of little military consequence. He dodged an immensely tall black pimp wearing a white suit and a broad-brimmed white hat and hailed a taxi.

# 4

It was nearly one-thirty when Flood arrived at the Central Park Zoo. He came in by the rear and walked to the cafeteria. He got a hot dog and a beer and went to the terrace. Sitting at a table where he could see the seal pond without being fully visible himself, he ate and drank and waited.

After a few minutes, he went inside and got another beer. As he paid he noticed that the cash register was full of change and asked the cashier whether she could spare three dollars in quarters. "For a telephone call," he explained.

"Don't matter to me if you're gonna swallow them," she said, counting out the coins and handing them to him with a surly look.

"Good to be back in New York," Flood said.

He went to a telephone and dialed 202 555-3121. When an operator said, "The Capitol," he asked for Senator Briggs's office. A brisk-sounding secretary answered there and Flood asked to speak to the Senator. He had no idea what he was going to say but he knew that Briggs was his only means of getting to Gilfedders. Flood was switched to another woman and again asked to speak to the Senator.

"Who's calling, please?"

"George Barrington," he said, using the name of his publisher; Briggs would certainly take his call.

"I'm sorry, Mr. Barrington, but the Senator is at the International Monetary Conference in San Francisco. He'll be back later tomorrow afternoon. May I have him call you?"

"That won't be necessary," Flood answered. "Can I reach him at home tomorrow night?"

"Yes."

"Fine." He hung up.

The Delacorte Clock chimed one-thirty and he

turned to look at it. Coming through the arch below the bronze clock with its bronze animals carrying bronze hammers to strike the bronze bell was a tall erect man. Flood started, then shrank down in his chair. It looked like McCade but he couldn't be sure because the man had on a hat. He paused and looked around, then continued walking, past the seal pond and up the steps to a row of benches. He sat down and took off his hat. He was bald. Had Marja brought him with her or had he followed her? It didn't matter, Flood thought. He was there. And he was facing Flood.

Half-crouched over the table, Flood peered through the leaves of the bushes concealing him and saw the man light a cigarette. Something was wrong but for a moment Flood couldn't figure out what it was. Then he had it: the man had lit the cigarette with his left hand. A right-handed man wouldn't do that, he knew as he remembered McCade in the cabin, the revolver in his right hand. A minute later a woman with a small girl came up and greeted the man on the bench and he got up and kissed them both. They left together and Flood sat up, letting out a long breathy whistle of relief.

When Marja came around the corner of the large brick building beyond the seal pond, Flood watched her to see if anyone seemed to be following. A couple of about eighteen came in behind her, then a black woman with a white baby in a stroller, then an old man, then a middle-aged woman. Marja went to the pond and stood with her back to Flood. He looked at her red-gold hair in the sunlight that had just broken through and scanned the area to see if anyone was watching her. Everything seemed all right but he was still too nervous to accept safety. If they were there, they'd be too clever to let him spot them.

A black boy of about twelve sauntered down the length of the cafeteria terrace, his white sneakers flapping on the tiles as he came closer. Flood called to him and the boy stopped, looking at him suspiciously, ready to bolt. Flood asked, "You want to make five dollars?"

The boy studied him. "Not from you, faggot."

"You got it wrong," said Flood quickly, feeling himself flush. "See that lady—the one with the reddish hair?" He pointed toward Marja and the boy nodded, still wary. "All you've got to do is take her a note." He took out a five-dollar bill.

The boy shrugged. "Okay, mother," he said. "Where's the note?"

Flood took out his notebook and quickly wrote: "Meet me at the side entrance of the Plaza Hotel— Central Park S. Ten minutes. F." He folded the slip of paper and handed it with the money to the boy. He started away but Flood stopped him. "Don't say anything to her and don't let anybody see you give her the note."

The boy looked at him contemptuously and left. Flood got up and walked quickly back under the arcade beside the cafeteria and waited. The boy went up to the railing a couple of feet away from Marja, then sidled to his left until he was nearly touching her. A second later he sauntered away. Jesus, Flood thought, he was good. The boy turned and glanced back at the terrace, shrugged when he didn't see Flood, and took out the five-dollar bill and grinned at it.

Flood watched Marja as she examined the note, then quickly walked off to leave the park the way she had come, out to Fifth Avenue. He hurried behind the elephant house to the path out of the park running parallel to Fifth Avenue in the same direction she would go. He walked very fast so that he would get there first and see if anyone was following her. Entering the hotel by the main doorway on the Plaza, Flood walked back through the lobby, past the Palm Court, where he averted his eyes to avoid the memory of that time when he and Ellen had gone there for brunch the day after the Pulitzer banquet, and headed for the side door. He left the hotel and walked a quarter of a block west, crossed the street, and came back up toward the hotel. A minute later he saw

Marja crossing Central Park South in long strides to make the light.

He swore out loud. It was impossible to tell whether any of the people behind her were merely behind her or were following her. As she turned toward the hotel most of the pedestrian traffic continued on down Fifth but a couple and a lone man turned in the same direction she had taken and another man hurried across Fifth and headed toward the hotel behind her. Flood waited. She paused by the entrance to the Plaza and the others continued on without a glance. Quickly Flood crossed the street and then Marja saw him. Her eyes widened slightly at the sight of his dyed hair but otherwise she paid no attention to him as he passed her and went up the steps into the hotel. A moment later she followed him. He retraced his path through the lobby and out onto the street in front.

"Taxi," he said to the doorman, gave him a dollar as he opened the door of a Checker, and waited for Marja, who was coming down the steps. She got in beside him. "Where's the car?" he asked.

"Sixty-second near Fifth," she said.

Flood leaned forward toward the open pane in the plastic divider of the cab and said, "Go up Madison to Seventy-ninth."

As the cab pulled away, he glanced at Marja, then looked out the back window. No one was following them. A woman came down the steps of the hotel and got into a cab and it started off but at Fifth Avenue it turned and headed downtown. When the Checker reached Madison and made the light just as it changed, Flood leaned back and looked at Marja.

"You look terrible," she said flatly. "Especially that hair."

The events of the night before and of that morning flashed through his mind and he smiled. "I could use a holiday."

"What's in the attic?" she asked in a quiet voice.

Flood stared at her in amazement and glanced at the driver and back at her. He leaned over and kissed her cheek. She began to pull away but he held her by the forearm behind the shield of his body so the driver couldn't see and whispered, "No one followed you?" He leaned back, watching her.

She shook her head. "And you?"

He nodded. "Part of the way."

Her green eyes widened again and he was surprised once more by their brilliance and depth. He looked away.

At 79th Street Flood told the driver to go over to Fifth Avenue and double back down to 62nd. He looked out the rear window as they swung around onto 79th and saw that the third car back, another cab, turned there, too. The Checker swung south at Fifth Avenue but the cab behind went straight on through Central Park. At 62nd Street Flood told the driver to turn again and this time no one followed them. They were clean.

Marja's car, a dark-green, two-door Ford, showed little damage from the fire except for a shadowlike scorching along the lower part of the driver's side. She unlocked the car and got in and let Flood in the other door. Following his instructions, she drove to the subway entrance at Seventh Avenue and 42nd Street and pulled up. Flood hurried down into the station, got his bag out of the locker, and a few seconds later was back in the car. "Straight on down Seventh Avenue," he said.

She drove at medium speed, moving expertly through the heavy traffic, and he thought, with gratitude, that he would be able to get some sleep on the way south. Neither of them spoke until they reached 14th Street and he told her to keep to the right and take the Holland Tunnel.

"That's to New Jersey, isn't it?" she asked.

"Uh-huh." He smiled to himself, wondering if he should warn her about New Jersey drivers, who were probably a greater peril to them than the KGB and the New Richmond Police Department combined.

After they emerged from the tunnel Marja said, "Are you going to tell me?"

Flood looked at her for a few moments. "No."

She glared at him. "Are you serious?"

"What you would know could hurt you very much —fatally."

"Being with you is perfectly safe, I suppose," she said.

"That's the next worst thing for you. You're with me only so I can convince those who might do you equally great harm—those on my side, you might say —to leave you alone."

"My providing you with safe transportation was only incidental of course."

He missed Sally.

They were silent for a few minutes, until Marja asked, "Why didn't you come to the Holiday Inn this morning as planned?"

Quickly Flood told her what had happened at the cabin and she listened, her lips pursed, her eyes on the road. When he finished she looked at him admiringly. "So you don't know whether he's alive?"

"No." He could understand that she wished McCade dead but there was something deeper than her desire for revenge.

They were silent again.

"You're getting good at this game," she said at last. "Keep it up and somebody will offer you a job."

"I couldn't keep it up another five minutes. Anyway it's a rotten thing to be good at." He meant that but he was pleased by her remark.

"What's wrong with being a survivor?" she asked.

Her voice was softer now and he turned and saw that she was smiling at him warmly. She understands, he thought with surprise. Even more, she seemed to care. He was flustered and to hide it he asked, "Have you seen today's *Herald*?"

"My satchel in back."

"Anything about Natalie or me?"

"No."

Tomorrow there was sure to be a story about Flower—and him. If McCade had escaped, the police would come after Flood. By now they probably had his prints. Rogers wouldn't be able to sit on the story for long. The police would talk—they always do, whatever the rights of suspects or the orders of the courts—and even though Flower had been hated by his fellow officers, they would go all out to get his killer; he had been a cop, they were cops, it was as simple as that. If the *Herald* played down the story, they would give it to the local radio-TV news staff and to the AP and UPI stringers at the university. Senator Briggs would know then—by tomorrow at the latest.

Flood closed his eyes and leaned back. He would never get to Gilfedders—not through Briggs anyway.

"Where are we going?" Marja asked.

"Keep on the turnpike until it says Garden State Parkway. Take that south. All the way south. We're going to the end of it." He spoke without opening his eyes and wondered if he was trying to exorcise the memory of Ellen or recapture it. The motel cabin, the cemetery, the seal pond, the Plaza, and now Cape May.

"Are we just running away or do you have some plan?"

"Both," Flood said. He wondered if he really did. Above all else he needed time to rest, to collect his thoughts, to be ready for Gilfedders. There was no way he could go in there feeling as he did—exhausted, distracted, frightened. If he got that far, they would want every detail—a so-called de-briefing—and he would have to be ready, not on the verge of collapse.

"Are you going to tell *anyone* what you found?" Marja asked.

"Yes." He opened his eyes and saw that they were going past Port Newark. On the left, in the distance, was an orange freighter and then there were loading derricks and ships' masts. An airport was on the right with a large radar scanner revolving.

"Who?"

"The President."

She turned, her eyes wide, and swerved out of the lane she'd been in.

"Jesus, look out!" he cried, sitting forward. A car

coming up on the right side honked at them and when Marja got back in the lane it sped by, the driver glaring at them. The car had a Jersey plate. Flood sat back. "You fit in here very nicely," he said, smiling at her.

She started to speak and to stop her from asking him again about what he'd found in the attic, he said, "What was it like when you got back to the house last night?"

"Bell was frantic of course."

"Any talk about arson?"

"If there was, I didn't hear it."

"Did he seem suspicious about the lights going out and then back on."

"He didn't say—at least not to me. I think he was watching me. He asked why I'd been gone so long. I told him I wasn't gone any longer than usual. It was true. He seemed to accept that. He was on the phone several times, I think, because he kept going up to his room. Did you see a phone there?"

Flood tried to remember but couldn't.

"Later, after he thought I'd gone to sleep, someone came to the house."

He sat forward. "Did you see who it was?"

Marja nodded. "My lights were out and the back-porch light went on. It lit up the ceiling of my room. I went to the window. Bell and a man came outside and stood for a minute. They were looking at the garage. My window was open but they were talking too quietly to hear. I thought I heard the name Cameron."

"The man claiming to be Wendy Cameron's husband?"

Marja nodded.

"What did he look like?"

"I couldn't tell. They were below me. He had dark hair and glasses and was wearing a dark raincoat."

The man on the bus and the train, Flood thought. He turned and looked out the rear window. It was pointless, he realized at once. With all the traffic anyone might be following; they could be back there in half a dozen cars and he'd never know it.

"There was no sign of McCade last night or this morning?" he asked.

"No."

"Did you go to the office?"

"No, I went straight to the Holiday Inn." She paused. "I was too frightened."

"Did you bring your passport?"

"Yes." She paused again, then added, "Actually I brought two of them."

Flood looked at her. "You've got a fake passport?"

She nodded. "I bought it a few years ago in London. It seemed like a good precaution, considering Bruce's background. He doesn't know of course."

"Don't tell me the name on it."

"I don't intend to."

"Any money?"

"I've saved quite a bit in the past few years. I've got it with me—in cash."

"Good."

"Should I have told you that?"

He grinned at her. "Yes."

Marja followed the exit to the Garden State Parkway and a little farther on got in line at a toll station behind half a dozen cars. A moment later they were jolted slightly from behind. Flood turned around. A man driving an old car behind them shrugged and smiled apologetically.

"Natives call New Jersey the Garden State," Flood said. "Others call it the Whiplash State."

Once they were on the parkway Marja said, "What happens to me when you leave?"

He didn't know what to say. If he told them about Marja, they would be sure to arrest her or at least take her into "protective" custody. If he didn't tell them, there would be no way to protect her from McCade. "Would you be safe in Europe?" he asked. "Do you know your way around well enough to hide, change your identity?"

She didn't answer for a time. Finally she said, "I think so. There are several places I could go." She paused and added, "Of course McCade's people—and yours—are everywhere."

Flood nodded. He knew the feeling. "I won't say anything to them about this part of the trip," he told her. "Just up to your helping me get into the house. I'll see how it looks, what their attitude is." He didn't mention that he might need her to verify at least part of his story.

"If you get that far."

"If I get that far." He turned and looked out the rear window again, and again he felt foolish as he saw a score of cars immediately behind them. "Do you mind doing all the driving?" he asked, turning back. "If we're stopped and I have to show my license—"

"I'm tired—hardly what you'd call a sound sleep last night—but I can manage. How far are we going—Washington?"

"No, Cape May. It's at the southern tip of New Jersey. Two hours, maybe two and a half, from here." An hour ago he had been anxious to get to Washington as soon as possible but now he was relieved that Briggs wouldn't be home until the next day. Flood hadn't realized how little thought he'd given to anything besides the next move. He had to slow down.

"Why Cape May?" Marja asked.

"It's safe. We can rest there. And we'll arrive in Washington by a route no one would expect. If they're watching for us, they'll be watching the northern route." He didn't want to tell her that his plan to go to Cape May had been formulated only a few minutes before. "We'll stay at the Cape until tomorrow sometime."

She looked at him in surprise but said nothing.

"The man I've got to see is away until tomorrow evening. He's the only one who can help—if he will."

Flood awoke as they were entering Cape May and realized that Marja had called to him. "How long did I sleep?"

"An hour or so."

"Did you call me just now?"

"Yes. I just murmured 'John' and you woke instantly."

"Maybe you shouldn't use my name."

"What should I call you—Trevelyan? Or Mr. Barnard?"

As they entered the old part of the town of Cape May itself, Flood looked with mounting pleasure, then with the sweet pain of nostalgic longing, at the Victorian richness of the place. The frame houses were gaudy with balconies, pillars, fish-scale shingles, widows' walks, ornate verandas, crowned dormers, myriad gables, and an endless profusion of latticework and gingerbread carvings.

"Nice," Marja said as she pulled up at a stop sign and looked around.

"The South. We're below the Mason-Dixon line. During the Civil War, New Jersey had strong Southern sympathies. It was the only Northern state to vote twice against Lincoln."

Ellen had told him that bit of history on the long weekend they spent in Cape May just before the end of his two-year assignment in Washington for the *Herald*. As a child she had spent summers in Cape May with her family, who came up from Virginia each July to a cottage just off the beach. On that weekend she rediscovered the haunts of her childhood with delight and lamented those that were gone.

He directed Marja through the town to its southernmost point, then told her to turn onto the street running along the ocean front. Suddenly, the sea was before them, glittering endlessly under the bright sun.

Marja gasped. "I never get used to that."

There was something different in her tone—softness, pleasure, a warm current running below the surface. Flood looked at her and back at the sea.

They drove north along the beach road. On their right was a broad macadam promenade, which, Ellen had told him, had been a fine boardwalk when she came there as a child, before it was washed away during a storm. On their left were some honky-tonk "amusement parlors," clam bars, the usual seaside gift shops with the souvenirs that are the same everywhere except for the location names printed and embroidered on them, old cottages that had survived the onslaught of commerce, a few grandly spacious Victorian hotels that were closed for the winter, several rooming houses with balconies running around three sides on each floor, and a couple of garish modern hotels that hadn't been there on his last visit.

He told her to turn on Howard Street and to stop at the hotel a block or so from the beach. It was the Chalfonte, a splendid century-old white-frame building sprawled out grandly under a red peaked-and-gabled roof; it had deep colonnaded porches around the first and second floors and long striped awnings shielding them.

"This is it," Flood said.

Marja looked at the hotel. "It's rather grand," she said. "I don't have the clothes."

He nodded. He knew he couldn't stay there again anyway. It had been nearly ten years since his weekend with Ellen but the wound was still fresh. "Let's go on," he said.

She watched him for a moment, almost studying his face, and asked, "Memories?"

Again he was surprised. Did it show that clearly? "Yeah," he said. "Let's go."

A few blocks away he saw a place that looked all right—a modest white-frame hotel with colonnaded porches around the first and second floors and a red mansard roof. It was called the Rudolph. Flood liked the name nearly as much as the setting—a hundred yards from the beach with clear views east and south.

A man of about sixty was painting the railing down the front steps and when Flood got out and asked if they had any vacancies, he smiled amiably and removed his painter's cap. He was wearing gold-rimmed glasses and had the tanned seamed face of a man much outdoors. "Only two rooms taken so far," he said. "Quiet this time of year." He was still smiling and Flood felt as if he had wandered into a Norman Rockwell painting. "The missus is out just now," the man said. "I'll show you what's available if you like."

"I'll ask my wife," Flood said. He hadn't meant to say that but it was out now. He had assumed, when he decided to stay in Cape May overnight, that they would take separate rooms. But he had also assumed that they would stay someplace large, where their comings and goings wouldn't be observed. In a place like this, having separate rooms after arriving together would look suspicious.

He went to the car and got in. "Congratulations," he said. "You just got married."

Her eyes narrowed and she frowned. "We could go somewhere else and arrive separately."

"We could," he said and fell silent, thinking. After a few moments he went on, "If we check in separately, it'll mean we'll have to meet outside somewhere even to take a walk or go to dinner. That might arouse someone's curiosity. I think we're pretty safe here. I need that feeling right now."

"Twin beds? A private bath?"

"They're bound to have some rooms with twin beds," he said. "But the bath I doubt. Not in a place like this. Bath at the end of the hall. Toilet next to it. Wash basin in the room."

She looked at him, then nodded, saying, "As long as you understand."

Flood grunted and got out. The man showed him several rooms and he finally chose one on the southeast corner of the third floor and went to get Marja.

As she got out of the car, she looked at him uneasily. Just inside the front door, she paused before the small sitting room; it had windows on two sides facing the porch and was furnished with white wicker furniture that had faded green and white and red floral-patterned cushions and matching curtains. She turned to Flood and smiled, almost reluctantly. "Nice," she said again.

He followed her up a narrow stairway with a red carpet and a polished wood balustrade and remembered how he had followed her sister like this. Jesus, it was only a few days ago, he thought, unable to believe it for a moment. Then he was assailed by guilt again at the thought of Natalie; if only he had left Treats earlier or had refused to help her.

The top-floor corridor was painted white and the doors to the rooms were double—the outer ones louvered to let air in. Marja paused. "Smell how clean it is," she whispered.

"There's no one else on this floor—not yet anyway."

Their room was pale turquoise, brilliant with the late-afternoon sun reflected off the sea. There were two beds covered with yellow chenille bedspreads, white cotton curtains, a white chest of drawers, a white table by one window, and two white straight chairs. In a corner was the wash basin he had predicted.

Marja looked around, then faced him, her smile more generous now. "I like it," she said.

"My kind of place," Flood replied. "The people who stay here drive five-year-old cars and work for a living."

He put the carryall down and took out his dirty clothes. It was time to be ordinary, he decided, and fished in the bottom of the bag for some of the packets of laundry soap he carried when he was traveling. He ran hot water in the basin, poured in the contents of two packets, and put the clothes in to soak.

Marja stood by the east window looking out at the sea. "I want to walk in the sand," she said. "But first I'd like something to eat. I haven't eaten since yesterday."

He looked at her high heels and said, "You need some sandals."

"I need everything."

The man painting the front porch suggested they might find a place to have a sandwich on the mall, a couple of blocks to the west, and they set out on foot. On the way they passed a yellow house that had gingerbread cutouts wherever they would fit and in some places where they wouldn't. Flood stopped and stared at the place. "They must have built that right after the jigsaw was invented."

Marja laughed and he looked at her in surprise. He hadn't heard her laugh before.

The mall was a tidy place with potted trees, benches, gas lanterns, and a few sidewalk cafés. They sat at one called the Gazebo and ordered grilled-cheese sandwiches and ale and watched the people passing by.

"Why do American women look so much older than their husbands?" Marja asked idly after watching half a dozen middle-aged couples pass.

"It's all those household appliances," Flood answered. She smiled at him and he went on. "The time they save is spent eating, watching television, and going to beauty parlors, all of which speeds up the aging process. Once they notice its effects, they spend their remaining free time looking in the mirror for new signs of age. Nothing makes one age faster than watching oneself age."

Marja smiled again and he ordered more ale. They drank in relaxed silence, watching the people on the mall. Finally Marja said that she would do her shopping and rejoin him there. He stood up as she left, then motioned to the waitress and ordered a double Jack Daniel's and water. When she brought it Flood sat back and had a long drink and sighed. For the first time in days he felt almost safe.

Half an hour or so later he was on his second drink, this one a single, when a woman wearing a bright-red bandana, a loose-fitting blue sweater, white-cotton pants, and white espadrilles and carrying a tan-canvas traveling case came down the mall toward him. She was the first interesting-looking person he had seen since his arrival and he sat up, watching her. She smiled at him and he saw that it was Marja.

"I got a nightgown, too, and underclothes and stockings and a toothbrush and toothpaste and a hairbrush," she said as she sat down. She looked very pleased with herself. Then she saw the drink in front of him and frowned. She averted her eyes, as if watching the people on the mall, and said, "I think I'll go for a walk on the beach."

Defiantly Flood picked up his glass and took a drink.

"All right," he said. "Leave the bag. I want to buy a couple of things, too, so I'll take everything back to the room and join you."

She nodded and rose, then paused and looked at him as if she wanted to apologize. "Don't be long," she said.

Back in their room, Flood rinsed out the clothes in the basin and hung them up on the makeshift closet— a pole that ran from the door to the far wall behind a white curtain. Then he changed into the clothes he had bought after Marja left: khaki pants, a yellow polo shirt, and a wine-colored V-neck sweater. As soon as he finished dressing, he swore and undressed, put a towel around him, and went across the hallway to shower. Ten minutes later he was dressed again, feeling better than he had in a long time, and looked around the room to see if he had forgotten anything. The gun. On the road south he had transferred it from his jacket pocket to a side pocket of the carryall, wrapped in the ski mask. Now he took the gun out and slipped it under the mattress, looked around again, and left.

Marja was a couple of hundred yards down the beach, sitting on the sand just above the reach of the foaming surf, her elbows on her knees, her chin on her hands. She turned as he approached and her eyes were very green in the light. She nodded approvingly at his outfit. "You look so different."

"Better or worse?"

She held out a hand to him and smiled. "Peace?"

He took her hand and felt it quiver slightly. "Peace," he said, smiling, too. As he sat beside her, he saw that she had taken off her espadrilles and that her toenails were bright red. Her feet were muscular, almost contorted.

She caught his look and said, "Ugly. All dancers have ugly feet. The polish is supposed to distract the eye."

"Yours or mine?"

She stretched and wiggled her toes without answering.

Except for the slow pulse of the surf, the sea was nearly calm now and Flood stared at it with a feeling of melancholy wonder. He thought of the bones of drowned mariners.

Marja sighed. "It's too mysterious. I hate things I can't understand."

"Just think if you understood everything. God must be bored silly."

She turned to him. "Do you believe?"

"Sometimes." He remembered his terror and how deeply he had believed then.

"What's in the attic?" she asked suddenly.

Flood looked at her in surprise. "You really do hate mysteries, don't you?"

She nodded, waiting, her lips open slightly, her eyes expectant.

He shook his head. "I can't. You don't want to know, believe me."

"I've got to. It's my right. They killed my sister."

"They'll kill you, too, if you know." He stopped, hoping she wouldn't object that they would kill her now anyway. He couldn't give her the real reason: that he wanted to be able to tell the people in the White House she knew nothing, so they would leave her alone. She had too small a chance of escaping as it was, without having both sides after her.

Marja picked up a handful of small stones and began tossing them into the water. She threw the last one and said, "That's what it's like."

"What?"

"Life. This sand is eternity. That ocean is another eternity." She picked up a stone and flung it angrily. "And that's me!"

"Or me."

She nodded. "Or anyone."

It was true of course, Flood thought. But he was different now; ever since he had seen the missile, he was different. Whatever happened, he wasn't going out with a tiny splash and sink unseen.

"What happened to you?" Marja asked abruptly, without looking at him.

"When? What do you mean?"

"What hurt you so?"

Jesus, not *that* cliché again, he thought, wondering what he should say.

"You act like a married man."

"I am." The words had popped out, without his meaning to say them. But he knew they were true: he was still married to Ellen. "My wife died."

Marja looked at him without speaking, then reached over and touched his hand for a second. He was grateful for that—and for her not saying those useless words, "I'm sorry."

Neither of them spoke for a long time. Finally he shifted his position and stretched out, one elbow in the sand. "It seems strange you're alone," he said. "A woman like you." He cursed himself. It had come out wrong.

She turned to him, anger glittering in her eyes. "Incomplete without a man, you mean?" she asked mockingly.

Flood didn't respond and after a moment she went on, more calmly now, "I'm quite capable of being without men. Long ago I taught myself not to need anything except food and clothing and shelter. If I want a man—not need but *want*—I'll take him." She paused and looked away. "That's how I took Bruce."

Flood stared at her in astonishment.

She turned back, smiling defiantly. "That's right. He was my lover. Natalie's husband."

That was what he had sensed in her that was deeper than a desire for revenge, Flood thought. Her betrayal of Natalie had made it possible for McCade to kill her.

"He loved Natalie, I think," Marja continued, her voice trembling now. "But she didn't want him anymore—not in that way at least. He needed someone, a release. You can imagine the tension he was living under. He was afraid to get involved with anyone outside. So was I. When he came to me I accepted. I even thought I might keep him for Natalie until she was well again. It was nothing—two animals coupling."

Flood stifled his disgust. He knew that if she ever faced the truth she would go mad; it might as well have been her hand that had plunged the ivory-handled knife into Natalie's breast. "Things like that happen," he said, trying to sound as if he believed it. "Three people in a house together. The wrong one sick or drunk or crazy."

"You don't know how it feels now," she said quietly.

He had to stop her from thinking that way. He sat up and said, "I killed my wife."

Now Marja stared at him in astonishment.

Flood began the story with the end of his two-year assignment in Washington. That time had been an unhappy one for Ellen and him. He had despised the journalistic politicking, the self-promotion of his colleagues, their cynicism, the contempt for the public held by politicians and journalists alike. And Ellen had been depressed by the pettiness she saw everywhere and, most of all, by what was happening to Flood.

Toward the end of his stint with the *Herald*'s Washington bureau, the paper's only columnist retired and the publisher offered Flood the job. He was delighted. It was time to get away from the trees to have a look at the forest, he told Ellen. And she suggested they should do what they had talked about for so long—take a camping trip out West before returning to New Richmond. Flood found a man in the Forestry Department who told him about a seldom-used trail in the Sierra Nevadas that led to a hidden lake where the trout were bountiful, the scenery was idyllic, and peace was total. He gave Flood a geodetic map of the area and marked the trail, saying, "You'll never regret it."

One morning just before dawn Flood and Ellen stood at the foot of the trail staring up at the lofty peak of the mountain in awe—the kind of awe that he later realized had actually been fear. They climbed for two days, stopping overnight at a rough hut built for hikers, and passed no one. The next morning Ellen complained of a pain in her side. "Only a stitch," he assured her. "Nothing compared to the way my feet feel." Late that afternoon they reached the lake. It was an unfathomable blue, clear a good twenty feet down, then receding into blue blackness. Surrounding the lake was a deep pine forest, the air was like the first gulp of breath in a baby's life, and they were alone.

Ellen's pain was worse, so Flood made camp alone and built a fire and cooked dinner. She felt better afterward and he gave her a little brandy with icy water from the lake. The next morning the pain was gone but as the day wore on it came back, worse than before, and by evening she was unable to eat. Assuring her that she would be all right in the morning, Flood said that he wanted to get in some fishing while the trout were feeding and went out to the edge of an enormous flat rock that extended thirty feet into the lake. He fished until dark, without a strike, and returned to the fire. Ellen was asleep and he took off his shoes and crawled into the sleeping bag beside her.

During the night she woke him. "It hurts so bad, John," she moaned. The moon was three-quarters and by its light he could see the fear on her face. He stroked her head until she fell asleep, then turned over and slept, too. In the morning Ellen was much better for an hour or two but after breakfast she crawled back into her sleeping bag. Looking at her pale frightened face, Flood was suddenly stricken by fear. He had always dealt with his own illnesses by ignoring them but now he was overcome by anxiety. To relieve it, he tried to comfort her but she turned away from him, huddled in pain. He waited in silence.

By two o'clock that afternoon she was so much worse that he knew he had to go for help. There were six, maybe seven hours of light left. It was almost all downhill. And later there would be the moon. But he realized that it would be almost impossible for him to return with help before noon the next day even if they started back in the middle of the night.

Ellen turned to him and asked, "Oh, John, do you think it's appendicitis?"

"I don't know," he answered. "All I know is I'm going for help."

"Don't go. I'm frightened."

Tears slid out of the corners of her eyes as he knelt by her and kissed her cheeks and hair. "Don't worry, my darling, you'll be all right."

It was nearly dark by the time Flood emerged on the road at the foot of the trail, bruised from falling repeatedly and scratched and exhausted. With each step down the mountain his fear had grown and now he flung himself into his car and drove with crazed speed to the nearest town. It was nine o'clock when he found the only doctor in the area, a burly young man with a heavy beard and rimless glasses, who questioned him in maddening detail about Ellen's symptoms. Finally he picked up a phone and said to Flood, "We can't get back up there on foot quick enough. And we'd have to bring her down by stretcher along that rough trail. Out of the question. The state police have a helicopter. One of the pilots, Shanley, knows these mountains like his wife's tits."

But it was hopeless even for Shanley, a lanky silent man who had flown choppers in Vietnam and ever since. The trail up to the lake was invisible from above, at least in the dark, and it was too dangerous to fly low enough to make the searchlights useful.

"You could have built a fire," Shanley said as they headed back for the base. "Or wasn't she well enough to tend one?"

Flood hadn't thought of that. He shook his head, without answering. Even the powerful flashlight they'd taken along would probably have been enough, he realized. If he'd only thought to tell her. Sickened by fear and remorse, he wondered if she had heard the engine as they flew overhead.

"Can't we try once more?" he shouted at Shanley. "You must be able to see that lake in the moonlight."

"There's dozens of lakes, scores of lakes, up here," Shanley said. "At night they all look alike."

The young doctor took Flood's arm. "She'll be all right," he said. "We'll be back up there at the first light of dawn."

They found Ellen then, within twenty minutes of taking off at dawn, and Shanley brought the copter down neatly on the great flat rock. The doctor was at her side within seconds, kneeling, talking softly to her. Ellen was writhing in agony and moaned as the doctor turned her gently onto one side, unzipped the sleeping bag, pulled up her heavy sweater and shirt, and pressed her abdomen wtih two fingers. She screamed.

Flood, kneeling beside her across from the doctor, took her hands and put them to his face. "Oh, my darling, oh, my darling," he murmured, kissing her fingers.

"We've got to get her in the chopper at once," the doctor snapped. "No time for a stretcher. Peritonitis."

He moved down to take her legs, Shanley crouched behind her head with his hands under her shoulders, and Flood slipped his arms under her back. As they started to lift her, she gasped and Flood took one hand out and touched her cheek. "It's all right, it's all right, my darling," he said. She turned her head and looked at him with anguish and rage. Then she screamed and bit his hand and died.

Flood stared at the row of tiny white scars along the side of his right hand. Without speaking, Marja reached over and took the hand and held it in both of hers. He was grateful for her touch and even more for her silence. Telling the story hadn't brought the relief he'd hoped for; in fact reliving it had made the pain of his remorse sharper. But he was glad that he had told her. Now he didn't feel so alone.

Unexpectedly he thought of Sally and wondered why. He saw her again—appealing and vulnerable. A moment later he realized that Sally lived as Ellen had taught him one must: ready to love even if it meant being hurt beyond endurance. He had forgotten that, he thought, and wondered if it was too late to try again.

"I feel close to you," he said.

Marja nodded, still looking at the sea. "I know."

She fumbled in the sand between her legs and picked up a stone. Wetting a forefinger with her tongue, she rubbed the stone clean and handed it to him. It was a pure, nearly luminous, white and shaped like a heart. Flood took it from her with a smile and put it in his pocket.

# 5

They had dinner at one of the modern hotels facing the ocean. The dining room—large, dimly lit, with a vaulted ceiling—was on the top floor and they got a booth beside a window overlooking the beach and the dark sea. A waitress brought their drinks and Flood looked around the half-filled room until he noticed a small dance floor not far away and, behind it, a bandstand big enough for three or four musicians. "Jesus," he said, "music."

"Of course." Marja sipped at a glass of white wine and put it down. "Americans must have their music—music in elevators, music in supermarkets, music in cars, music in shops, music at the hairdressers, music in restaurants—and all of it bad." She emptied her glass.

"You're cheerful tonight."

"You should see me in the morning."

Embarrassed by the realization that he was going to in a few hours, Flood averted his eyes. He poured some wine for her and as he looked up he saw that she was amused by his discomfiture. She turned to the window and her eyes went bright. Flood turned, too, and saw a half-moon just above the horizon. He felt that the contact they had made on the beach had broken and he wanted it back. Time, he thought, but knew there wasn't enough time.

"You don't like it when I attack America, do you?" she asked, still smiling.

That kind of discussion would only deepen the break, he thought. "Freedom includes the right to make fun of this country," he said. "Or to criticize or even misunderstand it."

"Do you understand it?" She looked serious.

He thought for a moment and shook his head. "I feel it." He wondered if what he felt was only a memory of a soaring idea, a few great men and women, turbulent aspirations.

Marja looked fondly at him. "You love it."

Flood was taken aback, then embarrassed again. It was true—he did love it. What would be lost if the missiles went off? he asked himself. Hope? "America's in my bones," he said and reddened.

"You can't expect me to understand," she said softly, her eyes averted. "I've known nothing but brutality. I see no reason to believe in anything—surely not in a country."

Flood nodded.

"You're a frightful romantic, Mr. Flood," she said suddenly and smiled warmly at him.

"True," he said. He sat back in the booth and stretched, then took a long drink of whiskey. "For some reason I want you to understand how I feel."

She looked puzzled. "Why?"

He shrugged. "I suppose being misunderstood is like suffering injustice. It hurts."

"Why do we have to understand each other?" She was watching him closely.

"Not understand. That was the wrong word. Accept is what I meant."

"Accept your faith?" she asked.

He felt his face flush and nodded silently. That was it of course, he thought, feeling absurd. Faith was all he had left—a blind dumb faith that if mankind had freedom and time it would triumph over itself. He picked up his drink and raised it to her.

"You're right," he said. "I'm just an aging romantic."

She touched his hand. "I accept that."

A blast of music brought Flood up out of his seat. Three men were on the bandstand—one behind a set of drums, one in front with a trumpet at his lips, and one at an electric organ. Diners—mostly stout and middle-aged—headed to the small dance floor and soon it was full of hefty bodies swaying to "The Way We Were."

Marja leaned forward and shouted, "Never before

has so much double-knit moved in such syncopation in one room!"

Flood grinned and when the waitress came and screamed, "Can I take your order?" he laughed outright.

They ordered and ate without speaking, unable to hear each other over the din. When they finished, Flood motioned to the waitress to bend over and said loudly in her ear that they would like brandy and a check.

Just then the band began playing "Stardust" and he leaned forward. "My misspent youth!" he shouted.

Marja smiled, her eyes gleaming, and shouted back, "Shall we dance?"

"I'm wretched at this," he said when they reached the dance floor, but as he took her in his arms he felt as if he had put on a comfortable old sweater and they moved easily around the crowded floor. After a minute he heard Marja singing softly and caught the words " 'when our love was new and each kiss an inspiration.' " He leaned back and laughed. "Did you learn that on the Danube?" She sang all the words all the way through and at the end they left the dance floor laughing and holding hands. They drank their brandy hurriedly and left.

The tide was in, beginning to recede now, and the moon was high and small. It should be full, Flood thought. Nothing was ever quite right. They walked along the wet sand nearly to a long stone jetty, where the sea crashed whitely, throwing a fine mist up into the moonlight.

"There's something else I didn't tell you," Marja said.

Hearing the tension in her voice, Flood stopped.

She took a few more steps, then turned and faced him. "I got pregnant, Bruce."

He took a deep breath and waited but she said nothing more. "When?"

"A few months ago."

"You're pregnant now?"

"No." She began walking again. He stood still and she paused and turned. "He made me get rid of it."

Flood stared at her in the dim light. "You wanted the child?"

She moved toward him, her face slack. "He made me have it killed."

Jesus, Flood thought, first her baby, then her sister. And her father had been killed because of his friendship with this man, her mother because of him and his tanks out in the forest. "You loved him?" he asked quietly.

She shook her head. "I wanted to love something."

She broke off and he saw that she was weeping. He put his arms around her awkwardly, knowing that she had put her bitterness aside and welcomed him. In spite of everything that had happened to her, he saw, she was willing to try.

He raised her chin. "Why do you want a child?"

Her lips trembled. "What else is there?"

They walked back to the hotel without speaking. He flicked on the light as they entered their room but she turned it off. She went to the window facing the sea and looked at the moon. Finally she turned. "Do you want to?" she asked.

"Yes."

"The act or the person?"

"They're the same."

She nodded and began to undress.

# Saturday

# 1

They had moved the beds together and when Flood awoke, Marja was facing him, still asleep, one arm across his chest. He studied her full lips, the heavy-lidded eyes, the cloud of bright hair, and as if aware of his scrutiny she moaned a little and moved her arm, revealing one of her breasts. He leaned forward and kissed her shoulder and lay back again.

The room was full of light but he decided that it must still be early, for there was no sound of traffic outside, only the thudding of the surf breaking on the shore. He lay for a few minutes listening to it contentedly, then sighed and quietly got out of bed. He turned on the hot water, letting it run in a small stream so that it wouldn't waken her. He shaved carefully, doused his face with cold water, and brushed his teeth.

He was combing his stiff hair when he heard footsteps pounding down the corridor toward the room. He turned off the water and someone knocked loudly on the door, shouting, "Flood! Stop! Flood!"

Marja sat upright, staring at him in terror. He took two steps to the side of the bed and thrust his hand under the mattress, feeling for the gun. They had been there all along, he thought frantically, waiting for the right moment. He swore and pulled out the gun. The pounding on the door resumed. He motioned to Marja to get out of the line of fire. She scrambled out of bed, pulling a blanket with her, and crouched in the corner, her eyes wide with fear. He moved slowly toward the door, holding the gun out the length of his arm, the muzzle chest high.

"Hey in there!" a man's voice shouted. "Turn off the water! There's a flood downstairs!"

Flood stared at the door, then at Marja, in stunned relief. She began laughing and put her hands over her mouth to stifle the sound. Grinning and trying not to laugh, too, Flood slid the gun back under the mattress and went to the door.

It was the Norman Rockwell man. Even now, despite his distress, he smiled genially when Flood opened the door. "The drain must be stopped up down below here somewheres," he explained. "Water's pouring all over the room underneath." He smiled again.

They had breakfast at the same sidewalk café on the mall. When they finished and started on their second cups of coffee, Flood opened a *Times* he had bought on the way and Marja picked up a Washington *Post*. Before he was halfway through his paper, she put hers down and said, "Nothing here." He smiled at her and went back to the *Times*. A minute later he found the article, datelined from New Richmond the previous day:

## POLICE LIEUTENANT SLAIN, EXECUTIVE HELD

Lieutenant Bertram Flower, a member of the New Richmond Police Department for 22 years and head of its Homicide Division for the past eight years, was found shot to death in a cabin at the Guardian Motel outside this city early this morning. The officer, believed to have been pursuing a lead on an unsolved murder case, was shot in the back at close range.

Police sources were reluctant to discuss the case, but it was reported by a reliable source that a suspect, a prominent businessman from New Richmond, was found unconscious near the scene of the crime. His identity has not been divulged, but he is believed to be under treatment at a local hospital and under close police guard.

In an unexpected development police officials disclosed that the motel cabin appeared to have been rented under an assumed name by Mr. John Flood, a well-known columnist for the New Richmond *Herald* and a Pulitzer Prize winner some years ago. Speculation among his colleagues on the *Herald* is that Mr. Flood was pursuing a lead on the same unsolved murder that Lt. Flower was investigating. Mr. Flood is being sought for questioning.

Flood handed Marja the paper and sat back. He drank some cold coffee and looked down the mall. He wondered if he had more time now. Someone on the *Herald* had misled the reporter in order to protect the paper from scandal for a day or two more, until it was unavoidable or until Rogers and Barrington had thought of a way out. That meant Senator Briggs might not hear about it when he got back to Washington tonight. He would probably go straight home.

Marja put down the *Times*. "He's alive."

"And under guard."

"He'll get away."

"I know. He probably has by now."

She looked around nervously.

Flood looked up, too, and saw a dark-haired man in a brown jacket and black pants watching them from across the mall. "Someone's over there," he said. "Looks like a cop. Don't turn now."

Marja caught her breath and sat back. After a moment she glanced across the way.

"Do you know him?" Flood asked.

"No, but he seems to know us." Her voice was flat.

Flood looked down the mall and saw a police car parked at a cross street. He swore under his breath. How had they found him?

The man walked toward their table. "Excuse me, sir," he said. "Do those bikes belong to you?"

Flood saw two bicycles chained to a tree near where the man had been standing. "No, they don't."

"It's against the law to have bikes on the mall," the man said sternly.

Flood nodded, trying not to laugh. "A good law, too."

The man glared at him and walked quickly down

the mall to the police car. A uniformed officer got out and joined him.

"They're going to call for reinforcements," Flood said.

Marja smiled in relief. The two policemen came toward the bikes and Flood saw that the one in uniform, a sergeant, was carrying a large pair of wire-cutters. The plainclothesman glared at Flood again, as if waiting for him to confess, then spoke to the sergeant, who clamped the cutters onto the chain.

"Jesus, a crime wave," Flood said.

Marja laughed and the plainclothesman turned to look at them in fury.

"Let's get out of here," Flood said. "I've got enough enemies." He paid and as they started up the mall he said to Marja, "Now I've got a federal rap against me, too."

She looked at him, perturbed. "For what?"

"Violating the Mann Act by transporting a female person across a state line for immoral purposes."

Her laughter rang down the mall. She said, "Let's go violate it again."


That afternoon they took the great white ferryboat from Cape May to Lewes, Delaware, across the broad mouth of Delaware Bay. The afternoon sun was hot, the water calm, the sky clear. Flood couldn't believe that he had this luxury of peace. They sat outdoors on the deck watching the other passengers in silence, their hands touching now and then, as if to make sure they were still together.

"What do you want?" Flood asked her.

"Nothing. Just this."

"For myself," he said, "I wouldn't mind a hamburger, some French fries, and a couple of beers."

She laughed and said, "Make mine the same."

They ate and drank greedily and watched other feeders—a flock of gulls that followed the ferry. A man at the railing was tossing popcorn to them, and the gulls—swooping, peeling off like fighter planes leaving a formation, then rising to glide, seemingly fixed in midair, a few feet from the man—scolded him with little cawing shrieks and snapped at the popcorn. Fascinated, Flood watched them for a long time with his arm around Marja's shoulders. It was almost like a honeymoon, he thought.

He must have stiffened for she looked at him and asked, "What is it, my darling?"

Her words were the same ones Ellen used, he thought, and shook his head. But the memory wouldn't go away—the omen that he had pushed out of his mind then and had kept buried. He hadn't thought of it until now and shivered as the recollection formed in his mind. Katie and Phil Briggs had stood up with Ellen and him at their simple wedding in a small church in the Virginia countryside and then the four of them drove off for lunch at the Briggses' house in Georgetown. Briggs was driving, with Katie beside him, and the Floods were in back. Suddenly a rabbit ran out from the bushes lining the narrow country lane. Briggs swerved but it ran under the car. Flood turned to look out the rear window and saw the rabbit's body flung out by the wheels like a floppy stuffed animal. "Is it all right?" Ellen cried, unable to look. Flood watched until the rabbit, lying still in the road, was out of sight. "Off it went—hippety hop," he said lightly, sickened by fear, and put his arm around her.

He took his arm away from Marja's shoulders. After a minute he got up and said, "Let's have a stroll." She rose and they started down the starboard side. Most of the passengers were inside the ferry, with a couple of dozen others sitting on benches or standing at the railing around the bow and down the forward sides. By midship the deck was empty. People were more interested in where they were going than where they had been, Flood thought as they reached the deserted stern on the main deck. That was natural of course. Then he realized that it was the opposite for him and he stared back over the widening wake toward the receding Jersey shore. Marja took his arm and they leaned against the railing in silence. Flood put his hand on hers.

"Marja!" a voice behind them called.

They turned simultaneously to face a plump florid man of about forty with thick curly black hair. He was holding a gun with a silencer. It was aimed at Marja's stomach.

"Willie!" she gasped.

"Sorry about this," he said mildly. "I tried to get out of the assignment." He looked at Flood. "So you shook Cameron. Hard to do. He didn't like that."

"You're one of them," Marja said. Her voice was listless, all hope gone.

"What the hell's going on?" Flood demanded, trying to sound angry but feeling foolish. No bluff could work now; it was one of McCade's men.

"Back up!" he ordered, motioning with the gun.

They moved against the railing. He stepped forward.

"Willie—" Marja began.

"No threats, no bribes, no begging," he said. "Spare me."

"Not you, Willie. I don't believe it. You're my friend!"

His trigger finger tightened. Flood felt nausea rising and tasted blood again. "Willie?" he asked dumbly. It was almost over now.

"The foreman where I work," Marja said. "He can't be—"

"The Colonel's not stupid enough to have someone there he can't trust," the man said. "The keys—to your car." He jerked the gun impatiently.

He must have followed Marja all the way, Flood thought. Then he had waited for the right moment. Not Cape May. Too many people. Bodies to worry about. Now. Two pops from the gun would fling them over the railing. It would be days before they were found. Maybe never . . . the tide. Flood looked around desperately. No one on the main deck within view. No one above on the upper deck.

"Don't try that one," Willie said, following Flood's eye movements. "The keys!" He looked at Marja. "Sorry, kid."

He wouldn't fire until he had the keys, Flood realized, frantically trying to think of a way to delay. The man must have left his own car at Cape May. Couldn't have a locked car on the ferry when it docked. He had hoped to take them here. If that failed, he would go with them in her car. A quiet byway in the woods later. Murder-suicide. No one would question that, not after Natalie and Flower.

"The keys!"

Marja reached inside her satchel. Willie grabbed her wrist and she cried out softly. He raised her hand slowly out of the bag. Dangling from her fingers were the keys.

An elderly couple appeared at the railing of the deck above and stared down at them. Flood realized they couldn't see the gun. "Hi!" he called to them.

Marja grunted in astonishment and Willie let go of her wrist and yanked the gun back to conceal it. The couple regarded Flood with disdain and moved back. Willie turned quickly, long enough to see them disappear. He backed up a step.

Flood jumped forward to grab the gun but stumbled and fell at Willie's feet. Willie jabbed the gun down toward him. Suddenly Marja leaned forward and grabbed his gun arm and jerked him forward. His feet hit Flood's legs and flipped him upward. He struck the railing on his stomach, his legs flew into the air, and in an instant he was gone. A muffled shout was all that was left of his presence as he hurtled, head downward, off the stern.

Flood scrambled to his feet and rushed to Marja's side. They peered down at the water. Nothing. Then Flood pointed a few yards to the rear, where the foaming wake was turning a frothy pink. He had been sucked into the propeller.

"*Dosvidanya*, Willie," Flood muttered.

Marja leaned over the railing and vomited. Flood held her, terrified he would lose her now that they were safe.

"*Mal de mer* on a day like this? Bless my soul!"

Flood turned and saw an old man wearing a black

suit and a black chauffeur's cap. He had a seamed face and was smiling at them.

"My wife's sick," Flood answered as Marja retched again. Had the man seen? he wondered. Was he Willie's backup?

"The best thing for the gorps is a bit o' luck, guvnor," the old man said, and thrust forward a gnarled hand holding a packet of New Jersey lottery tickets. "Try your luck?"

Marja straightened up groggily and Flood held her as she buried her face against his shoulder. He couldn't hear her above the ferry's throbbing engines but he could feel the sobs racking her body.

"Five for five!" the old man cried.

Flood shoved a hand into one pocket and brought out some singles. "Two," he said.

He drove off the ferry and on toward Washington while Marja lay face-down on the back seat, silent except for a low moaning cry now and then. She had hoped to kill one of those men who had filled her life with pain and terror, he knew. Now she had and she was torn by more pain and terror. Seeing the pink foam again, he wanted to comfort her but left her alone; it was her triumph, her desolation.

After half an hour, she sat up and blew her nose. "I'm all right," she said. "Maybe I should drive."

Flood nodded and pulled off the road. It would distract her. Besides, he thought, she was better at it.

At a little after eight-thirty that night Marja stopped in front of a small French restaurant off Connecticut Avenue not far from Du Pont Circle, in northwest Washington, and Flood got out. A few minutes later she put the car in a garage and checked in at the Jefferson Hotel, a quiet place he knew that had a self-service elevator and no doorman. She signed the register Mrs. Barnard Trevelyan. After showering and changing back into the clothes she had worn when she met Flood in Central Park, she took a taxi back to the restaurant. He was sitting at a small table near the rear morosely staring into a glass of whiskey.

"How long do we have?" she asked.

Flood looked at his watch: 9:20. "An hour." While she had been at the hotel, he had made sure that Briggs would be in all evening, by making an urgent appointment, through the housekeeper, under the name of an influential White House correspondent. Using the same reporter's name, Flood had also found out that President Gilfedders would be at work, as usual, in the Oval Office until his implacably set bedtime hour of ten o'clock. Nothing, it was said, had ever altered his retirement time and nothing ever would. Flood smiled; tonight would be different.

"What's in the attic?" Marja said suddenly.

"Stop. I can't tell you."

"Never?"

"Never." He realized that he must not even let her know his destination tonight. She probably imagined he was going to the Pentagon or the CIA. Let her go on thinking so, he told himself. If McCade found her, she would have nothing to tell him except that she had last seen Flood in Washington. Once McCade knew he was headed for, or had seen, the President, he would know that the secret was out. Then he would kill her.

They ate in silence and afterward Flood ordered coffee and brandy. She smiled at him, her expression full of wonder. Then they talked idly about places they had each liked in Europe. Indirectly, he knew, they were discussing the future. He wondered if there were any chance of a future for them together and then wondered if that was what he wanted. He didn't know, not yet.

"I think my favorite country is Switzerland," she said. "The peace is overwhelming."

"Stultifying is more like it," he replied. "There's something wrong with any country where you don't have to lock your car at night."

She laughed. "My kind of place."

God, I like her, he thought and looked away. "I've got to go soon," he said, turning back to her. "Tell me what you're going to do—not too much but something, so I'll know."

"I'm going to wait."

"How long?"

"Until you call."

His gratitude nearly brought tears to his eyes and he quickly said, "If I don't call by Monday, leave. When you get settled someplace let me know. But be careful. Not by letter and not at the paper. Through someone you trust."

Marja nodded. "You're not worried now, are you?"

"Just cautious," he answered. "A habit I picked up in the past few days." He stared at her longingly, then took out his billfold. It was ten-thirty.

She shook her head. "It's my treat."

Flood felt the tears coming again. "I wondered when you'd get around to paying me for last night."

"No, it's for this morning," she said. She tried to smile but her lips trembled and her eyes filled with tears.

Flood knew there was nothing more to say. He rose.

"Be careful, please," she said. A tear ran down her cheek.

Flood nodded. He bent down and kissed her and left.

# 2

Senator Philip Briggs's house—or rather Katherine Briggs's house—stood on a corner of one of the most fashionable streets in Georgetown. A spacious rose-brick residence of three stories with a large garden, the house was nearly covered with Virginia creeper, which was turning its autumnal red. Before going into politics, Briggs had been a successful tax lawyer and by the time he was thirty-three he had accumulated a modest fortune. But Katie Briggs had inherited six million dollars from her father and stood to get a lot more when her mother died. Katie Briggs was a decent woman and was passionately concerned about the social causes she supported. She was also passionately unforgiving when she felt betrayed. Flood hadn't seen the Briggses since Ellen's funeral. Katie had stared at him coldly and left without speaking. And the Senator had stood, torn by his loyalties, and had finally touched Flood on the shoulder, murmured, "Sorry, John, please forgive her," and followed Katie away from the grave.

Standing before the polished black door of the house, Flood thought of the cemetery below the river. He hadn't forgiven Katie or Phil. He shrugged and pushed the bell. He wouldn't let Briggs walk away now.

A maid answered and Flood identified himself by the name he had used over the phone. She took him into a serene oak-paneled library and asked him to wait. Flood sat down in a red-leather club chair and looked around—at the rich Oriental carpet and heavy red-velvet curtains, the wall of lawbooks, the large cherry desk with pictures of the Briggses' five splendid-looking children. Wherever Phil Briggs had ended up, Flood thought, he would have had a room like this. It announced his substance.

Briggs had been elected to the Senate at the age of

thirty-four and by the time he was re-elected, at forty, he was one of the most respected members of Congress. Although he hadn't been in the Senate long enough to become chairman of a full committee and had little direct power, his influence was large because his colleagues respected him for his decency, his plainness, and his unpretentious morality. As Flood saw Briggs, he was a man of ordinary integrity, but in Washington that made him extraordinary.

On one wall of the study was a photograph of the Briggs family at the victory celebration when he was first elected to the Senate. Flood recalled the event and remembered how the mayor of New Richmond, who had switched parties at the last minute and endorsed Briggs, introduced him at the celebration. In a rambling speech, the mayor dwelt on his own bravery in deserting his party and then got his concluding cliché wrong by saying, "It all goes to show you that the old adage is true: 'Politicians make strange bedfellows.' " Briggs jumped up from his seat on the dais and in mock alarm shouted, "No, no! It's politics that makes strange bedfellows, not politicians. I'm in enough trouble with my wife as it is!" He brought down the house.

The door to the study opened and the Senator came in. He was wearing an open-necked blue shirt, a dark-red cardigan, rumpled gray trousers, and dirty desert boots, and his old-fashioned horn-rimmed glasses were halfway down his nose. In the past few years Flood had often seen his picture in the papers and had occasionally watched him in televised interviews and Briggs hadn't seemed to have changed much. But as he stepped forward Flood saw how much he had aged, how worn he looked, how disillusioned.

Briggs peered over the top of his glasses as Flood got up, then stopped in mid-stride and lowered the hand he had extended. "John. What the hell—?"

"Hello, Phil. I'm sorry to have used that subterfuge to get in here," Flood said, holding out a hand. "It was necessary."

Recovering, the Senator clasped his hand warmly.

"I'm sorry it was necessary—or that you felt it was. You should know you're always welcome here."

Despite the warmth of his words, there was something evasive about his manner, Flood thought. "And Katie?" he asked.

Briggs frowned. "She feels bad about all that, John. So do I. We've talked about it a hundred times. We've vowed to get in touch with you. But you know—"

"It's the sort of thing one puts off. Is she here?"

"She and the kids are at her mother's for the weekend."

"Good."

"I'm sorry you feel that way." Briggs looked at Flood's dyed hair, then motioned him back to the easy chair and sat down in another across from him.

"It's not that I feel *that* way," Flood said, trying to sound at ease. "Under the circumstances it's better is all. I have to talk to you about something extremely sensitive and I have to ask you not to discuss it with Katie. If she's not here, that makes it easier."

"All right." The Senator looked at him in silence over the top of his glasses.

Flood wondered why Briggs hadn't said anything about his hair. It might be only his innate politeness if he thought an old friend was trying to look younger. Or it might be his uneasiness at the sudden reappearance of someone he didn't want to see. Or it might be that he had heard about the murders from his New Richmond office. Flood realized that he had no choice now but to explain.

"I'm in trouble, Phil—very bad trouble," he began.

The Senator waited calmly. He was a different man, Flood realized—a man used to trouble. He lived with it every day—political trouble for himself and the sea of troubles the nation always seemed about to founder in. Briggs was the kind of man who takes the country's problems more seriously than his own. That must be why he had aged so, Flood thought, waiting for some reaction. But Briggs gave no sign; he waited.

"I'm being framed for a murder, maybe two murders," Flood blurted.

The Senator's expression didn't alter as he asked, "And you want my help?"

Flood was insulted. Not that kind of help, he thought. And he was angry. Briggs clearly knew the story and was letting him writhe. "If they were just ordinary murders, no one could help me," Flood said, trying to keep his anger out of his voice. "I'd never ask you to intercede for me in something like that. It would finish you politically and it wouldn't help me. You should know that."

"Then?" Briggs had leaned forward a little but was still casual, seemingly unconcerned; they might have been discussing the World Series.

"You've heard about the charge against me?"

Briggs nodded. "George Barrington called an hour ago. He said you were implicated—'deeply implicated' were his words—in the rape and murder of a woman in New Richmond. He said you might also be implicated in the murder of a police lieutenant. George thought you might turn to me for help and asked me to let him know if you did. He wants to talk to you before the police do."

At least it was the publisher and not Rogers, Flood thought. Whatever the old man's flaws, he was fair. "Are you going to call him back?"

"What happened?"

"I can't tell you, Phil. I'm sorry. All I can say is I'm innocent." His voice trailed off; all murderers said that.

"You never trusted me, did you? Not really."

"I trusted you—and trust you—more than any other man, or any other politician I've ever known," Flood said firmly. "You hurt me is all. You and Katie. But I still believe in you. If there were ninety-nine other men in that Senate like you, I'd sleep better."

The Senator smiled. "But *I* wouldn't."

Flood grinned. "That's why I trust you."

"Not enough to tell me why you were framed."

"Not won't—can't."

"Can you explain that at least?" Briggs crossed his legs lazily.

"Someone thought I'd learned something. But I hadn't."

"That's real helpful. Come on, John—"

"They killed that woman because she *had* learned something and they thought she had told me. So they killed her and tried to frame and kill me, too."

Briggs shook his head in confusion. "What do you want from me?"

"You've got to get me in to see the President."

The Senator stared at him openmouthed. "You must be mad!"

Flood knew that he was going to have to tell him more, perhaps all of it. He was well aware that the last thing a politician wants to know is a true state secret; if it's leaked, he may be blamed and opponents are sure to attack him for betraying the nation's vital interests. Nothing, Flood knew, was more dangerous for a professional patriot than being accused of being unpatriotic. "I can't tell you," Flood said. "Believe me."

Senator Briggs got up and went to the telephone on his desk. "This isn't a threat, John," he said. "It's a fact. I'm going to call Barrington because I promised to. Then I'm going to call the Washington police because it's my duty as a citizen." He turned away and picked up the phone.

Flood took out the automatic and pointed it at Briggs's back. "Don't do that."

Briggs looked around and saw the gun. "You're not that much of a fool," he said coolly and began dialing.

"If I'm such a fool as to kill a helpless woman and shoot a policeman in the back, to dye my hair, to run away, to come here under an assumed name, to aim a loaded gun at your heart, I'm enough of a fool to pull the trigger. What do I have to lose?"

The Senator stared at him for a long time, then put down the phone. He went back to his chair and sat down. "Tell me what happened and if it makes any sense, I'll try to help. But first please put down the gun. Guns make me nervous."

Flood smiled. "You voted against the gun-control bill just last month."

"I'm a politician," Briggs said with a shrug. "A politician isn't worth much if he isn't in office."

"Over three-quarters of the American people want a strict national gun law but the gun nuts stop it every time," Flood said, his voice rising in anger. It was an issue he had written about repeatedly, without effect.

"In this business it's your enemies, not your friends, who count," the Senator replied mildly.

"So much for representative government."

Briggs looked at the gun and smiled. "If those things bother you so much, what are you doing with one?"

Flood looked abashed. He hadn't thought of that. Then he smiled, too. This was the only time the god-damn gun had been of any use to him, he thought— to stop a man, who wouldn't vote against the insane spread of guns in America, from calling the police to capture a man holding a gun on him. Flood grinned and lowered the automatic onto his lap.

"Thanks." The Senator sat back. "Anyway I'm sure you didn't come here to discuss Edmund Burke."

The remark took Flood back twenty-five years to the endless discussions the two young men had had at Yale on political philosophy. He looked at Briggs fondly, remembering him as he had been then. Now it was time to talk. "Is this room secure?" he asked.

"No room in Washington is secure. What the Russians don't have bugged, Gilfedders does. I wouldn't be surprised if the whole town was wired."

"I've got to see the President," Flood said, leaning forward.

"I've told you—you're mad even to suggest it."

"Even if the country's survival is at stake?"

"Tell me why."

"Believe me, Phil, you don't want to know."

"But what I should want," Briggs said, "is to get an accused murderer into the presence of the President of the United States."

Flood knew that he couldn't tell part of the story; it would have to be the whole thing now.

"Look," Briggs said, waving a hand. "Even if I wanted to help you, I doubt that I could. Gilfedders doesn't care for opposition from members of his own party and I've opposed him on some crucial issues. He doesn't like me. In fact he detests me. I ran into his wife at a party a couple of weeks ago and just her look gave me heartburn. She asked me if there was anything the President could do for me back home. You know how unpopular he is there with labor, farmers, businessmen. So I told her, 'Yes, he could publicly call me a son of a bitch.' "

Flood laughed.

"The White House sent me a note a few days later saying the President had my request under advisement."

Flood laughed again.

"Yeah, he's funny—if you like mean humor. He's meaner than hell and smarter than he is mean. He knows everything that goes on in this town and hates everything he knows."

Flood was beginning to relax. He needed time now before he told him. "Could I have a drink, Phil?"

Briggs looked surprised. "I heard you were up to your ears in the stuff," he said. "Do you plan to go see him as a drunken accused murderer?" He got up. "Still Jack Daniel's?"

"Yes."

"Be right back." He left the room.

Flood looked down at the gun. In a moment Briggs could be on the phone. Flood started to get up but sat down again. He hadn't realized before that putting a gun on a friend like that had taken all the will he had; he knew he couldn't do it again.

The Senator returned with a silver tray holding a bottle of Jack Daniel's, a bottle of J & B, an ice bucket, a flagon of water, and two tall glasses. "You let me go alone," he said as he put down the tray.

"I trust you."

"Don't. Trust no one in this town." He made two drinks and handed one to Flood.

"I've got to trust you," Flood said and took a long drink. "And you've got to trust me. Where can we talk safely?"

The Senator sipped his drink reflectively for a minute, then said, "Give me the gun." Without hesitating, Flood handed it to him and he put it in a drawer of his desk. "Okay," he said, "come on."

On their way out of the room, Briggs turned to him and asked, "Do you actually think you're going to see him tonight?"

Flood nodded.

"You really must be crazy. It's nearly eleven. You know he won't allow anyone to disturb him for *any* reason after ten. And on Saturday night?"

"That's what I waited for. Fewer people around."

Briggs looked at him suspiciously and went on. Flood picked up the bottle of bourbon and followed him—along a broad hallway to the dining room and out through some French doors into the garden. Briggs stopped at a wood table and put down his drink. He picked up a white wicker chair beside the table and nodded to Flood to do the same, then walked over beneath a large magnolia tree. He put his chair down and while Flood was placing his at an angle beside it, Briggs went back near the house and picked up a garden hose. He returned with the nozzle in one hand and when they were seated he turned it on. When a sizzling whooshing sound began, he nodded to Flood.

Taking a swallow of his drink, Flood leaned forward until his mouth was only a few inches from the Senator's ear. In a low voice, just above a whisper, Flood told his story as rapidly as he could, leaving out only Marja's presence on the way south.

Senator Briggs listened without interrupting until Flood described the nuclear missile. Then his head fell back against the top of his chair. "Oh my God," he said softly. He rolled his head slowly back and forth, his eyes closed, and again said, "Oh my God." From that point on, he listened with his head back, his eyes still closed, except when Flood told of his escape from McCade and the dog. Then he sat forward slowly and stared in admiration at his old friend. At the end he turned off the hose and in the sudden silence said, "I apologize again, John. I'm sorry for what you've been through."

Flood nodded and they got up and went back to the study. Briggs opened a thick address book, leafed through it, and dialed a number on the phone. "This is Senator Philip Briggs," he said after a moment. "May I speak to General Burkover, please?"

"You're not going to tell anybody else—" Flood began.

Briggs silenced him with a wave of his hand. He waited and a few seconds later he said, "General, I hope I haven't disturbed you but there's something of extreme urgency that has just come to my attention. I want you to call the President at once and ask him to telephone me at my home."

He paused, listening, then continued, "I'm well aware of his rule. I know it's absolute but this is more than an absolute emergency. I assure you, General, with no personal animus on my part, that if you fail to do as I ask you will be dismissed from the service within five minutes of the President's learning that you refused my request. The survival of the United States is at stake." Again he paused, then nodded. "Thank you, General." He hung up.

Without speaking, the two men resumed their seats and drank their whiskey and waited. In less than five minutes the phone rang.

Briggs answered and quickly pulled the receiver away from his ear as a series of shouted obscenities burst from it. As soon as they subsided, he said into the phone, "I will accept your apologies later, Sir." That set off another outburst and with a grin at Flood the Senator removed the receiver again. Finally he said into it, "Mr. President, naturally I would never have even considered disturbing you except for the gravest emergency. I trust that General Burkover—" Another stream of curses ensued and Briggs said, "Yes, Sir, but you chose him as military aide, not I."

Again he grinned at Flood, then grew serious. "Mr. President, a man whom I have known since boyhood has just come to see me with a discovery he accidentally made. It constitutes the gravest threat to this nation's survival in its history. . . . His name is unimportant right now, Sir. Your phone may be secure but I'm not at all sure mine is. I vouch for this man absolutely. I want to bring him to see you at once, so he can tell you himself."

Briggs pulled his head away from the phone to avoid another shouted imprecation, then said in a low voice that was almost menacing, "Mr. President, I would be criminally derelict in my duty as a member of the Senate and as a citizen if I had not done what I'm doing. And you, Sir, will be even more so and responsible for the disastrous . . . Nor do I *like* talking to you, or anyone else, this way, Sir. . . . All right, if you insist. The subject is an imminent enemy attack on the United States without any possibility of our retaliation."

That did it. A minute later he said, "Thank you, Mr. President," and hung up. He took out a handkerchief and wiped off his face.

"Well?" Flood asked.

"He'd be delighted to see you—in hell."

Flood slumped back in his chair.

"But he has agreed—you must have heard with what enthusiasm—to see you in person first. We have been invited to get our asses over there. He's sending a car."

Briggs looked at Flood appraisingly and said, "We used to be close enough in size to wear each other's clothes. I think it would be better if we get dolled up a bit. He's fussy as hell about things like that—considers anything less than impeccable an insult to the office. That is, to Gordon Gilfedders. He looks at everyone who comes into the place as if at any moment they're liable to piss on his carpet."

# 3

The two men were standing on the steps of the house —Flood in the first three-piece suit he had ever worn and Briggs in a double-breasted suit and a polka-dot bow tie—when the limousine arrived. They got in and it pulled away immediately.

"I'm almost as scared as when I saw the goddamn thing," Flood said quietly.

Briggs glared at him, with a warning flick of his eyes toward the driver, and Flood nodded, almost imperceptibly. He was annoyed with himself for the remark and miffed at Briggs for the reprimand. Both had been unnecessary. Briggs's cool demeanor made him feel like a schoolboy. Finally his irritation and the imposed silence drove him to speak. "I was pretty hard on you in my column on your vote against gun controls."

"That's okay," Briggs said. "You were right."

"You mean the piece helped you with your enemies, the gun nuts, but didn't hurt you with your friends?"

"There *is* that," the Senator admitted.

Flood could see his smile in the dim light and was infuriated. Would it be the same in the White House? he wondered. Feeling foolish but unable to stop, he went on, "A country that doesn't control guns can't possibly call itself civilized. And no man who votes against gun controls can call himself a fit representative of the people." It was out and he felt more foolish than before.

"You're probably right again," Briggs replied, unruffled.

"If you can't do that, why do you want to be a senator?"

"Most of the time I don't," Briggs said and patted Flood's knee, as if to remind him of their old comradeship. "If I vote for gun controls, I won't be there to vote for limiting nuclear weapons. That's the real issue. It's not the little guns, it's the big bombs."

"They're the same," Flood said angrily, remembering the missile. "Fire one and you're ready to fire the other." It was pointless, he thought and turned away.

The limousine swung onto E Street, sped around the rear of the White House grounds, slowed to turn into West Executive Avenue, and pulled up near the guardhouse on the right. A uniformed guard came around the front of the car and the driver rolled down his window and said, "General Burkover's guests." The guard looked into the rear of the limousine and waved them on. The car headed up the curved drive to a canopy at the South Portico and stopped.

Brigadier General Charles Burkover was waiting. In World War II Burkover had been an infantry sergeant at Anzio, where his actions under fire saved the lives of nearly a thousand men who had been sent to hold an untenable position by an inept commander. Sergeant Burkover was awarded the Silver Star and a battlefield commission and he decided to stay in the Army. He had been a good soldier and was a decent man—plain and trustworthy. It was said that Burkover couldn't betray anyone; it was also said that this was the sole reason President Gilfedders had chosen him as his military aide.

Burkover opened the rear door of the limousine and the two men got out. "Hello, Senator," he said, his voice deferential. "The President has asked me to join you."

"Good," Briggs said. "We're going to need you, General." He introduced Flood and added, in a low voice, "It might be better for now if he's not officially registered."

General Burkover nodded and led them to the double door and into a large foyer. As Flood stepped inside, he felt safe for the first time since he had left Treats on Tuesday night. Jesus, he thought, only four days ago.

A man in a dark suit who had a walkie-talkie in one hand and a radio-receiver button in one ear approached them. He had a hard wary face and Flood knew he was Secret Service. The General said something to him and he nodded and stepped aside, still watching them closely, and spoke into the walkie-talkie. Burkover led the other two toward an alcove at the left where there was an elevator and they got on in silence. At the second floor they emerged, turned to the left, took a few steps along a narrow corridor, and entered a long and broad hallway furnished like a living room. Another Secret Service man was waiting. He spoke into his walkie-talkie, then nodded to the group.

General Burkover led the way down the long room to a door on the far right, beside a large fan window at the end, and they entered a room about twelve by sixteen feet. It was painted pale yellow and a fire was crackling in the gray-marble fireplace. Two wing chairs in pale-blue-and-yellow-patterned silk were set at angles facing the fireplace at the edge of a rich Chinese rug in dove gray with a deep-blue border. Elsewhere in the room were a camelback sofa covered in a gray-blue velvet, a long coffee table in front of it, an antique pine table against one wall, and a couple of wood armchairs. General Burkover asked them to wait and left.

"The Lincoln Sitting Room," Senator Briggs said.

Flood looked at a picture of Lincoln over the mantelpiece and recognized it as the Gardner photograph, taken three days after the Battle of Gettysburg. Everything of Lincoln was in the picture: melancholy, simplicity, wit, kindness, sensitivity, and perhaps the most profound intelligence America had known.

"The poor bastard," Flood said, looking at Lincoln's eyes, which seemed to be fixed on some internal distance, as if he had been looking not at the camera but at the corpses of the thousands of men littering the hills and meadows at Gettysburg.

"This place is colder than Gilfedders' heart," Senator Briggs muttered and moved closer to the fire.

One aspect of the President's character that had particularly endeared him to the American people was his parsimony. He wouldn't spend a dime that wasn't essential to the survival of the Republic and had stripped the White House operation of all frills and many necessities. Among the latter was heat for the Mansion. His Scottish blood ran colder at the thought of spending money than at low temperatures, so he ordered the thermostats set at sixty degrees throughout the winter. To his less reverent aides, the President was known as Old Chilblains.

The door opened and Gordon Gilfedders entered, followed by Burkover. The President was not as tall as Flood had expected. Of medium height, he was broad-shouldered, with a bulging chest, his pugnacious face thrust forward belligerently. He had thick sandy hair parted near the center and bristling sandy eyebrows. Flood's heart pounded at the sight of him. The President, wearing blue-and-white-striped pajamas, an old brown-wool dressing gown, and black-leather slippers, snarled, "All right, Briggs, what the hell is this?" Without waiting for an answer, he sat down on one of the easy chairs and glowered at the Senator.

"This is Mr. John Flood," Briggs said mildly, looking at the President with unconcealed distaste. "He's a newspaperman from my state, a columnist on the New Richmond *Herald,* and an old and close friend. He has discovered something of uncommon interest."

The President grunted, "Get on with it, Mr. Flood."

Before Flood could speak, the Senator said, "If you'll allow me, Mr. President, I believe it would be better if you heard Mr. Flood's story in private. I'm sure that's the way you'd want it if you knew the circumstances."

Being told what he wanted was usually enough to send President Gilfedders into a rage, but now he merely stared balefully at Briggs and said, "You look like a flit in that bow tie."

The Senator smiled. "Flits don't wear bow ties, I'm told. It's my cover."

The President grunted again. "All right." He turned to General Burkover and said, "Charlie, you and Briggs wait outside."

"I don't think I'll be needed any longer," the Senator said. "If you want me, I'll be at home."

"Wait outside," the President repeated.

Burkover and Briggs left the room and President Gilfedders turned to Flood. "Sit down," he said and waved toward the other wing chair.

Wondering if there was any chance of getting a drink, Flood sat down stiffly and waited for the President to speak. He stared evenly at Flood in silence, his small blue eyes appraising his face, then shifting to his body and finally down to his scuffed brown shoes. The President looked as if he had just smelled something bad. His eyes snapped back to Flood's face and he ordered, "For God's sake, man, get on with it!"

Choosing his words with extreme care, Flood began slowly with the evening at Treats and left out nothing, not his drunkenness, not the sexual encounter with Natalie, nothing. As he got further into the story he spoke more rapidly, leaning forward with his forearms on his thighs, staring at the President who listened without moving or interrupting. The story took nearly half an hour. Flood finished it with a quick string of lies about how he had been so near collapse when he reached New York that he had taken a hotel room and slept for sixteen hours and then had gone by taxi to Newark and caught the train to Washington. As he finished, he leaned back, waiting expectantly.

"I can't think of anything else that would have justified your dragging me out of a sound sleep," the President said.

Staggered, Flood stared at him. He wanted to shout with laughter at this supreme egomania. Instead he nodded and clamped his jaw shut. The man was insane, he thought. Of course all Presidents were insane. One had to be crazy to want such a job, let alone to fight for it for years on end. American elections presented the voters with a choice between madmen.

"Then you're wanted for murder?" the President asked casually.

"Maybe two murders."

The President shook his head. "Terrific security

we've got around here." He got up and Flood jumped to his feet. Without a glance at him, Gilfedders went to the door and called the two men waiting outside. They came in and shut the door.

"You were right, Phil," the President said. "Thank you."

The Senator nodded without replying.

"Not a word, not a hint—anywhere."

"Of course not," Senator Briggs said. He looked indignant.

"All right, I'll call you if you're needed."

Briggs nodded, raised a finger in farewell to Flood, and left.

The President turned to General Burkover. "Charlie, we've got a bad one on our hands by the sound of it —maybe the worst. Get Admiral Whitfield and Billy Caldwell over here at once." Burkover started to leave but the President stopped him, saying, "As soon as you've reached them, come back here with that tape recorder."

"Yes, Sir," the General said and left, too.

Flood realized that he had left out one detail— his taping part of the story and putting the cassette in his safety-deposit box—and now he told the President about it.

Gilfedders nodded and sat down. He motioned to Flood to resume his seat and said, "I believe you could do with a drink."

"I could, Sir," said Flood, feeling better at once.

The President rose and went to the telephone. Flood was on his feet instantly. Gilfedders waved him back to his seat. "For Christ's sake, sit down," he ordered. Flood obeyed and the President said, "Sometimes I get up, sit down, get up—just to remind whoever's with me who is President of the United States. I gather you know who he is." He ordered drinks, then came back and sat down. "This woman—Marja Voll, you said?"

Flood nodded, waiting nervously.

"You're certain she had nothing to do with this operation?"

"Absolutely. I'd stake my life on it. In fact I did."

The President was silent for a minute. "I like that code name—*Dosvidanya*," he said at last. "The subtlety and irony and humor of it aren't what one usually expects from the Russians. About all I've heard from their leaders are the kind of Polish jokes that make your ears bleed. Or the bathroom humor beloved by children everywhere."

Flood wondered if the man was in a state of shock from what he had just heard. To ease him back into the subject, Flood said, "If it hadn't been for Marja Voll, I'd never have found that missile."

"I wish you hadn't," the President said distractedly.

The drinks arrived and a white-jacketed black man served them unobtrusively. "Thank you," the President said. "There may be more to do tonight."

"My pleasure, Mr. President."

He left and Gilfedders said, "That's about the only reward of this job—the service is good here."

Flood smiled and waited.

The President raised his glass—a third of it filled with neat Scotch—and said, "You've done remarkably well, Mr. Flood. I salute you." He drank half the contents quickly, sighed, and put down the glass. "Scotch whiskey has saved the world," he said. "If it weren't for Scotch whiskey, the Scots would rule the world."

Flood laughed and drank half the contents of his glass, too. He liked this man.

President Gilfedders looked up at the portrait of Lincoln, as if to ask, "What would you do?" Then he got up and went to the south window. He stood for a few moments and gestured to Flood, who joined him. In the distance he could see the brightly lighted Washington Monument. "There are no precedents," the President said softly. He turned to Flood and went on, "Unfortunately my recent predecessors in this office all too often used that phrase 'national security' to extricate themselves from every mistake, to conceal every vicious act. At the same time they lived in dread that something actually threatening the nation's security would occur and they wouldn't be able to handle it. After all that blather about national security, any President's failure to protect it could mean only one thing: impeachment."

Flood looked at him in alarm. Was that his main concern? He remembered something Robert Kennedy had revealed after the Cuban missile crisis: that he had told his brother the President that if he let the Russians get away with it, he would be impeached. In military terms the missiles had meant little, since we already had Russia ringed with missile sites and missile submarines. But politically the President could have been charged with sacrificing the nation's vital interests. So John Kennedy had risked a world war to stay in office.

"Dart missiles," the President said flatly and went back to his seat. "If what you found is borne out, it means they can deliver payloads to wipe out the United States in less than two minutes."

"I know." Flood sat down again and leaned forward. "But our missile subs and SAC bombers?"

"They have to get the attack order first," the President said. "Who'd give it?" He paused gloomily, then continued, "Our entire defense strategy for years has been based on the premise that there would be enough time after they attack for our retaliation. That's the deterrent of course. Two minutes isn't enough time."

There would be no White House, no President, no Joint Chiefs of Staff, Flood realized. There probably wouldn't even be the button to push. He recalled reading that out West somewhere was an immense cavern deep under a mountain, in which all the means of taking over if the government was wiped out—including another President, a complete military staff, a Congress, a Judiciary—awaited doomsday. Their time was near, Flood thought. But what would be left to rule? The arms race had come to its demented conclusion.

The President finished his drink and got up to make another. As he poured the whiskey, he said, "The nations of the world spend a billion dollars a day on arms. Imagine what the world would be like if that money went for food and clothing and education."

Operation Eden, Flood thought. He got up, too, and went to replenish his drink. He added ice and whisky but no water. "Excuse me, Mr. President, but what are you going to do?"

President Gilfedders took a sip of his drink and looked at Flood. "I haven't the foggiest."

room where Charlie Burkoverd—the President broke

# Sunday

# 1

General Burkover returned carrying a black-leather box about the size and shape of a woman's vanity case and put it on the table next to the liquor bottles. "Whitfield and Caldwell will be here within half an hour," he said. "Do you want this switched on?"

"Not yet," the President replied. "Do you have one of those forms?"

Burkover nodded and took a folded piece of paper out of an inside pocket and handed it to him.

President Gilfedders turned to Flood. "I'd like you to repeat to General Burkover what you just told me," he said. "There is no man in the United States I trust more. What you have learned will have to be restricted to a very small group of people—only those who have the vital facts on which my decision shall be based. The tape recorder is merely to simplify matters so you don't have to tell your story over and over. The others can listen to it, whether you're here or not."

Flood wondered where he was going to be but before he could ask, the President went on, "Since Watergate, of course, all taping done in this building or any building temporarily housing the Presidency or any Presidential aides is permissible only with the explicit agreement of the people involved. If you agree, please sign and date this form."

He handed the paper to Flood, who read it quickly:

This document states, under personal oath, that I, _____, approve the tape recording of the statement that I am about to make and accept that it may be transcribed and/or shown or played to persons explicitly authorized by the President or his delegated authority.

Signed: _____
Date: _____

Flood took out his pen and signed and dated the document and handed it to the General.

"Mr. Flood," the President said, facing him, "you obviously can't leave here and go out to be pursued once more by the police and the KGB, so for now we'll put you up on the premises." He turned to Burkover. "Charlie, after the recording take Mr. Flood to the Sub-Four Level residential quarters. Have Caldwell and Whitfield join you in the lounge there. Sandwiches, coffee—plenty of coffee. I'll get dressed and make a couple of calls and meet you in half an hour." He left.

"Would you mind sitting there, Mr. Flood?" the General asked, gesturing toward the sofa. Flood took a seat at one end and Burkover placed the tape recorder on the coffee table in front of the sofa and sat down at the other end. He leaned over and pressed a button on the recorder. "Please begin."

Speaking more calmly this time, Flood identified himself and then recited the story, again leaving out no details besides Marja's driving him to Cape May and Washington. He watched Burkover carefully and saw his eyes bulge out and the color leave his ruddy face as he described the missile and again as he told about McCade's murder of Lieutenant Flower. But there was no sign of surprise when he described his escape—to Flood the most stunning part of the tale. Of course, he realized, he was here, so he must have escaped, and the feat would surprise only him. After all, the stakes were the survival of the nation and his life meant little, nothing actually, to these men. He hurried on with his story, impatient to get it over with, almost tired of it now despite its enormity.

When he finished General Burkover said, "Would you please state your name again and the date and that you have given this statement freely, without coercion."

Flood did as he was asked and Burkover got up. "It's time to go," he said. He closed the recorder and picked it up.

They left the Lincoln Sitting Room and went back to the elevator. The General pushed a button and the elevator slid downward. The basement, Flood thought, they must have some sort of extra quarters there. When the door opened he followed the General down a hall-way past a door marked Situation Room—a British euphemism for "crisis," he assumed—to another cor-ridor. Burkover stopped before an unmarked doorway with a button at one side and two locks. He took out a key ring with many keys and selected two, inserted one in the top lock and turned it, pressed the button, then inserted the other key in the bottom lock and turned it. The door swung open.

Flood walked through the doorway into the muzzles of two gun barrels—submachine guns held at the ready by two Army men standing side by side and looking very much as if they were prepared to fire.

"Burkover for freedom," the General said calmly and the men snapped to attention, with the guns at their sides, muzzles down.

As Burkover and Flood passed them, headed for another door, the General said, "Ace High will be along soon. He doesn't like having guns pointed at him."

The nearest soldier, a sergeant, snapped, "His orders, sir."

"I know," Burkover said. "But he still doesn't like it. Be easy on him."

To Flood's surprise, the next door opened into an-other elevator. Without a word he got on and the General joined him. The control panel contained six buttons, arranged horizontally rather than vertically, and General Burkover pushed No. 4. The door slid closed and they descended again.

Jesus, Flood thought, an underground complex beneath the White House. It made obvious sense but he'd never thought of it before. Of course they would need a bomb shelter, an emergency command center, perhaps a complete War Room in case the Pentagon was knocked out in an attack. The complex must have been built surreptitiously over the years, the way prisoners-of-war dig tunnels below their barracks and carry out the dirt in bags hidden in their pants legs—only on an immense scale.

The elevator stopped and the door opened. Obeying General Burkover's gesture, Flood walked out—into a room about fifteen feet square and painted white, with a door on either side. The General started toward the one on the right and pushed another button at its side.

"Identify!" a disembodied voice commanded.

"Burkover for freedom," the General answered. "And captive."

Flood looked at him in alarm.

"Down here that means 'friend,'" Burkover explained in a whisper.

Flood hoped that no one identified him as "friend."

A panel in the steel door swung open and a Naval officer peered out. The panel closed and the door opened. The officer stepped aside and Burkover strode into a hallway with Flood at his side. The hall was painted white, too, and was at least a hundred feet long, with closed doors down both sides. At the end Burkover opened another steel door, this one unlocked and unguarded, and they entered a large room that was painted a pale yellow and furnished with comfortable easy chairs and sofas upholstered in bright colors, tables, scatter rugs on the parquet floor, and floral curtains drawn closed. Flood stared at the last for a moment, then turned to his escort. "Curtains? Five floors down?"

"For the illusion," Burkover answered. "They're supposed to help in case one has to stay down here for a long time. Or so the psychologists claim. Make yourself comfortable. Would you like anything to eat? Coffee?"

Flood sat down and waited to be offered a drink. He knew that he shouldn't have another but he wanted one just the same. When Burkover didn't offer any, he said, "Some coffee would do. And a glass of ice water if it isn't any trouble."

"Nothing's any trouble in *this* house," Burkover said with a slight smile. He pressed a button on a nearby table, a door across the room opened, and a man in a white uniform came in. "There will be a small group joining us in a few minutes," the General told him. "You'd better fix three or four kinds of sandwiches—enough for six or eight—and plenty of coffee and tea. Right now we'll have a pot of coffee for two and one ice water, please."

The waiter left and General Burkover went to a desk where there was a telephone. He dialed three times and said, "This is General Burkover. When Admiral Whitfield and Director Caldwell arrive, please send them immediately to the Sub-Four Level lounge with an escort. Thank you." He came back to where Flood was seated and said, "While we're waiting I might as well show you your quarters."

Feeling exhaustion setting in again, Flood rose and followed the General, this time to a door across the room from the one they had entered by. It had no lock but another door, half a dozen feet beyond it, did. It wasn't engaged, though, and Burkover opened the door and stood to one side as Flood entered the hallway beyond, which was also painted white and was perhaps forty feet long. There were four doors on each side.

"The rooms are identical," Burkover said. "You can have any one of them."

Without replying, Flood chose the one on the right side at the far end and opened the door and flicked on a light. The room was small, almost a cell, and spartan in its furnishings—a narrow bed with a Navy blanket, a Formica chest of drawers, a small Formica desk, a straight chair in front of it, and a small easy chair covered in vertically striped red and blue fabric; the curtains on a single fake window were made of the same material and the walls were a pale blue. At one side was a bathroom and next to it a closet.

General Burkover went into the bathroom and opened the medicine cabinet. It contained assorted shaving equipment, toothbrushes, toothpastes, shampoos, talcum, combs, brushes, nail clippers, skin creams, and several different kinds of shaving lotion. He closed it and checked the chest of drawers. In the top drawer were several sets of white pajamas and in the two other drawers were various sizes and styles of shirts, socks, and undershorts. He opened the closet door and Flood saw three different-length white terry-cloth robes. The General closed the closet and said, "If you're here long enough to need a change of outer clothing, we have a sizable store of things. Just ask."

Back in the lounge, they found coffee and ice water waiting. As Burkover poured the coffee, Flood drank the cold water quickly, gratefully. They took their cups and sat down.

They drank in silence for a time and then the General said, "I found your story almost incredible, Mr. Flood." He took a sip of coffee. "You've been through a very hard time. And you've done extraordinarily well. A man trained in such matters couldn't have done better."

Flood was moved by the man's plain decency and thanked him quietly. "It was clear where my duty lay," he added.

"Have you ever been a soldier, Mr. Flood?"

Flood smiled and shook his head. "I'm afraid that I'm a civilian down to my bones."

General Burkover nodded. "You thought like a soldier and behaved like a soldier. I suppose at times all of us have to be soldiers."

A moment later the door they had first entered by opened and two men wearing white coveralls came in; each of them was carrying a long-handled electronic device shaped like a small vacuum cleaner. They nodded to the General and passed on through a door directly across from the entrance to the kitchen.

"They're going to sweep the Talk Room," the General said.

Flood looked bewildered.

"There's no reason you shouldn't know, since you'll be in there with us," Burkover continued. "Through that door is a room with multiple walls—boxes inside boxes, so to speak, with spaces between each. As far as we know it's bugproof but you can never be sure what new devices our adversaries may come up with, so it's swept electronically before each use. Those men sweep the Oval Office every morning, too, and check all the phones to make sure no bugs were planted during the night."

The outer door opened again and two more men came in—one wearing a Navy uniform and a cap with a visor laden with gold braid, the other wearing a chalk-striped gray-flannel suit.

Admiral Jeremy Whitfield, Flood knew, the Chairman of the National Security Agency. In his late fifties, the Admiral had steel-gray hair cut short, a thin ascetic face, and silver-rimmed glasses. He had been the captain of a carrier off Vietnam during the war and since then had been desk-bound in Washington. It was said that he wanted to go back to sea—as he had put it, "to clear the pestilential vapors out of my nostrils."

The civilian was William Caldwell, Director of Central Intelligence, who was universally known as Billy the Spook. Fifty, plump, owlish-faced, black-haired, he spent most of his spare time reading spy novels aloud to his wife at their home in Arlington and playing scoutmaster for a local troop.

General Burkover introduced Flood to the men and they looked at him quizzically, as if to say, "Are you what we were dragged away for?" He was amused; they would soon wish they hadn't been reachable.

"The President will be along shortly," the General said. The four men sat down. A few seconds later they rose as Gilfedders came in. He was wearing khaki trousers, brown Italian loafers, a dark-blue open-necked shirt, and a V-necked yellow cashmere sweater. He nodded to the group without speaking and sat down across from Flood, who watched him covertly, wondering what horrors, what desperate alternatives he was weighing. The waiter returned, carrying a large tray with platters of sandwiches, pots of coffee and tea, and a large chocolate cake.

"I'd have some coffee, Charlie," the President said after the waiter left.

Burkover brought him a cupful of black coffee and the President hunched over it and slurped some noisily. Flood was put off by the man's need to assert his power even in these small ways: first by turning the General who served him into a servant and then by showing Whitfield and Caldwell his disdain for their use of manners as a basic measure of a person.

Finally Gilfedders put down the cup and said, "I've asked Springer and Wirkowski to join us." No one spoke and he went on, "Billy, who's that new fellow of yours in charge of clandestine operations?"

"Baker—Don Baker," the Director of the CIA said.

"I think we should have him here as well," the President said.

Caldwell nodded and went to the phone. He dialed, waited a few moments, then spoke in a quiet voice, his back to the others so they couldn't hear.

A born conspirator, Flood thought. He didn't trust even the President of the United States to hear him invite a subordinate to a meeting.

Caldwell hung up and turned to the President. "I think he was locked in coitus but he said he'd be right over."

Gilfedders grimaced at the schoolboy humor and asked Burkover for more coffee. As it was being poured the two overalled men who had been in the Talk Room emerged and when they saw the President they quickly left by the main door.

The group sat in awkward silence and at last the door opened again and a tall stooped man with receding wiry black hair, thick glasses, and a large mouth came in. Dr. Amos Springer, Flood said to himself with distaste. He had interviewed Springer several years before when he was at the Center for Strategic and International Studies and had found him arrogant, egocentric, and usually wrong. Since becoming Special Assistant to the President for National Security Affairs, Springer had proved Flood right. Now he watched the man cross the room and was dismayed at the prospect that he might be listened to in this crisis. Academics had demonstrated that they were a disaster when given political power. Bundy, Rostow, Kissinger, Brzezinski, Flood thought and shook his head slightly. To show their own toughness they had all advised the most ruthless course—and left death in their wake. They were absolved from the charge of mass murder because they hadn't given direct orders to kill; they had given only advice. As Flood watched Springer lower his long fragile body onto a sofa, he wondered if this man, too, had to destroy others to demonstrate his courage.

A few minutes later General Winfred Wirkowski, Chairman of the Joint Chiefs of Staff, came through the door with all flags flying. If General Wirkowski had proved anything during his career, it was the need for civilian control over the military. Among members of the press and even many of his colleagues, his initials were said to stand for "World War." A fat bald man full of bluster, he had the kind of self-assurance that is possessed only by the very stupid. He greeted the President effusively, ignored Burkover, nodded to Caldwell and Springer, and roared at Admiral Whitfield, "Hello, there, you old pederast!"

Whitfield winced and managed a wan smile. At Annapolis there had been an unsupported rumor that Cadet Whitfield had been seen in a peculiar position with a faculty member's young son; the story was untrue but he had paid for it for thirty-five years.

After fifteen minutes more passed, President Gilfedders looked at his watch irritably. "We can't wait for your man Baker," he said to Caldwell. "His role may not exist anyway. Charlie," he went on, turning to Burkover, "you've heard the tape already, so you wait here and bring Baker in when he arrives. The rest of us will get started. Gentlemen?" He got up and the others jumped to their feet and followed him as he headed for the door to the Talk Room. Wirkowski grabbed a sandwich off the food tray and had consumed it by the time he reached the door.

Burkover called to Flood and handed him the tape recorder, saying hurriedly, "Push that button to rewind, then this one to play back." Flood nodded and carried the machine through the door and down a short corridor to a series of three doors close together —the sides of the three boxes, he assumed—and into a fairly small room, most of which was taken up by a conference table surrounded by leather armchairs. President Gilfedders sat down at one end of the table and the others quickly jockeyed for positions close to him. When they were seated Flood took the chair at the end opposite the President and put the recorder on the table in front of him.

"What the hell?" Gilfedders said, looking at the recorder.

"General Burkover asked me to bring it in and play it," Flood said. Then, emboldened, he added, "I'm told the hours here are long but the pension plan is generous and there's always leftover food."

The President didn't smile. "What if you changed your mind and erased the tape?"

"It's too late to change my mind," Flood said. He reached out and pushed the rewind button. As the tape whirred back to its start, he heard the door behind him open and close.

Burkover and a tall blond man in his early forties with buck teeth and an open face came up to the table.

"Hello, Don," Caldwell said. "Quick work. I could hear it pop out."

"Hello, Billy," Baker said and grinned boyishly. "I live only two blocks away, you know. Target zero." He bowed slightly toward Gilfedders. "Mr. President." He sat down two places away from Flood.

Burkover took the recorder and set it in front of an empty chair.

"Gentlemen," the President said, "the recording you are about to hear was taped less than an hour ago. The speaker is the gentleman opposite me. His words will speak more than abundantly. All right, Charlie."

General Burkover pushed a button and Flood's voice came out. The four men who hadn't heard the story listened intently but none as intently, Flood noticed, as the President. It had been said that of all his abilities his ability to listen was the foundation of his genius. He not only listened, he heard—and he remembered. To the astonishment of others, he possessed an uncanny way of pulling the small fact that seemed unimportant or even irrelevant out of the recesses of his memory and placing it in precisely the right spot in the context of otherwise senseless information. Now he didn't look at the other men but stared at the recorder, as if only it could tell him the answer—as if the men around the table were superfluous except to share responsibility.

Flood looked at the man on the President's right—Admiral Whitfield, who was sitting stiffly, his gray eyes slits behind the lenses of his glasses, his elbows on the table, and his slender fingers formed in a V before his face.

Next to him, Springer sat slumped back in his chair, his coat bunched up at the back of his neck. As the voice from the recorder described the body of the woman in the alley, his eyes gleamed but then he made a moue of disgust at the mention of the vomit in the window recess. Flood was reassured about his appraisal: to this man the murder of an innocent woman was more acceptable than the contents of someone's intestines.

As Flood's voice went on to describe his attempts to destroy the evidence linking him with the murder, he looked at Baker, the clandestine operations man, and wondered if this part of the story, especially the evidence Flood had found planted in his apartment, reminded him of his own work. Baker was sitting with his elbows on the table, his chin in his cupped hands, his expression blandly innocent.

On the President's left was Baker's boss, Billy Caldwell. His benign face was impassive as he listened but when the story reached the description of Flood's break-in at the flag factory Caldwell sat forward. His lips curved in a slight smile at the account of how Flood found that the brass eagle came apart. When Flood told about fitting in the small transmitter, Caldwell's eyes widened.

None of the men made a comment or a sound until the voice told of the list of government buildings at which the eagles had apparently been installed. At that, General Wirkowski came halfway up out of his chair, his neck bulging out of his collar, his eyes starting. And when Flood described the list of military bases the General cried, "Holy Christ!"

"Be quiet!" the President snapped.

Wirkowski reddened with embarrassment at the reprimand; the President was the only person in the world who outranked him. "Sorry," he muttered and wiped his glistening face off with a handkerchief.

Caldwell stared at Flood with admiration and bowed his head slightly. Flood nodded in return. As long as only he had known of his feat, it had seemed little more than a blind flight through terror. But now that others knew he could feel pride rising in him as the voice went on calmly, without a sign of drama, to tell the rest of the story.

When the narration reached the garage fire and Flood's entry into McCade's house, all the men except the President and Burkover sat forward. He could hear Baker breathing heavily through his mouth. Flood was amused: now *here* was a clandestine operation to end all clandestine operations, he thought, suppressing a smile. The voice told about climbing the rear stairs and entering Bell's attic room, and Baker turned to Flood and swung his head slowly to one side and then back and emitted a low sigh. He's going to try to recruit me, Flood thought. He had stopped listening to the recording but a moment later was jerked back to it by the sound of his voice—urgent at last—as he described the missile.

General Wirkowski pounded a huge fist on the table. "The cocksuckers!" he bellowed.

President Gilfedders glared at him in disgust.

Admiral Whitfield removed his glasses and rubbed his eyes with the tips of his fingers. Billy Caldwell stared openmouthed at the President, then at Flood. Baker's jaw trembled and he began sucking the end of one thumb. Springer watched him, fascinated, clearly longing to see him break down, then his own lips started to tremble. "Oh my God," he mumbled.

The remainder of the tape went quickly and when the voice told of Flower's murder, McCade's preparations for killing Flood, his leap across the room to knock out McCade, the flight from the cabin with the dog pursuing him, Caldwell looked down the table at him with open admiration. The recording concluded with Flood's only deception—his faked journey to Washington. That part sounded unlikely to him, since he had been so careful earlier to avoid train terminals. But he assumed that his listeners would be too stunned by the story to notice such a detail—except perhaps Gilfedders. Flood looked at him as the account ended but the President's face was as inexpressive as a bulldog's. Burkover leaned forward and turned off the recorder.

"Operation *Dosvidanya*—brilliant," Caldwell said, as if it had happened somewhere else.

Wirkowski was slumped back in his chair, his face red, his breath coming in gasps. He said, "The goddamn fucking—"

The President waved him to silence. "I had the story checked as far as I could in the time at hand," he said crisply. "The New Richmond police confirm that a woman identified as Wendy Cameron was found murdered in an alley exactly as Mr. Flood described. The fire department there confirmed that the garage on property owned and occupied by a Bruce McCade, president of United Flags, was destroyed by fire on Thursday night, probably by arson. The murder of Lieutenant Bertram Flower was by way of a customized Mauser fitted with a silencer. The gun was found under the bed at the cabin at the Guardian Motel on the outskirts of New Richmond. McCade—or Colonel Emil von Hoffen if Mr. Flood's story is accurate—is unconscious and under guard at the Good Samaritan Hospital. I have asked the FBI office there to double the guard, under the pretext that McCade is a suspect in an interstate auto-theft ring. All this was accomplished without a hint of what we might be interested in."

He paused and slowly looked at each man in turn. "Everything that you do from this point on—*everything*—must be undertaken without a word, even a suggestion, a smile, a raised eyebrow that might lead anyone in any way to suspect what's going on. I cannot emphasize this too strongly. Nothing—I repeat, *nothing*—that you have learned here or that you learn as we progress is to be passed on to anyone, even the most trusted subordinates. Certainly not to wives or mistresses. Anyone who breaks this security in even the slightest fashion will be—ah, fully disciplined." He smiled thinly.

Turning to General Burkover, he said, "Charlie, two agents from the FBI office in New Richmond will be at Miller Air Force Base headquarters in one hour. I want you to take a helicopter to Andrews and a plane to Miller at once. I want the brass eagle at HQ there carefully dismantled by one of the agents to see if it's equipped as Mr. Flood's report suggests. I want this done in the dark—tonight—with a minimum of attention. Get the agents some Army fatigues so they're not conspicuous. Under no circumstances are they to know the meaning of what they find. As soon as you have an answer, call me."

Burkover got up without a word and left the room.

"Now, Mr. Flood, I'm sure everyone will have some questions," the President said. "First, though, I have to say that you've done a remarkable job. The nation owes you its gratitude." There were murmurs of approval and the President added, "At least I hope it does. Now for the only question I have at the moment. That list of mysterious numbers you found in the order books at United Flags. Where is it?"

Flood took the small notebook out of the inside breast pocket of Senator Briggs's suit. He leafed through it and tore out several pages and handed them to Baker, who passed them down to the President. He looked at the pages one by one for a minute, then gave them to Whitfield and said, "Do these mean anything to you?"

Whitfield read through the numbers and shook his head. "If I may send these to our cryptography division, I should have an answer for you within a few hours."

"Excuse me," Billy Caldwell said, smiling politely, "but I think we're better equipped for a job like that. The CIA has always—"

"For the love of God!" the President snapped. "We're not going to have interagency rivalry over this, are we?"

Whitfield passed the pages across the President to Caldwell, who studied them for a couple of minutes and passed them on to General Wirkowski. He peered at them, his brow furrowed, and gave them to Baker, who looked them over and shook his head.

"Here," Gilfedders said, reaching for the pages. They were passed down the line to him and after glancing at the numbers for a couple of minutes, he handed them back to Admiral Whitfield. "Not cryptography—cartography," the President said. "I imagine someone in your office can read a map. Figure the numbers are latitude and longitude. The first three columns are degrees, minutes, and seconds of latitude and the second three columns are degrees, minutes, and seconds of longitude. Or the other way around. Okay?"

The Admiral went to the telephone, dialed, and began speaking in a low voice. Of course, Flood thought, flabbergasted by the speed of the President's mind. It must be the answer. But how could he have known? Flood looked down the table, feeling renewed confidence. With a man like this in charge, there was a chance.

"Are there any other questions for Mr. Flood while we're waiting?" the President asked. His square jaw was set like a clamp and Flood saw that he was annoyed by his aides' lack of readiness. Flood, for his part, was amazed by their irresolution. Not one of them, he thought, could have done what he had done in the past four days.

"I have a question," Dr. Springer said finally. He pointed a long wavering finger at Flood. "Did you kill that woman?"

Flood stared at him in astonishment. "I—" he began.

The President jumped up and the others rose, too. "Do you seriously contend that he concocted a tale like this to cover up a murder?" Gilfedders shouted.

"Stranger things have happened," Springer said weakly.

"No they haven't!" The President sat down again and so did the others.

"I'm curious about those clippings from the *Times* you found in the safe at United Flags, Mr. Flood," Caldwell said calmly, as if the outburst hadn't occurred. "They covered only the story of the Great Blackout?"

"As far as I could make out."

"A temporary code source, do you suppose?" Caldwell asked, almost idly.

"Mementos," the President said, glaring at him. "Mementos of the biggest smuggling job in history."

They looked at him blankly and then Caldwell gasped. "My God! That's how they got the missiles in?"

The President nodded, without satisfaction.

Dumbfounded, Flood stared at him. How could that answer have occurred to him? he wondered. It was uncanny. Then Flood wondered who the genius was on the other side who had the idea originally. The brilliance of the operation was staggering.

"Wasn't the electrical fault at Massena, New York, near the Canadian border?" the President asked.

"Yes," said Caldwell, still staring at him in disbelief.

"The entire northeastern United States and two Canadian provinces were blacked out, as I recall," the President said. "Eighty thousand square miles affected. Thirty million people groping in the dark. The perfect time."

"Excuse me, Mr. President, but that doesn't make sense," Wirkowski said loudly. "A hundred crates, two hundred for all we know. Nope. The risk would be indefensibly large. Out of the question as a military move."

"So was every great military campaign," Gilfedders said.

"How long did you estimate the missile in the attic to be, Mr. Flood?" Springer asked.

"About twelve feet, I thought. Under the circumstances it was hard to be sure—"

"Quite," Springer cut him off. "Say a dozen feet. The guidance system in the nose. Behind that the payload. The rear is the jet engine. So it could come in three sections for easier transportation. By the General's estimate they would have needed three hundred to six hundred crates. By my estimate more like three thousand. After all, we have a thousand missile silos scattered around the country." He smiled indulgently at Flood and turned back to the President. "I'm afraid that's too ambitious a delivery even for smugglers as accomplished as our Russian friends. Remember. A thousand silos. They'd have to knock out every one."

"One thousand and fifty-four silos, to be exact," the President said curtly. "But they don't have to knock out every one of them by a long—or should I say short —shot. All they have to do is get most of them. Destroy our overwhelming superiority—a three-to-one superiority before this—and they've won the war."

"Too risky," General Wirkowski insisted.

"They could have brought them in at twenty, even fifty places," Gilfedders replied.

"Even riskier."

The President looked at him disdainfully. "The risk seems to have paid off, General. At least one missile is in place. That proves motive. The blackout provided opportunity." He stopped and gave a hollow chuckle. "The enemy is here and we are theirs."

The others looked at him in alarm. Was he cracking under the pressure? Flood wondered.

Caldwell broke in quickly. "It's true our ICBMs are scattered but they're scattered in clusters—ten here, twenty there, forty elsewhere."

"Which means?" the President asked impatiently.

"In itself nothing," Caldwell answered. "But I now understand some information we've gathered in the past two or three years that, I'm afraid, may have been misinterpreted. Bits and pieces of intelligence data that filtered through from various sources abroad suggested the Russians have succeeded in what all of us have been working on since the first nuclear weapons were produced—very small bombs with very high yields. Easier delivery of course and greater effect. Anyway they seem to have developed an extremely small warhead with tremendous explosive capacity. If that's what they've got in the dart missiles, one of them might be able to take out an entire cluster of our silos."

"You succeeded in finding out they had such bombs?" Gilfedders asked.

Caldwell nodded and smiled modestly.

"But you failed to find out how the bombs are made?"

The smile vanished. "So far, I'm afraid."

"So am I—afraid as hell," the President snapped.

"But we concluded they were intended as tactical battlefield artillery for use against infantry," Caldwell added hastily. "Since you can't kill soldiers more than once, we decided that the high dispersion factor was merely overkill."

"But now it seems—"

"We were wrong."

"Two hundred of our mobile MX missiles are now operational," Wirkowski said. "Since they're constantly moved around, they can't be hit, except maybe by a lucky shot."

Gilfedders looked at him wearily. "If the Russians have transmitters to home in on at every military installation in the United States, they have transmitters on the MX trailers, too," he said. "Think, man! The eagle. The eagle doesn't head for a fixed target always. If it's after something moving, it soars, it swoops, it dives—and!" He slapped the table with a resounding crack.

Flood could visualize the missiles falling on their prey. He turned to Caldwell and asked, "Was the

Russian fishing fleet off the Grand Banks during the blackout?"

The others looked at him in surprise but Flood ignored them, emboldened by his awareness that he was more than their equal. "As a matter of fact it was," Caldwell said. "When the first reports of the blackout came in we doubled our surveillance of that part of the Atlantic coast, including surveillance of their fleet."

"And our military components guarding that area?"

"They were quadrupled. Units were brought from bases to the south, out of the blacked-out area."

Flood nodded. He saw the President watching him curiously.

"You're suggesting?" asked Gilfedders.

"That it was a feint, to draw our forces away from the southern coastline and from the Canadian border to the west into the blacked-out area and leave those places open."

This time it was the President who nodded. "I think you're probably right, Mr. Flood." He glanced around the table and added, "But it's irrelevant how they got the goddamned things in. The apparent fact is that the missiles are here. At least there's one here—at New Richmond. That's our operative truth. If there's one there may be hundreds."

Admiral Whitfield rejoined the group and sat down. He took out a handkerchief and cleaned his glasses. The President glared at him impatiently and at last the Admiral said, "They've checked the first dozen sets of numbers and are continuing with the others." He handed the notebook pages back to the President. "The first dozen seem to be, as the President anticipated, geographical locations. Each one is within ten miles of an ICBM silo cluster or a SAC base."

General Wirkowski groaned.

The Admiral went on, "The thirteenth of those tabulated is near a Project Whirlwind installation. As you probably know, there are seven sites in that project."

" 'For they have sown the wind and they shall reap the whirlwind,' " Flood said to himself. Probably a plan to wipe out what was left of mankind after all the other weapons had been used. He studied the men around the table for a few moments. They're mad, he thought. As mad as the men sitting around a table at the Kremlin, maybe at this moment, debating when Operation *Dosvidanya* should be put into its final stage. He recalled something else Robert Kennedy had said, in an interview a few years after the Cuban missile crisis: that during it there had been eleven men advising the President—the most dedicated, intelligent, patriotic men a leader could gather around him at such a time—and that if any one of seven of those men had been President the world would have been blown up.

"If they know about Project Whirlwind—" Wirkowski began.

"Excuse me, General," Caldwell broke in. "Could you wait just a minute?" He leaned over to whisper to the President, who listened without expression.

Flood watched them, thinking that it wasn't only the Russians or the Chinese who threatened the survival of the race, it was *all* the leaders of the world. *They* were the enemies. Plots and counterplots, he thought, when every minute should be spent on finding a way to peace. They were all mad, he said to himself again as he looked at the men around him. Bullies in the schoolyard, responding to every threat with a bigger threat. Only now the threats weren't childish boasts, they were nuclear megatons delivering megadeaths. It was inevitable. These children around the table, other children around other tables, would hurl mankind to its doom.

Flood saw that Caldwell had stopped whispering and that he and the President were looking down the table at him.

"Mr. Flood," the President said, "we have reached the point of discussing top-level secrets. The Director feels, and I'm inclined to agree, that you should leave the room."

Flood listened, stunned. There could be no greater secret than the one he had brought to them.

"I agree," General Wirkowski said, glaring at Flood

as if he had just been caught pocketing some White House silver. Baker nodded and so did Springer. Admiral Whitfield gave no sign of his feelings.

A minute earlier Flood had wanted to get away from these men; any decision they made was bound to be bad and he was bound to be contaminated by it. But now their attitude angered him. He looked at them again and wondered, Who are they? Which of them could have done the job I did? Only Gilfedders, he thought. His anger rose. They had made it to the top but who would want such power? Surely no sane adult. Flood glared down the table. Children, he thought again. He shook his head.

The President looked at him in surprise. "You want to stay?"

"I think I should," Flood said, feeling reassured by the calm strength of his own voice.

"If I ask you to leave, will you keep quiet about what you've learned?" The President watched him closely.

"A reporter keep quiet?" General Wirkowski snorted.

"It's his duty *not* to keep quiet," Springer said.

Flood looked at them with contempt. Even Gilfedders had seemed momentarily unhinged not long before. All it would take was one mad moment. Flood hesitated, wondering if he could bluff it through. With him there they would have to act with care. He leaned forward. "I found the missile and nearly got murdered doing it," he said in a low voice. "I got here in one piece, with the secret intact, against immense odds. I stand to lose exactly what you do—my country and my life. Why shouldn't an ordinary man share in your deliberations?" He stopped.

"You're no ordinary man, Mr. Flood," the President said. "If you were, you wouldn't be sitting here now." He paused to look intently at Flood. "You stay and your silence is guaranteed?"

"Yes, Mr. President."

Gilfedders smiled thinly, obviously impressed by Flood's audacity. It was precisely this kind of power play that Gilfedders understood best. Then, as Flood watched him, he wondered if the President was using him for his own ends. After all, he possessed the big secret anyway and now the best means of assuring his silence would be by giving him part of the responsibility for the final decision. That must be it, Flood thought, marveling again at the man's unerring sense of manipulation.

Looking amused, the President glanced around the table. "Well, gentlemen?"

"Let him stay," Whitfield said. "I see nothing to be lost by his presence."

Wirkowski looked stunned and shouted, "Throw him out!"

Flood turned to him. "Tell me, General, what have you ever done for your country but fatten off it for thirty years?"

The President grinned. "All right, the ayes have it," he said. "You shall stay, Flood."

Flood knew that he meant it. If he hadn't he would have called him Mister Flood. The curt use of his surname showed that he belonged. He nodded and sat back.

President Gilfedders said to Caldwell, "You had no warning, not even a hint that such an operation might be mounted and you made no plans for countermeasures?"

"A feasibility study was prepared on the subject a few years back," the Director answered. "But it didn't contemplate the installation, within the United States, of nuclear *missiles* by a hostile power. The conclusion was that nuclear weapons of modest size—what the authors of the study called suitcase bombs—could conceivably be smuggled across our borders and secreted in population centers. It was assumed that the targets would be our cities, not military installations, because of the difficulty in concealment at military bases. However, it was concluded that such an operation would be far too risky for the Russians—"

"Of course!" cried Wirkowski.

"—because they would have to assume that any such

attempt, if aborted, would mean instant retaliation and annihilation of an estimated twenty to fifty million of their people. As we all know, both sides have always imposed on themselves limits of hostility."

"Far too risky," the General insisted.

The President lost his composure. His eyes blazing, he turned on Wirkowski. "For Christ's sake, stop talking like a Polish joke!" he roared. "The fucking missiles are here!"

The General's face went purple but he sat back silently, his hands clenched in his lap.

Professor Springer immediately moved into the silence. "In addition to those unknown number of missiles then, there could be an unknown number of suitcase bombs secreted in our cities. In all likelihood, a first strike by us would set off an instantaneous electronic signal as soon as our missiles reached their Early Warning System to trigger both the dart missiles and the suitcase bombs. In other words, within three to five minutes after our launching—or twelve to fourteen minutes before our warheads reach their targets —the United States would be hit."

The President looked at him incredulously. "Hit? You mean destroyed?"

"One could say that," Springer replied calmly.

Jesus, Flood thought, the man *liked* thinking the unthinkable.

"The premise we have been proceeding on seems so flimsy as to be useless," Springer went on. "The Great Blackout was so long ago—nineteen sixty-seven as I recall."

"November ninth and tenth, nineteen sixty-five," the President said. The others looked at him in surprise and he continued, "An operation like *Dosvidanya* would require the most meticulous planning and the most scrupulous care in execution. A very large number of people would obviously be involved. Businesses like United Flags had to be set up, construction companies formed. Houses or other buildings in precisely the right locations had to be found and bought. The reconstruction of them, even if they weren't as elaborately equipped with computers as in McCade's attic, would have taken a long time. Besides, we have no way of knowing at this stage how long the missiles have been in place. It could have been for years."

"Forgive me, Mr. President," Springer replied, with a slight smile, "but in that period the missiles would have become obsolete. We've found that the average life-use of missiles has been a little under six years." He looked triumphant.

The President glared at him wearily. "If we had installed a more recent missile system ourselves within Russia, obsolescence might be relevant," he said. "Since we had neither the nerve nor the sense to undertake such an effort, their in-place operational missiles are more practical than tomorrow's most advanced model. All the missiles have to do is fly ten miles or less following a radio beam. Under those circumstances the *Spirit of St. Louis* could do the job."

Crestfallen, Springer sat back in silence.

"Aha!" Caldwell said and leaned forward eagerly. "If the missiles have been in place for more than a couple of years—if the entry was made during the blackout, above all—the warheads couldn't be the new high-dispersion, high-yield type. Far less bang for a ruble in the old ones."

"How much does one of the new warheads weigh?" the President asked.

Caldwell looked deflated. "Five or six pounds," he answered, averting his eyes.

"A few thousand pounds at most then," Gilfedders said. "Half a million pounds of drugs are smuggled into this country every year."

Everyone was silent until General Wirkowski leaned forward excitedly. "In fourteen months the first stage of the Cruise Missile System will be fully operational. Three thousand sure-striking nuclear missiles. They're cheap, only a million dollars apiece, and a hundred percent foolproof."

"That's fortunate," the President said.

"And twenty-four months after that we'll have eleven thousand of them," the General went on, his excitement mounting. "The Russkies can't possibly match it. The cruise missile is an air-breathing, pilotless vehicle that flies at five hundred miles an hour five hundred feet above the earth. It has a terrain-matching, contour-matching guidance system that allows it to stay that low, far under the enemy radar screen. The first batch of a thousand missiles will be mounted in our B-Fifty-twos. Then we'll put another six thousand on modified military and commercial transport aircraft— the Boeing Seven Forty-seven, the Douglas DC-Ten, the Lockheed One Ten-Eleven, the Air Force C-Fifty-four. The third batch, of eleven hundred missiles, will be installed in our theater nuclear forces, mainly in Europe. The fourth batch, six hundred and fifty, will go aboard the Polaris and Poseidon subs and surface attack vessels. Land, sea, and air—we'll have them by the *cajones*." He sat back, looking around the table expectantly.

"Twelve hundred and fifty of your missiles are missing, General," President Gilfedders said mildly.

Flood stared at him in astonishment; his mind must have automatically added up the figures as Wirkowski spoke.

"Anyway," the President went on, "I believe we are all aware of the cruise missile's wondrous potential— except possibly Flood."

"It's all been printed over and over in the *Times*," Flood said.

"Those pinkos," Wirkowski muttered.

"Your office gave them the information," the President told him. "In any event, we don't have fourteen months, let alone fourteen months plus twenty-four months. We may not have fourteen days. And if all eleven thousand cruise missiles were ready to fly, they wouldn't solve the problem—even a hundred dart missiles with a two-minute strike time. Then there may be suitcase bombs." He paused and rubbed his eyes, as if unable to believe what he was imagining.

Wirkowski's eyes gleamed. "Enough of our ICBMs, our submarine missiles, our SAC bombers would get through—"

The President stopped him with a wave of his hand. "Few or perhaps none of our ICBMs would get off the pad. The darts would see to that. Only the small force of SAC bombers already in the air would have a chance—a very small chance since the Russians could forget about using their ABMs against our ICBMs and concentrate everything in their arsenal on our bombers and submarines."

Gilfedders shook his head and fell into a gloomy silence, his chin on his chest. Maybe the Bible was true, Flood thought: God had given man a brain and an opposable thumb and what he had come up with finally was Armageddon.

At last the President looked up at Wirkowski. "If you were sitting in this chair, General—or, for that matter, any of the rest of you—would you strike merely for post-mortem revenge? Would you try to kill as many Russians as you could, just ordinary people who don't want trouble any more than our people want trouble?"

Wirkowski glared at him. "I'd throw a tin pot at them from eighty thousand feet if that's all I had left!"

President Gilfedders nodded. "You would kill people who had nothing whatever to do with killing you?" He didn't wait for an answer but turned to the others. "Would it have any meaning to kill simply because we ourselves could not go on living? Wouldn't that be like a dying father killing his son? Does our race mean nothing to us?"

No one answered. Flood was impressed by the questions and wanted to speak up and build on them but refrained. He knew it wasn't time. The others would have to reflect on those simple and ultimate questions, if they were capable of it, before they would be ready for what he had to say. As he looked around at the men at the table, he saw confusion and belligerence in their expressions. Realizing that the President's questions had been too much for them, he knew that he had to say something to ease the tension and stop their urge to strike out from growing stronger. He raised a hand and Gilfedders nodded.

"I'm so unfamiliar with these things maybe there's something crucial I don't understand," Flood began, his voice faltering. "I wonder——" He stopped, his nerve failing him.

"What is it?" Gilfedders asked impatiently.

"If the dart missiles are operational and yet haven't been used, doesn't that suggest they are purely defensive?" The others looked at him in silence, so he went on, "Obviously the missiles could be an unbeatable first-strike force. Since they haven't been fired, couldn't that mean they were designed as an unbeatable defense system?"

"Or an attack system," Springer said.

"If you can't know which was the purpose but you do know they haven't been used for an attack, why not assume the presumable: that they're defensive?" Flood asked.

"Of course," Admiral Whitfield said. Caldwell nodded and the President looked at Flood appreciatively.

"I'm sorry, Mr. Flood," Springer said, hunching forward. "Though your point seems sound, there's a crucial flaw in it—namely, we can't be sure the dart missiles are fully operational. Perhaps once they are the enemy will strike."

"We can't be sure they're not either," Flood answered. "It seems pretty certain that one of them is, so it would be logical to assume others are, too."

"Nor can we take the risk of finding out," the President added. "Given the computer in McCade's attic, it seems likely they have a fallback system. If we try to simultaneously remove the transmitters from all the brass eagles installed around the United States, that might trigger the computer—as a built-in signal that we're onto them—and set off all the missiles. Although we know where the eagles are, we have no idea where any of the missiles besides that one is. Nor can we be sure the system is based on a permanent radio beam from the eagles to the transmitters hidden in other attics around the country."

Pausing, he hunched forward slightly and continued,

"Let's assume they had to face a major technological problem—the energy source for the eagles' transmitters —by installing special long-life batteries in the flagpoles. It seems unlikely they would plan on replacing them frequently. Of course they probably have regular service contracts with all purchasers, so they can check the equipment periodically and replace the energy source."

He stopped and shook his head. "On the other hand, maybe their attack must be executed before the batteries wear out."

"They could recharge the batteries with microwave transmitters," Caldwell said. "Wouldn't even need to get inside the bases. You can do that from a considerable distance. Remember they did that at our embassy in Moscow."

President Gilfedders grinned. "They seem to like our eagles," he said, sitting back and looking relaxed for the first time since the meeting began. "Right after the war ended in forty-five the Russian government presented our government with a beautiful hand-carved eagle as a present from a grateful people. Our ambassador there had the thing hung on the wall right behind him in his office at Spasso House, the official residence." The President laughed wheezingly. "Seven years later we found an electronic bug in the eagle's beak."

He looked at Caldwell and said, "Maybe our motto should be: 'Billions for intelligence operations but not one cent for intelligence.'"

Caldwell colored but before he could speak Flood interceded. "We've forgotten about the transmitter I saw in the attic. It could be there—as you suggested, Mr. President—to control all the dart missiles in the country. But it could also be there to activate the transmitter in the eagle. Let me explain. Let's say an attack is ordered. The transmitter in the attic sends a signal to a receiver concealed in the flagpole, which triggers off the transmitter in the eagle, which in turn sends out the homing beam for the missile. That way the eagle transmitter wouldn't have to be on con-

stantly, so the energy supply would last far longer."
Flood paused and took a deep breath. "That would
also suggest that the missiles are defensive."

"Shit," General Wirkowski said.

The President ignored him. "Flood, how would
you like to be Special Assistant to the President for
Common Sense?" he asked. "I could use one."

Looking both hurt and superior at once, Professor
Springer said, "If such an adviser's advice were wise,
it would go unheeded."

"So far the problem hasn't come up," Gilfedders
said.

"If you would like my resignation as of this moment—"

"All the rats stay aboard the ship of state," Gilfedders growled.

It couldn't be true, Flood thought. They weren't
going to bicker over the end of the world.

Turning to Caldwell, the President asked, "Billy, can
we find out how many missiles there are, where they
are, and whether they're operational without ransack-
ing every building within ten miles of a military installation?"

"I'm afraid not, Mr. President—at least not with the
state of the art in our present technology. If there were
something, almost anything, of distinctive size or shape,
we could spot it on our spy-satellite photos. As you
know, we've replaced Big Boy with Big Eye. It's fan-
tastic. You can see the hair on the back of a man's
hand from fifty miles up."

"But not a missile inside an attic."

"There probably isn't an observable seam for the
attic roof opening," Caldwell answered. "They would
have thought of that. The damnable thing about their
plot, Sir, is that it's so simple. Simplicity is the hardest
thing to beat."

"Then we should be miles ahead of them," Gilfedders said.

"There's just a chance," Caldwell went on. "If I
put a special group to work studying—"

"I thought I'd made that clear. No one outside this

room except Charlie Burkover"—the President broke off to look at his watch—"is to know anything. Now or later."

"I meant with your permission of course."

"Denied."

Admiral Whitfield cleared his throat for attention. "I appreciate your concern, Mr. President. Perhaps at this juncture the best we can do is consider what steps should be taken if the truth reaches the public." He didn't look at Flood but Flood knew he was the subject; so they still didn't trust him. The Admiral continued, "The panic that would ensue might be uncontrollable. It might even make a nuclear strike by the Russians unnecessary. What I mean is moral paralysis, a failure of will on the part of our people. They've become soft in the past generation, I think you'll agree. Vietnam proved that."

Jesus, Flood thought, it was a moral failure that got us into the war, not out of it.

"Then, too, there would be the collapse of our economy," Whitfield said. "One cannot expect the financial community—"

"You mean the fiber's gone out of our Wall Street soldiers?" the President asked sarcastically.

"Take away their profits and you take away their armaments," the Admiral said.

The President laughed shortly. " 'Merchants have no nation,' " he said. "That's Jefferson. As usual he was right."

"The Cold War is over," murmured Caldwell. "Good Christ!"

"As we all know, our present defense budget is close to a hundred and fifty billion dollars a year," Admiral Whitfield went on matter-of-factly. "If that were suddenly reduced or even eliminated by a hysterical Congress—"

"Those bastards!" General Wirkowski moaned.

Now Flood saw why Wirkowski had been invited to the meeting—why in fact he had been made Chairman of the Joint Chiefs. Gilfedders was trying to keep the military in its place; he had given it a role but made sure that role would be ineffective by making Wirkow-ski the military's spokesman.

"We can't just let everything go to hell," the General said.

"What would you suggest?"

"I say attack—now!"

"And blow everything to hell instead?" Gilfedders asked.

Flood listened with mounting dismay. Was Whit-field's point valid? he wondered. If the Cold War ended, would the country collapse? Jesus, no wonder it had gone on so long.

"It's after two o'clock," the President said. "We're getting nowhere and we won't get anywhere until Burk-over calls in. I suggest we all get some sleep. You are to stay here at least for tonight, maybe longer. Flood has been given a room in the private quarters. There's space for everyone. I'll speak to the steward on my way out. There are to be no telephone calls. If any of you didn't tell your wives or"—he smiled briefly—"anyone else who might be awaiting your return, tell me now and I'll have calls made for you." No one spoke and after a moment he said, "Very well then, gentlemen. We'll meet in the lounge outside at six. Calls will be left for you. Sleep well." He didn't smile as he said the last words but quickly rose and strode from the room.

Slowly the others followed. Flood was last and as he headed toward the doorway he smelled the room's stale air—the stink of defeat, he thought wearily. He shrugged. It wasn't up to him any longer. At least now he could sleep.

# 2

He slept deeply for three hours and awoke in terror.
A voice intoned commandingly, "It is time, sir!" Time
for what? Flood wondered groggily, trying to drag
himself out of sleep. There was no time, there were
only missiles. "It is five-fifteen, sir," the voice went
on. It was a disembodied computer voice, the inflection
unnatural, as if the words had been picked out of a
memory bank and strung together. "The President will
meet you at Sub-Four Level lounge in forty-five minutes."

Flood groaned and turned onto his back. On the
ceiling overhead was a small metal grate. He wondered
if that was where the voice had come from. Then it
said, more loudly, "Sir! Are you awake? Please respond by saying 'Okay' after the buzz signal." There
was a pause and a raspy buzz. "Okay, for God's sake!"
Flood shouted. There was another pause, then a
"Thank you, sir. Repeat: six o'clock in the lounge.
Breakfast is ready there. Have a nice day, sir."

Flood grimaced and sat up on the side of the bed.
The goddamned place was bugged. He might as well
be in the Kremlin.

He showered, shaved, and brushed his teeth. Ellen
had always been amused by the order of his morning
toilet, with the brushing last, but he had always done it
that way. He tried to put her out of his mind; the futility of his need for her was greater than ever now. He
dressed and left for the lounge. It was just five-thirty.

Donald Baker, the clandestine services man, came
out of his room as Flood closed his door. "Morning,"
Baker said, smiling toothily. "Sleep as well as Gilfedders suggested?"

"Dreams of goblins and blood on the moon," Flood
said.

They went to the first of the two doors to the lounge

and Baker tried to open it. It was locked and at the first half-turn of the knob a metallic voice went on again. "Name, please."

"Name: Donald Baker, CIA," Baker said crisply.

"Donald Baker, CIA," the voice repeated, "Name of person with you, please."

Baker turned to Flood, who said, "Count Leo Tolstoy."

The voice was silent for a few seconds, then said, "No guest by name Count Leo Tolstoy present. Correct, please."

Baker grinned and with a shrug Flood said, "Just testing you, O amiable machine. Name: John Flood."

There was another brief pause and the voice said, "Proceed, please, Mr. Donald Baker and Mr. John Flood."

As they went through the doorway, Flood asked, "How did it know there were two of us—a hidden camera?"

"No, the weight on the floor in two different spots," Baker answered. "An old device. Predates bugging."

"What if you can levitate?"

Baker laughed. "They don't worry about saints."

"They should—most of all."

They were the first in the lounge and a moment after they entered the kitchen door opened and a strapping black man in a white jacket came in. "Good morning, gentlemen," he said in a deep pleasant voice. "I trust you slept well. If you'd care to give me your orders for breakfast."

They ordered and took a small table set for two in one corner. After the waiter brought their juice Baker said, "You seem to have gone into the wrong line of work, Mr. Flood. You would have made a first-class agent. What you've accomplished in the past few days would have been an incredible feat even for a highly trained man."

He suspects I'm a double agent, Flood thought, and thanked him. "It was all done through courtesy of total fear."

Baker laughed. "Actually fear kills more men than

it saves. They get to the point where they can't endure it any longer and then they make a fatal mistake—literally fatal—in order to escape their terror. Frying pan into fire sort of thing. Panic is just another form of suicide."

Flood listened uneasily. This man had spent his adult life in a world of terror—creating it for others, eluding it himself. Yet he seemed so ingenuous, so calmly unconcerned. What did he believe in? Probably God, Country, and Yale. Flood thought of those young men he had known there—upright, idealistic, honorable—who had joined the Agency and overnight had turned their backs on everything they had been brought up to believe in.

"God, I'm hungry," Baker said. "Nothing like a crisis to whet the appetite."

Flood nodded and wondered if that was the answer: the good boy who was good in order to conceal the brute inside. Conveniently the Agency gave such people the chance to fulfill themselves—to lie, cheat, steal, kill—with perfect honor. They were patriots.

"I've been wondering why the FBI isn't here," Flood said. "Or shouldn't I know?"

A look of distaste crossed Baker's face. "Just between us?"

Flood nodded.

"Blundering dolts. They always want to burst in with guns blazing. To them the enemy is still Pretty Boy Floyd. No finesse." He fell silent, looking chagrined at revealing himself.

Flood suppressed a smile. When doomsday came men like Baker would finally get a chance to fight the real enemies—each other.

"I've often wondered why your people didn't try to recruit me at Yale," Flood said, hoping his disclosure would prompt a further indiscretion.

"You're Yale?" Baker seemed surprised but quickly recovered by saying, "So am I. Damn shame we didn't."

They shook hands across the table. Baker's skin felt dry and his clasp was noncommittal. Lifeless, Flood thought. He returned Baker's smile and marveled at his friendly innocent face. It was the perfect cover for an assassin.

Hoping to learn more about his companion, Flood said, "Maybe no one approached me because I stayed out of the clubs—not that I was so hotly pursued to join."

"That could do it," Baker replied. The waiter served their food and when he had gone Baker went on, "We like signs of that sort—you know, fidelity to abstract principles: brotherhood, ritual, secrecy."

In Flood's day Yale had been a hotbed of conformity—the ideal spawning ground for gentlemen spies, young men who dreaded the prospect of a lifetime spent in a bank or a law firm. Now it was God, Country, and National Security.

Baker took a mouthful of scrambled eggs and Flood dug into his corned-beef hash. After a minute he said, "I'm afraid I wasn't one of the good ole boys there."

"We look for that, too," Baker said with a nod. "Partly because we feel more comfortable with our own kind." He reddened a bit at the gaffe and hurried on, "Mostly, though, because they're less likely to go wrong."

The godhead of the establishment, Flood thought— the status quo. "You mean defect?" he asked.

"Right. Shame, disgrace to one's class, the old-school tie stained. That kind of thing. Too much for most of us. There've been some notable exceptions of course. Fortunately most of them in England. No surprise really. The starch is gone there. Socialism." He took a fastidious bite of toast.

Jesus, Flood thought, here was a child playing the deadliest game of all—reality.

"It had to come some time," Baker said. "This confrontation, I mean. In a way I'm glad. We'll survive, whatever happens. If the worst comes, we'll rebuild."

Flood tried to conceal his amazement. Rebuild what? he wondered. Freedom on a charnel house? But then he realized that to this man freedom was meaningless. To him democracy meant a big house on a hill outside town, a long green lawn, tennis and lemonade, beautiful gracious women. Baker killed for privilege.

Baker finished his food and sipped his coffee. "The forces of good and evil clashing by night," he said.

"More like zealots clashing in blindness," Flood muttered and took a swallow of coffee. Remembering Gilfedders the night before, he slurped it noisily.

Baker looked at him. "Zealots there, to be sure. But here?" His pale blue eyes were beginning to look dangerous.

"I don't see much difference," Flood said. "They're ready to kill half of us and we're ready to kill half of them."

"You don't believe in survival of an idea?"

"What idea could survive that?" Flood wished he hadn't spoken out. He didn't need this man's enmity just now.

"It is imperishable," Baker said.

The door to the sleeping quarters opened and the others came in. They nodded and said good morning and sat together at a large round table across the room.

The two men sat in silence, as if too absorbed in thought to talk. Finally Baker said, "I've enjoyed our chat, Mr. Flood. Now there's something I must ask my boss." He pushed his chair back and stood up. "Again my congratulations." He smiled, his short upper lip revealing a large expanse of pink gums. With a nod he walked off toward the round table in an easy stride—on his way to the tennis court, Flood thought—and took an empty seat beside Billy Caldwell.

Flood poured another cup of coffee and looked at them. They had their heads together and were talking —about him, he assumed. He scarcely cared anymore. If every citizen owed his country a debt, he had paid his in full.

# 3

At two minutes past six President Gilfedders entered the lounge, the five men waiting rose, and the group filed into the Talk Room. They took the same seats.

"I have a few things to report," the President said. "First, Charlie Burkover carried out an examination of the flagpole and eagle at Miller Air Force Base headquarters. The eagle unscrewed precisely as Flood described and it contained a highly developed powerful small transmitter. Fortunately one of the FBI men present is an electronics specialist. He said he'd never seen one like it but that it was clearly of foreign design. He tested it and found that it wasn't operating. A search of the flagpole itself revealed what Flood suggested might be the answer: a very small transceiver and a sizable battery supply. Presumably a coded signal from the transmitter in the attic activates the transceiver, which triggers off the main transmitter in the eagle. And presumably that transmitter emits a guide beam for the dart missile to home in on. We can't be positive because Charlie was naturally reluctant to do anything that might set off the missile. The men reassembled the devices and left them as they were. Charlie then proceeded, with the same agents, to the submarine base at New London to carry out a similar examination there. After that he will stop at Quantico, then return here to have a look at the eagles at the Pentagon and the CIA."

Why not the eagle atop the White House, too? Flood wondered. Or was Gilfedders afraid to know that somewhere in a nearby attic was a missile with his name on it? This time the President of the United States couldn't send thousands of men off to their deaths on some distant battlefield and sit back to grieve for them in personal comfort and perfect security.

General Wirkowski sat forward with a hefty lurch. "Mr. President, like everybody else here, I suppose, I didn't sleep too well last night and I—"

"I slept perfectly," the President replied.

Wirkowski nodded impatiently. "I didn't. I tossed and I turned and then I got an idea: why not mount a sudden covert raid tonight on that flag factory, get the list of places where those goddamn eagles are perched, and simultaneously dismantle every one of them. By nightfall I can have a hundred, two hundred teams ready—whatever's necessary." His small eyes were bright. "Without the guidance system the missiles are grounded."

President Gilfedders looked at him coldly. "I was under the impression we had dismissed that possibility. If the computer in the New Richmond attic has a built-in device to activate all of the missiles in the event that one or ten or all of the eagles are tampered with, then what?"

Abashed, Wirkowski sat back. "I still think—"

"Still?" Gilfedders asked with contempt. "What if the electronic guidance system is merely a secondary means of ensuring accuracy," the President continued, "and the missiles are able to reach their targets on their own without the beam?"

The General didn't answer.

Flood raised a hand and Gilfedders nodded to him. "How about the eagle here—on top of the White House?"

For the first time the President looked surprised. He sat back and smiled. "Now how could I have forgotten that?"

Flood didn't believe him; he had to have thought of it the first time he heard Flood's story. Sure that he was being made fun of, Flood said nothing more.

The President looked at him for a few seconds, then said, "Bruce McCade, or Emil von Hoffen, is dead."

Flood's head went back, his eyes closed. "Oh, no," he mumbled, sickened. Murder—self-defense but still murder, he thought. Now his life would never be the same. He shook his head sharply to clear the dizziness and saw Baker looking at him with curiosity. I'm like him, Flood thought.

"You needn't blame yourself," Gilfedders told him. "McCade was out of danger. He was fully conscious and his condition was fair. Someone put something in his drinking water—probably one of those new colorless and tasteless poisons. He went into convulsions and died within seconds."

Flood's relief was so intense he could only nod.

"The FBI and police guards?" asked Caldwell.

"They insist no one but those officially permitted in the room got into it. An FBI agent was present inside the room at all times. Three other agents, along with two to four local police officers, guarded the corridor outside around the clock. It was a doctor or a nurse or someone disguised as either."

"The Russians developed those poisons first," Caldwell said.

"That would seem the most plausible explanation—one of his own people," the President replied. "Naturally they couldn't let us interrogate him."

"Then they know we know about the missile," Admiral Whitfield put in.

"They can't be sure," the President said. "On my instructions the agents wore ordinary police uniforms so there would be no obvious federal presence. McCade's colleagues may simply have decided they couldn't take the risk."

"But he was a KGB colonel—probably in command of the entire operation," Caldwell said. "You don't go around killing your commanding officer merely on suspicion that the other side may be onto him."

"Don't you?" the President asked.

Jesus, Flood thought, no one was safe. He watched Gilfedders closely, then nearly gasped as he thought: Gilfedders is one of them. How else could he have come up with the map designations and the use of the blackout to get the missiles in? That was why he had pretended not to have thought about the eagles on top of the White House. Almost as soon as the suspicion arose, Flood saw its absurdity. This man alone stood between freedom and tyranny the world over. Flood smiled slightly as he realized that he was getting as paranoid as the rest of them.

"You are amused, Flood?" the President asked sharply.

"I was thinking of Bell alone in that house and wondering what the hell to do," Flood answered quickly. "I assume he can't fire the missile without putting a code sent from Russia into the computer."

"A safe assumption. But he isn't alone. I ordered the house put under surveillance immediately after our first conversation. Another man has moved in, presumably to take command. We don't know who he is or even who he's pretending to be. A dark-haired man in a dark raincoat. Probably the man who followed you from Albany and calls himself Cameron. Wears glasses."

Flood thought of Willie and stifled an urge to tell them about him.

"Whoever he is, I presume he killed McCade," the President said disinterestedly.

"Or Bell," Caldwell interjected.

Flood looked at Caldwell and thought, Jesus, he could be their man. Every intelligence apparatus in the world dreamed of getting one of its men installed at the top of the enemy's intelligence service. It would have been a simple matter for Caldwell to misdirect American military forces while the Russians smuggled in the missiles, Flood thought. And his disbelief that the KGB cell would have murdered its commander had been pretense. He had ordered McCade killed himself. Flood shook his head sharply to drive away the idea. Nonsense, he told himself. Pointless besides.

The telephone rang and Gilfedders went to answer it. He stood with his back to the table and as Flood watched him he was suddenly struck by another possibility: The Russians hadn't been trying to stop him from getting to Washington; they had been trying to make sure that he got to Washington. The missiles were operational and the Russians wanted the President to know it. They couldn't very well have their ambassador stroll into the Oval Office and say, "We've got the drop on you, old man," Flood thought. Governments didn't work that way. Too awkward. Made any future negotiations impossible. Everything always had to be done indirectly. A second secretary at the American embassy in Bucharest dropped a hint to a Rumanian military attaché who was known to be close to the Chinese, a series of stronger hints, then some outright messages went up the line through higher and higher officials, and at last, a year and a half after the first word was dropped, President Nixon went to Peking. That's how it was done, Flood thought. Idiocy. More children's games. Can't risk being rebuffed. No wonder the world was about to be blown up. But a moment later he realized that his idea was equally absurd. It was conceivable that McCade had killed Flower to let Flood get away, but the rest—especially Willie's appearance on the ferry—no, it was out of the question.

The President returned to his seat. "That was your man Clyde," he said to Admiral Whitfield. "All of the numbers from Flood's notebook are locations of ICBM and SAC bases, none are ABM sites. And all seven of the Project Whirlwind sites are targeted."

"That seems to wrap it up," Caldwell said.

President Gilfedders nodded and looked at him for a long time. "You know what causes most problems in the world, Billy?"

Caldwell waited.

"Secrecy," the President said.

The five men looked at him in silence and he went on. "Every government tries to get the upper hand over other governments through secrecy. Secret weapons, secret arms buildups, secret attempts to overthrow hostile governments, secret assassinations, secret deceit and manipulation, secret false promises, secret foul threats. It's been said that if one government told the truth for twenty-four hours, every government in the world would fall."

He paused and looked away for a minute, then turned back to Caldwell. "And it's all silly. The mere existence of a secret assures that it will be discovered.

Each side *has* to know what the other's doing and always finds out. They do it. And we do it. All the time. They commit thievery, blackmail, bribery, murder and we do the same. And when we try to stop them from getting our secrets, we destroy ourselves. We bug and tap and follow anybody who seems offbeat here at home. Anyone who doesn't conform is a suspect. To keep track of all those suspects we break our own laws. In the end we destroy freedom. That's what secrecy does."

Flood stared at him, stunned by his words. It was all true.

The President paused again and shrugged. "If I had my way," he said, "I'd make our government tell the public *everything* it does *all* the time!"

Caldwell glanced at Baker and the two of them looked at the President as if to say that they would go to unimaginable lengths to make sure he never had his way.

In all, the group had seven meetings that day. Except for the report from General Burkover, who had found the same sets of receivers, transmitters, and battery supplies wherever he went—including, at his last stop, the White House—the meetings were desultory and inconclusive. Toward the end of the last one, shortly before nine-thirty that night, Flood sat listening to the men around the table in a spirit compounded of boredom, exhaustion, and amazement. So this is how the country is run, he said to himself. It was a wonder the nation had lasted as long as it had.

Finally, President Gilfedders broke off the conversation, saying, "Gentlemen, I have reached my decision. I'll sleep on it and inform you first thing tomorrow. Good night."

Wondering how any conclusion could have been based on the erratic talk of that day, Flood rose with the others, wondering if Gilfedders had made up his mind long before, even immediately after hearing Flood's story in the sitting room, and had held these consultations to divide the responsibility. A lot of what politicians did, Flood knew, was done solely for "the record." But this time there might not be anyone left who would bother to read it.

On the way out of the room, the President motioned to Flood to join him. It was a slight to the others, Flood thought, but the President didn't pause in the lounge and the two men went back down the long corridors, through the room where the Army guards aimed their submachine guns at them until the President said, in a cracked voice, "Gilfedders for freedom," and on up to the Lincoln Sitting Room. A small fire burned in the grate of the marble fireplace. Then the President had planned this meeting in advance, Flood thought, and wondered why.

Gilfedders sat down heavily in one of the wing chairs. "There's drink on the table," he said, gesturing toward the pine table at one side. "Fix me a neat Scotch, no ice, third of a glass, and help yourself." He gazed pensively into the flames.

Flood fixed the drinks, handed one to the President, and took his own to the other wing chair. He sipped it for a few moments before realizing that it was his first drink that day. They sat in silence, staring at the fire.

Finally the President turned to him. "I asked you up here to discuss things that don't concern the others—not ultimately at least."

Flood nodded and waited.

"The first is that, on my instructions, General Burkover spoke to the chief of police in New Richmond. As you believed, they were after you—all out. They were convinced you murdered the woman and probably the lieutenant. Charlie tried to convince the chief that you had nothing to do with it and that it was a top national-security matter." He grinned. "It may be the first time in our history the claim was true."

The President sipped his drink reflectively for a minute. "The chief wouldn't buy it," he went on at last. "He didn't like being told how to use his police powers. He also didn't like having a couple of unsolved murders, including the murder of his own man, left on his hands. What he did like, I suspect, was the chance to make the President of the United States sit up and beg. That's what I did. I think he's satisfied. I promised it would all be explained in due course. It won't be of course. Right now Charlie's cooking up a theory about how McCade killed the woman and shot Flower, who mortally cracked McCade's skull before dying. Rough justice, you might say."

"That was extremely kind of you, Mr. President."

"Nonsense. Just tying up loose ends. Couldn't have them tracing you here." He paused and looked at Flood. "The chief showed Charlie a dossier they have on you."

"Because of the murders?"

"They've had it for years," the President answered. "Part of their covert intelligence operation."

"The bastards!" Flood took a long swallow of whisky.

"All policemen are bastards," Gilfedders said mildly. "But we need them. That's why they get away with being bastards."

The President went on to recount the contents of the dossier: Flood's "malicious and untrue" articles on the New Richmond city government, particularly its police department; his "baseless attacks" on the region's leading families, with no mention of the Pulitzer Prize; his "unswerving attempts to subvert public faith in American society" through his column; his heavy drinking; and his wife's "unnecessary" death, which was "highly suspicious."

Angered, Flood waited until the President finished, then said, "If that's the kind of crap you base decisions on, God save America." He heard the ice cubes in his glass tinkling and realized that his hand was shaking. He put the glass down on his knee.

Gilfedders smiled. "To some people that personal history would suggest unreliability," he said. "To some others it would suggest worse—mental instability. And to still others it would suggest a strong tendency toward disloyalty."

It was a bald threat to assure his silence, Flood knew, and was infuriated at Gilfedders' need to threaten him after all he had done. With deepening animosity, he realized that this man was capable of anything—anything except disloyalty to the country he led. He was President of the United States and he would take the nation crashing down with him into oblivion rather than betray it. So would the others, Flood told himself, and wondered if he would do the same. He knew that he would. But in a different way. It was absurd, he saw, but he wanted people to understand why they had to die before they died.

"Better Red than dead, Mr. Flood?" the President asked caustically, as if he knew what Flood was thinking.

Flood shook his head. "Are those the only alternatives?"

"Afraid so. For you there is that one choice. For me there is none."

Flood knew that he meant it. He looked at Gilfedders in silence for a moment, then asked, "And my police dossier? What does it mean to you?"

"Nothing—nothing at all," the President answered mildly. "All I think is that you have pulled off an astounding feat." He paused. "I give the orders here, Mr. Flood, so that's what everyone else is going to think, too."

Flood let his breath out slowly in a silent sigh. Now he saw what Gilfedders had been doing: He had been trying to make Flood nervous so that he would blurt out something he didn't want to say. He waited without speaking.

The President looked up at the portrait of Lincoln for a moment and said, "What do you suppose he would have done?"

"Made peace."

"A bloody neat trick, that," the President replied, lapsing into a heavy Scottish accent.

"He might even have opened up all the secrets," Flood said with a smile.

Gilfedders looked at him. "An even neater trick. Half the people I know like to lie and the other half like to be lied to."

It had all been rhetoric, then, Flood thought, disliking this man for the first time. He looked up at the portrait, then back at the President. "Tolstoy said Lincoln became great through his smallness. He said that compared to him all the others—Caesar, Napoleon, Washington—were only moonlight to his sun."

"Another goddamn Russian!" Gilfedders said. He laughed briefly. "No question about Lincoln's greatness. Just keeping that lunatic Cabinet of his together was a masterpiece of politics. But he had only a few million lives to worry about. The casualties on both sides in the Civil War weren't even a million men."

The President glanced at his watch and Flood looked at his, too. It was eight minutes to ten. Not even a million dead, he thought, and hoped the interview was over.

"One other thing," President Gilfedders said. "Also on my instructions, Burkover has ordered the Internal Revenue Service to impound your safety-deposit box first thing tomorrow. A tax matter." He smiled. Raising his glass to Flood as if in toast, he finished his drink and got up. "I'll have someone take you back to your quarters," he said.

Flood rose. "Thanks for the drink," he said, then grinned at the banality of the remark. There were so many things to say, he thought, and wondered if there would be time.

"Since you were the one to bring me the news, you should be the first to know my decision," the President said. "I'll see you in the morning before the others. Good night, Mr. Flood."

With that, he left the room. Flood looked at his watch again. At least tonight the President would get to bed on time.

# Monday

At five A.M. Flood was awakened, not by the computer voice but by a soft insistent tapping. It stopped. He got up and went to the door. The tapping resumed. "Who is it?"

"Baker," a muffled voice answered.

Flood opened the door to find a smiling, fully dressed Baker, who apologized for the early hour and explained, "The President wants to see you at once."

"I'll meet you in the lounge."

"I'll wait here," Baker said.

Ten minutes later Flood joined him. They responded to the computer's questions and were let out into the hall to the lounge. It was brightly lighted. They went on through it, not to the Talk Room as Flood expected, but out the main door, again down the system of corridors, and onto the first elevator. The Lincoln Sitting Room, he thought.

But Baker pushed No. 6 button and they descended. Flood looked at him questioningly.

"The War Room," Baker said curtly.

Flood looked alarmed. "Is that his decision?"

Baker didn't respond and a moment later the elevator stopped. They stepped out into an enormous low-ceilinged chamber filled with desks and tables and, along the far wall, a bank of computers.

Baker turned to the right, toward a door at one end of the room. Flood caught up with him and said, "Quite a complex."

"There is room—including sleeping quarters, kitchens, offices, dining facilities, conference rooms—to accommodate five hundred and eighty-two people down here," Baker replied.

Flood was surprised—not by the magnitude of the complex as much as by Baker's describing it to him at all.

"No reason you shouldn't know—now that you're practically one of us," Baker explained. "There's a large suite of rooms for the President and his family and servants, similar but smaller apartments for Cabinet members, senior military officers, and top White House aides. Barracks quarters for the others. Enough food and water and fuel to stay down here for a year. Special air filters to eliminate any nuclear seepage. A slanted runway shute up to a hidden exit on the South Lawn and a dozen supersonic planes stored here to take the family and other top people out. A dozen helicopters can be lifted by elevator to another exit. A storehouse of nuclear weapons in small concealed silos ringing the Residence to keep away any invading party at the time of escape. Quite nicely done, all in all."

"How could all that be done in secrecy?"

"The Agency did it with its own construction crews. Under cover, naturally. When the White House interior was rebuilt and the outer walls strengthened during the Truman Administration. That took two years."

Of course, Flood thought, in the early fifties—the start of the Cold War. He whistled appreciatively and Baker stopped and faced him. "This is where the nation finally lives," he said. "And here is where it will survive, come what may."

Once again, the leaders who sent their fellowmen to their deaths would escape, Flood thought. The final deterrent to nuclear war that he had always relied on most—the equal certainty of death for everyone—didn't exist.

Baker walked on and Flood followed him to the door, which opened onto a long corridor. As they started down it, Flood asked, "Do you know what his decision is?"

Baker nodded, without speaking, walking more rapidly now.

Hurrying to catch up, Flood asked, "What?" Gilfedders hadn't kept his word to tell him first.

"Nothing," Baker said, looking at him coldly.

Flood stopped short and Baker halted after a few steps and turned to face him.

"Nothing?" Flood asked, stunned by disbelief.

"That's right. We're going to do nothing—nothing at all."

Flood stared at him, aghast. Gilfedders had concluded that the dart missiles were defensive then, he realized. Otherwise he couldn't conceivably take such a risk. Nothing was to be done. Nothing was to be said even. The Cold War would go on. It *must* go on. Nothing would change—business as usual. There would be no war and no peace. There would be only continuing terror and one day, through madness or a mistake, there would be the end.

Baker turned and continued down the corridor. "We're late," he said.

Flood followed him around a corner and a few steps along a shorter hall to a door at the end. Flood thought of Ellen. She seemed close to him now and his mind raced as he wondered what she would tell him to do. He knew the answer even without asking: she would show him that he must tell the President he could not sit by and do nothing. The people must be told the truth. Only they could force their leaders to make peace. Any other course was madness.

A brass plaque on the door said WAR ROOM. Baker opened it and stood aside as Flood entered a large anteroom furnished with leather sofas and easy chairs. The floor was white marble and Flood tried to think what it reminded him of but failed.

"That door on the right," Baker said from behind him.

As Flood crossed the marble floor, he realized what it had set off in his mind: the luminous white heart-shaped stone Marja had given him on the beach. He must get out of here today, he thought, or get to a phone and tell her to wait for him. Suddenly, he felt different. Then he knew what it was. He had found his way out of himself through her. He was free of the past. He imagined Ellen and saw her gentle smile and thought how lucky he was to have had those years with her. Now there would be new years.

At the door, he paused, preparing himself for the confrontation. If the President refused to tell the people the truth, if Flood couldn't persuade him, he would have to do it himself . . . to free them at last. And then Marja. He had never felt so strong.

He turned to Baker, who seemed withdrawn, almost dreamy, and wondered again which side he was on. It didn't matter, though, Flood thought. There was little difference at the top.

"Through there, Mr. Flood," Baker said. "He's waiting."

Flood turned back and opened the door. He wondered if Marja was carrying his seed inside her and smiled.

There was a dim light at the far side of the room and Flood started toward it. At that moment a bullet tore into the base of his skull and exploded in his brain. In the instant of life remaining to him he realized that from the beginning he had known the end.

# The best
# in modern fiction from
# BALLANTINE